DARK AGES

TOREADOR

BY JANET TRAUTVETTER

Renaud's blunted sword bounced off his opponent's side, the force of the blow lessened by armor and the underlying monk's habit. Wheezing a little, the Teutonic Brother dropped to one knee, conceding the match. Rosamund applauded with the rest of the audience at Jürgen's court, though the monk's fellows seemed considerably less enthusiastic when a stranger defeated one of their own.

"Isn't there to be *any* blood tonight?" Erzsébet Arpad asked. "No steel?"

"Don't worry," Sir Marques assured her. "Sir Josselin is challenging the Lord Marshal of the Black Cross himself next. That'll be bloody for sure."

"Oh, *good*," Erzsébet exclaimed, just loud enough to make sure Rosamund could hear her. "But *whose* blood will it be, that's the question—"

Rosamund held her tongue. Apologizing once to Erzsébet had been bad enough. She was not prepared to make a habit of it. This, she was learning, was the most popular court entertainment in German Cainite society—the display of prowess at arms, either of mortals, ghouls or even of the Cainites themselves. More Cainites had come tonight than had attended court the night of her presentation—mostly male, and several more wearing the black Teutonic cross.

Janet Trautvetter

Dark ages
Toreador

AD 1224 to 1230
Ninth of the Dark Ages Clan Novels

What Has Come Before

It is the year 1224, and two decades of warfare and intrigue among the living and the dead show every sign of giving way to a third. A futile Fifth Crusade brought Germans and Hungarians to the Holy Land and sent them back with little to show for it; the French continue to war against the Albigensian heretics in the Languedoc; and the Teutonic Knights hold lands in Eastern Hungary to the increasing distaste of that land's king.

Away from the eyes of the living, in the shadowy world of the undead, matters are even worse. Alexander, the ancient vampire who has ruled Paris for many centuries, has been deposed by his own childe, Sir Geoffrey. Exiled into the east, Alexander heads into the Holy Roman Empire searching for support in his quest to avenge himself and regain his throne.

Among his company is Rosamund of Islington, who had been ambassador to Alexander's court from the Queens of Love—the vampires who hold domain over much of the rest of France. To Rosamund's dismay, it is now clear that the Queens were largely responsible for the plot that undid Alexander. They call his downfall justice for the long-ago murder of his consort Lorraine, who had been gifted to him by the Queens. That her mission of goodwill was a distraction came as a great shock to Rosamund, who now finds herself with few allies in exile. Alexander's own feelings toward her seem a mixed blessing—clearly smitten, the ancient and obsessive vampire has chosen to believe Rosamund's proclamations of innocence, but with every passing night he seems more determined to make her his new consort. Rosamund's existence may have been spared at the simple cost of her soul.

Meanwhile, few seem to remember the fall of Constantinople twenty years ago or the quest by some of the undead survivors of that blaze to restore it to its former glory...

Chapter One

Heidelberg, Rhenish Palatinate, Holy Roman Empire
Feast of the Invention of the Cross, May, 1224

"There, milord." The undead knight pointed to a tall house at the end of the block. "You find him there."

Sir Josselin de Poitiers took a moment to decipher his guide's bad French, and then favored the younger Cainite with a smile. "Thank you. And my thanks to your most esteemed sire as well, for troubling himself over a stranger's quest."

The German bowed from horseback. "Honored to serve, noble sir. Good night to you. I must return. Thank you."

"Milady might wish to thank you herself," Josselin suggested. "Surely your sire does not expect you back immediately, does he?"

"Yes. No, I cannot stay." In fact, he was already turning his horse. "God keep you, milord. Good even to you!" He dug his heels into his mount's sides. With a somewhat alarmed look, his ghoul escort turned to follow, carrying the lantern with him. Within a moment, they had turned a corner and vanished from sight.

"Milord?" Fabien looked at his master, and then at the house. "Was he afraid?"

Josselin turned his smile on his squire and saw Fabien's unease melt away. "There's no need to worry, Fabien. Come now, let us surprise milady!"

"Josselin! How did you—Holy Mary, it is good to see you!"

Josselin caught her rush and swept her up into his arms,

lifting her up off the floor—it was such a joy just to hold her and know she was safe. "Rosamund. My sweet lady, *ma petite fleur*," he said, grinning broadly, setting her down again and kissing both cheeks and then her lips with equal enthusiasm. "How could I not find you? All I had to do was follow the light of your beauty."

She smiled but didn't respond to his opening gallantries. "I have missed you so, Sir Josselin," she said. "Wait—wait. I mustn't forget. Margery."

"Milady?" Rosamund's mortal companion, whose smile was nearly as wide as her mistress's, rose from her seat, setting her needlework aside.

"Go and tell his Highness—well, tell Gaston to tell his Highness, that would be better. Tell him that my brother has arrived from—from Chartres."

"Yes, milady." Margery curtsied, and departed.

Rosamund took Josselin's hand and led him to a cushioned bench. "How are things at home? How is our lady? Tell me everything! The cathedral, how is the cathedral?"

"Sweet Rosamund. You cannot imagine how worried I've been." Josselin had trouble containing his relief just to see her again. "I did not want to leave you, you must believe that. When I heard about—"

She laid her fingers across his lips, silencing him, shaking her head. "Not now, Josselin," she murmured. "Please. The cathedral?"

Josselin had not existed for nearly a century in Cainite courts without learning when to recognize a warning, and the circumstance of their parting was clearly not a safe topic for conversation. "Still under construction, of course," he answered, taking her cue. "But they've been adding the saints to guard the buttresses. They're carved from the finest limestone, brought all the way from the quarries on the Seine, near Paris. And they each get their own little alcove, way, way up near the top, so they have a good view, each in their own little shrine with a roof over their heads to keep them from the weather. And the window—oh, Rosamund, you should see the window!"

"Oh? Tell me! Which one?"

"Over the west portal, up on the third tier. A great round window with a rose cut out of the middle of the stone, and twelve more little roses for the Twelve Apostles, cut around it in a ring. And the petals of each rose are filled with paintings in colored glass. Fabien tells me that in the sunlight, it is truly glorious. They even call it a rose window, because of the shaping of the stone."

Rosamund drew a deep breath. "I wish I could see it."

"You will," he assured her firmly. "They're still building the rest of it. It will be waiting for you, as patiently as only stone can wait."

"I miss it. I've missed you. I can't even recall when I last had a letter."

"Nor can I." Josselin's voice turned serious. "Which is part of what has brought me here. Our queen was concerned for you. So was I. We've had no word since a month after you left Paris."

"But I've written! I have! Let me see—once from Nancy, that was in August."

"Yes, I believe I saw that one."

"And then from Lebach, and from—oh, I don't remember the names of the towns, it's all a blur. But twice more since then, at least. I even sent one with my own Henry, before Christmas! I was writing another tonight, to send before we left Heidelberg. Peter told me he found a man to take it."

"Well, I have brought you a letter, *petite fleur*. Several letters, in fact. One from our sire, of course, but also others. It seems you have left many broken hearts in your wake."

"No, not those." She put her hand on his arm where he was reaching for the purse at his hip. "I'll look at them later. Put them away, quickly!"

"Rosamund?" Josselin took her hands between his. "You used to enjoy hearing from your admirers—no matter how atrocious their verse. I brought them all the way from Paris just for you."

"Yes, I know, Josselin, and I thank you. It's so kind of you to bring them for me. But I would much rather talk to you than read a bunch of moldy old letters. Letters will keep, won't they?"

"They'll keep, of course. Even the queen's letter will keep.

It's not like she expects an answer back right away! But tell me of your journey. How has the road treated you? Have you won any more hearts along the way?"

She smiled, but it lacked enthusiasm. "The road has been long, milord. Very long. Few courts have offered us welcome, or at least not sincerely."

"I daresay that's true, especially in the Empire. Does he think Lord Hardestadt will offer him sanctuary, then?"

"I don't know. But we know that Mithras of London will not." She paused, a faraway look in her eyes. "*Must* we speak of politics, Josselin?"

"What then would milady wish to hear?" he asked amiably. "The latest *canso* from Provence? A stroke-by-stroke account of my last melee with Sir Philippe d'Anjou? Or—"

She stood up, abruptly. "He's coming."

Alexander. Josselin suppressed a moment of near-panic—he had been forced to flee Paris on the eve of Alexander's over-throw, lest his knowledge of the plot compromise Rosamund's own innocence in it. How would his presence now be received by the exiled prince? But it was too late to change his course now, and courtly etiquette came to him as easily as riding; he rose to his feet and took two steps forward, going down to one knee as the door opened. Rosamund, already closer to the door, dropped into a deep curtsy.

The former Prince of Paris entered the room. His youthful appearance could be deceptive at a first glance. Alexander had been little more than a boy when brought to eternity, a slender adolescent with short-cropped dark curls and the face of an angel. Only his dark, brooding eyes, and his capacity for abso-lute stillness when not actually walking betrayed his immense age—Josselin had heard he was well over a thousand years old. Whatever the truth, the power fueling his personality drew the attention of onlookers like a lodestone. When Alexander was present, all other thoughts, desires or concerns simply ceased to matter.

Josselin caught himself staring, and quickly bowed his head. But the prince seemed to take no offense at his lapse of proper courtesies.

"Sir Josselin—what an unexpected pleasure." Alexander spoke French with just the faintest trace of accent, though of what Josselin was unable to tell. "How good of you to visit us in our exile. I'm sure milady Rosamund is quite delighted to see a familiar face—I know how much she misses the comforts of home."

"Thank you for your welcome, Highness," Josselin replied, raising his head now that he had been acknowledged.

Alexander appropriated the room's single chair and, as such, made it a throne. "We're glad you made it safely, of course. The journey must have been perilous indeed, for you to come armed into a lady's bower."

"I will disarm if you wish it, Highness." Josselin held out his hands, palms up in a gesture of peace. "And humbly beg your pardon."

"I do not fear your sword, sir knight. Keep it. We give you leave to go armed in our presence."

Josselin bowed his head again for a moment. "Your Highness is most generous."

"Come, rise, Sir Josselin. Gaston—bring a chair for milady and her kinsman. I would have him feel himself an honored guest in our court, however far from home we now sit."

Josselin rose smoothly to his feet and offered his hand to Rosamund, to escort her to the bench the mortal now set at the prince's side.

"Ah, ever the courtier," remarked Alexander, though he smiled when he said it.

"Courtesy to a lady is a pleasure, Highness, as well as a duty," Josselin bowed again, respectfully, before taking his own seat across from them, carefully lifting his sheathed sword to rest on the bench beside him.

"Of course," the prince returned. "Especially when the lady is so fair." He turned and smiled at Rosamund.

Rosamund seemed to relax somewhat in the light of that smile. Her posture, which had been far more stiff and formal, softened, though Josselin noted her hands remained clasped together on her lap. "You flatter me, Highness," she demurred.

"And you are modest as ever, milady." Alexander turned

back to Josselin. "Now, milord. Tell me how Paris fares these nights."

Josselin had rarely seen the Prince of Paris save during formal court occasions. During the last months of Alexander's reign, it had been Rosamund who had been the official ambassador, and he merely her escort. Alexander's gracious welcome surprised him; he was suddenly aware of the great honor of the prince's regard. "It—fares well enough, Highness," he answered, suddenly sorry he could bring no better news. He dug in his memory of court gossip for something better, to ease the sting. "There are those who say Geoffrey owes too much to too many—that he has mortgaged his power to gain it, and it is Queen Salianna who truly rules, over Paris and over him. He has driven the Heresy out of Paris; those who held to it have fled to the south. Those whom he caught, he burnt, both Cainite and mortal alike."

"I'm sure that God found the odor of such sacrifices most pleasing," Alexander murmured. "And what of the Courts of Love—do the other queens rejoice now that Salianna has come to rule over them?"

"No ruler rejoices to be ruled by another, Highness," Josselin remarked wryly, and felt a warm flush of triumph at Alexander's soft chuckle.

"Tell me then. How stands the alliance between Salianna and your Queen Isouda?"

Memories bubbled up unbidden, Isouda's sharp words pushing their way to his tongue alongside others spawned by his own dislike of Salianna, based on decades of mortal service. He thought instead of the cathedral and its silent saints before he made his answer. "Chartres stands but a hundred miles from Paris. My queen has her own domain and vassals to rule, and the Grand Court has acknowledged her sovereignty. There stands milady's alliance, as it must, your Highness."

"And what of the Countess Melusine? Does she still lick her wounds and hide in Mithras's shadow?"

This was at least a safer question. "From all accounts, she looks to Mithras to win back Anjou for her—which he seems strangely disinclined to do."

"You fought at La Roche-aux-Moines, did you not, Sir Josselin?"

"Yes, your Highness."

"No doubt your valor on the field of battle brought great honor to your queen. I'm sure she was appropriately grateful for your service afterwards?"

"She thanked me, your Highness. I asked for nothing more than to serve her well."

"You fought for me that night as well."

Josselin bowed his head briefly. "As milady commanded, yes, your Highness, I did."

"I don't believe I thanked you at the time—so allow me remedy that omission now." Alexander pulled a ring from his own finger and held it out. "Take this, as a poor token of my gratitude for your good service, Sir Josselin de Poitiers, and in hopes that one night you may serve me again."

Josselin slipped down from the bench to one knee at Alexander's feet, and bowed his head. "Your Highness honors me," he said. "If my queen so commands it, I will." He accepted the gift—to do otherwise would have been a grave insult—and slipped the ring on his finger.

"You are most generous, your Highness." It was the first Rosamund had spoken. "That was a most gracious gift."

"That it pleases you, milady," Alexander said, smiling at her again, "delights me beyond measure. But we are neglecting our duty as host!" He turned back again to Josselin, who had returned to his seat. "Sir Josselin, you have traveled far to find us, and we have not even offered you the means to slake your thirst! No doubt you wish to refresh yourself, and your squire as well. Gaston, are the rooms ready for our guest?"

The mortal seneschal bowed. "Yes, my liege, they are."

"Then do not let me keep you, Sir Josselin. See to your comfort, and that of your man. No doubt you will wish to see to your horses as well—you see, I know how dear you hold your mounts! There will be ample time to continue our discussion tomorrow night, I'm sure."

It was a dismissal, however politely phrased. Josselin rose to his feet and bowed, trying not to wonder what he had said to so offend the prince that he would be sent away so abruptly. He closed his fist over the ring, the reminder of Alexander's favor, and took comfort from it. "I look forward to it, your Highness," he said, "and I thank you again for your welcome to me. Good night to you, Highness." He turned slightly towards Rosamund. "My dearest lady."

"Good rest to you, milord," Alexander said.

Josselin followed the seneschal out of the room.

"So," Alexander leaned back, tapping fingertips restlessly against the carved arms of his chair. "We are entertaining spies this evening, milady? I suppose I should be grateful he was chivalrous enough to come so openly!"

All her fragile hopes crumbled at once. "Sir Josselin is not a spy, milord," Rosamund protested. "He is my brother in blood, he came only to see me."

"Oh, come now, milady," he snorted, and rose from the chair to pace, as if the humors boiling in him would not allow him to sit any longer. "Do not play the innocent with me—I know you better. Do you really believe Queen Isouda has only now noticed that you are no longer in France? If she was concerned for your fate, do you not think she might have responded sooner?"

"But it was Salianna—" *Milady did not betray me, she couldn't have. She wouldn't!*

"And what did your queen do then? Nothing. She abandoned you." He was walking around her, circling like a wolf with its prey. "Salianna gave you away, and Isouda let it happen. They cast you off because they were jealous. Yes, milady. It's true. They were jealous of you—of what you might become. They could see, as I do, what a magnificent queen you could make, and those jealous harpies will brook no rivals."

Rosamund sat still, her hands still clenched together on her lap. "No," she whispered. *Not milady. She always bade me to do my best, she gave me so much, so freely. She said she loved me.*

Alexander was behind her now. He put one foot up on the bench beside her and leaned close, his voice low and intimate. "Have you any sisters, Rosamund? Have you ever wondered why Isouda has chosen only men, except for you? You were so

young when you came to her. Unformed, like clay in the pot-
ter's hands. She thought she could mold you, shape you—control you. She sought to create perfection in woman's form. Then
she made your her pawn in the Grand Court, because she knew
I would be unable to resist you."

He reached out and slid his fingers through her hair, drawing it back from her shoulder. "But when she needed you no longer, she let you go. If she had asked for you, called you to return
even once, do you think I would have held you back? Haven't you
written her, as a dutiful childe should do? And what answer
have you received?"

"Nothing." The admission got caught in her throat halfway
out. It almost sounded like someone else's voice. She swallowed
to ease the tightness. *Nothing.* And then, Josselin's voice.

—*We've had no word since a month after you left Paris.*

"You see? Nothing. So why now would she send her favorite
knight all the way across Europe to visit you? Out of familial
duty? Affection?"

—*Our Queen was concerned for you. So was I.*

Blood tears welled up in Rosamund's eyes, and she let them.
They never got my letters.

Alexander sat on the bench beside her. "They are jealous
of you still," he murmured. "It was not enough to banish you,
no, they were not content with that. They fear what you will
become under my tutelage. And they know you will not suspect
him. You trust Sir Josselin. You still love him, don't you?"

"Yes." A cold, dark tear escaped and ran down her cheek.

"But he is bound to the Queen. You saw, didn't you, how he
could not betray her in his speech? How he tried to evade even
my simplest questions? At your hour of greatest need, did he
not desert you when she called? You know where his loyalties
lie, sweet Rosamund. He made his journey for her, not for you.
If you had mattered so much to him, you would have seen him
months ago. It would have been easy enough for him to catch
up with us in France. But perhaps you should ask yourself why
he didn't, if he cared for you so much?"

She listened for Josselin's voice again, but in vain. Alexander's
question echoed unanswered.

Alexander reached over and lightly caught her chin, tilting her face towards his. "My sweet rose." The warmth, the sympathy in his eyes was a soothing balm on her wounded spirit, her broken heart. "You have paid a bitter price for your faithfulness. We know, don't we, what it is to be betrayed by those we should have been able to trust above all? You deserved better from your queen than this, Rosamund."

Alexander's youthful face, his glittering eyes, and his smooth voice claimed all of her attention. "I know what sorrows you have borne, my rose. Abandoned, exiled, forgotten— and yet you bear it with such courage, such grace. As a true queen should."

Another tear stained her cheek, and Alexander caught it with a finger, then brought it to his lips, his tongue. "I will make it up to you, milady—my queen. They have cast us out, but we will endure, and together we will prevail. I will wipe away all your pain, and all these hard times will be nothing but a faded memory of a long-distant past."

He leaned close, taking her head in his hands. Gently he kissed her tears away, delicately catching them with his tongue. "You will have a court of your own, with ladies to wait upon you, and a garden, and musicians to play for you whenever you wish it. And pretty courtiers to dance for you, and to lie prostrate at your feet while they beg for the sweetness of your kiss—"

He kissed her, and Rosamund found herself responding, her hands seeking his shoulders, her body pressing closer to him, her tormentor, liege and lover. His arms enfolded her, held her against his shoulder.

"I will give you anything you desire," he whispered. "*Anything*—and what has *she* given you? What can *he* give you? *Nothing.*"

—*I have brought you a letter*, petite fleur. *One from our sire, of course.*

"Nothing," she repeated, obediently.

Chapter Two

Heidelberg, Rhenish Palatinate
The Feast of St. Monica, May, 1224
She did not have much time.

Rosamund didn't even stop to dress, but merely wrapped her mantle over her chemise and slipped as quietly as she could up the stairs. There was no sign of Gaston in the second-floor hall. Hopefully he would be too absorbed with his master to notice anything he might feel obliged to report.

Fabien, Josselin's squire, was somewhat surprised to see her, but he let her in without question. "He's still sleeping, milady," he said.

"Where?"

"In there, milady. I pulled the curtains and closed the shutters. Here, let me light a candle for you." He picked up a narrow burning taper and went before her, lighting a thick tallow candle on small shelf near the curtained bed.

She followed, and smiled at him as he retreated to give his lord and the lady what privacy he could. "Thank you, Fabien."

"Josselin?" She pulled the bed curtains back, carefully at first—it was never a good idea to startle a Cainite just coming out of daytime sleep—but he didn't stir. His wheat-gold hair had regrown to shoulder length during the day, and now lay in soft waves across the pillow. His features were elegant and finely cut, skin pale and taut over sharp cheekbones, a handsome effigy of life-like marble without the wry twist of lips or the sparkle of sky-blue eyes to animate them.

She sat on the bed beside him and leaned over to touch his

shoulder. "Josselin, wake up! I need to talk to you. Please, please, wake up!"

It took a minute, but he did finally stir. His eyes opened and he saw her sitting on the side of the bed. "Milady? So early—"

"The letter—please, where is the letter from our lady? I have to see it, Josselin!"

"What, now?" He pushed himself up on one elbow, ran a hand through his disheveled hair. "But last night you said—"

"This is the only time I know he can't hear. He doesn't rise until after full dark has come. It's the only time we can talk freely. Josselin, please, where is the letter?"

He pointed. "There. In the pouch. They're all in there."

She snatched it up, and brought it back to the bed, her fingers unnaturally clumsy with the fastening. Smiling, he took it from her, opened it, and then handed her a stack of thick, folded parchments, all sealed with wax.

Rosamund flipped through them, then found the one bound with a red ribbon and the familiar seal. "She did! She did write—"

"Of course she did." Josselin reached across the bed and snagged his shirt, pulling it on over his head.

She broke the seal and unfolded the parchment sheet. She drank in every word, from *My dearest Rosamund*, to the closing *by my hand, Isouda de Blaise*, as it if were the sweetest blood. The content was full of courtly pleasantries, reports on the progress on the Queen's precious cathedral, inquiries as to her well-being. No mention of particular concern over Rosamund's situation, or of Alexander, or gossip from the Courts. No discussion of politics, no sage advice, no acknowledgement that the letter had to travel further than a day's ride to reach her, nor even any chiding for not writing herself.

It was a letter to a stranger.

Josselin had risen from the bed and was tying his hose up over his braies. Fabien stood beside him, a tunic flung over each arm. One was a gambeson of padded linen, stained with rust; the other was a long cotte of fine blue wool and trimmed with edgings of cream. He offered both to his lord.

The knight considered for a moment, then took the blue wool. "What does she say?" he asked.

"Nothing." She took several slow, deep breaths, fighting blood tears that threatened to betray her, concentrating on keeping her voice light. "Just the usual court gossip."

He joined her, sitting on the bed. "What did you expect, *petite?* Or have you been away so long that you've forgotten how to read a letter properly?"

Oh. She *had* been away too long. She picked up the letter again and took it over to the candle. Very carefully, she held the parchment over the heat, until several lines of script began to appear on the letter's otherwise blank back.

My dearest Rose,

I pray that our loyal knight is successful, and this letter finds its way into your hands. I fear you have gone beyond the reach of my aid, save for my prayers and this my messenger—but know you are welcome to them. Indeed, he would not be contained, and so once again I send him to your side. I fear I cannot even advise you, so I will not, save to remind you that even the greatest and the least among us have their vulnerabilities as well as their strengths, and you are best served to make use of them both. There, I trust that is sufficiently vague to be of some use to you—the less said, the more learned. Write to me soon, my Rosamund, and let me know of your condition.

I remain, your loving sire,

Isouda de Blaise.

"Better?" Josselin asked, grinning. "Surely you can't believe she'd forget you, milady."

"No, no, of course not." Rosamund gave him as brave a smile in return as she dared and came back, folding the letter up again. *He lied. I have to remember it's a lie when he says it.* She started to hand it to him. "Keep this safe for me—"

"You don't want it? After all that?" He took it, but the slightest frown lines appeared between his brows. "Surely he doesn't object if you—"

"He mustn't know about this. It's complicated. Please, Josselin." She glanced towards the closed shutters—she did not need to see out of them to know that full dark was imminent.

"Now, that's a cruel trick," he said softly. "I think I know why we never saw your letters."

There was a light in his eyes that frightened her. "No! No. Don't you see, it's not important now! My letters aren't important. Only this one is. And you must guard it for me, so I can read it again whenever I want to."

"When he can't hear." He put Isouda's letter with the others yet unopened, and then slid them back into the pouch. "He frightens you that much?"

"Why would I be afraid of his Highness? He adores me. He wants to make me his queen."

"But you don't love him."

She couldn't answer him for a moment. *No. Yes—what does it matter?*

"I didn't think so." He leaned closer, laid gentle hands on her shoulders. *"Ma petite fleur—"*

"I must go. He'll be looking for me after he rises."

He pressed a kiss to her hair and released her. "They've already composed a *Lai de Lorraine*. Please don't add to it."

She gave him a harsh look. She knew the story backward and forward, of course—how could she not? Lady Lorraine, the fairest neonate of the Courts of Love, who became the betrothed of Alexander of Paris. But his love had turned to hate when she fled with her kinsman Sir Tristan. When he found them, his love turned murderous. The lays and *chansons* build around the tale were many, each adding its own permutation: Tristan had kidnapped Lorraine against her will; Alexander had trapped Lorraine's soul in a pure white rose; Tristan had cursed the ancient boy-king with his last words. One thing was now certain, the Queens of Love had never forgiven Alexander for Lorraine's murder and they had engineered his downfall some centuries later as delayed vengeance.

"I am not Lorraine, Josselin," she said.

"So long as you know that, *petite*, I am reassured. Go to him, if you must."

She pulled the mantle around her again and walked toward the door, but paused there and looked back at him. "Promise me you won't do anything foolish on my behalf, Josselin. Please?"

"I am your devoted servant, milady, and your kinsman. I would do anything you asked of me. But don't ask me to abandon you."

"Keep the letter for me." She stored his words away in her heart, for when she might need them again. Then she turned and left him, passing Fabien in the outer room without even a glance, slipping as quietly as she could down the stairs and back to her own chamber.

"Something else you might find of interest, milady," Peter reported, checking his *vade mecum* notebook again. "Fabien told me today that the Cainite who guided them last night seemed somewhat nervous—he declined to accompany Sir Josselin to the door, at any rate. It may be that our welcome here is getting a little strained. But I hesitated to broach the subject with Sir Gaston, given his reaction to my suggestion about the cushions." He looked up again. "Do you know how long his Highness plans to stay in Heidelberg, milady?"

"His Highness has not said anything about it, but if he does, I will inform you." Rosamund examined her reflection in the silver mirror Margery handed her, to make sure the circlet was on straight. It pleased Alexander when she wore his gifts.

"It may be soon. Gaston had word from Renaud today. Sir Olivier is expected to return tonight, and apparently he bears a letter from Hardestadt himself."

That was important news—doubtless why Peter had saved it for last. Alexander's one loyal childe had been sent to negotiate with the Cainite overlord of Germany for sanctuary and aid in the reconquest of Paris. "Did Renaud have any idea as to what was in the letter?

Gaston did not inform me one way or the other, milady." Her seneschal sounded aggrieved—Gaston preferred to hoard news and dole it out as favors, and Peter had little patience for such blatant inefficiency. "I bespoke the messenger privately, which is how I learned what I did, but he knew nothing more."

Blanche finished lacing Rosamund's left sleeve and tied it off. "There you are, milady," she said. "Now all you need is some music, and you'll be ready to dance."

Rosamund stepped lightly out into the middle of the room and did an exploratory hop and twirl, one arm out and hand curved just so. Her hair and the ivory brocade fullness of the kirtle both swirled out from the momentum. Blanche clapped with delight.

"It is good to see you dance again, milady," Margery said. "It's been so long since I've seen you so light on your feet."

"Is it Sir Josselin we've to thank for that?" Blanche asked, with a knowing wink. "He is a handsome one, I'll give him that."

"Blanche!" Rosamund tried to sound offended, but could not keep from grinning instead. "He's my *brother*, you shameless girl!" It felt so *good* to grin, even to laugh a little—how long had it been?

"Milady—" One of her mortal escorts came into the chamber and dropped to one knee before her.

"Yes, Thomas. What is it?"

"He's calling for you, milady. Sir Josselin is with him."

Rosamund paused just before she entered the hall, closed her eyes and took three deep breaths, extending her senses before her. Yes, there was Alexander himself... Josselin... Alexander's liegeman Sir Marques... and several mortal presences as well. She opened her eyes again as she came into the hall. Now their forms were rimmed in swirling colors that rippled outward as they spoke, their voices almost painfully loud to her ears, though none of them were actually shouting. The rest of the hall and its furnishings faded into indistinctness, overpowered by the brilliant spirit-halos of the occupants.

"Ah, here is milady," Alexander's silhouette was pulsing dark blues and pale greens as he turned towards her. Beside him, Josselin's taller form was edged with softer hues, sky blue swirled with green and occasional flashes of dark purple. The colors were reassuring—so far, so good. *He won't do anything foolish. He promised.*

She curtsied, letting the kirtle's full skirt flare out around her. "I beg your pardon, your Highness, my lords, if my tardiness has caused any inconvenience."

"It is of no matter, milady," Alexander held out his hand to her in invitation. "We must allow a lady sufficient time for her toilette! But come now, Sir Josselin has presented a proposal for our consideration."

Rosamund came demurely to the prince's side, letting the ghostly colors fade from her vision and the material world take on more clarity. "A proposal, milord? Of what sort?"

Josselin still wore his sword, but over his tunic and surcoat instead of mail, and he'd gotten Fabien to cut his hair to a more fashionable length. He gave Rosamund one of his more subdued courtly smiles and a perfectly executed bow as she joined them.

"It seems," Alexander answered her, "that Sir Josselin believes you are in need of a guardian."

"A guardian?" she echoed, carefully modulating her pitch so she sounded curious, but not dismissive.

"I have of course assured him that I hold you in the highest regard, and that you are safe and under my complete protection." Alexander had kept hold of her hand. Now he drew her closer to him so he could kiss it.

Josselin watched this stoically. "It is the desire of my queen that the Lady Rosamund remain safe, of course, both now and in the future."

"And that is my desire too," Alexander replied easily, smiling at Rosamund. "And I would think it would be your desire also, milord, as well as your queen's."

Rosamund wished she dared look, give Josselin what silent support she could, but the negotiation—for negotiation it was—was already delicate enough.

"It is, your Highness," Josselin admitted. "That is why I have traveled so far—to assure my queen and myself of Lady Rosamund's present and future well-being. It is the wish of her majesty, Queen Isouda, that I continue in this quest for as long as necessary, so I may continue to assure her, and ease her concerns over this her childe, now traveling so far from home."

Alexander turned to face the knight, and Rosamund was

able to do so as well. She could see Josselin's posture stiffen, heard his slight inhalation as Alexander's gaze fell on him.

But Alexander was not yet done with negotiating.

"I would be delighted beyond measure," he said, "if I could end her traveling and return her to her rightful home—indeed, give her a place of the highest honor at my side. Unfortunately, there are obstacles that prevent me from fulfilling the queen's desire to see her childe again—despite my best intentions."

"Those obstacles are not of my queen's making, your Highness, nor under her control."

"Aren't they? I should think that at least some of them might be manageable—she is, after all, still queen in her own domains, is she not?" Alexander's voice sharpened, and his eyes narrowed slightly.

Josselin flinched and looked away for a second. "I am not—not given authority to speak for milady on that matter," he said.

Alexander waited, as unmoving and still as a statue of marble, dark eyes staring without even blinking. He seemed totally oblivious to Rosamund at his side, though he still held her hand.

Josselin recovered. "Milady has not spoken her mind to me on these obstacles," he amended. "However, if my boon is granted, I would gladly serve as her continuing emissary in this regard, and convey your Highness's own missives with my own."

"It is a boon you ask, then," Alexander said at last. "For yourself, Sir Josselin, or do you ask on behalf of your queen?"

Josselin, no. Rosamund wanted to say something, interrupt, claim the boon herself if she had to, but her voice seemed trapped in her throat, just as her fingers were trapped in Alexander's hand.

"I ask on my own behalf, your Highness," Josselin answered. "I cannot guarantee what response my queen might give, only—"

"Then I will grant it," Alexander interrupted. "On one condition, which under the circumstances, I'm sure you'll agree is fair enough."

"And what is milord's condition?" Josselin asked, a bit warily.

"Our route takes us through the domains of many powerful princes. All who travel with me travel under my protection, and as such, all who travel with me must also swear an oath of fealty to me, an oath that is sealed with my blood. Will you swear, Sir Josselin?"

No! Rosamund dared to move her head sideways, just slightly, in hopes he'd heed her.

Josselin's eyes flicked to hers, and back. Alexander noticed.

"Yes, even my sweet Lady Rosamund. Those are my terms. Will you take them?"

But I haven't. Rosamund fought her paralysis, struggled to protest. *I'm sure I haven't. I'd remember—he'd want me to remember, I'm sure of that much....*

Josselin shook his head. "My oath is already given, your Highness. If I swore to you as well, that would render both oaths meaningless. How could you ever trust my word to you, when I had broken it to my queen?"

"I admire a man of honor, Sir Josselin. However, that does present you with a difficult dilemma—you cannot serve your queen's will unless you break your oath, but if you do not break your oath, you will fail your queen."

Josselin's entire body tensed. His fingers did not quite reach for the sword at his side, but his jaw tightened and his eyes went cold. He took several deep breaths, and then the sudden tension seemed to melt away and his hands relaxed.

"I cannot swear to you, your Highness," he said, "but I could swear to milady Rosamund."

"Could you? Would that not also break your oath to the queen?"

Josselin managed a slight smile, and his voice gained more of his usual confidence. "The task my queen laid on me was to serve and protect milady, who is also my kinswoman. To swear such an oath to milady only fulfills my queen's own will. And to serve her who serves your Highness—does that not fulfill your requirement as well?"

Alexander was silent for a long moment, considering—or perhaps simply taking his time responding because he could make them wait. Finally, he smiled as well. "You are very clever—yes. I think that will fulfill my condition admirably."

He released Rosamund's hand and stepped back. "Your boon is granted, Sir Josselin. Make your oath."

"Thank you, your Highness." Josselin bowed, giving Alexander all due respect, and acknowledging his boon as well.

Then he straightened back to his full height, and turned to Rosamund. The warmth in his smile penetrated to her bones, and it occurred to her that he really *was* going to stay, that she wasn't alone anymore. "My dearest lady." He came to her, went down to one knee at her feet. She held out her hands, and he took them, kissed her fingers, then looked up at her. "Will you accept my oath?"

"I will accept it, milord." The ritual was so familiar as to flow from her lips without thinking, which was a good thing, because she wasn't thinking entirely clearly at the moment. She took his larger hands between her own. "Swear."

"I, Josselin de Poitiers, childe of Isouda de Blaise, Knight of the Rose, do swear on my honor to serve you in all matters in which you may command me, or the need arise; to defend you against all enemies and manner of harm, even to my last drop of blood or my Final Death; and to honor you above all others, save the queen we both still serve. I am your faithful knight, your loving brother and your most devoted servant. This I swear, by my honor and my name, and by the blood you give me this night; in all things, I am yours."

—I would do anything you asked of me.

"Sir Josselin de Poitiers, you honor me with your service, which I shall honor in return, and accept with my deepest gratitude. Take then my blood, and be sworn to my service."

Her sleeves were close-fitting and too long, extending down to her knuckles, and the lacing awkward to undo one-handed. Gently he took her right hand, and found the right tie to pull. Then he unlaced her sleeve enough to expose a delicate white wrist. "You should probably sit down," he whispered to her.

"Peter, a chair," she called, spotting her seneschal among the small knot of servants. The mortal hastily obeyed, bringing it to her so that she might be seated exactly where she was.

She was aware of the witness of many eyes—those of her

own servants: her seneschal Peter, her attendant Margery, and her knight Sir Thomas Wyndham; of Josselin's squire Fabien; of Alexander's servant Gaston, of Sir Marques and his man Jean. And only a short distance off, Alexander himself, his dark eyes burning in his pale, youthful face, but otherwise totally still.

Josselin took her hand and turned it over, gently kissing her palm, and then her wrist. She rested her other hand on his shoulder. She felt his lips open against her skin, the pressure of his fangs. There was an instant of pain as he pierced her flesh, driving fangs in between tendon and bone. The thrill followed, moving swiftly through her veins up from her wrist to her heart, and then through her entire body.

Rosamund gave a little gasp—this was nothing like when she gave her blood to Peter or Thomas. They did not pierce her very nerves with pleasure bordering on exquisite pain, nor suckle on her flesh with such desire or sheer intensity. Josselin's eyes were closed, his expression rapt devotion. The slightest change in the pressure of his lips on her skin, the movement of blood in her veins called to answer his demands, sent a new tremor of delight through her.

She was still aware of her surroundings, rather like watching through a peephole into a scene she could only witness but not affect. The servants stared, some with their mouths hanging open; several had begun to sweat. Peter had wrapped his arms around himself, and was weeping silently. Margery rubbed tears from her eyes as well. In the doorway, Sir Olivier and his mortal vassal Sir Renaud stood transfixed, a puddle forming under their feet from water dripping off their cloaks. Gaston's eyes, however, were on his master. Alexander was motionless, like a statue of some ancient Greek hero, his dark eyes fixed on them, not even blinking. But they all seemed so removed from her—only Josselin was real, only he could touch her now.

Josselin withdrew, and she felt an immediate sense of loss. His tongue sealed up the wounds in her flesh, caught the last few precious drops of her blood. He kissed her wrist again, reverently, and then held her hand against his cheek. "I—I am yours, *petite fleur*," he whispered.

Rosamund bent down and rested her forehead against his.

"I know." Then she straightened and rose to her feet. She laid her hand on Josselin's bowed head. "I accept your oath, Sir Josselin, and welcome you to my service. Rise now, and join the others of my household until I call for you."

Josselin rose to his feet as well. He gazed down at her, and she could see the blood tears brimming in his eyes. "Milady," he murmured, bowed, and retreated.

"Graciously done, milady," Alexander found his voice at last, and returned to claim his place at her side. "I'm sure Sir Josselin will serve you—and us—very well indeed. If nothing else, our entourage is suitably enriched by the presence of another knight in our company."

Rosamund somehow managed to smile at him. *If nothing else? It was a sacrament, what he offered me!* She wasn't even sure if it was her own anger or Josselin's that she felt, somehow echoing through blood she had shared. "I have the utmost faith in my kinsman," she said.

But Alexander was already beckoning the new arrivals in. "Sir Olivier, Sir Renaud: Approach us. Do you bring us news from Lord Hardestadt at last? Has he responded to our request for an audience?"

Alexander's childe and liegeman bowed. "Your Highness. I do bring word, my prince. I bring a letter, from the hand of Lord Hardestadt himself."

"Come, come, milord—let us have the letter!" Alexander all but snatched it out of Olivier's hands. "Your negotiations went well, then!"

"I believe so, your Highness," Olivier replied. "I did not speak to Lord Hardestadt himself, of course—"

"You didn't? How then did you get this letter?" Alexander demanded. He ripped the seal open, unfolded the parchment and began to read.

"He would not receive me, but I did speak with his chamberlain, who spoke for his lordship. We had many good dialogues, your Highness, and he then bespoke his lord on our behalf, and then would come back again to talk with me. And in the end, the lord put the letter in my hands for you—"

Rosamund heard Olivier's voice falter, saw Alexander's

expression darken, and fought her own instinct to flee the growing storm.

"What *mockery* is this?" Alexander hissed. "You said your negotiations went well! Why then does he refuse to see me? A perilous precedent, he says? Does he think me a common *refugee*, that he can send me off like a beggar at the door?"

Olivier dropped to his knees at the intensity of Alexander's displeasure. "Your Highness, I—I did not know, please, I beg you—forgive me!" he cried. "He told me it was settled, he told me it was all arranged!"

"Who told you? His chamberlain? His *chamberlain?*"

"He said—"

"Out! All of you, *out!*" Alexander snarled. "No, not *you*, Olivier. We aren't done with you yet. The rest of you. *Out!*"

"But, your Highness," Marques protested. "If this chamberlain—"

Alexander bared his fangs and lashed out with one hand. His blow sent Marques careening backwards into the long table. Both Marques and the table slid another ten feet from the force of the prince's fury.

Mortal servants and Cainites alike fled before the prince's wrath.

It was not unlike being drunk—or what Josselin could remember of drunkenness, not having tasted wine save diluted in mortal veins in over a century now. To look on her now brought it all back again. Rosamund was Aphrodite herself, a goddess with hair the color of flame, copper and ruddy gold in the firelight, her features exquisitely proportioned, with just a hint of the girlhood not entirely left behind. He could gaze at her all night; the flawless perfection of her milk-white skin, the delicacy of her hands, the graceful way the skirt of her kirtle swayed when she walked, even pacing nervously as she was now. She was an angel walking on earth among common men.

That's her blood talking, whispering to you. But you knew what you were doing, didn't you? Didn't you?

Like drunkenness it was temporary, with but one taste,

but heady in its rush nonetheless. It was intoxication, and he savored it while he could.

"I am going to him," she said finally.

"No!" Desperation seized him, and he was on his knee before her in an eyeblink. "Don't risk yourself. I will go, and see what his mood is first."

"You will not know his mood until it is too late. I know him better. Josselin—" She knelt as well, to be on eye level with him. "Whatever possessed you earlier—I am grateful, far more than you could ever guess, for what you did for me this evening. I am honored that you would trust me so much, and I pray to the Holy Mother that you don't come to regret it. But you're not thinking clearly, I can see it in your eyes. I need you clear-headed, milord. I need your wits, not your worship."

Emotions churned in him, despair warring with exhilaration, fear for her safety colliding with the joy of her presence. He somehow managed to fight them all down. She needed him; she had said it. He had only tasted of her this once—his will and heart were still his own, if he would but claim them.

"I am recovered, milady. Mostly," he added, and saw her smile. "I regret nothing, *ma petite fleur*. I have always been in your service."

"I know." She let him help her back up to her feet.

"Milady," Margery said, curtsying apologetically. "Gaston is here. His Highness is asking for you."

"Tell him I will be there straight away."

"I will escort you, then." Something inside him wept to let her go from his sight, but he ignored the pang as best he could, and held out his hand to her.

She laid her hand in his, and he led her down to the hall. It was darker now; the fire on the hearth had burned down to coals, and someone had blown the candles out.

Someone was weeping softly, off to one side of the hall, in the shadows. Rosamund started in that direction instinctively; Josselin closed his fingers on hers and stopped her, then moved towards the sound himself. Rosamund followed.

Sir Renaud was huddled against the wall, rocking back and forth as he wept. In his hands he held Olivier's tunic, gritty with ash. The hose extended out of the tunic and into muddy shoes, but there was not enough left within them to give them shape. The mortal knight looked up at them; his face was smeared with ashes as well as tears. "It was promising news, he said it was," he said, wretchedly. "It *was*—"

"Holy Mary—" Rosamund whispered, and crossed herself. "Oh, no… Olivier… *Olivier*—!"

Josselin echoed the gesture, then took her shoulders in his hands, turning her gently away from the sight of Olivier's ashes. There were blood tears swimming in her eyes. "Poor Olivier…" she repeated, almost numbly.

"Don't go," he whispered, urgently. "Please, *petite*—"

His voice seemed to break her out of her grief for the moment. She shook her head, held a finger to her lips in warning. *Not when he can hear,* she mouthed silently. And then, *I must. Take me to him.*

The conflict in his soul nearly had him trembling. He released her, offered his hand again, and she took it. It took all the discipline in him to obey her, rather than sweep her up in his arms and flee—though to what sanctuary, he had no idea. Alexander was not one whose wrath could be outrun.

Her courage shamed him, and he took what comfort he could from her resolve.

Alexander waited for them in the solar, the quarters he had claimed for his own. "Thank you, milord, for bringing her," he said, shortly. The displaced prince held out his hand; it pained Josselin to see how easily she moved to take it.

"Your diligence is understandable, Sir Josselin," Alexander said, soothingly. Josselin didn't even remember looking into those dark eyes, but they caught him fast. "But unnecessary. I will see to Lady Rosamund for the rest of this night. You may return to your chamber."

Return to your chamber. Josselin bowed, and left them there, having no choice with Alexander's voice echoing in his mind, until he reached where he had been told to go. Such was the power behind even those simple words that once he arrived, he found himself trapped there as surely as a prisoner in a cell.

"I didn't mean to destroy him." Alexander's confession was in a soft, broken whisper. "I swear to you, milady, I did not."

Rosamund wiped a tear away from her own eyes with the backs of her fingers. Olivier had been a good companion on their journey from Paris, gracious, witty and steadfast, patient with both his sire's shifting humors and kind to her in her grief, fear and loneliness; he had done all he could to make her situation more bearable. "How did it happen?" she asked, daring to lay a hand on Alexander's hunched shoulder.

He looked up at her. His cheeks were streaked with dark tears, his eyes rimmed in red. "I don't even remember, that's the terrible thing. It's all a blur—everything happened so quickly. So quickly, and then it was too late."

She sat beside him on the bench. Alexander so rarely showed his heart to her—he had told her once how hard it was for him to let himself laugh or weep with true abandon, as she did. Yet at this moment she could see the boy he must once have been, before the gift of unlife that had so embittered him. How old had he been? She had been taken young, but he had been even younger yet. And she knew something of what it was like to be brought so young from life into undeath.

"I—I know he was dear to you," she said, softly. "He was ever loyal, even in—in times of trouble."

"Like you. Sweet Rosamund, so kind, so loyal—what would I do without you?" He took her hand and held it, stroking her fingers with his thumb. "You're all I have left now."

Rosamund wondered if she even dared ask about the letter. His moods were unpredictable; there was no way to know how he might interpret her interest in it. "You will draw others to your banner, your Highness," she murmured.

It was the wrong thing to say, of course, but if there was a right thing, she didn't know it. Alexander stood up abruptly, dropping her hand almost as if it burned him, and took several strides away from her.

"No one is truly loyal anymore," he muttered. "No one. You say the words, but in the end you're all the same—you will leave me like all the rest, I know it. He'll draw you away. That's what he came here for, to lure you away from me."

"No, your Highness—" she protested.

"He would steal you out from under my very nose, and you would go with him. Look how he manipulated you, how easily he made you into his co-conspirator. He thinks I didn't notice, of course. But I knew what he was doing—seducing you into trusting him, and in my very presence, too!"

His mood began to frighten her, especially the direction his logic seemed to be taking him. What accusations had he thrown at Olivier?

"Your Highness." It took all the nerve she had to approach him. *Soothe him. He wants to be comforted, give him what he wants.* "You mustn't believe that, milord. I am your faithful servant, always."

"My sweet little rose—" He smiled bravely at her, even as fresh tears streaked his cheeks, and held out his hands. She came forward and took them. "I do not blame you, milady. I have no right to lay claim on you—no reason to expect anything better."

The loneliness in his voice, the haunting despair she saw in his eyes, tore at her heart. *What a terrible burden he must bear—he grieves for Olivier as much as I. The Beast is at its cruelest when it robs us of those we love.*

"Trust is such a fragile thing." He raised one hand to caress her cheek. "Like loyalty. Like love itself. But unless loyalty is sure, there can be no trust. And without trust, how can there be love? It—it is so hard for me, Rosamund. It has been so very long since there was someone I could truly trust, who would trust me in return. You cannot know what it would mean to me, sweet little rose—"

His eyes drew her in. In their depths she saw pain that only she could ease, an aching longing that only she could fill. "Milord, you—you know I am your servant, in all things. What—whatever you would ask of me—"

—I am yours, petite fleur....

"Do you trust me, sweet rose?" Alexander's voice, his eyes, held her ensnared, but she could not find it in herself even to want to struggle. His voice soothed her, caressed her soul as tenderly as his hand caressed her cheek. "Trust me. Trust me, even as he trusted you."

His voice dropped lower still, to a whisper. "Will you swear, Rosamund?"

Chapter Three

Josselin awoke with a start and a snarl, fangs extended and a dagger in his hand poised to strike, before he recognized Fabien's pale face as his intended target. He tossed the dagger aside and held out his hand instead, taking several unnecessary breaths to calm himself. "Fabien—no, lad, come here, I'm not angry at you! I did ask you to wake me. Come to me."

Fabien came and sat on the bed, and Josselin took the trembling mortal into his arms. "There, that's better, isn't it? I *am* sorry, Fabien—I would never hurt you, you know that, don't you?"

Fabien buried his face in his master's shoulder, his arms encircling Josselin's ribs. "I didn't mean to—I tried to be gentle," he said.

"I know, I know," Josselin assured him. "You did the right thing, it's only me being a beast first thing in the evening— where did I put that dagger?"

It was all the hint Fabien needed; he scrambled across the bed until he recovered it and then presented it hilt first to his lord. His eyes shone, and his lips parted expectantly. "Please. Oh, please. It's been a month, milord. I'm sure it has."

"Yes, I believe it has. Only be still for a moment, I must check on milady."

Fabien obeyed. Josselin closed his eyes for a moment, *listening* as hard as he could. The beating of Fabien's heart pounded like a great drum, his breathing became a roaring wind. He heard mice skittering in the rushes, heard the clatter of plates and bowls being washed in the kitchen below from the servants' dinner. He heard faint voices—speaking German in the kitchen, a mixture of English and French in Rosamund's own chamber from Peter and Margery. He could not make out their words, but they sounded calm enough. He did not hear Rosamund herself, but perhaps she had not yet risen. It *was* early, even for her.

She's all right, then. If she were not, they would know, and I would hear it now. I would feel it, perhaps, in her blood.

Relieved, he brought himself back, letting the cacophony of sounds fade into the distance, until he heard nothing beyond the walls of the room, and his squire's breathing was a whisper rather than a roar.

He opened his eyes again, and smiled at Fabien.

"Choose where," Josselin told him, holding his arms open in invitation. As the mortal moved closer, he added, "Just remember that milady may walk through that door any moment, so perhaps a *little* discretion—"

Fabien's hands were pleasantly warm against Josselin's undead flesh, though the ghoul made his decision somewhat more quickly than usual—perhaps because he was simply eager, or perhaps because he didn't wish to share the intimacy of this moment, even with his master's lady. He leaned forward and pressed a kiss to Josselin's collarbone. "There."

"You *are* being discreet," Josselin observed wryly. He brought the dagger up, laid the point against his own flesh, and made a short, clean slice over the bone. Dark blood welled up in the wound. Fabien put his mouth to it and suckled greedily, pushing the knight back down into the pillows.

Josselin closed his eyes and enfolded his ghoul in his arms, though he kept his peripheral senses alert, just in case.

But Rosamund did not come.

Peter admitted him, albeit a bit reluctantly. "Good evening to you, milord," he said, bowing respectfully. "Milady is at her bath."

Josselin noted the curtain hung across the room, heard water being poured, smelled lavender and roses. "So I see. Thank you, Peter."

The seneschal bowed again and retreated to his books. Josselin approached the curtain.

"Milady—" He paused, thinking how to frame the question. *Why did he command me away like that? What did he want with you? Why didn't you come to me earlier?* "I was concerned for you. Are you well?"

She didn't answer him for a long time. He couldn't tell if it was because she could not, or for some other reason. "Rosamund?"

"I'm well, milord. Truly, I am. I shall be out in a few minutes, I pray you have patience."

He could hear her standing, getting out of the tub. Several minutes passed; he waited as patiently as he could. Then Margery came out and took the curtain down, admitting him at last to his lady's private sanctum.

Rosamund, now clad in a linen chemise, held out her hands to him. "You see, milord, I am quite whole," she assured him, with a wan smile.

He came and took them, bending down to kiss her cheeks. Her maidservant Blanche began to dry her hair vigorously with a towel.

"And I thank our Savior's own sweet mother that you are," he said fervently. "He sent me away—I had no choice. I couldn't—"

"I know. He can be a bit heavy-handed in his use of the blood sometimes. It's so easy for him, sometimes he forgets there are other ways."

"Heavy-handed? It was that, most certainly." He could not entirely suppress the anger in his voice. "It made me fear what he meant for you, that he should dismiss me like that. If he would murder his own blood with so little cause—"

"What happened to Olivier was an accident!" she said, just as fervently. "He—he didn't mean to. He was devastated with grief afterwards. I saw him weep, Josselin, and I've never seen that before."

"An accident?" Josselin echoed. It was possible, of course; any Cainite could lose control, and any Cainite could kill if the Beast ruled him. But it didn't ring true. Alexander had been Prince of Paris for centuries, and as far as Josselin knew, had never destroyed another Cainite *accidentally*. "How did this... accident happen?"

She looked away. "I don't know. Margery, I'd like the green cotte tonight, please. And the surcoat with the roses."

"What did he say, then?"

"We—we talked of many things," she said. "He talked of many things. I listened. That was what he wanted, really. He likes having a sympathetic audience."

Josselin frowned slightly. "Did he talk about the letter, then? What did Hardestadt answer him?"

"I didn't see it. He didn't leave it out and—under the circumstances—I didn't ask. He'll tell us when he's ready to, I'm sure."

Margery brought the green cotte, and for a moment, Rosamund's face was hidden under a swath of forest-green wool.

"Then what *did* he want to talk about?"

She didn't answer him for a moment, and he waited as the cotte was settled over her shoulders, and Blanche began lacing it up the back. She seemed absorbed in the buttons on her sleeve.

"Rosamund?"

"It was a private matter!" Rosamund snapped. "Must I tell you everything I do?"

The rebuke stung as if she'd slapped him. His protest died in his throat and his knees wobbled; he somehow managed to seat himself on one of her wardrobe chests rather than falling to his knees. An aching emptiness opened up somewhere under his heart from the sharpness of her displeasure. *This is the blood doing this to you*, he reminded himself, but knowing it didn't help. "No, milady," he said hoarsely. "Of course not. Forgive me."

"And in any case, there's nothing you can do."

It took a moment for her words to sink in, past the dull ache in his own heart at that moment, and develop meaning—and then blossom into further shades of meaning beyond that. His own pain was forgotten in less than a mortal heartbeat, and he looked up at her, letting his vision shift until the details of the room faded into a hazy blur and her silhouette darkened and took on a halo of pale, slowly flickering colors. Muddy colors, grays and dull orange and reds—colors he normally never saw on her.

"Nothing I can do," he echoed, "about what?"

An eddy of dulled orange rimmed her form as she turned towards him. "Nothing. It's nothing, Josselin. I—I'm sorry. I didn't mean to say that."

Josselin glanced towards Margery. The mortal woman's halo was far brighter, more distinct, pulsing with life, but showed colors similar to those of her mistress—flickering reds and orange fading to pinks. *Is she angry at me or at Alexander?*

"I am your servant, *petite*," he assured her, and saw relief ripple through her halo in a wash of silver-edged blue. Then he added, deliberately, "But I will not forgive him so easily. Not for what he has done to you."

Her colors flickered suddenly along the edges of her body—sputtering flames of muddy brown, dull blood red, tipped with orange. "He hasn't done anything!"

Margery's aura blazed with all the true colors of fire, angry reds, fearful oranges.

"He murdered Olivier," Josselin reminded her. "I was afraid for you, *petite*—"

"I told you, that was an accident! He would never—" For a moment Rosamund's aura flared nearly as bright as Margery's, brilliant blood red. "You have no idea how hard this has been for him. How lonely he's been—"

How *lonely*?

The colors in her halo were nothing compared to the crimson wave that flooded across his vision at that moment, the sudden fury that rose in Josselin's own heart as the patterns of words and colors fell into place. His fangs came down; he was trembling with the effort it took not to go hunt down Alexander and tear him apart, or worse, take out his rage on closer—much more innocent—targets.

Why didn't you tell me, petite?

"*Milady*—" A whispered warning from Peter, who realized much sooner than Rosamund did what was going on.

"Josselin?" Rosamund turned towards him, her colors rippling back to muddy orange and rust. "Josselin—look at me. Please forgive me, I didn't mean it like that. I know you were worried, *mon chevalier,* and I didn't mean to—to sound ungrateful."

She slowly started walking towards him, hands outstretched protectively, as if that gesture might protect the mortals behind her. "Josselin—please, what's wrong? Speak to me."

He focused on her. The soft nimbus around her silhouette swirled with muddy grays and orange, but her eyes bathed him in soothing blues. He felt her gaze wash over him, cool the burning in his blood. Part of him raged still, seeing her effort to calm him as additional evidence, proof of Alexander's violation of her; but the greater part of him welcomed the comfort and reassurance of her love, her approval, her concern. He savored it, drank it in as he had drunk her blood.

Her blood.

Her fingers were gentle and cool on his cheeks; he took her hands in his and kissed them, let the colors fade from his vision. The clarity of the room returned, the soft green folds of her skirt, her delicate fingers, rushes on the floor, all came back into focus. His anger faded too, but not entirely. This offense would not be so easily forgiven.

"*Ma petite fleur,*" he murmured at last, looking up at her. "It's not you I'm angry at. This—this cannot go unanswered, I can't—"

Rosamund put her fingers across his lips to silence him. "Yes, it can," she said. He could hear defeat in her voice, and it pained him. "It can, and you will allow it."

"Rosamund, *no,*" he pleaded with her. "I am here to defend you, I *swore* to defend you, to you and to our queen!"

"You *promised.* Do you remember?"

Words failed him. He remembered, and he nodded.

"Then listen to me. Keep your promise, Sir Josselin. We are not at Roncesvalles yet, this is not the time for tragic heroism. You know losing a battle does not mean the war. But I can't afford to lose my general, not now. I need you, Josselin. Please."

Rosamund's servants were clumped at the far side of the room, Blanche crying and Margery trying to soothe her, Peter's wary gaze flicking between the two Cainites, and Fabien, who stood frozen in the door, tears streaming down his face.

Josselin took a long, deep breath, and then another. Righteous anger warred with obedience; he was trapped between conflicting oaths and the sweet agony of Rosamund's blood in his veins.

Obedience won. He bowed his head. "I am your servant, milady."

Chapter Four

Heidelberg, Rhenish Palatinate
Feast of St. John at the Lateran Gate, May, 1224

To Alexander, once of Paris,

We have heard of the misfortunes fate has recently wrought for you, our cousin of Paris, and assure you that none within our realms had any part in the events which your emissary did describe for us. When a great prince has fallen, all of Europe must bear witness. Know that you have our sympathies in your time of troubles, but our responsibilities here do not permit us to meet with you at this time.

It would be a perilous precedent—indeed, contrary to the very Traditions of Caine our Father—to directly intervene in so distant a matter. In the greater interests of our Blood, a balance among the Eldest of our Blood must be maintained, lest the alternative destroy the fortunes of all. We offer to you, our cousin, the hospitality of our noble and beloved childe, Lord Jürgen the Sword-Bearer, at his court in Magdeburg. There you will find a safe refuge and such advice and assistance as we can extend, in the person of Lord Jürgen, who is both tried and experienced in the ways of war. We have made this our will known to him as well as to you, and expect him to welcome you as a kinsman should upon your arrival.

By our hand,
—Hardestadt, Lord of Bavaria, Saxony, Thuringia, and Overlord of the Fiefs of the Black Cross

"Magdeburg—eh." Sighard shook his shaggy head. His face was shaggy too, with a thick black beard that covered both cheeks up nearly to his eyes, which were yellow like a wolf's. He spoke broken French with a thick accent, occasionally interspersing it with some other tongue, guttural and fierce.

Alexander seemed to understand him, however. "Yes, Magdeburg," he said.

"You said Bavaria, not Magdeburg," Sighard growled. "I bring you Bavaria. Bavaria this way, nearer. Magdeburg is Saxony, that way, very far. North, past many mountains." He extended one long hairy arm to make his point.

"Do you know the way?" Alexander asked him coolly. "Or shall I find another guide?"

Sighard snarled. He was missing several teeth, but those that remained were all pointed and vicious, and his fangs seemed never to recede. "I know where is Magdeburg. Is dangerous road from this place."

"I want the fastest road. The most direct. I want to be there as soon as possible."

"That is most dangerous road, most direct. Manwolves in Steigerwald. Must avoid their villages."

Rosamund was grateful she did not have to bargain with the creature; Sighard had a way of looking at her that made her uncomfortable. But at least the discussion kept Alexander's attention focused on his recalcitrant guide, and away from her or Josselin, whose outrage had cooled but undoubtedly not died. Josselin's temper was slow to ignite, but once kindled could burn for a long, long time—especially over an injury done to someone he considered under his protection. Even if it wasn't an injury, exactly.

They were going to Magdeburg. Now that she had seen Hardestadt's letter, part of her wondered just how much say Lord Jürgen had been given in the matter of their invitation. Hardestadt had seemingly left him no choice, yet the Lord Jürgen she remembered was not one to bow easily to the will of another, not even his own sire.

Although Alexander, as she had cause to know, could be very persuasive.

The Cainites sat at the long table, with Alexander at the head, except for Sighard, who had hopped up, squatting on the table itself to carve crude maps into the scarred wood with one curved talon, the better to make his point. Marques, sitting in Olivier's old place by Alexander's right hand, snorted at Sighard's warnings. "You said the same thing about the Schwarzwald, if I recall," he said. "And yet we passed through it safely, and the only hairy beast we saw the whole time was you."

"Which is tribute to very fine guide," Sighard shot back, "so you should give more respect. You not know man-wolves. They *eat* little Cainites like you and spit out bones." He spat in Marques's general direction; the younger Cainite flinched, and the guide laughed. "And will my very fine guide continue to guide us to Magdeburg?" Alexander asked, ignoring Marques and focusing on Sighard.

"Is new contract, to Magdeburg," the Gangrel said. "Expensive."

"How expensive?"

Sighard didn't hesitate. "I want very good horse of dead knight, also his sword and fine cloak."

Olivier's horse... his sword... Rosamund felt her spine stiffen. *He talks as though what he asks for is little more than the spoils of war to be divided!*

"*What?*" Marques rose to his feet. "Do you have any idea what that animal is *worth*? Milord, we can find a better guide— or at the very least a less insolent one—"

"*Sit down* and *be quiet!*" Alexander snapped suddenly, turning to fix his coldest stare on Marques. The younger Cainite sat as if his legs had been chopped out from under him. "Or I will grant Sighard the pleasure of tearing out your tongue at the root."

He turned back to the guide, and just stared at him for a moment. Sighard didn't quite cower, but he did crouch a bit lower under Alexander's gaze.

But Alexander seemed to be thinking about it. "A knight's very good horse, his sword, his cloak—those are costly things, and in more ways than one. But why stop there? What about his mail and helmet? His clothing? What about his vassal, to serve you as he did his late master? If you're going to be a knight, you should have a retainer."

Sighard considered this. "Great prince can make me a knight?"

"Knights are made in many ways." Alexander rose from his seat so he could walk around the table as he spoke. "Some are born into families of rank and are trained from boyhood. Some not so advantaged are awarded the title on the battlefield after they have performed great deeds. But others earn the position through the fulfillment of a quest—a long and difficult quest, of course. Is that not right, Lady Rosamund?"

What is he up to? "That is correct, milord," Rosamund responded, a bit warily. "But a knight's quest is somewhat more—"

"Indeed it is, milady," Alexander agreed. "Indeed it is. But is not guiding a lady and her companions on a perilous journey a quest worthy of a knight?"

Josselin shifted restlessly in his seat; Rosamund laid a gentle hand on his arm.

Alexander turned towards the knight. "Sir Josselin—what do you think? You are something of an authority on this topic, I would imagine."

Josselin glanced up at Alexander, then fixed his gaze on Sighard, who was watching the exchange with keen, almost expectant interest. "If such a deed were enough in itself," Josselin replied coolly, "then he would be already worthy—but clearly it is not, if he must now bargain to gain it. Even the best horse and sword do not make a knight."

Sighard snarled at Josselin, inferring an insult; the Knight of the Rose didn't even flinch.

Alexander leaned against the table, and folded his arms across his chest. "That is quite true, milord," he agreed. "A knight must have courage, skill at arms, courtesy, generosity, honor, loyalty and nobility of spirit—all qualities which Sighard may have opportunity to demonstrate on our journey. Or perhaps be taught such virtues as he may yet lack, so that on our arrival he may prove himself worthy... even to you."

"Skill at arms may be taught, and even courtesy," Josselin replied, tightly. Rosamund could see the tension in the way he held himself, his hands gripping the carved arms of his chair. "But honor cannot be taught; it comes from within, from the heart. And once it is compromised, for whatever reason—then it is forever stained, and not even the greatest prince can wash the stain away."

Josselin, no—Rosamund wished she dared touch him, capture his attention with her eyes, *anything* to distract his temper and still his tongue without it being obvious to Alexander what she was doing. *He serves me out of love, I cannot compel him—not without making him weak when I need him to be strong.*

Alexander simply smiled. "So it is not unlike a woman's virginity, is that it?" Behind him, Sighard chuckled. Josselin did not respond.

"Milady Rosamund," Alexander continued smoothly, "the Courts of Love have always held that the noble ladies of the court are the true judge of knightly virtues—tell me, do you believe our loyal Sighard has the makings of a knight?"

—Your loyalty means so much to me. You're all I have left now.

Alexander's seductive voice in her memory, the taste of his potent blood on her tongue, his caresses, the glorious ecstasy of his kiss. Josselin's eyes following her, his uncompromising loyalty and unquestioning love. *Where is my honor now? Forever stained, lost like my virginity?*

Rosamund forced herself to smile, and rise from her chair. She approached Alexander and Sighard, and held out her hand towards the Gangrel. *I could face Guillaume; Sighard is nothing in comparison. He already wants what Alexander offers, so he will want to please me too.*

The Gangrel approached, still moving on all fours on top of the table, claws clicking on the wood. But as he drew near, he put one knee down and took her hand. His talons curled around her fingers, but did not prick her. He bent his head and kissed her knuckles furtively, almost shyly.

"Sighard, you heard the virtues that his Highness listed. Is it your desire to become a knight, to hold yourself to those virtues above all others? Or would you rather remain as you are, and settle for a fine sword and a very good horse?"

He raised his gaze to hers. The yellow eyes that had so unnerved her were wide with wonder, and the usual leer was missing from his expression. "Lady," he rasped, his broken French barely intelligible. "If you say I be knight, then I be knight in truth. I take you safe to Magdeburg. Is my honor."

She wasn't sure if he meant it was an honor to guide them to Magdeburg, or that in doing so he would prove his honor, but it really didn't matter. "Then guide us well, strive to hold yourself to those virtues, and seek instruction where you can. Prove yourself worthy of the accolade, and I am certain his Highness will grant it."

He nodded, bowed, and released her hand. Then he backed away, carefully easing himself off the table to sit on the bench opposite them.

"Very well done, milady," Alexander said.

Rosamund smiled and felt a flush of pleasure at his praise. "I always strive to please you, your Highness," she murmured, dropping into a brief curtsy before returning to her chair. But he caught her hand, and kept her by him. Out of the corner of her eye, she could see Josselin's jaw tighten.

"Tell me, milady," Alexander asked, drawing her hand up to his lips to kiss it. "What Sir Josselin said, about honor being compromised—do you believe that as well?"

Rosamund could not reclaim her hand, could not look away. "That—that is—is the knightly ideal, milord...."

"That seems an impossibly high standard... the slightest falsehood or momentary weakness might cast such a stain as to tarnish one's honor forever. But who is without sin, without weakness? How can anyone then meet that test? By such a standard, milady—is there any knight left who can still claim to have his honor?"

"How can *you* speak about honor?" Josselin was on feet in an instant, his chair shoved back nearly six feet by the force of his fury. "How dare you presume to judge, milord, after all you have done?"

Alexander's entire attention suddenly refocused on the

French knight. "So much," he said softly, "for knightly courtesy. My question was rhetorical, merely philosophical musing—but yours seems more accusatory. What exactly, milord, do you think I have done? Do you claim right to judge *me*, in my own hall?"

Josselin stood his ground, although not without some effort. Rosamund could see him shaking—though whether in reaction to Alexander's cold glare or his own anger, she couldn't tell. She couldn't move, couldn't speak—but she tried to catch Josselin's gaze nonetheless. *Please, please—Josselin, no, this is not the time for stubborn pride!*

"I can do no more than pray God will judge you, milord," Josselin said through gritted teeth. His fangs were down. "One time, it was your right. But not *twice*—she did not deserve such a penalty for her loyalty."

"Twice?" Alexander appeared surprised, even shocked. "You have misjudged my intentions, milord. Milady, can it be you did not tell him? Surely your loyal knight deserves an explanation?"

"I—" Rosamund was caught off guard, and trapped by Josselin's stricken stare. *Tell him? How could I tell him when I knew this would be the result?*

"What?" Josselin demanded.

Alexander merely smiled at her, and gestured her to continue. His support gave her strength; surely Josselin would understand. "It was but the one time, Josselin. We shared—he partook as well as I. I was afraid to tell you, I knew you'd do... something foolish." *You promised me, Josselin, please, please, don't take this any further. Yes, he lied. It's not worth martyring yourself!*

"Only one time—and he partook as well," Josselin repeated. His voice had grown icy calm.

"Yes," Alexander said softly. He reached out, ran his fingers through Rosamund's hair; startled at the unexpected contact, she flinched. "I confess, I simply could not resist—"

Josselin's sword slid free of the scabbard in one swift, smooth motion. "*No*," he said flatly. "You don't deserve her."

"Josselin, *no!*" Rosamund cried. Sighard snarled and leapt

to his feet; even the attending ghouls stifled cries of either terror or outrage.

Alexander didn't even blink. "So much," he said, "for knightly honor. Do you really mean to challenge me, milord?"

"No," Rosamund said quickly. "Milord, he doesn't mean—"

"Oh, I think he does," Alexander said smoothly.

"I meant what I said, your Highness," Josselin said. He had not lowered his sword, though his voice was calm enough. "You don't deserve her. She has followed you across half of Europe, endured rain and frost and long nights on the road, even been subjected to isolation from her own kin, and yet she has remained loyal. Any true knight would know that such a lady is to be honored, treasured—and above all, trusted and loved."

"You speak of love so glibly, Sir Josselin," Alexander mused. "But I do love her. How could I not?"

"Love springs from the heart, milord. Not the blood. Love is earned—not compelled."

"Ah, from the heart. Like honor, I suppose?" Alexander smiled. "Put aside your sword, Sir Josselin, and for your lady's sake I will allow you to beg for my mercy."

"You demand what neither honor nor love will permit. No."

"Josselin—" Rosamund had been frozen in place—whether by Alexander's will or her own fear, she wasn't sure. *Holy Mary, what can I do?*

Alexander looked more pleased than angered at Josselin's answer. "Very well. You leave me no choice but to accept your challenge as it stands. Gaston. Bring me that fine sword Sighard was admiring earlier."

Under Gaston's directions, mortal servants cleared the hall, moving the table off to the side. Alexander stood on one side, speaking softly to Sighard as he drew Olivier's sword and gave it a few experimental swings.

Fabien, his face white, unbuckled Josselin's belt and helped his master out of his surcoat, then removed the empty scabbard from the belt before buckling it back on. The squire only managed a weak smile as Rosamund approached them, but Josselin took her hands and kissed her fingers as if there was nothing wrong at all.

"Josselin, you don't have to do this," Rosamund pleaded with him. "Please—"

"And what would you have me do?" he asked her.

"You couldn't beg his pardon—forget your pride for this once? Josselin, you *promised*."

He winced, just a little. "I know—and all I can do is implore your forgiveness, *petite*. I have no excuse, save love itself. But let me also ask you: If I do what he wants, and beg for his mercy, do you think that will satisfy him? Or will he next demand that I take the drink I refused him before—or that you take yet another?"

"But I *need* you."

He was silent for a moment. "If milady commands it," he said finally, "I will kneel at his feet and forget all pride and honor. My own, at least, I will gladly sacrifice for your sake."

It was tempting. He would do it—but it would weaken him forever in Alexander's eyes, leave him vulnerable to even more humiliation. "No, I won't command it," she said at last. "You're right, he won't be satisfied. I don't know what else to do."

"Nor do I. But it seems my course is set." He glanced across the hall at Alexander; noted a blue scarf tucked into the prince's belt. "He carries your favor."

"He carries a bit of silk."

Josselin smiled and bent to kiss her hand.

"Are you ready, Sir Josselin?" Alexander called.

"Yes, milord. I am." Josselin released Rosamund's fingers, and took his sword from Fabien. Then he walked calmly out to the center of the hall, opposite Alexander.

The two combatants bowed to each other, and then began. Josselin was taller, had a longer reach and practiced the sword far more frequently, but Alexander was very quick. They circled, the first few blows merely testing their opponent's reflexes, each coming more quickly than the last, until mortal eyes could no longer follow the blur of the steel, or the undead flesh that wielded it.

Rosamund didn't dare even to blink lest she miss something. Her focus shifted with them, so that Fabien and Peter's anxious breathing and restless movements beside her seemed to slow to a crawl.

But then Alexander struck. First a horizontal slice that

Josselin had to twist to avoid, and then a vicious backstroke that struck his left thigh. There was a sharp crack of shattering bone, and Josselin fell, landing hard on his back. He blocked Alexander's next blow with his own blade, but the sheer power behind it drove his elbow against the stone floor with numbing force. Alexander's sword came slicing across faster than even Rosamund could see. There was a splatter of blood, and Josselin's sword went flying across the floor, his severed hand still gripping the hilt.

Alexander dug the point of his sword under Josselin's jaw. "Yield."

Josselin's fangs were down, his face twisted into a grimace. His left hand was drawn into a white-knuckled fist, his broken leg lay at a painfully unnatural angle, hose and tunic stained with what blood had been caught at the point of impact. His chest rose and fell as he struggled to master himself, to acknowledge himself beaten and restrain the fury of the injured beast within. "I... yield," he gasped at last. "My... lord."

"Lady Rosamund," Alexander turned towards her. "What say you, milady? Shall I spare him? For you?"

Her eyes swam with blood tears; she could taste her own blood where she'd bitten her lower lip clean through. "Yes, please, your Highness. Thank you, milord."

Alexander's eyes bored into Josselin's. "This time, for her sake, I will be merciful. Do not try my patience again."

He stepped back, turned and walked away. "Get him out of my sight."

Fabien was sleeping when Rosamund slipped into Josselin's chamber early the following evening. She did not wake him. Josselin had fed from his squire immediately after the battle, and the ghoul needed to rest in order to recover his strength.

Josselin's recovery required something more than rest, and she had brought that as well—one of the girls from the kitchen, whom Peter had thoughtfully cleaned up a bit before presenting her to his mistress. The girl, believing herself wanted for an entirely different sort of intimacy, waited outside the door as Rosamund went in to check on her knight.

"Do I look as bad as all that?" Josselin asked wryly on see-ing her expression. He pushed himself up higher on the pillows with his good hand.

She smiled. "Lady Genevieve would not approve of you in her chamber, I fear." In truth, he looked better than she had feared he might, but his eyes seemed sunken in their sockets, his cheekbones more pronounced, and his long hair tangled and limp. She couldn't see what his maimed arm looked like; it still lay under the sheet with which they had covered him.

"Ah," Josselin replied, "but she would order her ladies to prepare a bath for me, and bathe me with her own hands, and weep over my wounds, and beg me to tell her how I came to be so badly used."

"Well, I suspect you know her better than I." Rosamund sat on the bed beside him. "And what would you tell her?"

"Oh, that I was wounded defending milady's honor—but of course, I fell in glorious and noble combat...." He grimaced. "That would be the part I'd have trouble explaining. In all her favorite stories, the noble knight never failed in his quest because he acted the fool, or broke a promise to his lady."

"You didn't—"

"No, *petite*. Let me finish my confession. I was a fool. It seems whatever I do only makes things worse for you, not better."

"You do make things better. Just by being here."

"I wanted to save you from him. I can't." It hurt him to admit that, she could see it in his eyes. Josselin was not accustomed to defeat. "I failed you, milady, and I broke my word to you. And for those sins against both love and duty, I must therefore hum-bly beg for your forgiveness. I will fall on my knees before you if you like, once my leg is whole again, and accept any penance you assign me with a grateful heart."

"Josselin—" Rosamund took his hand, held it tightly for a few minutes. "For breaking your promise, *mon chevalier*, I do forgive you—I cannot fault you for your devotion. In that you have never failed me. And I thank God, our Savior and the most Blessed Madonna that you did not pay the ultimate price for it, for then I should have been robbed of all hope of deliverance."

"I can't promise you deliverance. I can't even offer you

hope." He shook his head. "He was playing with me, Rosamund. I never had a chance. He was *holding back,* and he was still so fast! It was so easy for him—if he'd wanted to, he could have had my head before I'd even raised my sword."

"But he didn't. You see? To have you still with me gives me hope."

"To owe my survival to his mercy—if you wish to call that a sign of hope, well—"

"You have no idea how alone I've felt—even your gossip about Genevieve gives me hope! And going to Magdeburg brings me hope, as well. Especially if you're there with me."

"It's thoughts of Lord Jürgen that bring you hope," Josselin remarked. "I recall you seemed rather impressed by him. I heard nothing else for months after you returned."

"Would that he had been that impressed with me." Rosamund shook her head.

It had been her first major duty once Queen Salianna granted her the title of Ambassador of the Rose, to attend the festivities surrounding Lord Jürgen's opening of Magdeburg as his new court seat, and to present to him a finely crafted sword as a symbol of the Courts of Love's esteem. When that blade had been revealed to be a cheap copy, the embarrassment had been devastating to Rosamund. That Jervais bani Tremere, erstwhile delegate from his order of blood-sorcerers, had ultimately been revealed as culpable, and that the original—and very fine—blade had been recovered and duly given to Lord Jürgen, had only partially salvaged the whole affair. Indeed Josselin's own childe Lucien de Troyes had played no small part in the ill-conceived Tremere scheme, and that wound was harder still to bear. The assembled Queens of Love had called a blood hunt on Lucien, over Josselin's protests. Rosamund had feared her career as an ambassador was over—until she had been sent to Paris last year.

"At least once we're in Magdeburg," she said trying to avoid bringing up memories of Lucien, which she knew could still cut Josselin to the quick, "Alexander will be focused on getting Lord Jürgen's support, making alliances for his return to Paris. We'll be among other Cainites whose good opinion Alexander will need to court, and he'll pay less attention to us."

"Will Lord Jürgen support him?"

"I don't know. And I won't let you distract me with talk of either Lord Jürgen or politics, Sir Josselin—there is still the matter of your penance."

"Speak then, milady, what quest you would demand of me—for I am anxious to be restored to your favor."

"You may think it cruel of me to demand it. I would have you apologize to Alexander. Make peace with him, I implore you, at any price but blood." She could almost see his spine stiffening as she spoke. "Josselin, listen to me. He knows you now, knows exactly how to wound you with words and little gestures, how to goad you until you cannot bear it any longer. He knows you love me, and he will use your love to destroy you—I beg you, by that same love, don't let him do that."

He freed his hand of her grip, reached up to touch her cheek. "Don't beg on my account, Rosamund," he whispered. He sat upright, pulled her close.

Rosamund hugged him, felt his arms—both of them— enclose her as well. He pressed a kiss to her hair. "I will do as you ask. *Ahh...* don't move, *petite*, I—" He shuddered slightly, and then slowly, very deliberately released her. "I fear even you are tempting me—my belly is a bottomless pit at present."

"I know." She could see that the stump of his right wrist now seemed more rounded, flesh and bone beginning to fill in for what was lost. "I've got someone waiting for you."

"Ah—good."

"She speaks only a little French. Peter said he didn't think Alexander had ever touched her, though Marques might have. Be gentle."

"Of course."

Rosamund went to the door. "Gude? You can come in now. My brother wants to see you."

The girl entered, smoothing back her hair nervously. She reminded Josselin of a rabbit venturing out in search of clover, ever wary of the fox. But then she saw him, and her eyes widened a little more. A shy smile crossed her face, and she bobbed in an awkward curtsy.

He held out his hand, and smiled at her. "Come, *lapinette.*"

Chapter Five

After such a long and uncertain journey, finally drawing near to Magdeburg almost felt like coming home. They were expected; messengers had been riding hard between their traveling company and Lord Jürgen, negotiating details of their sanctuary. A formal escort had met them the night before. Now, riding in the company of a half dozen knights bearing Jürgen's black cross, Rosamund had to wonder if the escort was to honor the former prince of Paris, or to oversee his compliance with the terms of his welcome.

Their escort did not bring them into the city itself, but turned off on a narrow dirt track that led through a stretch of dark, forbidding forest. It reminded Rosamund of the Schwarzwald. She noticed that Sighard constantly rode up and down the line of their caravan, very much on alert, and Josselin was careful to keep himself between her and the trees.

But they emerged after a short while into fields and orchards again, and approached a village nestled between the fields and a river. Set slightly apart from the village and overlooking the road there was a small walled keep, where torches burned at the gate, and the gate itself opened wide to welcome them.

Inside, more men in Black Cross surcoats stood watch on the walls and around the courtyard. Rosamund recognized Jürgen's own red-eagle banner hanging from the watchtower, and felt a small thrill of anticipation. Jürgen had come to greet his guests personally.

Josselin, ever the soul of courtesy, helped her down from the horse. "Well, here we are at last," he murmured. "And I see we are welcomed—" he nodded towards the keep's entrance. A woman in the white habit, wimple and veil of holy orders was coming down the stairs. She was escorted by two more of the Black Cross guardsmen. Rosamund recognized her at once.

"Lucretia," she said, in as low a voice as she could. "Jürgen's right hand."

Lucretia's height alone made her stand out—she was easily as tall as a man, taller than even Veronique d'Orleans, and carried herself with almost imperious authority despite her humble nun's garb. Humility, Rosamund recalled, was not a virtue Lucretia did well.

Alexander had dismounted as well, and now stood waiting to receive Jürgen's envoy. Sighard and Marques waited with him; now Josselin led Rosamund over to join them, fanning out in a small semi-circle behind the exiled prince. Behind them stood their retainers—one per Cainite, as arranged. Fabien and Peter followed and stepped into their places as well.

Lucretia glanced over Alexander's little entourage. If she recognized Rosamund she gave no sign of it. She curtsied formally to Alexander, who bowed—albeit not very deeply—in return.

"Milord Alexander," she said, in passable, if strongly accented, French. "On behalf of his Highness, Jürgen Sword-Bearer, Prince of Magdeburg, Lord of Saxony and Brandenburg, Protector of the Burzenland, allow me to welcome you and your companions to milord's capital of Magdeburg and this his manor and keep of Finsterbach. I am Sister Lucretia, of the Order of the Black Cross."

Rosamund noted the title granted Alexander—only Jürgen was a prince in Magdeburg, and they'd had to negotiate that in advance. The Courts of Love were reputed for their complex formalities, but even they had a hard time competing with the traditions of Clan Ventrue, the bloodline of both Alexander and Jürgen. Elders of that clan took rank very seriously indeed.

"Thank you for your welcome, Sister Lucretia," Alexander replied. "We are grateful for his Highness's hospitality to our company in our exile."

The agreed-upon formulae having been dispensed with, Lucretia's gaze traveled over Alexander's companions, and paused for a moment on a familiar face. Rosamund wasn't sure if having Lucretia remember her was going to bode well for their welcome or not. But the Saxon nun said nothing, and returned her attention to Alexander himself.

"You may bear arms, Lord Alexander," she continued, "by Lord Jürgen's grace, but your companions must disarm before coming into milord's court. That is our custom here with strangers to our domains."

"Of course, milady," Alexander agreed. He was, in fact, actually wearing a sword, which he rarely did. Rosamund herself carried nothing. Beside her, Josselin unbuckled the belt that bore both his sword and dagger, and handed it back to Fabien. On Alexander's other side, Marques did the same, handing his sword belt over to Jean. Sighard grudgingly started removing weapons belts from various places on his person—containing the sword, three daggers, a Turkish saber and a small axe—and handed them to Renaud, who looped them comfortably over his shoulders.

Once they were all disarmed, Lucretia nodded in approval. "Follow me, milord, and I will present you to Lord Jürgen. He will receive you in a private chamber—as you will see, we have other guests, who are not all privy to our business or our nature. Your discretion in this matter is appreciated.

"Know also that the language of milord's court is German. However, because you are foreigners, I will translate for you— unless you prefer to use your own translator?" She gave Sighard a meaningful look.

"Your assistance in this matter would be most appreciated by my companions, Sister," Alexander said smoothly.

Rosamund took Josselin's offered hand, and they fell in behind Alexander as he followed their guide up the stairs and into the keep. She did send one meaningful glance back at Peter, who *did* speak German. He nodded his understanding. He would listen and ensure not only that the translation was accurate, but pick up whatever else he could of the careless speech of others who might assume that they could speak freely in their own tongue if the foreign Cainites were using a translator.

A mortal youth waited at the top of the stairs. Lucretia bent and murmured something into his ear. The boy bowed and scampered into the darkness of the keep to tell his master their guests had arrived.

The keep had clearly been built with an eye toward defense—it was accessed only by a narrow, exposed stair up the outside wall to the heavy oak door on the second floor. The door, which was bound in iron, opened into a narrow passage off to the right that went by several angled slits in the inside wall. Josselin touched Rosamund's shoulder lightly and pointed up: The ceiling above them had murder holes, where the defenders could pour burning pitch or shoot arrows at invaders attempting to the entrance below.

The passageway ended after about twenty feet, and they came through another stout iron-bound oak door into the keep's main hall, though they were still hidden from the rest of the room by a wooden screen. Here Lucretia signaled them to wait, probably until Lord Jürgen was ready to receive them.

On the other side of the screen, Rosamund could hear the laughter and conversations of a number of mortals, the occasional clink of knives against plates, the begging whine of a dog or the legs of a bench scraped over stone. In the background, she heard a clear voice raised in song, and the soft rippling tones of a harp and a flute. She could pick out the smell of roast meat, of a fire burning on a hearth, and the sour odor of rushes left too long without changing.

Rosamund wasn't sure if she was looking forward to this meeting or dreading it—Jürgen must know by now she was a member of Alexander's entourage, but his messages to them had included no mention or salutation to her personally, as she might have expected. Given the debacle over the theft and substitution of the precious gift she had been entrusted to bring to Lord Jürgen during her previous visit, with the culprit being a kinsman and member of her own entourage, perhaps he was not so pleased to see her after all. The gift—a beautifully crafted sword—had been recovered fairly quickly, and Lucien's deceit unmasked, but it had still cast an embarrassing shadow over her first diplomatic effort abroad. Jürgen had not seemed to blame her for it, however, and for the rest of her visit he had been quite gracious.

But in the twelve years since her visit, she had never heard from him personally again. Her several letters had gone unanswered, though she knew Isouda had exchanged occasional diplomatic correspondence with Magdeburg's prince, and received replies.

The page returned and whispered to Lucretia. She straightened up again and looked over their company. "Lord Jürgen will receive you now. You will please follow me," she said, and stepped forward to lead them around the screen.

They walked down the side of the hall, behind the tables. There were perhaps two dozen mortals in the hall, though few now sat at table, where mostly empty plates testified to a feast well received. Noble guests stood in discussion clumps, servants were clearing plates, but all bowed low as the Cainites and their escort passed through.

Rosamund had to pull a little to keep Josselin moving. He was taking advantage of his height to scan over the assembly. She spotted the object of his search at the same moment he did—the singer, a cherub-faced young man with rumpled dark curls and a plain dun tunic, standing with the harpist at the far corner of the hall. Then their procession swept through the doors on the other side of the hall and began to climb up a spiral stair into the keep's upper chambers.

Lucretia announced them in German, in a strong, ringing voice as they entered the chamber, and then repeated herself in French. "Your Highness, Lord Alexander of Paris and his companions beg leave to enter and approach, and so present themselves."

This room was but half the size of the hall below, and more sparsely inhabited. A dozen or so individuals, most of them mortals, waited here. But Rosamund's gaze immediately went to the tall, regal Cainite standing apart from the others on the far side of the room, who now sized up their party in a glance, waiting until all had entered before making his response.

Lord Jürgen, however, spoke in accented but passable

French. "Lord Alexander has our leave to approach. Let him come and be welcomed."

They bowed, then walked forward. As they had in the courtyard below, they spread out behind Alexander, Sighard and Marques on one side, Josselin and Rosamund on the other, with their mortal servants trailing a few steps behind.

There were other Cainites now taking their places with their lord, but Rosamund's eyes were focused on Jürgen himself. Lord Jürgen was the kind of man who drew attention by just being there. Tall, lean and powerful, he reminded Rosamund of the lion she'd once seen in a bishop's menagerie, including the tawny gold hair and beard, and the way he could appear relaxed and yet be fully alert to everything going on around him. There was no doubt he commanded both men and Cainites.

Tonight he had not, as he sometimes did, taken on the image of the warrior monk. His tunic was a dark wine-red, and he wore a mantle of rich blue, bordered with a broad band of crimson and gold embroidery and lined with ermine. Rosamund recognized the sword that hung at his side—it was that very same beautifully crafted weapon that she had delivered to him from the Courts of Love, twelve years ago.

Alexander stopped ten feet shy of where Jürgen stood, and bowed again. Lost in her reverie, Rosamund was brought back to the present by a warning squeeze on her hand from Josselin, and bowed with the rest.

"Your Highness, we are grateful for your kind welcome to these your domains," Alexander began. "Unfortunate circumstances have driven us from our own city of Paris, and forced us to wander across Europe—"

Rosamund let her gaze wander to Lord Jürgen's advisors, who were unfamiliar to her. There was a thin-lipped priest in a plain cassock, who studied them down the length of his aquiline nose. On Jürgen's other side stood a serious-looking young brother of the Black Cross, who wore mail under the order's surcoat. And squatting near the priest's feet, there was a round-cheeked fellow in the bright tatters and belled cap of a fool, who studied them all with detached amusement.

Alexander had finished his description of their circumstances and begun introductions. "Sighard, who has guided us well to your lands; Sir Marques de Langres, of whom I have written to your Highness; Lady Rosamund of Islington and Sir Josselin de Poitiers, of the Clan of the Rose."

Jürgen's eyes lit on them all in turn, but when they reached Rosamund seemed to linger just a little longer. "Lady Rosamund is known to us," he said. "It is a pleasure to welcome the Ambassador of the Rose back to Magdeburg." Rosamund curtsied again in response.

Then Jürgen turned his attention back to the business at hand. "Indeed, milord, it grieved me to hear of the circumstances of my distant kinsmen."

This was all arranged, as Rosamund knew. Neither Jürgen nor Alexander had any desire to be surprised in open court, so their entire public meeting had been scripted in advance—although Jürgen's acknowledgement to her had not been in that script, and had doubtless surprised Alexander as much as Rosamund. *He acts as though I'm here in an official capacity. Didn't Alexander tell him?*

And then: *What if he didn't?* A tiny seedling of hope took root in her mind, and then her sire's voice from some long-ago lesson in Cainite diplomacy.

—In court, a prince deals only with public faces, the formal masks we all wear, not the reality behind them. And in truth, Rosamund, a prince prefers the fiction of pretty masks—of respect, loyalty, alliance, even adoration. Even if he knows it to be a lie, it is still easier to deal with the mask you are wearing than the reality beneath, for if he ever acknowledges the deception, he must then act on it. Only be careful what mask you choose....

Now Marques stepped forward to bow low to Jürgen. "Your Highness. If I may be so bold—"

"Speak," Jürgen said easily.

Marques went to one knee, the position of a supplicant. "On behalf of milord and for myself, your Highness, I most humbly request and petition your Highness for sanctuary and refuge within your domains, and offer your Highness my fealty and most faithful service."

Rosamund's fingers tightened ever so slightly on Josselin's. He glanced down at her without moving his head and met her eyes. He couldn't read her thoughts, but perhaps he could at least tell she thinking beyond Alexander's script. His nod was almost imperceptible, the return pressure of his fingers on hers reassuring.

—I am yours, petite.

"Lord Alexander," Jürgen continued. "Do you give your leave for this your vassal to swear fealty to another lord?"

"If it so pleases you, your Highness, of course," Alexander returned. "Let it be done."

"Very well, then," Jürgen said. "Come then, and make your oath."

Marques rose and then knelt again at Jürgen's feet, and the prince took Marques's hands between his, much as Rosamund had done for Josselin. "I call upon all here to witness this oath is freely given, and with Lord Alexander's grace," Jürgen said. "Let there be no doubt whom Sir Marques serves."

Marques lacked Josselin's poetic spontaneity. He made his oath in Latin, with the traditional text that bound him in obedience and in blood to Jürgen's service, and Jürgen, in German-accented Latin, made the traditional response. The young monk of the Black Cross stepped close to unbutton Jürgen's sleeve and fold it back, and then offered his lord a dagger, hilt first. Jürgen drew the blade across his own wrist in one swift motion and then offered the bleeding wound to Marques to drink.

Josselin moved his hand and flexed his fingers slightly, and Rosamund realized her grip on them had grown so tight it had to be painful. She gave him an apologetic look and forced her fingers to relax. *Do I dare presume? Would Jürgen have named me Ambassador of the Rose if he knew my circumstances? Dare I take him at his word—what will Alexander say, will he dare challenge my status if Jürgen grants it?*

Alexander stood as he had for Josselin's oath, unmoving as a statue, watching his young vassal take oath to another lord. Even though the substitution was merely a diplomatic gesture to acknowledge Jürgen's sovereignty without requiring Alexander to swear such an oath himself, Rosamund did not envy Marques the task of soothing Alexander's offended pride later.

Dare I not seize whatever chance I can to be free of him while I still can muster the will to do so?

The wound healed, and Marques took the last drops of blood and released Jürgen's hand. "Return to your companions now, Sir Marques, and hear my answer to your petition," Jürgen said. Marques rose, bowed, and returned to Alexander's side, though his gaze was now focused on the German prince—it was almost as if he was now unaware there was anyone else in the room.

Lord Jürgen's voice took on a more formal tone. "To my vassal, Sir Marques de Langres, I grant leave to dwell in this my domain of Saxony, and do further grant to him this keep of Finsterbach, and its villages, lands, and all the living who dwell within, for his support and that of his guests.

"To my esteemed and noble cousin, Lord Alexander of Paris, I grant sanctuary within my realm, and commend him to the hospitality of my vassal Sir Marques de Langres, Lord of Finsterbach."

Now.

At her slightest movement, Josselin picked up her cue, and escorted her forward, going smoothly down to one knee at her side, but still supporting her hand as she bent into a deep, formal curtsy of her own. "Your Highness. I bring you greetings from Queen Isouda de Blaise and the Courts of Love, and pray that you once again accept me as their official emissary to your Highness's court."

Jürgen turned towards her. "Milady." He studied her for a moment. He knew she was departing from the arranged protocol, and was surely thinking of what to do about it. "I thank you for your greetings, Lady Rosamund," he said at last. "It has been too long since I entertained an embassy from the Courts of Love. I am sure we will have much to discuss. Indeed, I look forward to it."

"I thank his Highness." She curtsied again. Josselin rose to bow with her, and then their formal audience—such as it was— was over.

"This keep is now yours, Lord Marques," Jürgen said, briskly.

He was already unfastening the clasp of the regal, but heavy, fur-lined mantle. A mortal squire wearing the black cross came to take it from his shoulders. "Those who feast below are here for your pleasure, and that of your guests. Your steward here is Herr Gerhard, and he will provide you with more particulars at your leisure. If the available vessels are insufficient, let him know and he will see to it you are adequately supplied with the viands of your choice."

Marques was still caught up in awe from the effect of his oath and being elevated to a domain-holding Cainite lord—if still a minor one, given the size of the estate—and could barely manage the presence of mind to bow to his new liege lord, much less stop Jürgen from ending their audience then and there.

Alexander was not so distracted, however. "Your Highness," he began smoothly. "At your convenience, there are matters we must discuss."

Jürgen nodded. "Indeed there are, milord. But you have only just arrived, and it would hardly seem gracious of me to drag you into discussions before you had even dined, or been given the welcome due your rank—it is not often we host such an august visitor, and I would not have you think our hospitality less than that of Paris! We will address those matters at length, I promise you, but not tonight."

Alexander offered a short bow. "Of course, milord," he said smoothly. "I will look forward to it."

"And so shall I," Jürgen assured him, and then turned to face her and offered her his hand. "Lady Rosamund. Might I have the honor of your company?"

"It is I who am honored, milord," she replied, giving a short curtsy of her own before Josselin handed her over to him.

Josselin stepped back, and allowed the prince of Magdeburg to take Rosamund towards the stairs, followed by Alexander, Marques and the others of his court. Only one brought up the tail end of the procession, and Josselin bowed almost from reflex and held out his hand to Sister Lucretia.

"Milady. Might I—"

"Thank you, but that won't be necessary." She started to pass him by.

"As milady wishes, of course, but surely one so fair—"

"*Herr Ritter!*" She turned towards him and the ice in her glare chilled his poetic ardor in an instant. "You forget, sir knight, I am in holy orders. I should hope that would be sufficient grounds for respect, even in France."

She turned and was gone before Josselin could recover even enough either to be insulted or to muster an apology. All right, she wasn't *that* beautiful—rather plain, really, especially in comparison with Rosamund. Still, he could count the number of times he'd encountered a nun out of her cloister in his entire existence on one hand, and this was the first time his charm had failed on any of them.

He hoped this wasn't an omen of what his future in Jürgen's domain would be like. Was it even *possible* to woo a lady properly in that harsh tongue of theirs? But then he remembered the singer. With that thought to cheer him, he followed the others downstairs.

"Walk with me, milady?" Jürgen asked her, and led her out of the hall, to a narrow passage and steep circular stair that wound up and up inside the walls until it opened up on the very top of the keep itself, a narrow walkway between peaked roof and the crenellated stone of its outer walls. The wind was chillier up here, lifting the strands of her hair out from her shoulders and nipping at her cheeks.

The view from up here was tremendous—would be even more so in daylight, though Rosamund could still see the faint sheen of moonlight on the river, the shadowy shapes of trees near the village, and of course, the activity around the bonfire in the courtyard below.

No one followed them. Lord Jürgen was one of the rare princes who did not feel obliged to surround himself with either sycophants or bodyguards at all times. If he wanted to speak to someone alone, he did exactly that.

"So, Lady Rosamund," Jürgen said. "Once again, you bring me a gift from the Courts of Love."

"I fear his presence in your domains is no gift of ours, milord." She did not say Alexander's name—she was never sure just how well he *could* hear, and she didn't want to risk catching his attention. "It was Lord Hardestadt who sent us to your gates."

"I wasn't speaking of him." He smiled at her. "You see, milady, I am not all cold armor and sharp-edged steel."

"It was never I who said you were." She had not forgotten that smile—or the force of personality behind it. Having the full light of his attention focused on her was nearly as hazardous as the dawn. "I see you bear our last gift to you. I trust it has served you well."

"It has indeed—far better, I fear, than the Courts of Love have done. But I suppose this latest gift is more Geoffrey's doing."

"In part. But he has the support of the queens as well."

"I heard that it was Geoffrey who spared his sire's very existence."

"Geoffrey holds his honor highly."

"More highly than Queen Salianna, apparently—I suspect she was not pleased at his generosity."

That was putting it mildly, as Rosamund recalled. "Most probably not."

"And what did *you* do to offend her?"

"Milord?"

"I've all the pieces of this puzzle save one—why *you* are in his company. If the Courts of Love supported Geoffrey's coup—why then hand over their fairest ambassador to an ousted prince?"

Rosamund could almost see the chain of logic constructing itself in his head: Was she still his connection to the courts in France, or only the plaything of a potential rival? Did she serve her sire or a vengeful exiled prince? Could she help him deal with his uncomfortable guest or was she merely a pawn and useless to him? *What am I to him now?*

"By Queen Salianna's grace and my sire's will I am in his company," she said, searching out just the right words that would neither cause him to dismiss her, nor claim authority she could not maintain. "And so I am in Magdeburg by their will as well, however convoluted the path, and can assure you, milord, of their continued support even now."

"And what of your support, Lady Rosamund? Your queens are far away, but their refugees are here, within my walls. Their support is of little use to me. Yours would be invaluable—if it is yours to give."

"What is mine to give, Lord Jürgen, be assured that you have. I would be remiss, however, if I did not caution you that it may not be all that your Highness might wish. I confess to you, milord, that my arrival here was not anticipated—I have no letters of introduction, no proper documentation for my position. But wherever I am, I still serve milady, and the Courts of Love."

"Not anticipated—I see." He didn't say any more, but Rosamund had the feeling that Jürgen understood exactly what her situation had been, and why her claim to be the Courts of Love's emissary came without proper diplomatic credentials.

The prince was silent a moment and rubbed at his beard thoughtfully. "Do arrange for the documentation, milady," he said at last. "I will put one of my own messengers at your disposal. I am very interested in maintaining good diplomatic relations with my allies in France."

A messenger Alexander cannot intercept—I hope. "I thank you, your Highness, for your patience, and your generosity. I will have appropriate letters prepared as soon as possible."

"Excellent. I hope, milady, that your current knightly companion serves you better than your previous fellow did."

"Sir Josselin is my brother in blood," she said firmly, "and sworn to me, not his lordship. He has my complete trust, which I assure you Lucien never did."

"Good." He extended his hand, and she laid hers on it. "I think I had best return you now, so neither your knightly guardian nor his lordship has cause to doubt my intentions."

And those intentions are—? But Rosamund did not ask. It was enough for the current night that he accepted her claim to emissary status. The more serious hurdle was yet to come.

Rosamund. Come.

Alexander wasted no time brooding. Rosamund felt his summons as soon as Lord Jürgen and his escort had passed out of the gates. Some echo of it must have reached Josselin as well, for he caught her arm as she turned to go.

"I have to answer him, Josselin."

"I know." He hesitated. "I have something for you. I brought it from Chartres, actually, but I'd forgotten—until you spoke up in court." He reached into the leather pouch at his belt and drew out a short length of green silk, embroidered with the white rose of a Toreador envoy.

"Oh…" Rosamund touched the silk, smiled at him. "You forgot *this*?"

"I've never been granted the right to bear it, *petite*. I brought it for you." He went easily down to one knee and tucked the favor into her girdle. "There. *Now* go to him—as an Ambassador of the Rose, not an errant serving girl."

—*Only be careful what mask you choose.*

Rosamund gave him her bravest smile and smoothed the silk of the favor with one hand. Then she turned away and walked gracefully towards the stairs, her back straight and her head high.

If Alexander thought she had taken too long to respond to his summons, he gave no sign of it. He did, however, clearly notice the badge she wore from her belt. "So, you show your true colors now that there is another to dance attendance on you. Will you never be satisfied, Lady Rosamund? What chance has any man of earning your regard, much less your fidelity, unless he be emperor of the world?"

Rosamund sank into a deep curtsy, but came up again with the most hurt look she could muster. "Milord? But I did it for you—it was all for you! Surely you could see that!"

"What I *see* is the hand of Salianna, pulling your strings even now, when I had hoped to free you from them once and for all. Rosamund, what madness is this? A piece of embroidered silk does not make an ambassador—what do you think Jürgen will do when he discovers the truth? How can you expect me to protect you when you insist on throwing yourself on the mercy of those who have long abandoned you?"

"How can *you* expect Lord Jürgen to support your endeavors unless he thinks you still have allies back in France?"

That came out a good bit more heated than she had intended—perhaps it was the old accusation of abandonment that did it. But there was nothing for it now but to keep going, present her whole argument, and hope Alexander could still see reason in it.

"Lord Jürgen will want me to write to my sire, and to Queen Salianna, of course. And they will not dare abandon me then. They will endorse me, because they must, because I am already here, and they have no other agent so well situated. And that is to your advantage too, milord—because I *am* their emissary, and I am in your company. As merely a follower in your train, your Highness, I am of little use to you—little more than a bauble to hang on your arm. But as a legitimate emissary of the Courts of Love, as your ally and advocate, then I can stand with you and carry the weight of my office, to speak for you here, and with my queen back in France."

She allowed herself a pause for breath, and to check his response—he was in one of his totally motionless stances, watching her. She hoped that meant he was thinking as well.

"I do most humbly beg your pardon, your Highness, for the unexpected nature of my declaration in court—I must plead that it only at that exact moment became clear to me how I might best serve you and your cause, and could not let the opportunity slip by unanswered. If I have erred, milord, it was in love, and I can only beg your forgiveness for it."

Rosamund pulled the favor with its white rose from her belt and held it out to him. "I wear this in your service, milord, and cherish it only as it allows me to serve you. If it offends you, I beg you to declare it, and I shall fling it into the fire for your sake."

Alexander moved then, coming closer and plucking the favor out of her hand to study it more closely. "My sweet rose," he murmured. "How I wish I had your faith—your ability to believe in them, even after all they have done. Do you really believe, milady, that the Courts of Love will grant you that legitimacy when they know you are in my company? Having cast you away, will they now dare confess their error and declare you their voice in Jürgen's court?"

He handed the favor back to her and turned away. "Salianna has never admitted a mistake in all her nights, never taken back what she has said, no matter how foolish or ill-advised it might have been. What makes you think she will change for you?"

"Because it is in her best interest to keep all avenues open." Rosamund held the favor in her hands so that she could see the rose, remember what it meant, and who had originally granted it to her. "Queen Salianna will know we are here in Magdeburg, but she cannot predict how Lord Jürgen will receive your suit, whether he will help you or not. She cannot know his mind, or yours—and therefore she cannot afford to ignore the possibility that he might support you—"

"He *will* support me," Alexander said sharply. "He m*ust*. That is why Lord Hardestadt sent us here."

"Exactly, milord. With his support, you can defeat Geoffrey, take back your throne. That is the possibility she must account for—and hold the way open to abandon Geoffrey and make her peace with you again. She will want an emissary here, who has both Lord Jürgen's ear, and your own."

"But are you so certain, sweet rose, that you are the emissary she will trust?"

She went to him, dared touch his shoulder, take his hand. "We will know soon enough, my prince," she murmured. "Can you not trust me until then?"

Alexander turned back to her, dark eyes holding hers even as he lifted her hand to his lips and kissed it. "My own Queen of Love. I must do as my heart commands me—and how can my heart refuse you now?"

"No more than mine." Rosamund felt herself falling into his eyes, swept up by his need, his adoration, even as he gathered her into his arms. He kissed her, and she could not resist him, nor did she want to, not with his blood already singing in her veins. His lips strayed to her cheek, her jaw, and then the hollow of her throat, and her chin lifted for him without her even willing it.

She hung suspended by expectation, caught between fear of him and a mad desire for the very thing she most feared. For an instant, she *wanted* him to take her; she hungered for his kiss even more than she hungered for the incredible potent fire of his blood. If he had offered himself to her, she would have taken him as well—the longing echoing in her blood was that strong.

But then he shuddered and raised his head, then drew her close against his shoulder. "No," he whispered. "Not yet, my rose. He was right, your loyal *chevalier*—love must spring from the heart, not the blood. I do love you, so very much—and I will prove it to you. I will earn your love, Rosamund."

Her free hand clutched the favor as tightly as she could; that piece of silk was her lifeline, the memory that the blood threatened to wash away. It was hard to muster words, to know what to say to such a heartfelt confession—when the wrong words could very well turn his adoration into fury. "I believe you," she managed at last.

"Sleep with me today."

"—Milord?"

"Just—just sleep with me. Share my bed when dawn comes, rest in my arms like mortal lovers do. Can you not trust me even that much?"

There was only one answer she could make.

He looked so innocent when he slept, more like the boy he must have been centuries ago, before his sire condemned him to be a boy for all eternity. Alexander's head nestled against her shoulder, his arm draped over her, his hand curled gently over her breast. *Like mortal lovers do,* he had whispered, before the lethargy of the day had overcome him, and left her alone with her thoughts and his cold, dead body pressed close to her own.

—A lover can never have enough of the solaces of his beloved.

This isn't love, she reminded herself. No matter how charming his smile, no matter how pleasurable his caresses, or enthralling his kiss. It was the blood and Alexander's Cainite gifts, not love, that made her weak in the knees when he gazed at her. She knew the power of those gifts too well—she used them herself.

—That which a lover takes against the will of his beloved has no relish.

But when the will itself was suspect, tainted by Cainite blood or overwhelmed by a powerful Cainite's own will—how could anyone ever know if what a lover felt was real? Could Cainites ever know love at all, or would it always be tainted with Caine's own curse?

Was this what Josselin felt when he looked upon her? Was it only the blood that made him so fierce in her defense, so sensitive to her whims? Was it only the blood that made Peter and Margery so devoted to her?

Like mortal lovers do. Some mortals, at least, knew what love was. She could hear it in Margery's voice when she and Peter lay together, entwined in each other's arms, or when they made love in the pre-dawn hours, in the private quarters to which Peter's status as her seneschal entitled him. Rosamund always felt guilty for listening in, vicariously sharing their carnal pleasures, but she could not resist. Their very passion drew her. They *felt* something, and it came from inside, not imposed on them by dark gifts. There were times she almost envied them that little bit of happiness—even as flawed as it was, between Peter's guilt at breaking his monastic vows, and Margery's hurt at his refusal to marry her—their love and mortal desires reminded her of the life she had once known, and had lost with Isouda's Embrace.

Instead, she lay in a cold bed, trapped by the weight of Alexander's unmoving corpse and growing obsession, and waited for whatever comfort the oblivion of the day might bring.

Chapter Six

The Priory of St. Paul in Magdeburg had served as Lord Jürgen's haven since he had first made his court here on the edge of the Eastern Marches in 1212. Although known as a general above all, Jürgen took the condition of his soul quite seriously, as befitted one who drew his most loyal supporters from an order of military monks. Slumbering and holding court on hallowed ground—humble though the blessing here might be—was but one more sign of his piety. The presence of his confessor Father Erasmus at his side was another.

Tonight, it was Erasmus who read the letter Jürgen had received from his guest at Finsterbach: "—And I would be most grateful to have opportunity to discuss the matter of Paris with your Highness at greater length, for I most fervently believe that the rebellion there is a canker that may well spread beyond that one unhappy city and endanger the natural order of things among our kind across Europe. Such blatant disregard for the traditions of Caine and lack of respect for their elders cannot go unpunished, or the Furores will see it as a weakness and rise up against all elders in other lands, other domains, possibly even here in the Empire."

The priest looked up from the letter. "Milord, might we interpret that last as a threat, should you not see fit to accede to his demands?"

"I suppose I should find it flattering to be considered an elder in his eyes," Lord Jürgen said dryly. "I suspect milord sire would categorize me somewhat differently—and if it was Lord Hardestadt's army that Alexander was trying to woo, I could find myself quickly categorized as Furore. No, that's not a threat, not yet."

"Not until you refuse him." The Cainite priest gave the parchment a withering glare.

"*If* we refuse him," Jürgen corrected. "However, we cannot refuse him until he actually asks. And he will not ask until he knows whether or not we will refuse him. Whatever our answer, he must then be prepared to act on it—and so he will not ask until he knows what the answer will be, and is in fact prepared to act."

"That is very true, milord, but how long do you think you can stall him? Alexander has never been known for his patience."

"He will be forced to develop some, then," Jürgen said, flatly. "He is in *my* lands now, and I will not be dictated to. Not by Lord Hardestadt, and not by him."

"If you don't write him back, he'll have to write to someone else." Wiftet didn't often speak up in serious discussions; in fact, Jürgen wasn't sure Wiftet even listened half the time. The Malkavian fool's attention wandered far afield—except in times like this, when he cut right to the heart of the matter.

"That is, unfortunately, true." Jürgen agreed. "And once lords like Balthasar and Baron Eckehard learn of his presence here, there will be no lack of letters, I suspect."

"Can you not forbid it, milord?" Ulrich asked. "Cut him off, isolate him from any possible allies? Leave him as he is, bottled up in Finsterbach, with his followers."

"Come now, Brother," Father Erasmus snorted. "Do you honestly believe Baron Eckehard would obey such a stricture? Would you have Lord Alexander think his Highness is afraid of his own vassals?"

"His *vassals* should be obedient to his will," Ulrich snapped back.

"Oh, *do* open your eyes, Ulrich—" Erasmus began, but fell silent when Jürgen raised his hand.

"Baron Eckehard *is* obedient to my will," Jürgen said firmly. "However, his obedience relies a good deal on never being ordered to do something he doesn't want to do. A prince walks on a precipice, Ulrich—for he rules only so long as his vassals do not become desperate enough in their anger to forget their feuds with each other long enough to rise against him. Therefore it is wise never to give a direct command unless you know it *will* be obeyed—or are willing to do whatever it takes to *ensure* it be obeyed. Therefore I will not command Baron Eckehard or any other of my vassals not to speak to our guests—it would be like asking the stallion to leave the mares alone."

Wiftet chuckled; Ulrich shot him a dark look. "Be silent, fool."

"In fact," Jürgen continued, "I think it is time to introduce them to our court. It's better to have them conspiring in front of our eyes rather than in secret—and we will see how long it will be before Lord Alexander asks the question he does not yet know the answer to."

"As you will, of course, milord," Erasmus bowed. "They will soon see Magdeburg is no place for simpering French courtiers."

"She's very pretty," Wiftet murmured. "Like an angel."

Ulrich laughed. "You are a fool indeed if you think she'll look at the likes of you."

"God looks after fools," Wiftet replied. "And angels are his messengers."

Jürgen nodded. "Then God looks after us all."

Lord Jürgen held a formal court on All Souls' Night, two weeks after receiving Alexander's letter. "Lady Rosamund of Islington, Ambassador of the Rose from the Courts of Love in Anjou; Sir Josselin de Poitiers, Knight of the Rose."

There were perhaps a half-dozen Cainites in the priory's hall and perhaps twice as many mortals, mostly monks; all fell silent as the two Toreador entered.

Rosamund had learned to accept it, this awe she inspired wherever she went, but she wondered if she'd ever get used to it. She had that effect on people, sometimes whether she wanted to or not. Isouda had told her it was simply not in the blood of Clan Toreador to be ignored; the gift of Arikel, the clan's legendary progenitor, drew the eye and caught at the heart even without her descendents thinking about it. All it took was to walk into a room where first impressions mattered and to be announced, and the rest was as natural as walking.

Josselin's fingers tightened ever so slightly on hers as they paused and bowed to Lord Jürgen and the others assembled there. Several had the wit to bow back. Then Josselin led her up to Jürgen, where they bowed again.

Jürgen spoke in German—some kind of welcoming phrase, Rosamund guessed. Then Josselin led her to the side where Marques and Sighard already waited.

I must learn his speech, Rosamund told herself.

"Lord Alexander of Paris." No further honorifics were necessary. Rosamund was certain everyone knew very well just who Alexander was and how he had come to be in Magdeburg. When Alexander stepped into the room, Rosamund was, at least for that moment, forgotten. Slim and elegant, dark and youthful, Alexander's beauty was that of a young god. His white tunic and mantle with its broad trim of imperial purple recalled the majesty of Rome. The Cainite closest to the door bowed first, then another, and another, leaving only two wearing Jürgen's black cross still standing. Rosamund felt her own knees buckling as Alexander crossed the hall and, beside her, Josselin dropped down to one knee, a little less gracefully than usual, as if he'd been fighting the impulse and had lost.

Jürgen still stood straight and tall, and even managed to look natural about it. As Alexander drew closer, the sheer power of his charisma eased, until it was possible to move, stand up again, even to look away.

Alexander made a slight bow, an acknowledgment of Jürgen's rank but no more. If Jürgen took it as insult, his voice did not betray it. He greeted Alexander cordially in German, and Alexander responded, made another half-bow, and then retreated to the opposite side of the hall.

Jürgen spoke a few words to the hall, and then the formal audience was ended.

Josselin leaned close. "Now the fun begins," he murmured, his voice barely audible. "Look to the left, you've made a conquest already."

At the foot of the dais, the fool sat in his colorful patched tunic, clutching his belled cap in his hands, his eyes fixed on Rosamund. When he noticed her regard, his eyes widened, and his mouth made a little round O of surprise. Then he started to stand, tripped on his cap, fell forward into a surprisingly graceful somersault, and somehow ended up on his knees practically at her feet. For an instant she was looking down into wide blue eyes, and then he crossed himself quickly and bowed low, touching his forehead to the stone floor at her feet.

Josselin chuckled, and even Rosamund found a little laugh escaping. There was something so earnest about the fool's performance.

"Wiftet." Father Erasmus, the priest Rosamund had learned was never far from Jürgen's side, nudged the fool with his foot and said something further in German, and then switched to French. "Your pardon, Lady Rosamund, he can be a bit odd. It's his blood, I'm afraid." The fool scuttled sideways on all fours, out of the reach of the priest's foot, and then rose up to knees again and smiled up at Rosamund. "Not a saint, Father," he said in French, "an angel. God told me you wouldn't believe it, but I do."

Rosamund laughed again. "I'm afraid I'm not an angel, master fool," she said.

"Shhh!" Wiftet held his finger in front of his lips, and then whispered theatrically. "Well, if you want to keep it a secret, I won't tell anyone."

"Enough," Father Erasmus said, irritably. "Go annoy someone else."

Wiftet pouted, and said something in German that Rosamund suspected was either insulting or rude, and the priest sighed. "*Go.*"

The fool fled, scrambling on all fours and dodging other occupants of the hall as he went.

"He seemed harmless enough," Josselin commented, watching the fool's progress across the hall.

"Harmless, yes, but quite mad. Don't expect to get anything but nonsense out of him." The priest steepled his fingers in front of his chest. "I suspect this is not the sort of court you're used to, milord, milady. We do things differently here in Magdeburg."

"Every court is different to some degree, Father," Rosamund replied easily. "I can already see that I must learn the language of this one, or I shall have far fewer opportunities for conversation."

"Perhaps milady would like me to recommend an instructor in the German language?"

"I would greatly appreciate it, Father. Preferably someone conversant in French, of course—my seneschal speaks something of the language, but a talented interpreter would be a welcome addition to the household."

"I will be happy to make some inquires for you, milady."

"Who is that?" Josselin asked, as if he was totally unaware of what the conversation had been about. "With Lord Jürgen, over there."

Father Erasmus glanced in that direction. "The holy sister? That is Abbess Hedwig of Saint Mary the Magdalene in Quedlinburg."

"No, no, not the abbess. The monk. I've not seen him before."

Rosamund looked as well. The abbess was a short, stocky figure in black and white, her carmine lips the only spot of color on her pale fleshy face, and her expression sour enough to curdle milk. The Cainite monk who stood between the abbess and Lord Jürgen, however, was tall, slim and well-favored, with dark brown curls cropped short around his ears, and wearing the habit of the Black Cross, with a sword belted to his side.

"Ah. That would be Brother Christof, Lord Marshal of the Order of the Black Cross. A most diligent and devout Cainite in Lord Jürgen's service, and in God's."

"And the lady there, who is she?" Rosamund asked, looking across the hall at a young woman richly dressed in exotically patterned silk, her mantle trimmed in fur, her dark hair bound in gold netting under a jeweled circlet.

Father Erasmus glanced in that direction. "Ah, that is the Hungarian ambassador, from the prince in Buda-Pest, who is a clansman of Lord Jürgen's. The Lady Erzsébet Arpad. Would you like to be introduced?"

The Lady Erzsébet had her chin raised at a haughty angle

Rosamund recognized all too well. *Lovely. A Ventrue and a princess, no less. But the Arpad are Jürgen's allies in his wars to the east. It would do no harm to cultivate her if I can.*

"Thank you, Father," Rosamund said with a pleasant smile. "I would like that very much."

It wasn't until they were halfway across the room that Rosamund realized Josselin had not followed them.

"There is a difference, Herr Josselin, between the tournament melee and the reality of war," Brother Ulrich said.

Josselin had sought Brother Christof's further acquaintance. Unfortunately, Ulrich seemed intent on both fixing himself to his superior's elbow and making himself as obnoxious as possible in the process, as if his status as Lord Jürgen's childe made up for his lack of experience and arrogance all at once.

"You say that, Brother, as if you believe I've not seen the reality," Josselin said dryly. "We do have wars in France, you know."

"You have not seen what we face in Hungary, milord."

And you have? Josselin privately suspected not. "Hungary seems rather far away from your borders here to be of interest even to Lord Jürgen."

"Should we not expand the borders of Christendom?"

"Is *that* what it is you're doing?" Josselin inquired. "I thought the Hungarians were Christian already."

"Not in the eastern marches of Transylvania." Brother Christof allowed his younger brother to carry the bulk of the conversation, but clearly occasionally felt the voice of experience was required. "In the mountains there, they still hold fast to their pagan ways, and the Tzimisce lords rule their domains openly as petty gods themselves—save that they are more like to devils than anything else."

"I have heard stories about the Tzimisce." Which was true, although Josselin didn't credit even half of what those stories had claimed.

Brother Christof nodded. "I think you would find the reality far worse than any tale you've heard."

"I have no particular desire to see the reality," Josselin

admitted cheerfully. "I am no crusader. I leave that glory to you, Brothers."

"You would not take the cross, milord?" Ulrich interjected. "Even against the heretics in the Languedoc?"

Especially not in the Languedoc. Perhaps it was the memory of Aimeric, who had scant patience for fools, that inspired his response. Or Ulrich's naïve assurance that no true Christian knight could possibly refuse a call to crusade. "Someone must remain at home to defend the ladies, Brother," he explained, with a wide grin. "And to entertain them, which is often a more difficult and strenuous task than defending them."

"I'm sure you can be quite entertaining, Herr Josselin," Ulrich snorted. "But what could *you* possibly defend them from?"

"*Ulrich.*" Brother Christof's voice cracked like a whip, and the younger monk winced as if he'd been struck.

Josselin smiled. *Quite entertaining.* "If you doubt my skill with the sword, Brother," he said smoothly, "there's only one way to find out for sure, isn't there? If you have the courage to face me."

Had Ulrich still breathed, he might have turned red; instead, he bared his fangs and reached for his own sword. But Brother Christof's hand caught Ulrich's wrist before his hand closed around the hilt.

"No," Christof said sharply. "You will kneel before Herr Josselin, and beg his pardon for your lack of courtesy."

Ulrich started to protest, but Christof silenced him with a look and one raised eyebrow. The younger monk struggled for a moment to regain his composure, took several long, deep breaths, and then went down on one knee in Josselin's direction. Christof immediately went up several notches in Josselin's estimation, to not only demand such obedience, but actually to get it.

"I most humbly beg your pardon, Herr Josselin," Ulrich said in a low voice. "My words were improper and disrespectful, and unbecoming of a servant of God."

Josselin hesitated just long enough to give the impression that he had to think about it. "Since you ask for my pardon,

Brother, you have it," he replied. "I bear you no ill will."

"I thank you, Herr Josselin," Brother Christof said quietly. "I'm sure Brother Ulrich will mind his tongue better from now on."

"I trust he will," Josselin replied, already in a better humor. Ulrich rose to his feet, but looked considerably subdued.

"But *I* will face you, if you're still willing."

Brother Christof's words were so calmly delivered, that Josselin almost missed their meaning. "Brother? We have no quarrel."

"No quarrel," Brother Christof replied, though his voice was cool. "Call it curiosity. I'm curious to see if you're really as good with your sword—even for a courtier—as you seem to think you are."

In Christof's quiet, measured voice, the words stung far more than Ulrich's crude insult. For a moment, at least, Josselin regretted baiting Brother Ulrich, if it lost him Christof's respect.

"I will meet you, Brother," Josselin replied. "Whenever it's convenient."

He held out his arm, and Christof grasped it firmly, sealing their agreement as one knight to another. But what caught Josselin's eye was Christof's right hand; the outer two fingers were only stumps, making it all but impossible for him to wield a sword.

Christof noticed Josselin's gaze. "I fight sinister," he said. "I hope that will not inconvenience you."

"Not at all. I like a challenge." Josselin noted that Christof wore his sword on his right side, just as he wore his own on the left.

"Good. I shall endeavor to give you one."

Alexander had left the hall; Rosamund remembered that even in Paris he had not cared to mingle among his guests at court receptions, where it was never certain who might overhear one's conversations and the use of the prodigious gifts of his blood was as much hindrance as help. He much preferred intimate audiences where he could command the full attention of those around him without distractions.

A servant appeared at her elbow. "Please, milady. Milord would speak with you privately, if you would come."

"Your lord?" she asked. She didn't recognize him.

"Yes, milady. *The* lord," he repeated, emphasizing slightly.

Jürgen. "Oh, of course. Yes, I'll come."

He led her down the stairs and out of the priory house, down the cloister of the small abbey beyond, and then through a narrow door. Beyond that was a small Lady chapel. It was lit only by several small candles flickering at the Virgin's feet.

Jürgen knelt before the shrine, his head bowed in prayer, but as she came in, he crossed himself and rose to meet her.

"My apologies, milord," she said, curtsying deeply. "I did not mean to interrupt your devotions."

He smiled a little. "Don't apologize, milady. I was expecting you. I only took advantage of the moment and the setting to pray for the safety of my men in Hungary. Since I cannot be with them right now to guide them, it seems only fitting that I beseech the Holy Virgin to do so in my stead."

"How goes the war in Hungary?" Rosamund asked. "It seems so far away."

"It is. I would not have hazarded such a campaign but for the support of the Arpad Ventrue in Hungary's eastern kingdom. And now they waver, and the Tzimisce may strike again at any time. I should be there—not here."

"A general should be with his troops."

"A general should. A prince, however, sometimes has other concerns—such as ensuring the security of his own throne. It is sometimes easier to be a general."

"Why do the Arpad waver? What does Lady Erzsébet tell you?"

"Politics." He pronounced the word with loathing.

"Yes, of course, but what politics? Why did they support you before, and what has happened to make them less committed to those goals? What do they stand to gain or lose through what you do?"

"It's complicated," he muttered.

"I'm sure it seems that way, on the surface. But it may be there's one simple underlying cause that remains unspoken, yet is crucial to the entire matter. Once you can identify that one cause, all the others may simply fall into place. Deal with that underlying question, and many of the others burn away like the mists."

"And is that what happened in Paris? One underlying cause that triggered all the others to fall into place—or out of place, as it were?"

"I'm sure it was," Rosamund admitted. "Unfortunately, by the time I got even the slightest hint of what was really going on, it was over. And then we were exiled, and—" she stopped, suddenly aware of what she'd just said. *Damn. Why am I telling him this?*

"Exiled—even you, Rosamund?"

She gave him a brave smile. "I never said I was *Geoffrey's* ambassador, milord. I am afraid I was... unfortunately connected... with his sire in his eyes, and so..." she gave a little shrug. "Here I am. And the rest you know. We are here, milord, because this is where Lord Hardestadt sent us. What he will do now... I must confess, I do not know, not yet."

"Oh, I know what he'll do," Jürgen said darkly. "The question isn't *what*, but *where* and *when*. And this does indeed have one underlying cause, milady—in that, your theory is indeed quite correct."

"My theory, Lord Jürgen?"

"Let me tell you something I have learned, Lady Rosamund, about our kind. It is that those who rise above their fellows, who strive to rule rather than be ruled, once they have *attained* that august position, are never again content to be anything less. If, may God forbid, I should ever be forced from my place here and survive that disaster, there is nothing—*nothing*—that would dissuade me from doing anything in my power to regain everything I had lost."

He shook his head. "He was Prince of Paris for longer than I have walked the night. He cannot bear to be nothing, a beggar in a foreign court. He will want a throne. Which throne, though—that is the question."

The passion in his voice captivated her.

"Paris. It is Paris he wants, milord—and revenge against

Geoffrey and Salianna. There are nights he speaks of nothing else."

"And he expects me to help him get it. And if I cannot, or won't—what then? Will he then cast his eye on the throne closer to hand—whether to hold or merely use as a base for his conquest of Île de France makes no difference to me." He paused, as if he was himself surprised at what was passing his lips. "Why am I telling you all this?"

"You speak your thoughts aloud, milord, because you wish me to know your mind, and trust you."

"I did not ask you in here to discuss politics—you know the situation as well as I. Better perhaps. You know his mind."

"I think your Highness knows his lordship's mind as well as I do at present."

He did not reply immediately. The silence stretched out between them just long enough to notice, and then he changed the topic entirely. "I kept your letters."

Rosamund was only caught off guard for an instant. She had an arsenal of practiced replies for any possible social situation, although this particular one was certainly unexpected. "Did you? I am flattered, milord."

He reached down and picked up a leather courier's pouch from the floor where he had been kneeling, and took out a small stack of folded parchment, bound together with a ribbon. Rosamund recognized her seal.

He kept my letters, but never answered them?

"They took a while to reach me in Hungary. Two of them even arrived together with the same messenger, though they were dated a year apart." He tapped the letters against his palm as he spoke, almost as if he needed something to do with his hands. "I meant to write back. I started to, several times. But then the Tzimisce would attack, or someone would come into my tent and require my attention, or I would realize that it was close to dawn and I'd still not managed to put more than three lines on the parchment. And it just seemed a waste to send a letter from the marches of Hungary all the way to France with only three lines—hardly a real letter at all."

Jürgen turned the stack of letters over, and eased the bottom one out from under the ribbon; this one was a single piece of parchment, folded neatly but without a seal. "But I suppose three lines are better than nothing, and I no longer have the excuse of distance preventing its delivery."

He extended his hand, offering it to her. "With my apologies, milady, for its tardy delivery and its unfortunate brevity. I fear I am more adept with the sword than the pen." Rosamund stepped closer and accepted the folded parchment. "My thanks to you, milord—and to your messenger." She smiled up at him, and saw the faintest hint of a smile in return. Then she unfolded the letter.

To the Lady Rosamund of Islington, Ambassador of the Rose, in Chartres, France:

Your letter finally found me today, here in my camp in Hungary. The nights here have been cold and damp of late, but your missive seems to have been the herald of summer, for even though the rain still falls, I now feel warm.

"It's not finished," Jürgen said.

"It doesn't need to be," Rosamund assured him. She refolded the letter and held it in her hand. "I am glad, milord, that my letters pleased you."

"They did. Then they stopped coming—and I wondered if I had perhaps angered you."

Angered me?

"No, milord," Rosamund managed to keep her tone even and her expression pleasant. She did not laugh. "I—I confess I was not certain my letters were well received, that is all."

"Of course they were. Why shouldn't they be?" He sounded honestly surprised.

"Milady Isouda received responses to her missives to you within eight months of sending them. I realize those were, of course, affairs of state—"

"Yes. That was just diplomacy, not the same thing. You're saying I should have written."

"Well, yes. But it is of no matter—I have your letter now,

milord, and it pleases me as well."

"Good. Perhaps we should start again, milady—and I shall attempt to be a better correspondent now that the distance is not so great."

No. No letters, that's the last thing I need. Not with Alexander watching me like a hawk. "Now that the distance is not so great," Rosamund stepped closer and offered him her warmest smile, "I find a letter alone does not suffice, milord. A letter, after all, is but a poor substitute for the sound of your voice. Surely you will not banish me to the country and expect me to be content with letters alone?"

"No, milady." Jürgen smiled, apparently not immune to courtly flattery—or flirtation. "As much as I enjoyed your letters, I believe your conversation far more intriguing, to say the least. Do feel free to visit my court, such as it is, any time you like—though I would still recommend a letter to ensure I am in residence to receive you."

"I will accept your Highness's kind invitation," Rosamund said. "And I hope I may take frequent advantage of it, so long as you do not tire of my company."

"I look forward to it, Lady Rosamund," Jürgen said. "But regretfully, I suspect I should return you to the hall—I wouldn't want Lord Alexander to believe I had abducted you."

The possibility of Alexander thinking exactly that wasn't at all funny, but Rosamund laughed, because Jürgen clearly intended his comment to be humorous. All the same, she was greatly relieved when Alexander was not in the hall when they returned, and Peter told her that the former prince of Paris had not returned while she was gone—hopefully he was too busy courting his own support to notice.

Meanwhile, she put Jürgen's long-delayed letter into Peter's document pouch for safekeeping.

...for even though the rain still falls, I now feel warm.

She was already feeling warmer herself.

Chapter Seven

Magdeburg, Saxony
All Souls' Night, November, 1224

"Peter. May I see the letter I gave you?" Rosamund sat sideways on the edge of the bed, clad now only in her shift, while Margery sat behind her, braiding her mistress's hair.

Peter dug into his document pouch and brought it out for her. "Here it is, milady."

She unfolded it, and then showed it to Margery. "This doesn't seem at all like his usual style," Margery murmured. "But it looks like his hand. This is Lord Jürgen's hand, isn't it, Peter?"

Peter peered over Margery's shoulder. "Looks like it, yes. But he didn't sign it."

"He never finished it," Rosamund explained. "But he gave it to me this evening."

"It looks like he was trying to write a love letter, milady." Margery said, handing it back.

"Or maybe he's just talking about the weather," Peter put in.

"Peter!" Margery poked his arm. "The weather, indeed!" Peter grinned at her.

It was the faintest of noises, the tread of shoes in the hallway outside, but Rosamund heard it.

"He's coming. Quickly, here, take it!" She thrust the letter at Margery, and sprang up to her feet, reaching for her mantle.

Margery nearly dropped the letter; Peter grabbed it, put it back into her hands and then hurried to answer the knock on the door. Margery quickly shoved the folded parchment inside her surcoat.

"Milord." Rosamund dropped into a deep curtsy; behind her, Margery did the same. "I thought you had retired."

Alexander smiled and offered her a hand to aid her in rising. "I fear I've neglected you shamefully this evening, my love."

"Nonsense, milord," Rosamund assured him. "You have been concerned with far more weighty matters than my amusements, that is all. I can hardly begrudge you what we have come so far to seek. That will be all, Peter," she added. The code phrase meant *Leave me alone now*, and both her ghouls moved to obey.

"No—" Alexander held up his hand. "Let them stay, milady. Perhaps they may be useful to us."

Rosamund nodded, and the two mortals took their places off to one side, Peter guiding Margery gently with his hand on the small of her back.

"How was your evening, Rosamund?" Alexander asked, taking no further notice of the two ghouls. "Did you enjoy being in a real court again—such as it was?"

Rosamund smiled. "I did indeed, milord. As did you, I trust?"

"Whom did you find to speak with?"

"Oh. Well. I spoke with Father Erasmus for a while—and I met his lordship's fool, who is quite clever."

"And what did you talk about with Father Erasmus?"

"He offered to find me an instructor in German, so I might better serve your Highness by learning the language of this country we find ourselves in. And he also offered to introduce me to some others in the hall, and so he did."

"How very thoughtful." Alexander began to pace around her in a circle. "Who did you meet?"

What's he after? "I met the ambassador from Hungary—Lady Erzsébet Arpad, and her cousin István. I also met Baron Eckehard and Abbess Hedwig, and Brother Ulrich—"

"What did you talk about with the Lady Arpad?"

"Not—not much of interest. She was making cutting remarks, and I refused to rise to them. And then Lord István came to tell her she had a message that had to be attended to at once, and she fled."

"You really must learn to get along with people better, my

dear, if you're ever to be an effective ambassador."

"She—" Rosamund took a deep calming breath.

"Of course, milord, I know."

"The Arpad are a noble house in their own country, and they can be powerful allies for our cause. Surely you don't think that because they are not French, they aren't worthy of your respect?"

"Of course not, milord, but—" *But Erzsébet is a spoiled little bitch.*

"You wouldn't want to jeopardize a possible alliance with powerful allies, would you, Rosamund? No, I didn't think so. You will apologize to Lady Erzsébet at the next possible opportunity. In front of witnesses. You'll do that for me, won't you?"

"Yes, milord." There was nothing more she could say. *Erzsébet must have promised him the world, whether she's authorized to do so or not.*

"You didn't mention Lord Jürgen in your list."

"No, milord—you asked whom I had *met*...."

"So you did speak to Lord Jürgen. Were there witnesses? I do hope you haven't offended him too?"

"No, I have not. He was most gracious, milord. He did ask about your plans."

"My plans. And what did you tell him, my sweet?" Alexander stood behind her now. He started to play with her hair, slowly unraveling the braids.

"I told him you wished nothing more than to return to Paris and reclaim your rightful place there. He seemed to be concerned you might cast your eyes elsewhere—to a throne closer to hand. I assured him that was not so. It's not, is it?"

"And what else did Lord Jürgen wish to talk about?"

"Nothing else of importance. He waits to learn more of your plans, milord; you are a far greater concern to him than I am."

"Allow me to be the judge of whether something is important, milady. You might be surprised what I find to be of interest. So, no secrets between us, Rosamund. What else did Lord Jürgen want?"

"He asked if our accommodations were adequate—I assured him, of course, they were."

"Of course. I fear I've undone your hair, milady. Your woman will have to braid it again. You. Come here and fix milady's hair."

Somewhat nervously, Margery stooped slightly to pick up the comb from the travel chest, and came to where they stood. The parchment rustled slightly inside her surcoat.

"Now this I wouldn't have believed of you, Rosamund," Alexander said softly. "Using your servant to hide your secrets— a poor defenseless mortal woman. You. Give me the letter."

Margery cringed away. "L-letter, milord?" On the other side of the room, Peter stiffened.

"Give him the letter, Margery," Rosamund said quietly.

"Yes, milady." Margery drew it out and Alexander snatched it from her fingers, unfolding it and scanning the brief contents.

Rosamund turned to face him, carefully putting herself between Margery and Alexander. "It is nothing, milord," she said.

"Nothing. It's not signed, milady. He's had this a long time— and he only gave it to you, when? This very evening? To what letter does he refer?"

"A letter I wrote long ago, milord. After my first visit to Lord Jürgen's court—long before I came to Paris or met you."

"Why even *bother*, after all this time?" He stared at the few lines of script. "Nothing, you said?"

"Yes, milord. It's nothing. Just a bit of—"

"Good." He took two strides over to the table and held the letter out over a candle. The edge smoldered, then caught.

Margery's hands clamped down on Rosamund's shoulders, reminding her to stand still. Rosamund patted her hand, then guided that hand to her hair. *Do what he told you.* Fingers trembling a little, Margery set to work.

Alexander stared at the flames licking at the letter now, spreading down its edges, almost as if the fire itself entranced him. Only when the flames nearly reached his hand did he take two more steps to fling it into the ashes of the fireplace.

Rosamund watched the letter burn. *It's just a letter. I remember what it said, I'll remember it forever. Jürgen won't ever know what became of it. I should have given it to Josselin straight away—*

"There. That's much better, don't you agree?" Alexander

smiled at her, and Rosamund felt her heart lighten. He wasn't angry, not really. Everything would be all right.

"Yes, milord. Much better."

"Good. You know I would never cause you distress, milady." He came closer, laid one hand gently against her cheek. "So warm," he murmured. "You accepted Lord Jürgen's hospitality—what that whey-faced woman had to offer?"

"She seemed quite kind to me, milord. Yes, I did—did you find nothing to your taste, then?" It was a delicate question. Ventrue like Alexander could be very touchy about their personal tastes—it was, or so she had been taught, the height of discourtesy to even ask what one's "taste" might be.

"No," Alexander said softly. "I did not... at least, not yet. There is an old custom among those of my blood, dating back to the days of Rome. We have many such customs, of course, but this one is special. The *Auctoritas Cibus*—the Right of Sustenance. Have you heard of it?"

"No, milord. What is it?"

"It means that a Ventrue may, if need arises, claim feeding rights on any single mortal chattel of kinsman or ally that happens to meet his peculiar needs. Any single kine, even the personal servant of the prince himself—for none may deny to one's kinsman the right of sustenance. And he may have rights to that kine so long as his need may require, and the kine survive. A very practical custom, the very essence of hospitality, wouldn't you agree?"

"It sounds very practical, milord. Will you go to Lord Jürgen then, to claim your right?"

"I suspect Lord Jürgen cannot fill it—I've seen what his hospitality offers. It does not suffice. Fortunately, the *Auctoritas Cibus* does not apply to Ventrue alone."

A cold sinking feeling began to form in the pit of Rosamund's stomach. "Doesn't it?"

"Surely you would not deny me that right, my sweet Rosamund? You have fed—can you deny me the right to do so as well? Would you have me hungry and weak, vulnerable to the ravages of the Beast? When it is within your power to give me what I need?"

"No—" Rosamund managed. "No, milord, I would never deny you—if you would but tell me what you require, I shall do all in my power to acquire it for you—"

"It's not that difficult, my rose. She stands at your very shoulder."

Margery gave a little gasp and dropped the comb. "Milady—"

"Margery is my personal servant, milord," Rosamund protested. "Surely there is some other who—"

"'Any mortal chattel,'" Alexander quoted softly. "Surely you cannot believe I would *hurt* her—you know how hard it is for me even to have to request this of you. Is this so very much to ask, after all we have shared together?"

Margery cast a desperate look across the room at Peter; the seneschal's face had gone pale, and his lips formed Margery's name.

"Margery." Rosamund turned and took the mortal woman's hands in hers.

"I'll go, milady. Please. No need to fret on my account, I'm sure I'll be fine." Margery's voice was firm, but her hands trembled a little. "I'll be back before you know it."

Rosamund gave her hands a gentle squeeze. "Yes, you will." She turned back to Alexander. "Margery is at your service, milord," she said, as calmly as she could, ignoring Peter's stricken look on the other side of the room. "I pray you treat her gently, for she is dear to me."

"Of course." Alexander said, with a little smile. He didn't even look at Margery. "Send her to my room. I will be there shortly."

Rosamund nodded. Margery bent slightly, pressed a kiss to Rosamund's hair, curtsied to the two Cainites, and then walked quickly out of the room. She didn't look at Peter.

"You cannot know how much this means to me, my love," Alexander told her softly. "Be sure I will treat your woman as if she were my own kin." He leaned closer, tipped Rosamund's chin up to meet his kiss, which was long and lingering. "Never forget," he whispered against her lips, "how much I love you."

Then he was gone.

Peter stared at her across the room. The fear and worry she

could see in his eyes tore at her heart. She could think of nothing to say to him, no words to excuse either Alexander's actions, or her own.

"I'll—I'll go wake Blanche for you, milady," he said finally, and left her alone.

Sir Renaud found Peter in his chambers in the late afternoon, when he knew those who shouldn't hear would be slumbering and insensate. "How is Margery doing?"

Peter shut his ledger with a authoritative *thump*. It helped only a little. "She's asleep." he said, shortly. Then he added, "Her color's better. She had some soup at noon. Blanche is with her."

"Thanks be unto God," Renaud murmured and crossed himself; Peter did so as well. "I only just heard—Fabien told me."

"I see our Fabien's become quite the gossip, hasn't he?" Peter muttered darkly. "Did he tell you she won't see me now? Not that I blame her of course."

"She won't see you?" Renaud stepped fully inside the room, closed the door.

"She won't even speak to me. She let Blanche see to her when she came back this morning—she was barely able to stand, but she wouldn't take my arm. But then, she knows me for a coward now. I just *stood* there, Renaud. I didn't do anything, I didn't even protest—"

"And because of that, you're both still alive," Renaud interrupted, sharply. "Listen to me, Peter. Listen very carefully—I know of what I speak. He is the very devil in Cainite flesh. You cannot prevail against him. God's teeth, *they* can't prevail—you saw what he did to Josselin! And—and to milord Olivier." Renaud's voice broke for a moment, then he continued on, with even greater fervor. "Your lady risks her existence every time she's with him—now think what *your* life is worth to a monster like that. We are *cattle* to him—worse than cattle. Chickens squawking in the yard, good for nothing in the end but the pot."

"*I know!*" Peter snapped back, and then sank down on a bench. "He's punishing milady, I think." he said finally. "That's why he took her. He's hurting Lady Rosamund by hurting us."

"Possibly." Renaud sat down beside him and lowered his voice. "But that's not why he took Margery. He took her because of *you*. Because she loves you, Peter."

"He feeds from women, I know that much—"

Renaud leaned closer, his voice dropping even lower. "Not just any women. I had to hunt for him, you see. So I know what to look for. It is the flavor of love he savors. She has to be in love with someone. Anyone, it doesn't matter who. That's the secret. That's what he needs."

"In love—"

Renaud nodded. "You should have married her, Peter. Love can't exist in marriage, it's in all the rules. If she was married, she'd be safe from him."

Peter closed his eyes, fighting the tears burning behind his lids. "And now it's too late. There's nothing we can do."

Renaud laid a hand on his shoulder. "Pray, my friend. Pray that God will have mercy on us all, and count these nights as time in purgatory—for surely as we still breathe, we are in the devil's hands."

Chapter Eight

Lucretia awoke as she always did, to the faint music of the bell ringing vespers in the Commandery and Hospital of St. Mary of the Teutonic Order. She rose promptly and left the cramped sleeping chamber, opening the hidden panel to enter her modest cell. Sister Agathe was already there waiting for her with a pitcher of hot water—one of the few luxuries Lucretia allowed herself—and a towel.

"Good evening, Sister," Lucretia greeted her doppelgänger. Agathe had been a rare find—a woman close enough to her in appearance as to be her sister, and both willing and able to take on the difficult role Lucretia required of her.

"Good evening, madame," Agathe curtsied.

Lucretia pulled her shift off over her head and handed the garment to Agathe, who set it aside to be washed with her own. "Will you be attending the services this evening, madame?" the nun asked.

"No, Sister," Lucretia told her. "You may attend for me, as usual. And if one of the sisters is available for me, I'd be most grateful."

"Yes, madame," Agathe nodded, obediently. "It is my turn, madame."

"Is it? Good." Lucretia bent over the basin and began to wash her face and arms. The hot water brought the blood to her skin, infusing undead flesh with the illusion of life.

"Yes, madame." Agathe sounded pleased. She was one of the

few sisters to know Lucretia's true nature and needs—though very little else—and took satisfaction in knowing she did God's will in providing for it, so that her mistress might be spared from sin. That she also believed Lucretia spent most of her nights in solitary prayer in the crypts below was more regrettable—but necessary. Lucretia had not lived as long as she had by letting her more vulnerable servants know her full business. "Will you be needing the bindings tonight?"

"Yes, I will." Lucretia finished drying herself, and ran her fingers through the unruly curls of her hair, which had grown out in tangles down to her shoulders during the day. "Thank you."

"Yes, madame." Agathe brought out a narrow length of clean white linen, and began to wrap it tightly around Lucretia's upper chest, binding her breasts as flat as possible against her ribs until she was nearly as flat-chested as a boy, and tying it off.

Agathe sat down on the narrow bed, and unpinned her veil and wimple, laying them neatly aside, while Lucretia pulled a clean shift on over the bindings. Then she joined Agathe on the bed. The mortal nun leaned back against the Cainite's shoulder, closing her eyes as Lucretia's arms came around her, and making a little cry of pleasure at her mistress's kiss.

Lucretia gently guided Agathe to lie down afterwards. Then she rose, put a plain dark kirtle on over her shift, and slipped a pair of shoes on her bare feet. "I do not know if I will return before dawn," she said. "I pray you do not worry if I do not greet you tomorrow evening. I shall send word if I am delayed longer."

"Thank you, madame," Agathe murmured sleepily. "Have you any messages for Brother Christof, should he ask?"

"Not at this time. Thank you, Agathe." Lucretia bent over the bed and kissed Agathe on the cheek. "God grant you sweet rest."

"And you also, madame."

Lucretia went out the same hidden panel door, but this time bypassed her bed and opened a second panel door on the other side. Working confidently in total darkness, she found the rung of the descending ladder with her foot, and closed the door behind her before she started down.

The passage below was narrow, sloping down and then running alongside the crypts of the commandery's chapel, where a number of the dead and undead found their own rest. It ended in a narrow, winding stair leading upwards. Lucretia slipped out of the kirtle and hung it on its accustomed peg before ascending the stairs and emerging in another plain cell much like the one she had left, save that she was now in the dormitories of the Teutonic Knights themselves.

Brother Hildiger awaited her there, with a pan of hot water, comb and pair of shears. "It's almost time for holy office, Brother," he said sternly, sitting her down on a stool and draping a towel over her shoulders. "Best you start your penances now, while I work."

Lucretia closed her eyes and began murmuring the Latin prayers while Brother Hildiger took his shears to her tangled locks. With the ease of long practice he cut away the excess lengths, until a pile of dark brown curls lay on the stone floor at his feet, and the rest lay neatly combed and cropped to a length no longer than the lobes of her ears. He walked around to face her, tilted her chin up and studied his handiwork. "Yes, that'll do," he nodded approvingly.

"Which of the brothers stand for bouts tonight?" she asked as he carefully gathered up the towel from her shoulders and began to sweep up the hair trimmings from the floor into a bowl for burning.

"Brothers Gerhard, Albert, Stefan, Johannes the Tall, Benedict, and Rorick," Hildiger ticked them off on his fingers, then added slyly, "I also understand Brother Christof himself has accepted a challenge from a French knight—perhaps to teach him some manners, or so it is rumored in the brothers' dormitory."

She got up from the stool, brushed a few trimmings off her shoulders and sleeves. "Have the brothers nothing better to do than discuss the doings of their superiors?"

"Brother Christof is much admired among them. Our Lord Marshal has even given his leave for all who desire to watch the bouts tonight."

"The *Hochmeister* will also be watching this evening—I trust the younger brothers will remember *their* manners as well, no matter what they believe about the French."

"I am certain they will, Brother. Just as I am certain that you will not disappoint them." He set the bowl of hair trimmings aside, and with a reverence bordering on ritual, laid out a wooden board, stained with old blood and slightly gritty with ash, and scarred from frequent use. Beside the board, he laid a small hand axe, its edge polished and honed nearly as sharp as his shears.

"That is in God's hands, Brother Hildiger." She came to the table and its implements, took a deep breath.

"Yes, Brother." Hildiger turned away, closed his eyes. He didn't like to watch.

Lucretia laid her right hand down on the board, curling the first two fingers under her palm and letting the outer two splay out at just the right angle. She picked up the axe in her good hand, hefted it comfortably to get just the right balance, and aimed carefully. It had taken several weeks of practice to get the same cut every time.

Then she brought the blade down on the wood and her own hand with a solid *thunk.*

About fifteen minutes later, Brother Christof was fully dressed. He left his cell to go join his brothers and sisters at holy office, the stumps of the two outer fingers on his right hand now healed over without a scar.

Renaud's blunted sword bounced off his opponent's side, the force of the blow lessened by armor and the underlying monk's habit. Wheezing a little, the Teutonic Brother dropped to one knee, conceding the match. Rosamund applauded with the rest of the audience at Jürgen's court, though the monk's fellows seemed considerably less enthusiastic when a stranger defeated one of their own.

"Isn't there to be *any* blood tonight?" Erzsébet Arpad asked. "No steel?"

"Don't worry," Sir Marques assured her. "Sir Josselin is challenging the Lord Marshal of the Black Cross himself next. That'll be bloody for sure."

"Oh, *good*," Erzsébet exclaimed, just loud enough to make

sure Rosamund could hear her. "But *whose* blood will it be, that's the question—"

Rosamund held her tongue. Apologizing once to Erzsébet had been bad enough. She was not prepared to make a habit of it. This, she was learning, was the most popular court entertainment in German Cainite society—the display of prowess at arms, either of mortals, ghouls or even of the Cainites themselves. More Cainites had come tonight than had attended court the night of her presentation—mostly male, and several more wearing the black Teutonic cross.

The opening matches had been bouts between ghouls, in armor and using blunted swords. Renaud, whom she did not remember as a particularly impressive swordsman, had demonstrated a new, almost savage aggression, easily winning three bouts.

"Sighard's blood," Marques muttered. "It's ruined him—he's turning into an animal himself."

Erzsébet, hanging on his arm, was quick to agree. "And you told me he was once in the service of Lord Alexander's childe? The poor fellow *has* gone down in the world."

Rosamund ignored her. She suspected Erzsébet would be far less bold if Sighard was actually within earshot—but sooner or later she was bound to get careless and forget just how well those tufted ears could hear.

Fabien had not done so well. Josselin's squire had been matched against a Teuton who was both taller and outweighed him by a good thirty pounds, and Rosamund privately suspected Josselin did not drill his squire on foot combat as forcefully as he could. Fabien was breathing hard and holding his side as he returned to the mortal spectators' side of the hall, and did not seem to mind Margery and Blanche fussing over him before he went to help Josselin arm for his own bout.

Rosamund looked for Peter, and found him standing with the victorious Renaud some distance away. It was odd—usually her little family stuck closely together. But during the past week, Margery had shared Blanche's pallet in Rosamund's room, and she and Peter had seemed to say no more to each other than their duties demanded.

Alexander sat beside Rosamund, ignoring the conversation going on around him, barely moving—she wasn't sure if he was actually watching the matches.

Fabien, doing his best to ignore his own injuries, helped his master strap on the shield, which bore Josselin's own heraldry: azure, three swans naiant argent. Josselin bent close as his squire whispered some last-minute encouragement, and then accepted his newly honed sword from Fabien's hands.

Steel. Unlike the mortals, they were fighting with bare steel, with shields but without armor, clad only in their shirts and hose, with not even the padding of a gambeson between their opponent's sword and their own flesh. For a Cainite, such a fight posed only minor risk—what might incapacitate or cripple a mortal would be considered a fair blow given the recuperative powers of the blood, and a fatal blow would not be permitted. Their white shirts would show the stains of their wounds, allowing all to keep score.

Rosamund had seen such bouts before, in France. They were popular—the knights liked the thrill of actually blooding their opponent, the risk of taking such wounds themselves. Not all such bouts ended quickly; some required one combatant to be incapacitated or actually surrender, and such matches could go for hours while the combatants sliced each other into bloody ribbons, refusing to acknowledge themselves beaten while they still had blood to heal themselves, and were still capable of standing.

Neither Josselin nor Brother Christof, however, seemed intent on proving himself invincible. This bout would likely be quick.

Lord Jürgen himself stood as judge and marshal of the Cainite match. He wore the habit of the Black Cross tonight, his dark gold hair cropped to his jaw line and beard neatly trimmed.

Rosamund wondered if the prince's garb was intended as a not-so-subtle sign of partisanship. She had already noted Brother Ulrich standing with the others of his order, clearly relishing the thought of their marshal facing down the foreign challenger. She had little doubt that Josselin was relishing the bout as well.

"This match will be to three strikes, and strikes will be to blood only," Jürgen said. "Is that acceptable, Sir Josselin? Brother Christof?"

They both nodded. "Yes, milord."

"Then make yourselves ready."

Josselin raised his sword in salute. Brother Christof did the same.

Lord Jürgen signaled, and the page holding the banner between them lifted it and moved quickly out of their way.

The handsome monk was good, Rosamund was forced to admit very quickly. Nor did Christof react impulsively as Josselin had told her Marques sometimes did, anxious to prove himself. *Not so young as he appears, either.* He was quick and agile, but his strikes did not move into speeds beyond normal perception; therefore Josselin did not do so either. And when his sword, moving at normal speed, got past Josselin's guard and slashed through his sleeve, the French knight dropped to one knee. "Hit," he admitted. "Very good, Brother."

The monk nodded and returned to his place. Josselin healed the wound—it was little more than a scratch—and did the same.

The same move did not avail Christof again. This time Josselin's shield blocked it, and they circled again. Another flurry of blows, and Josselin's sword flicked out under Christof's arm and sliced across the monk's ribs. The tip of his sword sliced through fabric and undead flesh, but did not penetrate past bone. Christof inhaled sharply and then let his sword arm go down. "A hit, Herr knight," he said. He sounded almost surprised. "Good."

Rosamund found herself chewing her lower lip again, and forced herself to stop. Her hands were clenched as well, she relaxed them. Three seats down, she could see Lady Erzsébet's eyes following the combatants' every move, the tips of her fangs showing behind her lips.

It seemed to Rosamund, at least, that Josselin's success had startled the monk somewhat. Of course, it had also made him more determined. The third round was more cautious, both combatants less willing to take risks, more focused on defense. Still, they moved quickly. Rosamund found herself accelerating her own perceptions just to slow them down enough to see. As it

grew slower, the swordplay became more deliberate, more graceful; the two combatants moved in their elaborate dance of strike,
dodge, strike, parry, circle, feint, strike, parry....

Because she was watching them so, she saw the end coming before they did. Christof's low feint suddenly moved high,
and his sword sliced across directly at Josselin's unprotected
neck. She knew the instant he recognized his danger, made the
swift decision which way to move—extremely hazardous if he
guessed wrong and moved *into* Christof's blade instead of away.
She saw Josselin meet his opponent's eyes, and then freeze in
place—letting the sword come at him unhindered.

She didn't even have time to scream.

The monk's sword stopped just as the edge touched Josselin's
throat. A thin rivulet of blood ran down from the edge of the
blade to stain his shirt. Josselin dropped his sword and went
down on one knee, Brother Christof's blade still poised at his
neck. "I yield."

The brothers of the Black Cross were on their feet, cheering
the victory. The rest of the audience applauding as well. Across
the hall, Margery gave a vastly relieved Fabien a hug. Rosamund
clapped as well, trying not to shake at how close that could have
been. *Josselin could have dodged that. He could have blocked it. Why
didn't he?*

Christof tossed his sword aside as well and offered his opponent a hand up. Grinning, Josselin accepted it. The two men
spoke together for a moment, then parted to pick up their swords
and return to their respective sides, both to warm welcomes from
their supporters.

"That's that, I suppose," Erzsébet said. "Until next week's
matches, anyway."

"To be honest," Marques told her, "I've seen him lose more
often than win—"

That could not be borne. Rosamund turned to face him.
"Have *you* ever dared challenge him, milord?" she asked. "Shall
I inform Sir Josselin you wish to face him next week?"

"*I* have nothing to prove," Marques said, although from the
look on Erzsébet's face, Rosamund suspected he'd be persuaded
otherwise soon enough.

"You should go to your brother, milady," Alexander said. It was the first time he'd spoken all evening. "No doubt his pride needs your tender consolation."

Josselin didn't look particularly in need of consoling—he actually seemed to be in very good spirits indeed—but Rosamund didn't feel like disputing Alexander's impressions. "Yes, milord," she said obediently, and left the dais without regret.

She found Josselin kneeling next to Fabien, more concerned with his squire's injuries than his own performance. A massive purple bruise was spreading across the mortal's side, and he gasped in pain when Josselin had him bend this way and that.

"You've cracked a rib, I think," Josselin told him. "We'll have to wrap that up so you can ride."

"I can *always* ride," Fabien insisted, stubbornly. "Yes, but we can at least make you less miserable while you're doing it." Josselin gave Fabien's shoulder an affectionate squeeze. "Ah, Margery. Thank you—"

"I'll see to him, milord," Margery had her basket of herbal simples, bandages and poultice makings. "I think milady wants you."

"Milady!" Josselin noticed her now and rose to his feet.

"And how are the wounded warriors?" Rosamund asked, offering her warmest smile.

Josselin chuckled. "Barely scratched. Right, Fabien?" Fabien grinned at her over Margery's shoulder.

Rosamund glanced around. "Where's Peter?"

"You've not seemed your usual self of late, Peter." Alexander's voice was soft, soothing, his expression one of grave concern. "I was wondering if there was something I could do to help."

Among the mortal servants of the house, Alexander was not known for his charity, and to be summoned by him was never a good thing. Peter concentrated on remaining calm. "I thank his Highness for his kind concern," he said carefully, choosing to flatter the deposed prince with his old title and the most deferential tone he could muster. "However, I would assure his Highness that I am quite well and content in my service to milady, and his Highness."

"Are you indeed?" Alexander began to walk around him in a circle, as he'd done to Lady Rosamund a few nights before. "I would not have thought so the other night. You seemed quite distressed, in fact—did you think I wouldn't notice?"

Don't look him in the eyes. It was his litany, his only hope. When Alexander's circling brought him in front, Peter averted his gaze, hoping not to be too obvious about it. "I—I was merely concerned for—for milady," he stammered. "I meant no disrespect to his Highness. If I have offended, I beg—"

"*Don't* beg." Alexander cut him off sharply. "Not yet. When it's time for you to beg, be sure I will let you know."

"Yes, your Highness." Peter clasped his hands in front of his stomach, fighting the habit of his monastic youth to hide them in his sleeves.

"I am sorry you were distressed," Alexander's voice was smooth and silky again. "Was it merely your concern for your lady that so moved you? Or was there someone else who perhaps held some small claim to your affections?"

"Yes, your Highness."

"Yes? To which? You must confess it in order to be absolved—isn't that what they taught you at Notre Dame de Chartres?"

That Alexander knew that much of his past sent a cold chill down his spine, and put a sharper edge on his reply. "Absolution can only be pronounced by an ordained priest, your Highness, and confession is for sins alone." He knew as soon as the words escaped him that they were a mistake—he sounded lacking in humility. And to apologize immediately would merely draw the error to Alexander's attention, demand retribution. "I have nothing I need confess."

"Don't you?" Alexander asked. "Forgive me, Brother, but—is not fornication a mortal sin?"

Pride goeth before a fall, Brother, Peter reminded himself bitterly. "Yes, your Highness. It is." Somehow he kept his voice calm. He realized he was wringing his hands; he forced himself to stop.

"And you have sinned, Peter. It's no secret—the entire household knows who shares your bed. Even Lady Rosamund knows—she's far too well bred to speak of such shameful behavior, of course."

Peter could think of nothing to say. It was true, he *had* sinned. And of course, everyone knew, that was hardly a surprise. Even Renaud had known, and he'd been away at Hardestadt's court half the time.

—*You should have married her, Peter.*

"Why didn't you marry her?" Alexander asked. "Did you think the flavor would go out of it then? They do say, you know, that love cannot abide in marriage."

"I—I was under vows—" he whispered. Margery had been disappointed, he knew that. But he could not bring himself to break that final vow—just as he could not bring himself to give up the pleasures of her company in his bed.

"You were *pure*, Peter. Weren't you? Before she touched you, corrupted you. You sacrificed that purity of God for the stain of carnal sin, and for what? For *her?*"

"—What?" He didn't want to hear this, he didn't want to know—but he found himself listening, hanging on Alexander's every word.

"Open your eyes, Peter. See what kind of woman you have so blindly given your heart to. Didn't you see how willingly she came to me? Do you believe it was you she was thinking of when she lay naked in my arms? Did she not give herself to Sir Josselin when he was wounded—did she even *hesitate* to offer him her most intimate comforts? Did you not see her fawning over Fabien this very evening?"

The images were too clear: Margery leaning close to Fabien's ear, her hands on his shoulders; Margery's knowing smile when Sir Josselin kissed her hand and thanked her for her kindness to him; Margery lying on Alexander's bed, waiting for the deposed prince's sweet kiss—

"*No!*" Peter sank slowly down to his knees, sobbing. "No... no..."

"All I'm suggesting is that you think about it, that's all," Alexander murmured leaning over him. "Consider it well. Is that woman really worthy of all you have sacrificed for her— would you let such a common whore keep you from the glories of heaven? Is she really worth your immortal soul?"

Peter was so wrapped up in his own private agonies of the

spirit, he never even noticed when his tormentor left in search of other, more challenging prey.

Lucretia knew he would come, as soon as their guests had departed for their intown lodgings. Jürgen would want her counsel, and for her to listen as the prince thought aloud. It was the way they had worked together for several decades now, and Alexander certainly was something that had to be talked about.

But it was not Alexander that was foremost in Jürgen's mind when he came to Lucretia's chamber.

"Well, Brother," Jürgen said. "Tell me, did you enjoy yourself this evening?"

Lucretia grinned, and folded her arms across her chest. "Well, partly, yes. He's very good. Much better than I expected, in fact. It's almost a pity his blood is not of our line. He would have beaten Ulrich, you know."

"You should have let Ulrich learn his lesson. This Knight of the Rose damn near beat *you*."

"As I said, he's very good. Not as good as *he* clearly thinks he is, but..." She scowled, and couldn't quite control the annoyance in her voice. "He *let me win*, the bastard."

"I thought he should have parried that last stroke."

"I asked him why. He *claims* he thought it poor diplomacy for a stranger to defeat the Lord Marshal of the Black Cross—especially in front of half the brethren."

"A very diplomatic answer, considering you likely would have won anyway. You don't sound as though you believe him, though."

"I'm not sure. I suppose it's good diplomacy. He's got balls—he didn't even flinch when my sword was coming down. What he'd be like in a real fight, though—"

"At least three times as fast, and considerably less diplomatic," Jürgen said dryly. "But he's Lady Rosamund's man, not Alexander's. Sir Josselin is not the one I'd worry about."

"You're not worried about Lady Rosamund?"

"On my list of worries, Rosamund is nowhere near the top," Jürgen said dryly. "Alexander asked about troops tonight, finally. He seemed content with my answer—for now."

"Good—for now. It's the truth anyway. It's not like we can just pull another army out of our purse."

"It won't hold him off forever, but at least the first exchange is complete. I doubt he'll get even that much of an answer from Eckehard or any of the other barons just yet. They'll all be cautious, watching to see what we do, and what he does in response. No matter how sweet his promises, they'll not make commitments to him… at least, not yet."

"Nor can you sign Geoffrey's treaty. Not with his usurped sire at our gates."

"Geoffrey's treaty fortunately has other issues preventing its signing besides Lord Alexander. Negotiations will continue, of course. He won't send a personal ambassador so long as Alexander is here, and therefore we are not required to send one to him. Nor will he use Lady Rosamund as his emissary, because in his eyes she is compromised. Therefore negotiations will likely take a very long time indeed—years at least."

Rosamund again. Lucretia fought down her own rise of irritation and considered her response carefully. "Is she not compromised in your eyes, milord?"

"She's an envoy of the Courts of Love, who have been and still are our allies. That she arrives with Lord Alexander is a bit irregular, I'll admit, and curious—"

"Very irregular, considering it was the Courts of Love who aided in engineering Alexander's overthrow. Her credentials, milord, are worth the parchment they're inscribed upon right now—and until we see those and verify their authenticity—"

"Are you implying that Lady Rosamund would *lie* to us?" Jürgen was a little surprised at the irritation in his own voice. "She has been faithful enough in the past—the debacle over the sword was none of her doing."

"That's true, Jürgen, but it happened, and she was there. Just as Alexander's overthrow happened, and now his arrival in Magdeburg happened—whether she's *responsible* for it at all is, I grant you, highly unlikely, but again, here she is."

"She was not responsible, Lucretia. And until her diplomatic credentials actually do arrive, we will take her at her word—it certainly does no harm."

"True," Lucretia agreed, and then added carefully, "Her presence may even distract Alexander's attention away from far more dangerous things he could be concentrating on."

"Dangerous for whom, is the question," Jürgen replied, pensively.

Lucretia noted that Alexander wasn't the only one being distracted. While this did not please her, it was hardly a surprise. Jürgen had found the Ambassador of the Rose particularly fascinating even a dozen years ago. He could not afford such a distraction now, not with Alexander here, and the forces of their enemy Vladimir Rustovitch on the move again in Hungary—Václav's latest missive had warned of a possible new offensive that their current forces there might not be able to contain.

Well, that was why she stood at his right hand—no matter which habit or name she bore—to watch for the things he could not spare an eye for. Especially when his eyes were captivated by someone far more alluring than herself. "Yes, milord."

Chapter Nine

Magdeburg, Saxony
Soon after the Feast of St. Cecilia, November, 1224

"It starts out with eight steps to the left, like this," Rosamund said, and took Josselin's offered hand to demonstrate. "One. Two. Three. Four. Five. Six. Seven. Eight. Then count eight the other direction…. Then the lady goes around her escort, to the right—"

The little circle of mortals and Cainites—mostly mortals, as the brother-knights of the Black Cross did not attend court for frivolities like dance instruction—watched and attempted to follow instructions, even given in French. It was a relatively simple carole, and most seemed to be mastering it easily enough.

"No, to the left," Josselin called, exercising his growing German vocabulary. "That's your shield arm, not your sword arm, Herr Augustin."

The mortal quickly corrected his step, grinning foolishly, pleased at any acknowledgement from a Cainite, even in correction.

Lady Erzsébet, having come into the hall during the last set of instructions, watched the dancers moving in a circle, but did not join in. "Is that what they're dancing in Paris these nights?" she asked coolly, in French. "I think my grandmother learned that one from her grandmother."

"It's such a pity *you* were never able to master it, milady," Wiftet interjected from his place in the circle. The fool's eyes then went wide and he put his hand over his mouth. Most of the circle laughed.

"I'll dance, master fool, if and when there's something worth dancing *to*," the Hungarian retorted, but she had lost that round; the laughter had defeated her.

Across the circle, Wiftet winked at Rosamund. She smiled back and then went on to instructing the next section of the dance.

Then the dogs began to howl—one at first, then another, and then it seemed like every dog in the city, of all sizes, took up the chorus. "What?" Rosamund looked up at Josselin, who looked as puzzled as she. The circle began to break up, as Cainites and mortals stopped to listen and exchange speculations.

"That's not natural," Renaud murmured, his head cocked slightly sideways to listen. "But what would—"

There was a commotion somewhere downstairs, and then the hollow clatter of hoofbeats on stone. "That's coming from *inside!*" Josselin left her side immediately, followed by Fabien and Renaud, running for where they had laid down weapons.

A mounted knight burst into the room, knocking the wooden pantry screen aside and sending mortal servants running for cover. He rode into the middle of the room—Rosamund and those left of her dancing circle backed away as the fighting men drew weapons and stepped forward to form something of a protective line in front of the non-combatants.

The great black horse reared, pawing the air. Its eyes glowed red, and its teeth included a pair more at home on a wolf than a grazing beast. "Lord Jürgen!" the rider called, in sharply accented German. "Come forth! I am the herald of Vladimir Rustovitch, *voivode* of *voivodes.*"

"Speak, herald." Jürgen entered the hall, strode to the dais. A half-dozen of his knights, including Brother Ulrich, followed him, with Sister Lucretia trailing behind them. "I am Lord Jürgen. What is your message?"

The dogs' howling stopped, as suddenly and eerily as it had begun. Rosamund peered around from behind Josselin and Fabien. Wiftet somehow ended up beside her, also safely behind their guardians; he hunched down on the floor and covered his head with his arms, whimpering softly. Peter found his usual place at her shoulder as interpreter, advisor and loyal defender, ready to protect her with his own body if necessity demanded it.

"The *voivode* would finish this, Lord Jürgen," the herald declared in a ringing voice. "Thus says Vladimir Rustovitch: 'It is a poor general who sends his army to fight when he remains safe at home. His men lose heart, and then they lose much more. By midsummer there will be no Saxon left either breathing or undead in all my lands. Victory will at last be ours.' The *voivode* discovered three of your men wandering lost in our forests. In hopes of convincing you of his sincerity, he bids me now return them to you." The knight reached up and undid the clasp of his dark cloak, then with a sharp gesture, swung the mass of fabric free and sent it sailing upwards in a slow spiral, to land in the rushes near the base of the dais.

The lining of the cloak was not silk, or even fur. It was made of human skin, tanned and pieced together without seams through some foul devil's art—and, to make its nature all the clearer, there were three *faces* still preserved within it, their faces frozen forever in a rictus of agony. Nor was the blasphemous thing unmarked: Latin words were written on it, in a bold hand, and spelled out in blood.

It was Peter, literate in four languages, who read it aloud for the benefit of those standing near him, his voice hoarse with the sheer horror of it. "Thus shall all be served who dare trespass on my lands. Let all Saxons beware."

Even those who could not read the message felt the impact; there were sharp hisses of anger and bared fangs all around the room. Rosamund crossed herself and ducked behind Josselin's solid back, unable to bear the sight any longer. Instead she peeked around at Jürgen himself, to see what he would do.

The Saxon prince looked up from the desecrated remains of his men, trembling with fury, his eyes blazing with such fire that everyone in the room, whether living or undead, ally or not, felt the force of his rage like a great invisible wind. Mortal servants whimpered and fell to their knees in terror, and battle-hardened Cainites took an instinctive step or two backwards. Even the monstrous horse backed up, half-rearing and attempting to flee despite its foul rider's will.

"Down, you craven cur," the rider snarled, yanking on the reins, taking out his fear on his beastly mount. Bloody froth dripped from its jaws, and its eyes showed white, but it obeyed. "Do you have a message for milord Rustovitch?" the rider finally asked.

Jürgen's initial wave of near-frenzy had abated, though his anger had not. "Yes, herald. I have a message," he said, his voice carrying throughout the hall. "Tell Rustovitch that we fought him before out of duty, but now we come for justice and vengeance for his atrocities against not only our own people, but those wretched souls held captive under his tyrannical rule. We were armed before with our honor, courage, and well-honed steel; now we face him armed with the righteous wrath of God, and even though he raise up armies out of the very bowels of Hell itself, *he shall not stand against us!*"

The black horse reared again as the brothers of the Black Cross and all those gathered in the hall, down to the last mortal servant, raised their voices in a roar of support for the prince and fury at the Tzimisce's messenger. Indeed, they began to take a few steps forward, towards the herald, those bearing weapons raising them with purpose.

"Wait." Jürgen's voice was soft, cold, but it carried, and it demanded obedience. "He is but the messenger, not Rustovitch himself. Go, herald. Tell your master my message. Tell him to prepare to face God's own judgment, for most assuredly we will be sending him there very soon, and I am certain he has many sins on his soul to atone for ere that night comes."

The herald glanced around the room, then offered Jürgen a stiff bow from his saddle. "I will tell him, milord," he said, and wheeled his horse around. Cold, angry faces surrounded him, but at a signal from Jürgen, they backed away, leaving the exit clear. With a shout, the herald dug spurs into his steed's sides, and galloped out of the hall.

At a soft word from Lucretia, two of the Cainite brothers bent to fold the cloak and its terrible lining so that the tormented visages were no longer visible, and carried it away. All eyes turned back to the prince then.

"We will not let this go unanswered," Jürgen said at last.

"We have been too long absent from where our stalwart kin and brothers in arms hold the line against the depredations of the Tzimisce barbarians. It is time this was indeed finished—and Rustovitch and his cruel, blasphemous jests will be finished as well. And we *will* end it this time, make no mistake of that.

"I call all those pledged to my service, all vassals, knights, and brothers in the Teutonic Order to join me in this effort, this one last crusade against the godless pagan terror clawing at our gates to the east. We will crush this serpent's head beneath our heel and put all his devil-minions to such a flight that they will be knocking on the gates of hell, begging for refuge there from our wrath. This is our decree—let it be answered by all of good Christian faith and noble heart, bearing arms or not, to crush the adversary's forces, for Christ and the Virgin, and the holy Church!"

The roar of approval from those gathered there left no doubt of their support for their prince and his crusade.

"I will fight with you, milord, for chastisement of this barbaric monster and for the glory of God!" Ulrich dropped on one knee at Jürgen's feet, lifting his sword, hilt up like a cross. The rest of the brothers of the Black Cross, even Lucretia herself, followed his example, falling to their knees, pledging their swords and their loyalty.

"I will fight with you, milord! You have my sword!" Several other knights, both mortal and Cainite alike, came forward, drawing their swords and holding them up as well, calling out their own declarations of loyalty.

Rosamund grabbed Josselin's hand and held it tightly—*no, don't go, Josselin, don't leave me!* His fingers curled gently around hers. Fortunately, he seemed to be in no hurry to join the furor of Jürgen's new crusade.

"Milord Jürgen." Alexander walked up the length of the hall with all the dignity of a king going to his coronation. Marques and István Arpad, along with several of their mortal retainers, followed in his wake. "Must one be a monk to take part in this little lessoning you seek to hand down to the fiends in the East?"

That started a murmuring among the brothers of the Black Cross which ceased when Jürgen raised his hand. "No, milord

Alexander," Jürgen informed him. "Only to swear by the Cross to see the matter through to the end, and accept my complete and total authority, under all situations that may arise—without question."

"Then I, too, will fight with you, milord," Alexander said smoothly, offering a slight bow. "And so will those in my service—four Cainites and their retinues now, ten by the time we arrive in Hungary."

Jürgen's eyes swept over Alexander's current retinue. "You are, of course, welcome, Lord Alexander, to take up the cross and join us in our holy endeavors—but unless my eyes mistake me, I only see two Cainites with you."

"A moment, milord—" Alexander smiled and turned towards the gathered spectators, and beckoned. "Sighard. Renaud. I believe I still hold your oaths, do I not?"

Sighard didn't look nearly as enthusiastic about this as Jürgen's own men had been, but he offered a stiff bow, a slightly deeper one to Jürgen, and then strode to take his place behind Alexander. Renaud looked even less happy, but he followed his master without a word.

Then Alexander's dark eyes swept across the room to focus on Rosamund. "You owe me a boon, Sir Josselin."

"Yes, milord," Josselin agreed. "If milady permits, I will ride with you, milord."

Alexander glanced at Rosamund. "Milady?"

There was little she could say other than the expected. The boon was a fact, and Alexander was within his rights to demand it of Josselin, and herself. Whether Josselin wanted to go, or whether she really wanted to send him, was irrelevant; he was a knight, trained for war, and his honor would not permit him to refuse the debt. "Of course, milord. Sir Josselin, you have my leave." Rosamund released Josselin's hand. He bowed to both Alexander and Jürgen, and then joined Sighard in Alexander's train, Fabien following at his heels.

Jürgen nodded, approvingly. "Then your company is for now complete, milord, and we thank you for your resolve. We will gather all the brothers of the Order, and whatever other knights of noble mien would join our company, and travel swiftly south, ere the winter overtakes us. Rustovitch boasts he will have us defeated by midsummer—I do not intend to give him anywhere near that much grace, for he does not deserve to see even one more night more than it takes for us to destroy him and his foul minions, and cleanse the land of their filth."

Rosamund chewed her lip nervously. Peter came up beside her and took her cold hand between his warm ones, comfortingly.

Wiftet came up on her other side. "I'll protect you, milady," he offered.

"Thank you, Wiftet," she managed, and smiled at him.

Chapter Ten

The Burzenland, Eastern Hungary
During Lent, March, 1225

Josselin dictated conversationally, forgoing poetry as his sister had requested months ago. "We have finally arrived in Kronstadt, as big a town as one finds in the Burzenland, which is not saying very much. It is a fortress settlement, the largest of seven fortresses that the German knights have built to guard the pass against the Cumans, and the Tzimisce. But it is little more than a country town, save for the number of armed men, both mortal and Cainite, who dwell within its walls. We have fought two night skirmishes to get this far already, though neither was sufficient to do more than delay our progress. Brother Christof tells me we have not yet seen any real Tzimisce strength, so we should expect far worse to come.

"Fabien writes this for me, as usual, and I am grateful for his assistance—"

"Do you want me to write that, that I'm writing this?" Fabien asked, looking up from the parchment. "It sounds funny. She knows I'm writing it for you, doesn't she?"

"Yes, she knows, and yes, you should write that." Josselin rolled over on the narrow cot, coming up against Fabien's back. Pushing himself up on one elbow, he tried to look around Fabien's arm at the writing board the squire balanced on his lap. As usual, the slightly smudged lines of text on the parchment failed to divulge any meaning. "I'm giving you credit, *cher*, in appreciation of your assistance."

"You could just thank me then, and spare me writing all

those extra words. This parchment isn't that big."

"Oh. You can leave it out, then," Josselin agreed amiably, and then added, "But I am grateful, Fabien, and I thank you."

Fabien grinned; a slight flush rose on the back of his neck, nearly as red as his hair. "You're welcome. Hold a moment, the quill's gone mushy again." He reached for the penknife.

Josselin heard unfamiliar footsteps coming down the corridor, and rose from Fabien's cot before he offended any monastic sense of proprieties.

"Herr Josselin?" Hesitantly, one of the Black Cross knights— Brother Gerhard, if Josselin remembered correctly—came into the barracks reserved for the secular knights and their men, and offered him an abbreviated bow. "Sir. The *Hochmeister* requests your presence in his chambers."

Lord Jürgen's chamber was actually quite crowded; he must have summoned most of the Cainites in his company. Josselin spotted Sighard and Renaud, and made for them. "What's happened?"

Sighard snorted and offered him a piece of parchment—it looked very official, written in an elegant hand, with the King of Hungary's seal at the bottom. Josselin handed it back. "What does it say?"

"King Andras has ordered the Teutonic Knights to leave Hungary," Renaud replied, dropping into French. "Effective immediately."

"*What?* Who the hell let *that* happen?"

Renaud's voice dropped to a whisper. "The impression I'm getting, milord, is that his lordship has no good agent of his own in the king's court—and somehow this little matter seems to have slipped through Arpad fingers."

"Well, they're just a slippery-fingered lot, aren't they?" Josselin muttered. What he had seen of the ruling Ventrue house of Hungary had failed to impress him in the least.

"You watch," Renaud shook his head. "When Lord Miklós finally gets in here, he'll know nothing about it, and be terribly shocked and appalled."

"And then he make big offer, like he go to fix, and he ride

away," Sighard growled. "Cowardly snake."

"Let's pray you're wrong, my friends," Josselin murmured. "But I fear you're dead on." He headed for the table.

Lord Jürgen leaned over the table, studying the map. Brother Christof was moving troop counters and checking a list.

"How many at Marianburg?" Jürgen asked.

"That we can trust? Not nearly enough, *Hochmeister*. Of the thirty brother-knights, only eight are of our brotherhood, and only two of those Cainites. Perhaps twenty-five at most of lesser rank we can call upon."

"We can't hold it, then. Heldenburg?"

Christof checked his roster. "Ten brother-knights, six of them Cainites, thirty of lower rank."

Jürgen scowled. "Not enough. Schwarzenburg?"

"Thirty brother-knights, ten of them Cainites. Fifty or more of the lower ranks, depending on how well Brother Adhemar has done in his recruiting effort."

"How many total, Christof? Assuming the worst?"

"Assuming the worst..." Christof flipped through his notes, thought a moment. His expression was grim. "Without the mortal fighters and support personnel of the Teutonic Order, our forces will number approximately eighty to ninety Cainites, two-thirds of them knights, and between three and five hundred mortal troops, one third of whom are knights, and at least one hundred of whom are non-combatants."

Those gathered had fallen silent at Jürgen's question. Christof's words carried throughout the room.

"Call them all in, Brother Christof," Jürgen said at last. "I want everyone in either Kronstadt or Bran in three nights' time. They are to bring with them as many of those not yet in our brotherhood as they can—recruiting them if at all feasible, and by any means necessary. Tell Václav he's to hold Bran, send him our forces from Kreuzburg, Eulenburg and Rosenauer Berg. Tell all the others to come here. They are to travel by night only, and at their best possible speed. I do not want any Cainite traveling in a box by daylight unless there is absolutely no other choice."

There was a murmuring of agreement across the room. Josselin studied the map. A string of seven fortresses across the valley, but without the mortals of the Teutonic Order, not enough men to hold them, nor protect the Saxon settlements in between. *And how many does Rustovitch field in this, his home territory?*

Lord Miklós Arpad, tall and darkly elegant, strode into the room and executed a perfectly graceful bow. "Ah, Lord Jürgen. I was wondering where everyone had gone. Have I missed anything?"

Someone handed him a copy of the proclamation. He read it, and his eyebrows arched nearly into his hairline. "What? I was not informed of this! This is absolutely appalling! Clearly something terrible is going on in Buda-Pest, milord! I will send word—no. I will ride there at once myself and straighten things out!"

The Hungarian started out, but paused at the door and looked back at István, standing at Alexander's shoulder. The younger Arpad hesitated, but when Alexander laid a hand on his shoulder and spoke to him softly, István smiled and resolutely turned his back on his sire. Lord Miklós shrugged and left him to his fate.

Across the room, Josselin caught Renaud's eye. The ghoul knight made a little gesture, the tip of his index finger hitting his palm like an arrow hitting the mark.

Dead on.

Over the following weeks, Josselin had much reason to reevaluate his guess that the stories he had heard of the Tzimisce were exaggerations. Alexander led Marques, István, Sighard and him—along with ghouls and others—on a series of raids against the enemy. An enemy who seemed to be closing in on Kronstadt with every passing night.

On the night of the Feast of St. Gregory, they faced off against a large pack of what the men had come to call hellhounds, twisted beasts that might once have been wolves. They were fast and savage, but an hour before dawn, the last of them whimpered and died. Josselin wiped his sword blade clean of ichor and resheathed it, then whistled for Achilles. The hounds were far too fast to fight on horseback.

The scream that wafted out of the woods was like no animal

or mortal Josselin had ever heard, a many-voiced wail that sent chills down even a Cainite spine. The breeze brought with it the foul carrion stench of an abattoir.

Whatever it was, it terrified the horses. Achilles reared suddenly, jerking the reins out of Josselin's hands, and tore away, oblivious to his master's summons. Alexander's white tossed its head and stamped, held in place by the sheer force of its master's will. Sighard had remounted, but he was barely holding his gray. Even Fabien was having trouble—Whitefoot turned in tight circles, fighting his rider's control.

"Back!" Alexander shouted, and the command was repeated down the line.

Then a great hulking *thing* came lurching towards them out of the trees, and Josselin felt his blood turning cold, his limbs suddenly too heavy to move, out of sheer terror. It was taller than a peasant's cottage. It had four arms that ended in claws as long as sword blades, multiple eyes glittering across its shadowy bulk, and multiple mouths, all of which were screaming. It was a monster out of hell, and suddenly Josselin realized that none of the stories he had heard had even come *close* to the truth. As he watched, still frozen in horror, the thing reached out with one of those taloned limbs and scooped a fleeing man from the ground, plucking the shield from his arm and tossing it away like a discarded bit of offal. Then it brought the struggling mortal up to its gaping maws, tore off one flailing arm, and began to feed each mouth in turn.

It was the very opposite of the rapture, but the same effect: Josselin couldn't move, couldn't turn away, couldn't stop watching. Somewhere in the distance he heard someone calling his name, but he couldn't take his eyes off the horror before him.

"*Josselin! Don't just stand there, idiot Frenchman, move!*"

"*Milord! Josselin!*"

"*Fabien! Get him!*"

Suddenly his view was blocked by a black neck and mane; Fabien grabbed the back of his master's surcoat and hauled him bodily up over the pommel of his saddle. The squire kicked his gelding's sides, and Whitefoot was only too glad to flee.

Fabien released him when they caught up with some of the

others, letting him slide to the ground. "Milord." He was panting for breath. "Are you hurt, sir?"

Josselin shook his head. "What—what the hell *was* that thing?"

"Tzimisce war-ghoul," Sighard growled, riding up. "Not natural, their creatures. Renaud! Over here!"

Renaud galloped up to join them. "Lord Alexander's having us regroup at Schwarzenburg. I think he has a plan."

Fabien extended his hand. "Come on, mount up behind me, we'll find Achilles later."

Josselin took Fabien's hand and swung up behind him, wrapping his arms around the mortal's ribs. "Thank you." he said.

Fabien grinned. "Anytime."

They could still hear the monster screaming behind them as they rode away.

Chapter Eleven

The Burzenland, Eastern Hungary
During Pentecost, April and May, 1225

The rack had been all but useless with this one. The prisoner could lengthen its limbs as easily as the rack could stretch them. So Jürgen had ordered the prisoner's arms and legs chopped off entirely, which had certainly stopped its flesh-twisting tricks, but not improved its cooperation.

The translator repeated Lord Jürgen's question for the prisoner's benefit.

The Tzimisce snarled, baring a mouthful of jagged teeth. It was all the creature could do—it was now secured to the table by two great spikes through its shoulders and several heavy iron chains. Jürgen signaled, and the leather-gauntleted Brother Farris took a pair of iron tongs heated red-hot from a brazier and held them where the prisoner could see them.

"Right ear," Jürgen said. Brother Farris grabbed the prisoner's ear with the tongs—the Tzimisce screamed, and there was an acrid stench of burning carrion.

"Milord! Milord!" A young brother-squire came rattling down the stairs. "There's word from Marianburg! A messenger from Brother Henricus!"

Jürgen stood up. "Tell him to think carefully," he told the translator. "My patience wears thin."

The messenger was a dirty, exhausted peasant boy, no older than fifteen, half-naked and terrified out of his wits. "Milord. *Hochmeister*," he gasped. "They're dead. They're all dead, I saw it. The demons killed them all…."

Jürgen regarded him warily. "Who's dead, boy?" he asked. "What happened?"

"Everyone!" he gasped. "They surrounded the village, the keep. Monsters came out of the woods, breathing Greek fire. There were giant wolves with teeth like spikes. Men in armor, riding terrible horned beasts. Too many, too many of them." He was crying. "He told them to let me live. He said I had to bring you the message."

"What message?" Jürgen demanded. "*Speak*, boy!"

"Milord." A short, cloaked figure, its face hidden under the shadows of its hood, appeared beside the boy. It bent and turned the boy around, pulled away the ragged mantle he clutched over his shoulders, exposing the boy's bare back. "Here, I fear, is Rustovitch's true message."

There was a man's face there, embedded in the boy's flesh, caught up in a rictus of total agony, blue eyes staring blindly, mouth gaping, the remnants of a graying beard still bristling around what had once been its chin.

"Brother Henricus." Jürgen spoke through gritted teeth; his fangs were down, and he was all but trembling from fury. The boy began to cry.

It took several minutes for Jürgen to master the crimson fury in his soul, to regain control enough to speak without screaming, move without succumbing to the Beast's need to lash out and destroy. "Thank you, Akuji," he said at last, then glanced down at the boy. "Herr Michael. Kill it."

The knight closest to the wretched messenger nodded grimly, and drew his sword. Jürgen turned and stalked back downstairs.

"Out!" he snapped at Brother Farris and the translator, and they fled.

Jürgen and the prisoner locked eyes for a moment. The Tzimisce's eyes grew wide, and he started to babble in a mixture of Slavonic, German and Latin, but it did him no good. The Sword-Bearer was no longer interested in listening.

Lord Jürgen picked up the discarded leather gauntlets, put them on. Then he picked up the tongs in both hands and rammed the red-hot metal through muscle, sinew and bone to tear out the Tzimisce's unbeating heart.

"Sighard, childe of Cuno, come forward and stand before us."

Sighard had grudgingly consented to a shave and hair trimming; even with the yellow eyes and wolf's teeth, and the curved claws that protruded from his gloves, he looked more human than Josselin had ever seen him. He wore a knight's surcoat over his leathers, green with two running wolves in white, the device he had chosen himself, though it was Fabien who had stitched it together for him. The Gangrel came to the front of the hall, bowed, and then stood stiffly before Lord Jürgen.

Alexander formally presented him with Olivier's sword, horse and armor that he had already held for so long. Two brothers of the Black Cross put the white belt around his waist, and attached the spurs to his heels as best they could, for Sighard wore no shoes. Sighard knelt, repeated the words of the oath as Jürgen gave them to him, his hand on Lord Jürgen's sword. His pronunciation of the Latin was less than perfect, but that hardly mattered.

Jürgen then raised the sword and lightly tapped Sighard's shoulders with it. "I dub thee once, I dub thee twice, I dub thee three times knight. Rise, Herr Sighard, and receive the buffet. Let this be the last blow you ever accept unanswered."

Sighard rose, his grin exposing all his teeth. Jürgen struck him in the middle of his chest, hard enough to knock him back a step, but not knock him down. The assembled witnesses, mostly members of the Black Cross, broke into applause and shouts of congratulations in three different languages while Jürgen clasped Sighard's forearm and congratulated him personally.

Sighard's was the first but not the last knighting that evening. Twelve squire-brothers of the Order also received the accolade, but for five of those, the occasion was even more significant, for they were led off by senior brothers in the order for a further initiation—the Embrace, to replenish the ranks of Cainites lost in the fighting.

Jürgen took the last parchment from the stack Brother Christof had been holding, and read it aloud. "Fabien d'Auxerre, son of the Seigneur de Conches, come forward and stand before us."

Fabien didn't react at first. Then his eyes widened and his mouth hung open in total astonishment. Josselin nudged him. "Go on, Fabien, don't keep him waiting."

"But I—I'm not—"

"If you're not worthy, *cher*, then no man is. Go."

Fabien squared his shoulders and went to accept the accolade of knighthood.

Lord Jürgen let a drop of his blood fall into the glob of wax, and the scribe pressed the seal into it before it cooled. Three letters, three couriers, one very important message.

"The Tzimisce hold Rosenauer Berg, and have infiltrated the woods near Eulenburg and Bran. Rustovitch seeks to divide us. Instead, we will trap him between us. Send the messengers out one hour before dawn. We will stage a sortie at that time, to draw Tzimisce attention, and give them a chance to get through the sentries."

"Whom should we send?" Christof asked.

"Ask for volunteers, and weed out any whom you think can't make it through. Bring me the names, and your recommendations. Don't tell them where they're going yet. I want those who are willing to run to Constantinople if I ask it of them, not just ride a few miles to Bran."

"Yes, *Hochmeister*."

"He's late." Renaud wiggled into the angled opening in the crenellations of Kronstadt and leaned out as far as he dared, as if that would stretch the range of his sight even a few feet more, but the heavy fog rendered everything not within three strides all but invisible. Sighard had left three nights before to carry Lord Jürgen's message to Bran.

"Careful." Fabien hooked his fingers in Renaud's belt, just in case. "It's a *long* way down on this side."

"He should have come back by now," Renaud muttered. "What's taking him so long?"

"The fog, maybe?" Fabien shrugged. "Josselin, can you see anything?"

The Cainite joined them, took Renaud's place himself. Fabien hooked his fingers into Josselin's belt as well, just to be safe.

"No," Josselin began, and then held up his hand. "Wait—the fog's lifting. There's a fire—no, two fires—on the hill over there...."

"Sorcery," Fabien murmured, and crossed himself.

"*Holy Mary*—" Josselin growled, pulling back out of the opening. His fangs were down. "Lord Jürgen must know about this."

"What?" Renaud pushed forward; Josselin caught the ghoul by the shoulders, blocking his view for a moment.

"Renaud—" Josselin hesitated, but the grief in his eyes said as much as was needed. Renaud cried out, shoved past Josselin and all but threw himself into the opening, staring with horror at the spectacle across the river.

"*No!*"

The fog had vanished as mysteriously as it had come. On the hill across the river, three tall stakes had been set up, between two great bonfires—clearly the Tzimisce wanted their victims to be recognizable. And indeed, he did recognize all three, but it was the one in the middle whose agony drew him in, and cut the deepest into his heart.

Sighard had been impaled from below, the stake passing up through his belly, his heart and into his skull. His jaw with its wolf's teeth hung open, but the yellow eyes blazed in fury—though wounded and paralyzed, the Gangrel still survived.

But only for the moment. One of the Tzimisce took a flaming brand from the fire and held it up, setting the prisoners' clothing alight. And even as Renaud cried out in horror, there came the clamor of horns, horses, and the clash of steel from across the river, and he spotted mounted knights in white wearing the black cross. The Tzimisce were under attack. *Václav! He got through. Sighard got the message through!*

Behind him, the keep's bell began to ring; men scrambled for weapons and horses. "To arms! To arms! Brothers, to arms!"

Renaud left the wall, and ran to get Ghost from the stable, moving with a grim purpose that overpowered, at least for the moment, the soul-wrenching agony deep inside him. *This* time, at least, vengeance for the master he had loved was not beyond his reach.

There was an acrid taste of smoke in the air; the vestiges of the bonfires still smoldered on the hillside. Josselin did not look up at the charred remains of the impaling stakes—of their victims, nothing but ashes remained now. Rustovitch had not been prepared for an attack—this time. Next time, their numbers would be greater, whereas Jürgen and his knights could not afford to lose a single man. Still, there was a certain grim satisfaction in the price the Tzimisce had paid for their arrogance.

Josselin spotted Marques's red surcoat and urged his mount in his direction. "Have you seen Fabien?" he called.

"Who?" Marques handed his bloody sword down to his squire to be wiped clean. "Jean, my mail will need to be sanded and cleaned by tomorrow night. And I'll want a vessel at sundown. See if you can find a prettier one this time."

"Sir Fabien, who serves me." Josselin struggled to rein in his temper. "Have you seen him?"

Jean pointed out into the darkness. "Last I saw him, sir, it was by the river. There were trees. His horse went down—"

Josselin wheeled his horse around and galloped towards the river.

The ground was a morass of churned mud and blood, littered with discarded gear and strewn with corpses, several of them bearing the black cross. Sorel shied as one of the wretched Tzimisce-bred horrors, mortally wounded but yet breathing, made a pathetic swipe in their direction. Josselin dismounted to dispatch it, severing the beast's head from its hunched shoulders.

Josselin let his vision shift, seeking any sign of life yet flickering among the carnage at the ford. There—was that something? *You bear my blood, Fabien, where are you?*

There. A living halo, however faint. Josselin refocused, made out the hulk of a horse on the ground, a black with one white foreleg. "Fabien!"

Whitefoot had fallen, the gelding's carcass pinning his rider, who lay twisted in the muck. Josselin dropped down to his knees, gently removing Fabien's helm, then unlacing the chin flap of the mail coif beneath and easing it free as well, so that his fingers could seek the artery in the mortal's throat. "Fabien. Fabien, *mon cher*, can you hear me?" There was a pulse—but it was weak, so very weak.

Josselin drew his dagger, slashed his wrist and held the wound to the pale lips, opened the mortal's mouth to let the blood trickle in. "Fabien. Please, *please*, Holy Mary—"

Fabien's eyelids flickered, and he swallowed, but he barely had strength to suckle. *How much blood has he lost? Dare I even think of it—would Alexander allow it? Or would I be making the same mistake all over again?*

"—Josselin." His voice was little more than a breath. "I—I knew you would come."

"Of course I did." Josselin assured him. "I'll have you free in a minute. Drink."

"I'm cold. I—I can't feel my legs. Or—or anything."

"Just—just cold."

Fabien's skin was nearly as cold as Josselin's own. Gently Josselin probed under where Fabien lay, and his hand came away soaked with blood.

There were some wounds not even the blood could cure— though its power could keep a mortal alive and lingering when he should have died hours before. *Even if I dared Embrace him— would he then spend eternity crippled or whole?*

Fabien tried to lift his head, failed. "I—I beg your mercy, Josselin. Please."

Blood tears welled in Josselin's eyes, streamed down his cheeks. "I should get you a priest."

"No. Just you. Pray—pray for me."

Josselin leaned down and kissed Fabien gently, felt the mortal respond, tasted his own blood on Fabien's lips. "Every night, I swear it, as long as I endure."

Fabien smiled. He gave a little sigh as Josselin pierced his throat one last time; his heart went silent soon after.

A Tzimisce envoy arrived at Kronstadt under a flag of truce a month to the night after the mass sung for the souls of Sighard, Fabien and the rest. It had not been a good month for the Saxon forces, with communication between Kronstadt and Bran now almost impossible and every night bringing word of another atrocity. The fiends were burning every village that had once been home to a German settler. The arrival of an envoy seemed hardly propitious to Jürgen.

Still, the diplomat arrived with only a token mortal escort, whom he permitted to be disarmed without protest. He was no monster, but a slender well-spoken young man who wore robes in the Greek style rather than armor, and spoke German with the accent of Byzantium rather than the barbaric tongue of Rustovitch's hordes.

"You are outnumbered, milord. Your men are valorous, your strategies are well thought out, but you cannot afford to lose a single man—the *voivode* will chip away at your defenses, taking a man here, two men there, a Cainite here, and you will not be able to replace them. He has forces to spare, he is in his own country, and he can afford to be patient and play with you as a cat with a mouse."

"Do not tell *me* how to wage war, Greek," Jürgen snarled. "Did he send you here to test my mettle, Tzimisce? How many pieces would you like to be returned to your master in?"

The Tzimisce took a moment to reply, no doubt considering his words more carefully. "Lord Rustovitch," he said finally, "threatened me with much the same thing, even though we have been allied in the past. He seemed to think I wished to rob him of his victory.

"But in truth, milord, his situation is not as strong as it may appear. Those who believed his promises, who allied in his cause and gave him the men and monsters with which to wage his war, grow impatient, for the victory he promised seems out of his reach. Your numbers are fewer, yet you persevere, and it makes him look... less than entirely competent. Damek Ruthven, lord of Sarmizegetusa, grows impatient. The one the Tremere call Ioan the Butcher grows impatient. Noriz, who fought the legions of Rome, grows impatient. Even the most patient Radu of Bistritz grows impatient."

"Patience is a virtue, Greek. If it will mean Rustovitch's destruction and my victory, I can be very patient indeed."

The Tzimisce shook his head. "Patience will not give you victory now. I am here to tell you that there can be no victory, for either side. Other forces beside your own are gathering in the night. Rustovitch knows this as well, and seeks to harry you out of these lands before either he, or you, must fight a war on two fronts."

Jürgen's eyes narrowed. "What forces are you talking about? More Tzimisce?"

"The Gangrel of this land are led by a powerful warrior queen named Morrow—"

"I know what she is," Jürgen growled.

"She has many followers. If she calls them to war, she will be quite formidable—and they will give no quarter."

"What business is this of hers? Will she support Rustovitch, then?"

"She supports no one but her own kin, milord. She cares nothing for Ventrue or Tzimisce, neither for the Church of the Latins nor the Greeks, nor for Saxon, Szeklar, Cuman, or Vlach. She cares only for the land, the forests and mountains and the beasts—and I tell you, milord, your conflict here has made the land bleed until it cries out in its torment for those who can hear."

"Those who can hear? Sorcery and devilry."

"*I* am Tzimisce, Lord Jürgen, and *I* hear it. This land has drunk our blood for more centuries than even the Church can count. Morrow hears the voices of the birds and the beasts, and the cries of her childer. She is angry, but she is clever also. She will let you and Rustovitch tear and worry each other until you are both exhausted, and then—" the slim shoulders shrugged. "She will have the ultimate victory, unless you act now and end it."

"If you do not serve Rustovitch, whom *do* you serve?"

Again, the Tzimisce appeared to weigh his words before replying. "Those whom I represent claim a different lineage, that of my own ancestor the Dracon, late of Constantinople. Most are scholarly monks, who desire little of the world save a place to pursue their studies in peace—but in these nights, such peace has been hard to secure. It is my hope, milord Jürgen, that

I may serve your needs as well as my own—and assist in some small way to the forging of a peaceful settlement of this dispute, before it is too late."

"So I should give up my claim to this land that my men have fought, bled and died for, and just *give* it to you and your heretical monks? Don't make me laugh, Greek!"

"If the thought displeases you, milord, I can but offer my apologies—it is the only plan I have to offer that might work. But I can assure you, milord, that Lord Rustovitch will like it even less."

"Hmm..." Jürgen considered, studied the Greek more carefully. "What did you say your name was again?"

The envoy smiled. "Vykos, milord. Myca Vykos."

Chapter Twelve

Magdeburg, Saxony
The Ides of May, 1225

With Lords Jürgen and Alexander both in Hungary, along with the bulk of their immediate vassals, Magdeburg had become a very quiet place indeed in the spring of 1225. Rosamund was able to act more freely, but found there was precious little to act upon—the war in Hungary occupied all thoughts, especially with the poor news of the expulsion of the mortal Teutonic Knights. Without their cover, the common wisdom went, Jürgen and the rest could not stand against the Tzimisce. It seemed to Rosamund, that much of Saxony and several interested parties in Île de France were waiting to see if anyone would return from the Burzenland at all.

Thus, she had little reason to expect trouble when Wiftet appeared before her. "An admirer, milady," he said. "Will you receive him?"

"Of course. Please, show him in."

Wiftet bowed again, and then trotted off on his errand.

The admirer was cloaked and hooded, his face obscured. His bow was perfect in its grace, even down to the flare of his cloak, and his French carried the accent of the Champagne. "Milady. I am but a humble messenger who begs leave to present his master's petition for your perusal. Will you accept it?"

A cold knot began to form somewhere in her belly at his first words; it was his voice, not his words, that captured her attention. A beautiful voice, and a familiar one.

After all these years, he dares present himself to me again?

"Lucien."

Her visitor pushed back his hood, revealing a youthful face with rounded cheeks, a disheveled mop of brown hair, and haunted lapis-blue eyes. "So, you do remember me. I was afraid you would."

"How could I forget? How dare you show your face here of all places?"

She could almost see his spine stiffening. "Well," he said, "to be perfectly honest, milady, I am here because Lord Jürgen is not, and as I said, I bring a message. I've gambled my unlife on your mercy, Lady Rosamund. Or will you call for your servants and carry out Isouda's sentence yourself? Cut off my head? Drink me to ashes? Or just stake me out for the sun so you don't have to hear me scream?"

"*Stop it*, Lucien."

"As milady wishes." He held out a roll of parchment, sealed and bound with a red ribbon. "Will you accept my master's message?"

Wiftet stepped forward to take the parchment for her, taking his responsibility as her guardian quite seriously, but Lucien withdrew his hand even as the Malkavian reached for it.

"No. Not you, fool. This message is for milady's hands alone."

"Wiftet." Rosamund spoke quickly, raising her hand to wave the Malkavian away. "It's all right." Wiftet bowed and obeyed, although he didn't go far.

Lucien held out the parchment again. "For you, milady. Will you take it?"

She rose from her seat and approached. Lucien was trembling a little as she came up to him; he dropped down to one knee as she took the parchment from his hand. "Who is your master now, Lucien?" she asked. Then she saw the seal. "Holy Mary."

"What other choice did you leave me?" he asked bitterly. "The blood hunt called against me in France—the news traveling to every court in Europe: 'Lucien de Troyes is outlawed, cast out from the protection of the Traditions and the Blood. Let his existence be forfeit and his blood reclaimed, let his name be blotted out and even his memory be brought to ashes.' He has a copy of the proclamation, you see, and he reads it to me now and then, just to remind me of where I stand. I sold my soul to the devil, Lady Rosamund, and his name is Jervais bani Tremere."

She broke the seal, and unrolled the letter.

A week after Lucien's unexpected visit, Rosamund sat on her chair on the dais like a queen on her throne, receiving a humble petitioner. Her guest was Jervais bani Tremere, and humility did not come easily to him, but it was a lesson she felt he much needed to learn, lest he forget his place again in the future. She looked at the petition he had sent ahead of his visit. "This request is best directed at Lord Jürgen, Maestro, not to me. I am but a guest in Lord Jürgen's domains."

"I have sent it to him previously, milady, and made other overtures to him in Hungary," Jervais answered. "He has yet to favor me with a reply."

"Lord Jürgen is on crusade, Maestro," Rosamund pointed out. "I doubt he has very much time for such matters."

"Yes, milady," Jervais agreed. "I am freshly returned from travel through those lands myself, and I can bear witness to the stout opposition Lord Jürgen faces there. I fear that upon his return—if return there should be—he will be all the more disinclined to receive me, due to our past misunderstandings."

"Misunderstandings, Maestro? You conspired to sour relations between the Courts of Love and Lord Jürgen, stole the very blade my queen had entrusted to me to gift to Lord Jürgen, and did a very good job of souring my own position here. I think perhaps you address your petition to the wrong person."

"I sincerely hope not, milady," Jervais said. "It was a great misunderstanding on my part, at least, for which I have been most ardently corrected by my superiors in the clan, I assure you. It is at their direction, and out of the remorse of my own heart at the unwarranted difficulties and embarrassment I caused you, that I come before you this night to offer my most humble apologies." It was not quite groveling, but it was likely as close to it as the Tremere would come.

Rosamund found it satisfying, but not satisfying enough. "I find myself searching for a goodly reason to accept the apology of one who has wronged me so, Maestro. What penance do you bring?"

Jervais glanced at Lucien, who stood behind him. "I understand that my humble servant Lucius is under severe penalty for his part in that affair."

"That is no secret." Indeed, Salianna had made quite sure that every court from London to the Holy Land knew of the blood hunt against Lucien de Troyes for conspiring against the courts.

"Then, milady, may I make the formal offer to return Lucius to your custody as a token of good faith and a first meager step in returning to your good graces?" A look of sheer horror crossed Lucien's face and Rosamund felt it echo in her own heart. Were she to accept that offer, she'd have very little choice but to execute the former troubadour who was her brother's only childe. *Josselin would never forgive me.*

"If it would better please you, milady," Jervais said, "I could surrender Lucius to Lord Jürgen upon his return. Or, I suppose, I could simply keep him discreetly in my household."

Rosamund had to fight to maintain control. Jervais had read her perfectly—he had obviously learned a great deal since his blunders in Magdeburg thirteen years ago.

"Your offer is appreciated but unnecessary, Maestro. Your apology is accepted."

"Thank you, milady. I am your most humble servant."

She did not miss the look of incredible relief that passed over Lucien's face, kneeling in his master's not inconsiderable shadow.

Jervais clasped his hands over his broad belly with an almost feline smile of satisfaction. "Now that we're on more diplomatic terms, milady, might we discuss my petition to Lord Jürgen? Given the situation, it occurs to me that perhaps what Clan Tremere most needs at this time is an advocate in the court, someone of impeccable credentials who has his lordship's ear and might be persuaded to speak on our behalf."

Chapter Thirteen

Near Buda-Pest, Western Hungary
Eve of the Feast of St. John the Baptist, June, 1225

For the first time in too long, Sir Josselin dictated a letter:

"It is over at last, *ma petite*. I admit being more than a bit surprised—and grateful to Our Lord that I have survived these last few months here in this blood-soaked land. But there is little rejoicing here. I think we are all too weary of the killing, the blood, the fear and horrors we have endured in this place. That we are done with it all, that we are at last returning home to more peaceful pursuits and civilized lands does not yet seem real enough to celebrate. It is almost as if to do so would be to dishonor those who suffered and gave their very lives in our endeavors. Perhaps in a few weeks, once these mountains fade behind us in the shadows and we hear German spoken on every side—or maybe even some good French!—our hearts will find time to mend.

"Lord Jürgen keeps much to himself of late—even Brother Christof seems concerned for him here in the lands of the Arpad, where we have made camp after leaving Transylvania. I think the price we have paid for our survival—for even though there is peace now, no one favors it with the term victory—weighs most heavily on him. He is a strong man, and his men love him—that we survived at all is much a testament to his leadership, courage and tactical skill. Our Lord Alexander was most valiant and bold in our defense as well—and I am told that he and Marques held back a great force from taking Bran during our last sortie into the terrible woods of this land. I will have more to say of this when I return, little sister, so I beg you to be patient until you hear it from my own lips. For now I come to the hardest part of my missive.

"My heart is weary, Rosamund, and there is a great emptiness within it, and at my side. I did not have heart to tell you before—my sweet Fabien was taken from me into the hands of Our Lord some six weeks past. He was ever more to me than a servant, and was my closest and most trusted companion these past ten years. I was proud as any father to see him dubbed knight by Lord Jürgen himself, and I have pledged myself to pray for his soul throughout eternity. Now his bones will rest in Hungary—the Greek monks have promised me that his grave will be tended as befits a good Christian, even though they are not of our faith, and I must be content with that. But I would entreat your prayers for him, and also for the soul of our stout-hearted Sir Sighard, who received his wish at Lord Jürgen's hands at long last, and was as true-hearted a knight as ever I knew, and far better even than many in our own country who have never yet tested their steel in such a forge as we have been tested in here.

"My good friend Brother Renaud writes this for me, not for any service he owes to me, but out of the Christian kindness of his heart, and I am grateful for his assistance...."

"Josselin—please. Give me a moment." Renaud broke in. There was a tightness in his voice that matched Josselin's own. "I—I find I hard to write of him and not weep."

"I know," Josselin murmured.

"Does it ever... get easier?" Renaud wore the surcoat of the Black Cross over a plain white habit; his hair was neatly cut in a clerical tonsure under the order's white coif, but he had retained his beard in honor of his late Gangrel master. He had seemed to find some peace in his new existence, though, and Josselin was glad to see it. *Though Alexander has still not forgiven Jürgen for allowing it, nor Christof for bestowing it, even as desperate for new blood as we were in those damned woods. But I think Olivier would have approved.*

Josselin walked over to where Renaud sat at the copydesk

and sat on the long bench beside him. "Only if you let it, Brother. That is your human heart aching—do you really want to lose it?"

"Never." Brother Renaud spoke it as seriously as he done his vows. "If this is the price, then I will bear it throughout eternity. I—I would not be like *him*, Josselin, not in a thousand years."

Josselin put a hand on the white-clad shoulder and gave it a slight squeeze. "I pray God protect us both from such a fate, my friend."

Renaud crossed himself, a gesture Josselin echoed. Then the young unliving monk wiped the blood tears from his eyes. "Go on, Josselin. I'm ready now."

"Good. Where were we? Ah... My good friend Brother Renaud writes this for me...."

Chapter Fourteen

"Your Highness." Lord Hardestadt's envoy was an elegant Lombard, whose mantle was of black silk velvet lined with a darkness that eddied and flowed in a most disquieting manner, like some sort of animate ink. He bowed respectfully, Rosamund observed, but not too deeply; perhaps he wished to remind Lord Jürgen that he represented the prince's sire and liege—or perhaps it was simply pride. "Allow me to congratulate you on your recent safe return from the wilderness of Hungary—I bring greetings from your most sovereign liege, Lord Hardestadt, Monarch of Bavaria, Swabia, Franconia, Savoy, Lorraine, Bohemia, Saxony, Lombardy, and Thuringia."

"We thank you, milord Ignatio, and welcome you to our court," Lord Jürgen said evenly. He was wearing his order's habit this evening, the white surcoat with its black cross over well-polished mail, a white mantle lined in sheepskin, and a white linen coif over neatly trimmed hair. The contrast between the humble garb of the military order and the almost decadent finery of the Lombard envoy was hard to ignore.

"Your Highness, it would please milord Hardestadt to renew and strengthen the ties between his court and your own with an exchange of envoys; by milord's grace and with your Highness's permission, it would be my honor to serve as milord's envoy in your august court, and I present to you my commission from his own hand, and bearing his seal." He proffered a rolled parchment, bound in a ribbon and sealed with wax.

At a signal from Sister Lucretia, Brother Renaud went up to receive the parchment. Lord Hardestadt's envoy studied him curiously for a moment, then nodded, and handed the document over. Renaud brought it back to Lucretia, who examined the seal before proffering it to her lord. Jürgen broke the seal, gave the top page of the document a cursory glance, and then passed it to a brother who was acting as his secretary for the evening.

"Let it be recorded then, that we accept Lord Ignatio Lorca of Pavia as the official envoy of our sire, Lord Hardestadt," Jürgen pronounced, and the clerk made notes in his book. "We welcome him to our realm, and grant him leave to dwell herein and claim such rights of us as befits his commission and rank, which shall include the house set aside for such purposes and those who dwell within to be his lawful chattels."

Lord Ignatio bowed again. "I thank your Highness for your welcome and your generosity."

Rosamund had once heard Sighard, in one of his more expressive moments, refer to a Cainite court as a gathering of vultures waiting for one of their number to die so they could devour him. Rosamund had experienced the full attention of such vultures when she had arrived in Paris. Despite the fact that Magdeburg was but a quarter the size of Paris, a frontier outpost on the eastern marches of the Empire, the vulture analogy was no less true here. The vultures were fewer in number, but that did not make their hunger any less. Particularly after the less-than-decisive Hungarian campaign, which had broken Jürgen's long string of military successes, vultures seemed to abound. Lord Ignatio was but one of several such new arrivals, though Rosamund privately thought he looked by far the hungriest. The way shadows clung to his form marked Ignatio as being of Lasombra blood—so although he served Hardestadt, he did not share the high lord's blood. He thus likely had more to prove. That he might be more than willing to do so at Lord Jürgen's expense did not escape Rosamund.

Alexander had come back from Hungary with renewed purpose and new sycophants to compete for his approval and regard. Marques still claimed the position at his right hand, but Lord István's cleverness and wit often made him look the fool, and when István's guile failed to charm, Herr Konrad, a Saxon of Brujah blood who had found himself displaced from his domain near Kronstadt by Lord Jürgen's treaty, could make his mark through the threat—and sometimes the reality—of sheer brute strength.

Josselin, however, had come back alone. He had been extremely fond of Fabien, more so than Rosamund remembered him being with any who had served him in the past, and it was only with reluctance, and out of sheer practicality, that he agreed to search for another squire. Sighard's destruction and Renaud's Embrace meant that those he called friends besides herself were all among the Brothers of the Black Cross, not in Alexander's household.

Lord István had even had the temerity—once—to suggest to her that perhaps Josselin might consider taking vows himself. She had merely laughed, but the idea that István might be speaking Alexander's own mind worried her more than she liked to admit.

When the formal court broke up, Alexander wasted no time making the acquaintance of Lord Hardestadt's envoy, who seemed equally eager to meet him as well.

"Lord Alexander. My pleasure to meet you in person at last. Sir Olivier spoke so highly of you. I was hoping to see him again, actually—"

"I regret to inform you, milord, that he perished on our journey," Alexander said smoothly.

"My most sincere condolences, milord," the Lasombra replied. "I most enjoyed my discussions with him while he was visiting Lord Hardestadt's court. He was a most able advocate on your behalf."

Alexander smiled. "He did me good service, milord. His loss was most difficult to bear."

The two Cainites walked away together.

Rosamund found herself clenching her teeth, and forced herself to relax. *Olivier is gone, and God will judge Alexander for it, even if it is not any night soon. It is to those who yet survive that my duty lies.* Schooling herself to smile, she went to speak to Baron Eckehard.

"We were desperate, in the last few weeks before the truce," Marques's voice carried just well enough for Josselin to hear, which he suspected was the entire point. "That's the only reason he was Embraced. They were choosing anyone who could be spared, really."

Josselin knew exactly who Marques was referring to—he seemed to have taken Renaud's passage into undeath as a personal affront, an action intentionally taken just to deprive Marques of the servant he had long coveted. It wasn't entirely untrue, either, which Josselin knew full well; although it had been service to Alexander that Renaud had been seeking to avoid when he sought sanctuary from the Order of the Black Cross. So far, Marques had not yet been foolish enough to make such statements when Renaud or Christof could hear—but his audience was Hardestadt's envoy, and he was all but challenging Josselin to contradict him.

Josselin had to forcibly remind himself that anyone who took Marques's word for anything was likely not worth Hardestadt's time, and Ignatio likely knew spiteful gossip when he heard it. What he'd do with it, of course, remained to be seen, but the insult was not his to respond to, no matter how highly he regarded Christof's newest childe. He turned away and left the hall, seeking the fresher air of the garden.

"Herr Josselin!" A booming voice, in accented German, heralded a mountain of a man in a Teutonic habit. It did nothing to hide the fact that Václav had been born to be a warrior, not a monk. "You're a hard man to track down—one would think you *liked* this court rabble."

"Good evening, Brother," Josselin said, clasping Václav's powerful arm. "I do like it—usually—although I wouldn't describe it quite that way, of course."

"Of course." Václav grinned, revealing teeth missing from some fight in his mortal years. His long hair and beard were trimmed tonight, although even that did not manage to make the big Bohemian truly look monastic. "I am leaving soon," he said, his voice rumbling from his barrel chest. "The Duke of Masovia has asked the Teutonic Order for aid to drive the heathen Prussians out of Chelmno, and the Emperor has given his blessing to the crusade. With milord sire's leave, I'll go where there's a real fight. I've no patience for courtly prattle—I like to break my enemies, not pretend I wish to talk to them."

"Then I wish you God speed, Brother," Josselin said. "It was an honor to serve with you."

"You could come with me," Václav suggested, although there was a twinkle in the pale eyes; clearly he knew where Josselin's heart lay. "You're a good man in a fight. And after Rustovitch's foul lot, the Prussians will be nothing."

"Thank you, Brother, but my duty lies here," Josselin answered, smiling. "I'm sure you and God can handle the Prussians well enough without my help."

Václav laughed. "I'm sure we can! Well, there will always be another fight. To be honest, I almost wish we were sent further north, to Riga. I've heard rumor of a new warlord among the pagan tribes there. Some Tartar chieftain out of the east. Might be more of a challenge than what's in Chelmno."

"A new warlord?" Josselin asked. "Mortal or Cainite?"

"With the stories they tell, who knows? But it's Chelmno for me. Riga will have to wait." He clapped a broad hand on Josselin's shoulder. "Then God's blessing on you, my friend, and my best to your lady. Keep a good eye open, though. I don't much like those grasping young bloods his lordship surrounds himself with now."

"I'll be careful," Josselin assured him. "God keep you."

To Lord Jürgen Sword-Bearer, Prince of Magdeburg, We rejoice to hear of your safe return to your domains in Saxony, after such terrible ordeals in Hungary, of which we have heard in full detail. We share your great disappointment in the end results of your campaign against the tyrant Rustovitch. It is regrettable that such noble purposes should be thwarted by so simple a matter as mortal politics. But the Arpad, as you know, are notoriously factional, and can be most unreliable when it comes to putting another's interest above their own petty rivalries. We also share your grief at the loss of so many of those loyal to you, who fought and died under your command, and regret there could not have been a better result of their sacrifice on your behalf. Still, it is our most fervent hope that you did indeed gain some measure of wisdom from your recent experiences, albeit at such a price we would have never wished you pay.

We note as well the continued presence of our cousin Alexander of Paris in your realm, and commend you for your generous hospitality to him. We do not need to remind you how delicate the Parisian situation remains, and how unwise it would be for you to pursue any alliance or diplomatic contact with Geoffrey while the prince he forced into exile remains a guest in your court. Indeed, it is for your own good we advise you to have as little to do with even the Courts of Love or their current representative as possible, lest such a gesture be misinterpreted by your guest as being unworthy of your position as his host.

By our own hand,

—Lord Hardestadt, Monarch of Bavaria, Swabia, Franconia, Savoy, Lorraine, Bohemia, Saxony, Lombardy and Thuringia.

Jürgen resisted the urge to throw Hardestadt's letter into the fire. *Disappointment.* How very like his sire, to offer support with one hand while stabbing and twisting the knife with the other. He could just *imagine* how disappointed Hardestadt was.

Had it been arrogance, then, to answer the Arpad plea for aid against the Tzimisce? Arrogance to hold fast to what he had claimed, with Arpad blessing, even when their support vanished like a mountain mist? Arrogance to believe that his men were capable of meeting whatever hell-spawned forces Rustovitch could call up? Arrogance to think that the fiends would do as they had long done, and fall to squabbling?

"I was arrogant, Erasmus," he said aloud. "And as Lord Hardestadt so righteously points out, it is others who have paid the price for my folly and shortsighted ambition."

The Cainite priest studied his lord carefully. "Do you wish to make confession, milord?" he asked. "No matter what Lord Hardestadt may believe to the contrary, it is only God who can grant absolution from sins, through the blood of Our Lord, not that which is passed down from sire to childe. And you know that Our Lord is always ready to hear sincere repentance from His lost lambs, even such as we."

"Is ambition a sin, Father?" Jürgen asked.

Father Erasmus considered this a moment. "It was the ambition of Saint Paul to bring the word of Our Lord to Rome itself, and he did. It was the ambition of the Emperor Charlemagne to united all of Europe under one Christian crown, and he did—though only for his lifetime. And it was the ambition of the Fourth Crusade to liberate the Holy Land—but at the end, it was Constantinople that burned. It is not the desire to prove ourselves, or to do great things that is in itself a sin, milord. It is to what ends that desire leads us, and the means by which we strive to achieve it, that is where we may be judged. For God sees not only what we do, but the motivations of our hearts."

Jürgen crossed himself and knelt by the priest's feet. "Then I would confess my sins, Father, and ask absolution."

Several nights later, Jürgen still felt the sting of his sire's letter, and found himself walking along one of the upper halls of the Priory of St. Paul. He stopped when he heard Rosamund's voice coming from the gardens below one of the windows.

"Herr Augustin, I'm so glad you came!" she said. "What do you have for me this evening?"

"I wrote a poem, milady," said Augustin in the garden. "In—in French. I'm afraid it's not very good. It's hard to find the right *words* in French. German is so much better for poetry."

She laughed. "And yet the troubadours would have us all speaking Provençal, while the Italians swear by the tongue of the Florentines. Let me hear it, and I shall judge."

They were alone in the garden. *A tryst*, Jürgen realized, and he could well guess why—since Augustin's primary function at court was hardly for his poetry, nor were his family connections or skill at arms anything extraordinary. He had all the social grace of a gangly puppy, and yet Rosamund favored him with her kiss.

Augustin cleared his throat.

"In a moonlit garden is the fairest rose,
Beyond the reach of mortal men she grows,
Her petals soft as a dove's white wing,
For her sweet kiss I'd do anything,
To pluck her free from her thorny bower,
And in my heart to forever flower."

"Oh, that's so sweet," Rosamund murmured. "Do you truly think I am beyond even your reach, Augustin? Or would you dare the thorns to claim your reward?"

She flattered him, and Augustin basked in her regard, willingly falling under the spell of her voice, her charm, her beauty. Jürgen knew he should move on, that he had no business eavesdropping on what was developing below. Yet he found himself lingering—in fact, his own fangs were already lengthening in his jaw in anticipation of what he knew was coming.

"I would dare anything, milady. Anything at all, if it would grant me your favor."

"And what do you know of gardening, Augustin?" she asked him. Her voice dropped in volume and register; Jürgen focused his hearing so as not to miss a single word.

"Not as much as I should like, milady," Augustin admitted, though there was clearly hope in his voice.

"Let me show you...." She moved closer to him on the bench; Jürgen could hear the hem of her gown catching on the dead leaves under her feet. "Roses require a lot of gentle handling... a light touch... like this. Yes, that's right...."

"So cold," Augustin whispered. Jürgen had to concentrate to distinguish Augustin's words from the increased throbbing of the mortal's heart.

"Then you must keep them warm."

"Yes..."

Talking ceased when they kissed. The soft wet sounds of it vied with the Augustin's occasional gasps for breath and Rosamund's low murmurs of pleasure. In the passageway above, Jürgen clenched his fists and closed his eyes, trying not to imagine just what liberties she was allowing him, and failing miserably. Nor did he dare look to see how close his imaginings came to the truth. And yet he could not tear himself away from the window, could not resist sharing, however clandestinely, Augustin's pleasures.

"Roses have thorns as well as velvet petals, sweet gardener," Rosamund said at last, in a low, husky voice, thick with desire. Jürgen did not need to see her to know she was nearly as aroused as her prey, and her desire could take but one kind of satisfaction now.

"I know." Augustin was all but panting now under her touch. "I... welcome... their prick... *oochhhh*—" His voice trailed off in a soft moan of pure bliss.

Jürgen had never imagined he'd be jealous of Augustin for anything, but at that moment he had to fight an intense urge to leap through the window down to the garden, tear the hapless mortal out of Rosamund's arms and take his place. Jürgen's arms hungered to hold her, his fangs positively ached to taste her sweetness for himself, feel the prick of her fangs in his own flesh.

With a tremendous wrench of his will, Jürgen tore himself away from the window and strode as swiftly as he could while still maintaining some appearance of dignity towards the underground levels of the priory. There, an unfortunate Vlach prisoner who had once served in Rustovitch's hordes was forced to serve the hunger that the Lady Rosamund and her mortal suitor had aroused in him—but his desire for her would have to remain unsatisfied, at least for now.

Distractions, he reminded himself, dropping his prey's body to the straw, realizing only belatedly how extravagantly indulgent his eavesdropping had been—he did not have so many proper vessels in his captive herd that he could afford to waste one on a frivolous bout of passion. Nor could he take the time now to raid east and accumulate more. *I cannot afford to let her distract me now. There are too many other matters needing my attention. She is the least of them—why then does she usurp a higher place in my thoughts?*

To his credit, Brother Farris did not say a word about the loss of one of their limited stock of war captives, nor did he inquire why his lord had been so careless as to drain one. Jürgen left terse instructions to give the dead man a proper Christian burial and arrange for the usual number of masses for his soul, and then took himself to the priory chapel to pray for the state of his own.

Chapter Fifteen

Magdeburg, Saxony
Feast of St. Mary Magdalene, July, 1227

"I will need more light, madame, if you would be so kind? It *is* after dark, after all." Peter didn't even look up from his notes as he spoke. Margery set another candle on the table in front of him and lit it, without speaking or acknowledging him. His request had nothing to do with the amount of light at any rate; it was a merely a code phrase. But still, Rosamund was not pleased to witness the manner of it. She tried to remember the last time she had heard them exchange a kind word, and could not.

Peter handed her a wax tablet, where he had noted: *He entertains Ignatio and Balthazar tonight. Again.*

She nodded, and picked up the stylus herself. "Do you know when my brother will return?" she asked, while she wrote: *Lord Jürgen should know.*

"I don't know, milady." He took the tablet back and stuck the flat side of the burnisher in the candle flame for a few seconds, ignoring Rosamund's wince; then rubbed away what they had scribed in the wax. "I do not think his heart is in his search—he still mourns for Fabien. It would be hard to ask any man, however promising, to step into such beloved shoes." He picked up the stylus again: *Write to him. I shall take it.*

"That, and he still hopes for one who speaks French." She wrote back: *No. I will go.* Then, before he took the tablet back again, she added: *Why don't you talk to her?*

He scowled and rubbed the words out, barely heating the burnisher first. He didn't say anything, merely scribbled *No*, and then: *Don't go, it's too dangerous.* But the look he gave Margery then, who was busy helping Blanche put Rosamund's bed here in Alexander's keep of Finsterbach to rights, was as hurt as it was resentful.

"Perhaps you could make some inquiries," she said, claiming the tablet one more time. "Surely there are some young French men who are looking for a good position somewhere in the empire." *She loves you still.*

Rosamund laid her hand on his; he wouldn't meet her eyes. "I—I'll see what I can do," he muttered, not entirely sure himself what he was agreeing to. "Is that all, milady?"

"Thank you," she whispered, and rose from the table. Peter bent over the tablet, staring at what his mistress had written before stubbornly rubbing the words out of the wax, as if that would erase them from his memory as well.

"Milord, I—I find I must beg your forgiveness yet again," Rosamund said as humbly as she could, falling to her knees at Alexander's feet. "I pray you, please have mercy—"

"My sweet rose." Alexander extended a hand to bring her to her feet. "What could you have possibly done to warrant such a display of penitence?"

"I am ashamed even to say it, milord," she whispered, ignoring the approach of Alexander's servant Gaston. "Here you have been so very good to me, so kind and loving, and I have been so ungrateful. Pride is such a dreadful sin, milord—and God's own word teaches us to respect our elders, and yet—"

Gaston cleared his throat, meaningfully. "Milord, your guests—"

"A moment, Gaston," Alexander said. "Sweet Rosamund. We will talk later, I'm afraid I have pressing business to attend to."

Rosamund kissed his hand. "Might I then at least go to confession, milord? My sins weigh heavily on my soul, and I must ask God's forgiveness as well for my wickedness, for I am keeping your Highness from his duties.

Go, then. We'll talk later, my love—do not be so hard on yourself! Rest assured you will always have my forgiveness for the asking."

"I most humbly thank your Highness." Rosamund bowed low; Alexander's hand lightly brushed her hair in benediction, and then he was gone, following Gaston to his all-important guests.

As soon as the door closed behind them, Rosamund was up and running to the stables, where Peter had already arranged to have her palfrey saddled and ready for her, and his own and Sir Thomas's mounts as well. Less than a quarter hour later, they were on the road towards Magdeburg, and the Teutonic commandery and hospital of St. Mary.

The guesthouse was plain and spare, as befitted a military monastic house, being mostly a large dormitory, but there were two private windowless chambers for the use of Cainite guests, and it was in one of these that Father Erasmus kindly heard Rosamund's confession. When she had also confessed her true purpose, and asked for parchment and a pen to write a short letter to Lord Jürgen, Erasmus had listened gravely, and then departed to find what she needed.

But when the chamber door opened, it was not Father Erasmus with the promised scribing supplies, but Lord Jürgen himself.

"Milady. This is an unexpected pleasure." Jürgen bent over her hand, brushed his lips over her knuckles. "Father Erasmus tells me that you had a message for me—he thought it best I hear it myself."

"Milord. I thank you for seeing me—in truth, I did not know you would be here. I thought only to leave word for you." Now that she was here, it was no easy thing to say what she had come for. *If I betray Alexander's trust, even for his sake, will Lord Jürgen ever trust me after? Where does my duty lie?*

"And what is that word? Speak, milady, I listen."

She told him.

"I suppose I should not be surprised," he said at last. "Ignatio Lorca is a snake, slithering about looking for heels to sting, and

Balthasar has never been shy about keeping his options open. And Alexander, I imagine, grows restless—but is it Paris his eye is fixed upon, or something closer and more convenient?"

"I don't know. He does not confide such things to me."

"Your position, I think, is already known."

"Would you have it be otherwise?"

"No, milady. I prefer candor. Among our kind, it's almost a novelty. So what business has Balthasar with Alexander?"

"If I may say so, milord, since you value my candor—"

He raised an eyebrow. "Go on, lady."

"Your vassals grow restless because you have spent more time with your attention outward—on crusade in the Holy Land, or in Hungary—than inward, to your own domains. They are princes in their own territories, and they have grown unaccustomed to having an overlord, to the point where some wonder if they have need of one at all. Some even dare imagine what it might be like to claim an even greater domain than merely their own. And you must realize that Lord Ignatio serves his own purposes as much as your sire's. He seeks dissent, but he has little trouble finding it. Such conditions toppled Alexander."

"Do you make a comparison?"

"No, milord. I offer a concern for your consideration. Believe me when I tell you this, Lord Jürgen—you are nothing like Alexander."

"That, at least, is gratifying to hear," Jürgen said dryly.

Had she still breathed, she would have blushed. "I—I didn't mean it *quite* like that—"

"What do you think my sire's purposes are?"

"I think—" She hesitated, now unsure of his mood. "I think if he had truly meant to show his support for your rule here, he would have sent a different messenger. But it does him no good to undermine you—so that's not it, either. This is more of a test, isn't it? Like sending Alexander to Magdeburg in the first place."

"Quite probably."

As was sending me with Alexander. "It never ends, does it? They're never satisfied."

"No. But neither am I. Be assured, milady. I do not plan to sit idly on my throne and let some Lombard snake burrow into its foundations. But I do not do this for Lord Hardestadt's amusement. He did not put me on this throne. I do not need his support—such as it is—to keep it."

Jürgen was standing directly in front of her. His very nearness overcame her defenses. The full intensity of his charisma had been meant for the battlefield or open court, not the confines of this spare little guesthouse cell. "You see, milady." His voice was soft, but it still thrummed in her very bones; she was held captive by the intense blue of his eyes. "In the end, it's not their desires, their ambitions, or even their satisfaction that drives us. It is our own. The will, the courage, the ambition to become more than we are, and all we can be *must* come from within. It cannot be taught—only acted upon."

His passion was contagious. In that instant, Rosamund felt herself almost able to stare back at Salianna, at Geoffrey, even at her own sire, hold her head high and defy the fate they had sentenced her to. Almost. *I am not Lorraine,* she reminded herself. *I will not be trapped as she was. I will not make her mistakes. I must not.*

"You must act, then, milord," she said. "Either to crush the snake, or strengthen your foundations. Or both, for there are always more snakes."

"Indeed, my sire has an endless supply of them." He held out his hand to her. "Walk with me, milady? It is too fine a night to spend it within such confining walls."

Smiling, she laid her hand in his, and let him lead her out to the main hall of the guesthouse, where Peter and Thomas were waiting. The mortals rose to their feet expectantly, and Rosamund remembered her purpose.

"Milord," she said, turning to Lord Jürgen regretfully. "I cannot stay. I must return before he wonders where I've really gone."

Jürgen studied her for a moment. "Perhaps I have been remiss," he said, thoughtfully. "I should have arranged for you to have a haven of your own here in the city. The Ambassador of the Rose should have an embassy, after all. And she should answer for her actions to no one save her queen and the prince she serves."

"Your Highness is most generous," she said. "But it is enough that I have your leave to do so—in the interests of diplomacy, it would be more proper for an Ambassador to make her own arrangements. I could not have brought you such news as I did this night had I been in any other place but where I am—and in these difficult times, I must be in a place where I can best serve your Highness and my queen."

"I see." Jürgen suddenly took note of the witnesses, Peter and Thomas standing by, waiting patiently for their mistress to finish her business. "You may get your lady's horse ready," he told them, and it was not a request. "I will bring her out to you presently."

Rosamund turned slightly and nodded. Both mortal men bowed and left to carry out their instructions.

"I would not have you place yourself at risk, milady, not in my service or your queen's," Jürgen said when the two mortals were gone. "You are not my only eyes watching the comings and goings at Finsterbach. Though I also confess it... pleases me... that you would think so highly of me that you would come personally and tell me where my duties lie."

She dropped her gaze immediately. "Milord, I did not mean—"

"Rosamund, no—I didn't mean it that way, either." He was still holding her hands, so she couldn't escape. Now he took her small white hands between his own, one above and one below, as if in shielding them, he could shield her as well. "Allow me rephrase that, milady. I am pleased that you came, and I promise you, I will take your advice to heart. But if you are in any sort of danger because of it, I will not be pleased. You are under my protection here. If you or your brother *need* that protection, please do not hesitate to ask—I promise you, it is yours."

Rosamund didn't even want to think what colors her halo might be blazing in right then. Decades of practice kept her emotional turmoil—she hoped—from revealing itself on her face; she looked up and smiled at him. It was hard to avoid his eyes—or to want to avoid them. There was something in her that wanted to let herself fall into them, let him protect her. *And then what would Alexander do?* That gave her the strength to resist. "Thank you, milord," she managed. "Be sure, if I need it, I most certainly will."

He brought her hands up, and kissed her fingers, first the right hand and then the left, and then let them down again. "Thank you, milady."

Then he took her out to her horse and held it for her to mount.

"She doesn't understand, does she, Margery?" Alexander's voice was a soft whisper in her ear as they lay together on his bed in the darkness before dawn. Ignatio and the other delegates had left Finsterbach two hours before. "I love her so much. No one will ever love her as I do. All I want is to make her happy."

"Yes, your Highness," Margery replied. She had learned months ago that Alexander didn't actually want conversation from her, merely her submissive affirmation. She had hoped that during the year he had been away he'd forgotten about his claim on her, but such had not been the case. At first she had come only because she had no choice—she feared what he might do to her, her mistress or Peter if she dared refuse.

Peter had never understood this, of course. Still, Alexander's absence during the past year had allowed most of the breach between them to heal. It had been easier to work with him, discuss their lady's business and concerns, do the little things she had always done for him, preparing the liniment for his joints that ached in Magdeburg's cold winter, presenting him with a new shirt at Easter. For a short while after that it was almost as if nothing had ever come between them; old troubles, while not forgotten, could still be set aside, as distant from their lives as Alexander himself.

But it was not to last. Now it seemed Peter once again looked on her as if she was some common tavern-woman, who offered her body for a penny, speaking to her only when his duty demanded it, avoiding her close company, spending more time out of the house during the day. As if what she had given him had lost its value—as if he thought she had *wanted* Alexander's cold hands on her body, or to shudder in pleasure when he demanded of her that which he could not ask of her mistress, suckling on her as if he could taste Rosamund in her very blood. In the past few weeks, that little bit of pleasure, however it came, had been all that sustained her from one week to the next, and gave her to strength to present a bright face to her beloved mistress, and to face Peter's accusing gaze at all.

When Alexander at last succumbed to the day, she slipped out from under his arm, put her clothes back on, and made her way back to Rosamund's own chamber.

Peter was sitting on a bench outside the door. She pretended not to see him, and headed straight for the door, but he rose to his feet and stood in her way.

"Margery—"

"I'm very tired, sir," she said, trying to keep her voice even. "Please let me by."

"I—I wanted to talk to you. Please."

He sounded awkward, hesitant, almost like the first time he—Margery suppressed the memory firmly. "I don't know what there is to say—"

"Some things I should have said a long time ago. And I didn't, and this is all my fault."

"You've said quite enough," she said, and couldn't keep the bitterness out of her voice. "Let me pass, please."

"I—I know. I don't know why I—I never meant it, Margery. I never wanted to hurt you."

"Yes, you did. You meant every word of it, and it was all true. Now will you get out of my way?"

"I still love you."

The words hurt; stinging salt on half-healed wounds that other words of his had cut into her. *Temptress. Whore of Babylon. Witch.* Did he think he could heal what he had ripped apart so easily as all that? "Do you really?" she asked, fighting the tightness in her throat, the tears burning behind her eyelids. "What would an apostate monk know about love?"

Stunned, he stared at her. She pushed past him, slipped inside her mistress's chamber and shut him out.

Margery listened at the door until she heard his footsteps trudge wearily away down the corridor. Then she curled up beside Blanche and cried herself to sleep.

Chapter Sixteen

Magdeburg, Saxony
During the Fifty Nights of Pentecost
April and May, 1227

"I want to show you something," Alexander said. There was such a bright sparkle in his eyes, his smile brilliant enough to light the entire room, that she could not resist. He led her out of the solar, out of the keep itself, and down the stairs to the courtyard. "Come with me, hurry!"

Whatever it was, he seemed ecstatically happy about it, and his enthusiasm was contagious. But there was only one horse waiting.

"But—" she started.

"You can ride behind me. Give me your hand." He pulled her up to sit pillion behind him, her arms around his waist. "There. Hold on tight, now, we're going."

The horse took off at the slightest touch of his heels, causing the guards at the gate to duck quickly out of its path, and for her usual escort to get their own horses hurriedly and catch up as best they could.

Josselin and Thomas caught up when they were half-way to the city, but hung a few lengths back, content to follow, although Rosamund could imagine Josselin's annoyance at being relegated to mere escort.

Alexander took them inside the city, the city guards opening the gate for him without questions, and through the streets. "There, my rose," he said. "See? That one, with the banner?"

Rosamund looked where he was pointing: at a steep-roofed,

four-storied house on the end of the street, with a gate leading down between the house and its neighbor to the stable and
yard beyond. Over the door hung a banner of dark silk, proudly
bearing the insignia of the white rose. "What—?"

"It's for you, my love. An embassy for the Ambassador of
the Rose." Alexander lifted one leg over his horse's neck and
slid down to the ground, then turned and held up his arms for
her. "Come, I'll show you."

She reached for him and let him lift her down. "For me?"

He did not release her from his arms right away. "An ambassador needs an embassy, doesn't she? And there's even a garden
in the back, with roses growing up the wall. I saw that and I
knew it had to be for you. It's a perfect choice, isn't it?"

"Yes," Rosamund agreed, suddenly radiantly happy, bathed
in the glow of his almost boyish delight in pleasing her. *He
understands. It's going to be all right now.* "It really is perfect."

"Come in, see the inside," he urged, and she was more than
happy to follow.

Josselin and Thomas pulled up outside, as Alexander and
Rosamund disappeared inside the house, the door closing
behind them.

"That's... very generous of his lordship, isn't it, milord?"
Thomas asked.

"Yes, it is," Josselin agreed. But he couldn't help feeling a
twinge of uneasiness as he looked up at the banner hanging
over the door and noted the location, only a few blocks from St.
Paul's church and its priory. "Very generous indeed."

It took a good many weeks of work before the new Embassy
of the Rose was fully prepared. The building was cleaned
from cellar to attic. The servants, both Rosamund's own stalwart staff and those new to her service, most of whom she had
hand-selected from those available to her from Finsterbach,
were coached on their duties, what was expected of them and
what was not. An ongoing exchange of correspondence that had
first begun while Jürgen and his forces were still in Hungary
had now come to its next expected level. Lord Jürgen himself
would not meet with the representative of Clan Tremere, but

by his leave the Ambassador of the Rose would, and see just how badly the usurping warlocks wanted to make amends for Jervais's diplomatic faux pas of fifteen years ago—a faux pas with which the ambassador herself was intimately familiar.

That her interest—and that of her loyal guardian—in this meeting was personal as well as diplomatic made this a bit more difficult, of course, but even more necessary.

"I want to see him, Rosamund." Josselin, predictably, was far more interested in the fate of Lucien de Troyes than Jürgen's diplomatic relations with the Tremere. "I have that right, don't I?"

"It won't change anything, Josselin. You can't help him anymore. What's done can't be undone."

"He never even had a chance to speak in his own defense. Salianna condemned him out of her own petty spite."

"He betrayed our trust, conspired with the Tremere to undermine our diplomatic efforts here in Germany, stole something of great value, and when he was in my custody he broke his word yet again, and he ran away. I didn't want to believe it either, but I was *there*, remember?"

"*I know!*" Josselin snapped, and then, more gently, "I know, *petite*. I'm not disputing his guilt. I know what he did. But he does not deserve the Final Death for it. That is not justice."

"You still love him, don't you?" Rosamund laid her hand over his, where it rested on the back of a chair. He laid his other hand on top of hers.

"He's still—" He stiffened, raised his head, and stood straight up again; Rosamund, also catching the sound of the door being opened down below, did the same. There were a few words, and then the creak of the stairs as their guest ascended to the solar where they awaited him.

"Ah, milady Rosamund. So good to see you again." Jervais positively beamed with good humor as he mounted the top stair and turned to bow politely; a great bear of a man with a neatly trimmed dark beard, whose smile, Josselin noted, did not quite reach his squinting eyes. "And this must be the noble Sir Josselin de Poitiers! I've heard *so* much about you, milord. It's such an honor to meet you at last."

"Sir Josselin," Rosamund said formally, "may I present to you Master Jervais, of the High Chantry of Ceoris."

Josselin offered the very briefest of bows, barely a nod of his head. "Master Jervais," he said coolly. His eyes were drawn to the nervous Cainite standing in the Tremere's rather substantial shadow. "Lucien."

"Well, my dear Lady Rosamund," Jervais held out one fleshy hand. "Why don't we leave these two to get reacquainted? I'm sure we can find a few things to talk about to occupy ourselves—"

Rosamund did not miss the sudden look of panic Lucien gave his master—she suspected this was not a reunion he had requested. "Of course," she agreed, as graciously as she could. "Milord, we'll be in the garden, when you're ready to join us."

Josselin nodded and gave her a half bow as she laid her hand on that of the Tremere and allowed him to precede her down the stairs and out of the solar.

Their footsteps receded. Neither Josselin nor Lucien spoke for nearly a whole awkward minute after that.

Finally, Lucien took the plunge. "Are you going to destroy me, milord?" he asked.

"What the hell kind of question is that?" Josselin found himself raising his voice for the second time in a quarter-hour and concentrated on calming himself.

"Will you do it? Carry out her sentence, take back what you gave me? If anyone has the right to unmake me, you do. God knows I've not turned out the way you wanted." Lucien paused, took a quick breath. "Whatever nobility you saw in me that night, I've tried hard to find it. But I think it died as I did, in your arms."

Red flared across Josselin's vision, and he struck, sending Lucien flying back against the wall. The young Cainite fell, but Josselin was there, grabbing a handful of his hair and tunic, yanking him up to his feet, forcing his head back so his throat was exposed.

Lucien was trembling, but he didn't resist. Instead he arched his head back farther yet and closed his eyes. A single blood tear ran down his pale cheek. "Do it," he whispered. "End my misery. Finish what you started. Your queen comma—*ahh!"*

Josselin sank his fangs into Lucien's throat. Cainite blood, rich and full, flowed over his tongue. *My own blood—he is my own creation, I made him, how can I unmake him now? My own childe, however illegitimate—*

He forced himself to withdraw, to lick the wound closed. Lucien was weeping; Josselin let him go, eased him down to the floor and followed to kneel beside him. "No. This is not justice, and I will not be party to it. Lucien—"

"It was a good idea," Lucien mumbled. "It almost worked. I would have liked to end my nights under your kiss—swept up by the rapture of it, not even noticing when the last spark of unlife left me and my body crumbled to ash in your arms. I'm a coward, you see. I'm afraid of the end if it's going to hurt."

"Why did you run away? Why didn't you come to me?"

Eyes. Dark eyes, framed in lashes nearly as long as a woman's, set in cheeks that would never know a beard. Margery felt the will behind those eyes pushing at her own, like storm winds battering rain against the shutters. It was all she could do to hold on to her own identity, remember her name, against the onslaught.

"Don't resist me, Margery. It only hurts when you resist. And you're tired. So tired. Don't hurt yourself any more...."

Then the shutters broke and the sea poured in.

"Madame Margery? Are you all right? You look pale."

I'm fine, Blanche. Thank you." She looked at the spindle in her hand, the wool she was spinning. Its operation was unfamiliar, and irrelevant. She laid it aside and rose to her feet. "Where is our lady?"

Blanche looked puzzled. "She has a guest, madame. I believe Sir Josselin is with her also."

"Of course. I remember now." Margery leaned down to stare into Blanche's wide blue eyes. "Forget I even asked."

"Yes, madame." Blanche went back to her spinning, the conversation already forgotten.

Margery went to the window, and sat on the cushioned seat, bringing her knees up and wrapping her arms about them. It was cold, but she ignored the discomfort. Instead she closed her eyes and listened. Blanche's softly whirring spindle became a thrumming roar; her own heartbeat echoed like a drum. But then she concentrated, let her attention drift through the keep, picking up snatches of conversation here, the snores of sleeping mortal servants there. There—there was a familiar voice.

"Why did you run away? Why didn't you come to me?"

"What else could I do? Trust Salianna's mercy? You of all people should know better than that! Not even Isouda stretched out her hand to save me. What could you have done?"

"I did speak for you. I asked for mercy—"

"And we know just how highly Salianna values your counsel, don't we?"

"I am sorry, Lucien. You're right, this has not turned out as I wanted. How does he treat you, this master of yours?"

Lucien? Margery remembered Josselin's childe—but what was he doing in Magdeburg?

"No worse than I deserve, I suppose. Better than he treats his chattel, but worse than he treats his apprentice—I'd still not be Tremere myself for all the gold in the Templar treasury."

Tremere! The expression flitting across Margery's face was not her own, the cold fury in her eyes foreign to her nature. Exactly *who* was Rosamund's guest?

She let her attention drift, leaving Josselin consoling his errant childe. Rosamund. Where was Rosamund? Ah—there. The garden.

"He is our kinsman, Master Tremere. Surely you can understand our concern for his welfare?"

"My dear lady, when he came to me, he seemed utterly convinced that his kinsmen were out to destroy him. There was the little matter of a blood hunt called against him in Chartres—has the queen lifted that sentence?"

"No. No, she has not. Josselin and I hope to persuade her yet."

"Was it not by your testimony he was condemned?"

"I never wanted him hunted for it. And there were... extenuating circumstances, of which you are well aware. Lucien did not act alone,

nor entirely of his own will. Be sure, Maestro, that I have not forgotten that, either."

"Of course. Of course, milady, I do understand. I hope you also understand my position. Those of my blood are not so welcome across much of Europe and it would hardly help my position to confide my servant to your care in a secret manner. If you wish me to make the formal surrender I had previously suggested—"

"That's quite all right, Master Tremere. I'm sure Lucien appreciates your protection, Maestro. Considering the price at which it came."

"Regrettably necessary, milady—you have no idea what an untrusting lot my brethren are. Not to change the subject, milady, but have you any news for me? Has Lord Jürgen accepted my petition?"

"I gave it to him, Maestro. You must be patient. I'm sure you understand that he might not be eager to receive you."

She was conspiring with the Tremere. *Conspiring with the Tremere!* So *this* was what the little harpy did when he was away, and in the very house that *he* had given her! *This* was how she repaid his trust, his leniency.... She would pay for this. She would have to be punished. She had to learn....

Margery felt a stabbing pain behind her eyes; her entire head throbbed and the room spun crazily. "Blanche—"

"Madame?"

She attempted to rise, but the darkness rose up and swallowed her. With a little cry, Margery collapsed to the floor.

Chapter Seventeen

Magdeburg, Saxony
Near the Feast of St. Augustine, August, 1227

*D*ark eyes. *Piercing her, sharper than any Cainite's fangs. Cold hands, cold lips, and a burning in her blood. Hot, dry humors that needed to be cooled, the fire quenched…*

Margery was well regarded even by the native German servants in the household; she was a kindly mistress and had provided salves for burns and tisanes of herbs to soothe fevers and other ills even back in Finsterbach. The dawn was lighting the horizon when she came down to the kitchen, but Hans and his wife Eva were already up, stoking up the coals and preparing for the day's work. It was nothing to pour a cup of cool ale for madame's medicine, and of course he hoped she would feel better soon. She accepted it with thanks, and then sat in a far corner of the kitchen with her basket of medicines and poultice makings. A tiny vial with a tightly sealed cap provided what she needed: She poured its contents into the ale, then packed it away again. The taste was odd, unfamiliar; it burned in her mouth and sent tingles over her entire body as she gulped it down. Surely she had used this before—perhaps the ale flavored it oddly. Most of her medications did work better in wine. She was suddenly hot, sweating… her hand fell on a piece of parchment at her side, English lines written in her own hand, the ink still fresh:

I am so sorry. Please forgive me. I cannot bear this any longer, the weight of the sins on my soul. Please tell Peter I never…

A cold fear suddenly washed through her. She remembered then exactly which vial she had taken from her basket, and knew then what her fate would be.

"Peter!" She struggled to her feet, but her legs would no longer support her, and she fell to the rush-strewn floor. *"Peter!"*

She was dimly aware of someone calling her name, of Eva come to her aid, but oil of monkshood worked too quickly. By the time he came, running down the stairs in a very undignified manner to fall to his knees beside her, to cradle her in his arms, she could no longer speak. When he bent to kiss her, it took all her remaining strength to turn her face away, knowing how that would be the last and cruelest hurt she would inflict on him, but better that than he taste his own death from her lips. *Peter... my love... milady... what... have I done?*

Josselin knew something was wrong even as he passed through the city gates—he couldn't put his finger on it, but there was a darkness that touched his soul as he rode slowly through the empty streets. The house showed lights within, but no lantern on the gate—and even that oversight was foreboding.

Anton the groom, one of the servants whom Josselin himself had chosen, met him in the yard, took his steed Sorel's reins and whispered the news fearfully, as if he wasn't sure he was even allowed to talk about it. Josselin thanked him, left Sorel in his care, and then hurried to Rosamund's chambers.

"Where have you been?" Rosamund demanded, when he came in. "You said you'd only be gone a few nights!"

It had been three years since he had tasted her blood, but her anger still cut him. "I'm sorry, *petite*. I only just heard."

"I *needed* you," she managed. Tears were already welling up again in her eyes. "I needed you *here*."

He came and sat beside her on the bench, drew her into his arms. "Rosamund. My sweet lady. I *am* sorry, *ma petite*. But I'm here now." He glanced around the room. Blanche hovered nearby, her own eyes red and weepy. "Where's Peter?"

The girl shook her head. "I don't know, milord. He rode out this morning, right after she—" Blanche swallowed hard. "He was distraught, milord."

I can imagine he was. Both Peter and Margery had been in Rosamund's service a long time—her first mortal attendants, and always the most devoted to their mistress. There had been bitterness between them of late, Josselin had observed, which he had found puzzling, but hadn't thought too much about. Now he wondered if he should have done something, spoken to one of them, tried to help. "Do you know why she would want to do such a thing?"

Rosamund raised her head from his shoulder. "Bring me the note."

Blanche brought it. He glanced at it, then held it for Rosamund to see. "What does it say, *petite*?"

She read it aloud to him.

"Please tell Peter she never what?" he asked. "What sins?"

"I don't *know*, Josselin! I don't know why she—she did this, I don't know why Peter—" She swallowed, tears welling up in her eyes, and reached for him; he held her close and let her mourn. His own heart ached as well. Margery had always been kind to Fabien, for which he was grateful, and generous to him; to Rosamund she had been so very much more.

His full attention was focused on Rosamund's grief and his own, but when Blanche dropped to her knees, he looked up. Alexander himself stood in the door way, clearly having let himself in, or ignored the efforts of servants to announce him properly. His youthful features showed deep concern and sympathy.

"My poor rose," he murmured, holding out his hands to her as if he expected her to jump up from the bench and run to him. "I just heard the news. I'm so dreadfully sorry to hear about poor Margery. Whatever possessed her to do such a thing, and to you? Especially now, when you needed her the most!"

Josselin nudged Rosamund gently, turning her a bit so she would notice their lord's presence. Even in her grief, however, she knew her duty; reluctantly she rose, left her brother's arms, and went to Alexander's. Josselin fought down his own irritation, feeling himself and Rosamund intruded upon, her grief trivialized like a child crying over a broken toy. Alexander had known Margery only for her blood. What Margery had been to

Rosamund was a relationship Josselin suspected that Alexander would never understand.

Alexander kissed Rosamund's cheeks, lapping up her tears, murmuring softly to her. Then he seemed to realize Blanche and Josselin were still standing there, watching his performance. "Go on, girl," he said to Blanche. "I can see to milady well enough. I'm sure you have other things you should be doing."

Blanche was not the brightest of girls, but she knew a dismissal when she heard one. She swallowed hard, curtsied, and fled.

Alexander turned to Josselin, whose irritation was already growing into something much far more virulent. Rosamund, however, kept her wits, and forestalled the likely confrontation before it began. "Josselin. Please—could you find Peter for me? I'm worried about him."

—You promised, Josselin. It can be borne, and you will allow it....

Josselin met her eyes, took a deep breath, let it out. "I'll find him, milady." He took refuge in action; he bowed, strode out, and then managed to hold his anger down until he reached his own chamber below, where he drew his sword and, in one blow, split the table in two.

Fifteen minutes later, he was once again mounted. He thought for a moment—where might Peter have gone? But he could think of only one likely refuge. Josselin urged Sorel towards the west gate, paid his toll to be let out again, and then was on the road towards the Teutonic commandery and hospital of St. Mary's.

"He arrived sometime this morning after Prime, Brother Abelard told me," Brother Renaud said, "and spent practically the whole day prostrate on the floor in the church, in great anguish of soul, even during the day offices. I finally persuaded him to come to my cell and rest. Strictly speaking, we're not allowed to have visitors there, of course, but under the circumstances the *Hochmeister* gave his permission."

Josselin had never been in the monks' quarters, even in Kronstadt; the secular knights and their men had kept to their own quarters, whose limited amenities had still been considerably more luxurious than those he suspected the monks enjoyed. Now he glanced around him with an outsider's curiosity at the interior courtyard of the Teutonic commandery of St. Mary, with its cobbled paths winding between small bushes, an herb garden and a statue of the Virgin, surrounded by the vaulted brick cloister and the tall, soaring walls of the church and the main keep.

"Has he said exactly what happened?" Josselin asked. "Milady did not have opportunity to give me more details."

"Some, but his grief has not allowed him to say very much as yet. I hadn't the heart to press him too hard."

Renaud led him down one side of the cloister, and then through what Josselin guessed was the refectory for those of the order who needed mortal sustenance. Here they went down a circular stair and then down a long, tall passageway with very few doors. At the end of this there was a turn, a short, straight stair down, and then a small antechamber and a broad door leading to a large chamber beyond.

The Cainites of the order did not have private cells but, like their mortal brethren, slept in one large dormitory. This chamber, Josselin guessed, was under the church itself; it had a great vaulted roof and a number of thick pillars supporting the floor above, which provided a number of neatly separated, if not private, alcoves the brothers used as their sleeping chambers.

Renaud's own alcove was near the door, a bare little nook with a narrow cot, an unadorned chest for his monk's garb and mail, and a few hooks on which to hang a white mantle, his sword, and a white shield with the order's black cross. Peter sat slumped on the bed, eyes closed, lips moving as his fingers counted the beads on a rosary.

"Peter?" Josselin said softly, waiting for the brief pause after a paternoster, not wishing to interrupt Peter's devotions more than he must. Peter didn't respond, though he did not move on to the next bead, but sat there unmoving.

"Peter." Josselin went down on one knee beside the bed and its silent occupant, and laid a gentle hand on the mortal's arm. "Our lady asked me to find you. We've been worried about you."

Peter's eyes were red and swollen, his face smeared with

grime and the tracks of his tears, his thinning hair in disarray, his clothes dusty. "Well, milord," he said finally, in a voice a bit hoarse from weeping, "here I am."

"Are you ready to come back?"

"Hans told me she called my name," Peter murmured. "She wanted me beside her... but by the time I got there, it was too late. There—there was nothing I could do."

Josselin laid a hand on his shoulder. "I'm sure you did all you could, Peter. It's not your fault."

"They won't even let me bury her in consecrated ground..." Peter whispered, eyes closed. "Not as a suicide. It's a mortal sin. So many sins... I should have married her, it's all my fault...."

"We will find a resting place for her, I promise," Josselin told him. "Come back with me."

"I—I suppose milady needs me," he murmured, rubbing at his eyes wearily. "Can't waste any more time, then. Too many things to do. Must—must go—"

Josselin, his own heart aching at Peter's misery, was about to suggest that perhaps he *could* stay a night or two at St. Mary's if he wished, to rest and pray, but Renaud forestalled him.

"She does need you, Peter," the younger Cainite said, before Josselin had his thoughts together. "How can she not? Who else can she depend on at this time? You know how useful Blanche is going to be, she's far too fleece-headed to handle anything of import on her own. Lady Rosamund needs you, Peter, now more than ever."

Josselin saw Peter's back straighten up, and only then remembered what it had been like to be a mortal in service under the blood, to desire more than anything else his lady's approval, and to be *needed*. "She needs you, Peter," he said, picking up on Renaud's instinct. "Our Savior knows *I* can't write her letters for her."

That almost got a hint of a smile, and Josselin continued. "And she needs you to help her with Margery. You know what has to be done, and how Margery would have wanted it. You are milady's right hand, and she cannot manage without you."

Peter stood up, and Josselin rose with him. The mortal rubbed at the grime on his cheek, then brushed at the dirt on his tunic. "If I might prevail on your kind hospitality one more time, Brother Renaud, for water to wash my face? I—I would not appear before milady looking like a beggar."

Chapter Eighteen

Magdeburg, Saxony
Feast of the Nativity of the Blessed Virgin Mary,
September, 1227

"Milady, please. I beg you. This is—is quite—" It had been a long time since Rosamund had heard Peter so upset that he had trouble finding words for his thought, even in his native English. "Quite *unacceptable*," he finished. "I will *not* have it. She has *no right* to—this is *not her place!*"

"Peter, I know. I know." His pride would not let him weep in front of her, but his eyes were red and swollen, and his cheek, when she laid her hand on it, was flushed and hot. Rosamund focused her gaze on him, drawing air into her lungs, letting the air out again and, with it, soothing, calming thoughts. *I do understand, Peter. We've barely buried Margery, how can you accept anyone else in her place?*

He took several ragged breaths himself, recognizing the comfort she was offering him and accepting it, her personal attention and concern the exact soothing balm his wounded spirit craved.

"It's not Katherine's fault, either," she reminded him gently, when it seemed his temper had been once again reined in. "Nor is it yours—you know how much I rely on you, now even more than before. Alexander apparently thought I needed someone, so—"

"He sent her here to spy on you, milady," he said, bitterly. "You know he did."

"Then I will rely on you to ensure she finds nothing suspicious to report, and to keep our Blanche from talking too much. Maybe Thomas will consider renewing his affections with her—that will distract her adequately, I suspect, and I don't think he'll mind."

"Most likely not," he agreed. "Will you be giving her—Madame Katherine, I mean—the elixir, then?" Mortals in Cainite service had many names for the blood—even those who knew what it really was.

"Perhaps, in a week or two—with your approval, of course."

"*My* approval?" he echoed, a bit doubtfully.

"You are still my seneschal, Peter. I value your judgment."

That finally got something like a smile, even if it was a bit grim. Rosamund suspected Madame Katherine would be put through her paces—but that was Peter's prerogative, and she would not take that away from him. "And speaking of the elixir—how long has it been, Peter?"

"I—I don't even remember, milady. I should check my *vade mecum*...." But even as he said it, she could see the hunger in his eyes.

Rosamund took his hand and led him to the window seat, then sat down beside him. "Write it down later," she said. Her hand still lay in his; a tiny nod gave him permission.

Peter raised her hand to his lips and kissed her palm, and then unlaced the first few inches of her sleeve almost reverently. She sliced across her wrist with a small knife, wincing a little—no matter how many times she did this, it still hurt—and he suckled greedily on the open wound like a babe at its mother's breast. While not as intense as the kiss of one of her own kind, it was still pleasurable to feel him drawing on her, forcing the blood to move sluggishly through her veins.

But it was not Peter her thoughts perversely chose to dwell upon, triggered by his lips on her flesh. Jürgen, of course, would hardly need a knife. She could almost imagine the sweet pleasure and pain of it, his fangs in her flesh, the blood rushing through her veins to fill his demanding mouth, his blue eyes burning through her—

"Milady?" Peter asked, hesitantly.

Rosamund suddenly realized her fingers had closed tightly enough over his to hurt. The wound in her wrist had ceased to bleed, and her own fangs had descended. The sudden spasm of hunger-desire that gripped her then must have shown in her eyes. Peter's own eyes widened and the former flush in his cheeks fled, leaving them nearly as pale as her own. Yet even so, he closed his eyes and lifted his chin, offering himself to her in perfect love and submission.

He gave the softest of moans when she took him, relaxing totally into her arms, helpless in the throes of her kiss. His blood, hot and rich, spiced with her own essence, poured over her tongue. Even as she savored his surrender, guilt stabbed her as well: *This was not what I meant to do—how will he ever forgive me?* She reined herself in, withdrew, forced the sweet flow to cease with her tongue, laving the marks of her violation of him away from his skin, and then held him close. "Peter—Peter, I'm so sorry, I didn't mean—I wouldn't hurt you for all the world, please forgive me—"

His arms went around her as well; he pressed kisses to her temple and stroked her hair, assuring her he was neither angry nor hurt. "Lady, my sweet lady, it's nothing, you would never hurt me, you know I am your servant in all things—"

For a few minutes it was difficult to say who was really comforting whom. Then they both recovered their relative dignity and remembered their places and parted, save for his hands, which she kept in hers, and he did not object. "Peter," she said at last. "What would I ever do without you?"

"I honestly don't know, milady," he said, in perfect seriousness.

There was a knock at the door of her chamber. At her nod, Peter went to go answer it, and schooled his sudden scowl quickly into something more neutral as Katherine entered, carefully bearing a long, thin box of carved wood, wrapped around with a white silk ribbon. Her bow was court-perfect, her knee very nearly touching the ground, spine straight, eyes respectfully on her mistress. "Milady. A messenger just delivered this for you, from his Highness."

"Oh?" Rosamund had to remind herself to maintain her

own courtly manners, and not to act as she might have with Margery, forgetting her dignity as mistress of the house. "Thank you, Katherine—please, put it on the table there."

"From *which* Highness, madame?" Peter put in, his own spine suddenly straight as a lance.

"From his Highness Prince Alexander, of course," she replied, as if that should have been obvious from the first—what other Highness had any place in giving her mistress gifts?

Katherine laid the box on the table, and Rosamund, who enjoyed presents of any sort, carefully undid the bow, unhooked the tiny brass clasp and opened it.

Her initial smile of delight froze in place. She hoped it wasn't obvious to Katherine, at least—Peter, of course, simply knew her too well. "Katherine," she said, softening her smile into something more natural. "Would you be so kind as to find my brother Sir Josselin and ask him to attend me, please?"

"Of course, milady," Katherine said, executed another court-perfect curtsy, and departed at once on her errand.

Only after the door had closed, did Rosamund take the delicate creation from where it nestled in the velvet cushioning of the box: a beautifully sculpted rose of ivory-colored silk, its stem of carved and painted ash, complete with thorns and green silk leaves, each petal perfectly cut and shaped, surrounding a center spangled with knotted gold thread and the whole of it giving off the sweetest scent, as if it were indeed a real blossom instead of an exquisite work of craftsmanship. Beside it in the box was a note, in Alexander's own hand: *For my most faithful rose, to match her heart's own purity.*

"All this time..." Rosamund whispered. "All this time, I had always thought he had given Lorraine a *natural* rose...."

Chapter Nineteen

Magdeburg, Saxony
Not long before Christmas
December, 1228

It was Christmas Court, and the hall was adorned with greens, bright with candles. The great hearth housed a ruddy blaze that no Cainite went near, yet which warmed the backs of those mortals fortunate enough to be invited to witness the spectacles presented there for their masters' amusements. On the other side of the hall, Cainites from the local domains, the rest of the Empire and even beyond gathered to attend Lord Jürgen's annual Christmas Court, and enjoy both the prince's hospitality and the entertainments provided for his guests.

Some guests, such as Count Balthazar, the Lasombra prince of Bamberg, or Abbess Hedwig of Quedlinburg, were less welcome than others, but Lord Jürgen did not hesitate to use this occasion to remind them of his sovereignty, simply by commanding their presence in his court. Other guests included emissaries from Cainite courts as far away as Buda-Pest, Copenhagen, London and Milan, plus at least one from a clan few who had fought with Jürgen in Hungary had any liking to see.

"He must be getting less choosy about his allies," Josselin whispered, his voice a mere breath in her ear, but his distaste plain, "if he's meeting with the Tzimisce."

From the stories Rosamund had heard of the Tzimisce, she expected to see a multi-headed, tentacled monstrosity. Instead, she saw a slender, elegant, dark-haired Cainite in long Byzantine robes speaking with Alexander and Marques on the far side of the hall. "Tzimisce?" she repeated, as he drew her back out of the hall into the antechamber beyond.

"Vykos," Josselin explained, after bringing her to a secluded window alcove. "The Greek Tzimisce who arranged for the truce. He claims he's not allied with Rustovitch, but his monks are of this monastic order from Constantinople—"

"Vykos? Myca Vykos is *here*?"

Josselin spun around sharply, his hand on the hilt of his sword, and Rosamund took a step backwards herself. Before them stood a hunched figure, hooded and cloaked in the robes of a mendicant monk. His face was hidden in the shadows of his hood, but the gnarled, twisted hands he raised to show himself unarmed left no doubt as to his blood.

"My pardon, milady, milord," he said in strongly accented French. "But you spoke a name I have not heard in some years, nor expected to hear in these lands. And if what you say is indeed true, then I know why God's hand has led me to these lands."

Josselin relaxed, moving his hand away from his sword. Rosamund braced herself not to wince as the figure raised his hands and lowered his hood to reveal his ravaged visage. The Nosferatu's skin was drawn painfully tight over the bones of his hairless skull, the surface cracked and peeling and tinged with gray, but he held himself with pride, and his eyes were wise. "My name is Malachite."

Alexander sat in a place of honor on the dais at the Christmas Tourney Jürgen had organized as part of the festivities for his many guests this season. He was relaxed in his chair, staring straight forward, his body totally motionless. He seemed oblivious to his surroundings; in fact the exact opposite was true, for he was quite attentive to everything going on throughout the entire hall. He was aware of Lord Jürgen two seats down, his chair in the middle of the raised dais taller and more prominent than anyone else's, talking to Baron Eckehard on his left. He was aware of Lady Rosamund, walking among the participants in tonight's martial spectacle, exchanging gracious words and accepting compliments, playing her part as Queen of Love.

He could, in an instant, locate anyone who had ever tasted his blood: Marques, testing the sharpness of his sword in preparation for a long-awaited match against the traitor Renaud; István, in conversation with two Lasombra from Hamburg; Konrad, sullenly watching the brothers of the Black Cross; his mortal servants and agents throughout the hall. He picked up snatches of conversation here and there, recognizing not only several dialects of German, but French, Hungarian, Danish, Latin, even Slavonic and Greek, sifting the talk he could comprehend from that he could not. He listened idly for something to trigger his particular interest, absorbing, sorting, evaluating what he heard according to its relevant merits, then tucking the words away for later consideration or letting them fade into oblivion.

—*"I want it sharp enough to split a hair, Jean. I will see his blood on that damnable white habit, by St. John, I will."*

—*"Be sure, Brother, I shall remember I have promised you a true fight to the last this time."*

"Be sure, Sir Josselin, I shall hold you to it."

—*"I heard the one they call the Khan defeated the chief of a rival tribe in single combat, and now he intends to drive the Christians totally out of Livonia."*

—*"So, this is what passes for court entertainment among the Latins. I think I shall perish of boredom, Myca."*

"I think you'll find the real swordplay goes on among the spectators, Ilias."

—*"Two Cainites met the Final Death—both merely fledglings, of course—but surely you can see what a potential danger there is, should these Knights of Acre extend their crusade into the Empire."*

—*"No, the Heresy has no adherents in Magdeburg, not anymore. Lord Jürgen and his Black Cross brothers would never tolerate them. Bishop who?"*

—*"But that's just the thing. If a lord determines to be feared rather than loved, how then can he ever trust his vassals, whose fear may at any time drive them to act against him? Then does not the lord himself exist constantly in fear? What does your teacher say to that, Frederich?"*

—*"Milady. I would promise to win this tournament in your name, but alas, I fear I would find myself foresworn, and would not be so for any price—yet I would be bold nonetheless and beg the right to wear your favor—"*

Alexander's attention sharpened suddenly, focused. *There she was,* speaking to a mortal knight; he could hear the man's heartbeat increase as she smiled at him, could all but smell the sweat break out under his gambeson, just from gazing on such perfection.

—*"You underestimate yourself, Herr Augustin. Is it not better to fight to the best of your ability, and with honor? Any man here has that opportunity—yet only one can win. If you fight well and honorably, then you fight for me, and I shall feel honored by such noble service."*

—*"Lady, I would gladly die for one kiss from your sweet lips."*

—*"That much honor, Augustin, I can do without. But wear this, and be certain if you do yourself and me good and honorable service, I shall grant you what you would die for."*

—*"Lady, I am ever your most devoted servant—this I shall keep safe by my heart."*

He could see what she handed him and what he kissed so reverently, as if it were a relic from a saint: a braid of her very own hair, entwined with ribbons. *Her own precious hair.* A cold fury gathered in his long-atrophied belly; his eyes took in every detail of this impertinent mortal who dared ask so much of a goddess. If Augustin wanted to die for her... well, that could be arranged.

But some hours later, when he had a chance to search the mortal's body and effects (Augustin having died when his opponent's lance glanced off his shield and penetrated his mail and his torso—much to the dismay of his opponent, who did not understand why his arm had moved to the left just as his lance impacted Augustin's shield), the precious relic was nowhere to be found.

After court, Malachite sent a carefully worded letter, written in Greek and requesting a meeting, to the house where the Obertus emissary was staying. The answer that his messenger brought back was, for Myca, uncharacteristically terse.

I will be at the Sign of the Dragon this evening.—MV

Still, it was an answer, and so Malachite found his way to the dockside inn and tavern whose hanging sign was painted with a chipped and fading red dragon. A mortal servant showed him to a private room where the Tzimisce awaited him.

In the nights before the Bitter Crusade had sacked Byzantium, Myca had never been one of Malachite's allies. Still, the Tzimisce brood from which Vykos hailed had benefited from the Dream—the city's grand undead society—as much as either of the other leading clans. A worldly scholar whose range of interests extended beyond the usual pursuit of salvation and self-discipline over the Beast his brothers in the Obertus Order were known for, Vykos had since made a name for himself among his clan as a politician and emissary. Indeed, the scattered remnants of the Obertus Order now boasted monasteries and other holdings in Hungary and Bohemia, and a growing role in the Cainite politics of the East.

"I had heard you were in Paris, seeking the new Dream," Myca said, once formal greetings and the serving of refreshments had been dispensed with, and the provider of the refreshments had been taken away to rest and recover from his participation in the formalities. "I also heard that your messiah was more than a little reluctant to don the raiment of heaven for the sake of the survivors of Byzantium—or do you still follow him, hoping to persuade him to accept his destiny?"

Malachite snorted. "Alexander? He has no part in the Dream, he cannot restore it."

"And who can?" Myca responded, without expression. "You? Antonius the Gaul is ash; Michael the Archangel is ash. Yes, the Dracon still walks the night… but clearly the obvious has not occurred to you: If the Dracon *cared* about your precious Dream, he would have returned. Why has he not, pray tell?"

"I don't know," Malachite admitted. "When he spoke to me, it was of God's judgment upon Caine's childer, and destiny—"

"How could the Dracon ever have spoken to *you?*" Myca interrupted, sharply. His eyes glittered, his entire frame was tense. "He left Constantinople long ago, centuries before the Latins came. Do you claim so many years or such status to be his confidant from those distant nights? Why would the Dracon speak to *you* and not to—" He caught himself before he finished, and Malachite wondered what he had nearly said. *To me? To his own descendents?*

"I do not know, Myca." *Why shouldn't he speak to me? It did not shame Michael to do so.* But Myca had always been hard to read, his thoughts and emotions masked, even the colors of his halo muted and indistinct. He could not know the Tzimisce's mind so easily, nor judge him. Malachite reached inside his robes and brought out the tile fragment he had carried so long, laid it on the table and untied the silk of its wrappings. "It was in a cave in the barren hills of Anatolia, near Mount Erciyes, that he spoke to me, in the guise of a holy hermit. This I have carried from the ruins of Constantinople."

Myca leaned closer to study the tile. "I have seen this image," he murmured. He reached out a graceful, long-fingered hand as if to caress the elegant features of the Christ depicted in the ivory. Yet, before his flesh made contact with the surface of the tile, the outstretched fingers halted and then curled back, as if their owner feared contact might singe them. "And where is this Christ, this holy hermit now?"

"I do not know that, either," Malachite admitted. "Tell me, what connection does the Dracon have with Archbishop Nikita of Sredetz?"

"Nikita?" Myca allowed his lip to curl. "The heretic pontiff? An accident of blood, and little else. He repudiated his kinship with our line long ago."

"There is more. In Paris—" Malachite stopped.

Myca sat up perceptibly straighter in his chair. "In Paris?"

Clearly Myca was not as indifferent to the subject of his ancestor as he would like Malachite to believe. "Archbishop Nikita was in Paris when the hair star blazed in the sky. He spoke of destiny and judgment as well, in words much like those the Dracon spoke to me. He also spoke of traveling east. But that was eight years ago. The east is wide and the trail has grown cold."

"So now you seek Nikita," Myca mused, "in hopes that he could lead you to the Dracon?" There was a calculating tone to his voice that had not been there before.

"I am not sure," Malachite admitted. "But I believe Nikita may have some of the answers, when all I have are the questions."

"And one of your questions, then, is where to find Nikita. What will you do with that answer, Malachite, Rock of Constantinople?"

"To preserve the Dream?" Malachite lifted his chin. "Whatever I must."

One dark eyebrow arched, the only expression on the Tzimisce's fine-boned face. "Then there is one answer," he said, "with which I may be able to provide you."

Chapter Twenty

It was a council of war, although the war was far away. Brother Klaus von Aderkas wore the red cross and sword of the Livonian Sword-Brothers, not the Teutonic black cross. But his war was of great interest to Lord Jürgen, and news of the growing power of the pagan warlord who opposed him of greater interest yet.

"So he is a Cainite, then," Jürgen stroked his moustache thoughtfully. "How many does this Qarakh lead?"

"It seems to vary, milord, from month to month," Klaus replied. "They don't stay in one place for long—if they had anything like a permanent settlement, we would have found it by now. Many of his Cainite followers appear to be Gangrel, based on the reports I've received from survivors, and you know what *that* blood are like. Master Abelard believes Qarakh is likely Gangrel himself. A Tartar barbarian, from the eastern steppes."

"What the hell are they *feeding* on, out there?" Brother Johann asked. A veteran of many a crusade, from Acre and Damascus to the long Hungarian campaign, he grew restless and edgy in monastic peace. He had been lobbying to go to Prussia; but now Jürgen was hoping he'd consider a different battlefield entirely.

"Slaves. They take mortal captives whenever they can. Mostly from native tribes—Livs, Letts, Estonians and others. Men, women, children, doesn't matter to them. And livestock, horses and cattle, especially. But that's not the problem, really. The problem is the cult."

"The cult?" Jürgen asked. This hadn't been in Klaus's letter.

"The cult of Telyav. It's some kind of pagan death-cult, from what I've been able to figure out. But the priests are all Cainites. The natives think they're half-divine, of course, and attribute all kinds of powers to them. They've been around a long time, but now they've allied with Qarakh's tribe of raiders, which gives him considerably more legitimacy even among the mortals there. I'll tell you, Brothers, we win by taking the tribes one at a time, and helping one against another, because they hate each other worse than they hate us. But if Qarakh and the Telyavs can unite them, or even attract enough of the Cainites in the region to form a real fighting force—there might be no stopping them then.

"So Master Abelard believes we need to move against him in force, deal with these Telyavs before they get too much of a following. The trouble is, we've not got the force just now. We're spread thin indeed, between Livonia and Estonia, now that the Danes have deserted the field, and this isn't a battle mortals can fight alone. I was hoping to find Václav here, to be honest, milord—twiddling his thumbs and spoiling for a fight."

"Václav is in Prussia, unfortunately," Jürgen admitted, "although he's doing good work there, from what I've heard."

"I'll go," Johann sat up straighter in his chair, eyes alight again, as if he already smelt the blood of battle. "If the *Hochmeister* will allow, of course," he added, remembering proprieties.

To his credit, Jürgen kept a straight face. "I think that can be arranged, Brother," he said. "As it happens, Brother Klaus, I believe we can spare a few of our own troops for Christ's cause in Livonia—"

There was a knock on the door, and Jürgen paused. "Come in."

"Oh—I beg your pardon, milords," Renaud bowed, respectfully. "I didn't know you were busy—"

"No, come in, Brother." Jürgen beckoned him in. "Brother Klaus, this is Brother Renaud, one of our more experienced novices. Renaud, this is Brother Klaus von Aderkas, of the Order of Sword-Brothers in Livonia. And you know Brother Johann, I believe."

Bows and formal greetings were exchanged, and then Jürgen got back to business. "Brother Renaud, I sent for you for a reason. The Order of the Black Cross is sending a supplemental force on crusade to Livonia, to assist our brothers there. It's tough country, and a dangerous enemy—you've heard the rumors, no doubt."

"Yes, milord."

"They're true," Klaus put in dryly.

"Brother Christof recommended you, Renaud," Jürgen continued. "Are you interested?"

Renaud paused only a moment. "Yes, sir. I'll go."

It was obedience, not enthusiasm, Jürgen realized—but that was good enough. "Good. Sit down, Renaud. We've got a few other matters to discuss."

When the council had disbanded, Jürgen returned to his own simple, solitary cell and prepared for his day's rest. He knelt at the small portable altar and said his devotions to the folding triptych with his personal saints: Mary and the Holy Child, of course, but also St. Michael and St. Maurice, both in their armor.

As he stood up again, his gaze fell upon a small casket sitting in a special place on a shelf. His hands reached for it without his even willing it, and opened the lid. Within, coiled carefully in a nest of dark green velvet, was a slender coppery braid of silken hair, bound with blue ribbons. Something of her scent still clung to it; when he closed his eyes and stroked its length he could see her as she must have been that night, sitting on her bed, clad only in her white shift, while her maidservant's deft fingers wove the braid, tied it off and then cut it free. There was something of Augustin still here as well, for the unfortunate mortal had loved both the gift and its giver, but those impressions he ignored. It was that intimate glimpse of Rosamund herself he savored, that faint scent, the sweet silky coolness of it sliding between his fingers, imagining how it must feel to run his fingers through the bright waves of that same hair as it tumbled over her shoulders….

Enough. His fangs had come down, and though he had fed earlier this very evening, the mere thought of her aroused his hunger again. Carefully he laid the braid back in its casket, closed the lid, and forced himself to return it to its place on the shelf.

The braid was not his to keep, but he kept it nonetheless. It was the distraction he allowed himself, as if, by giving it a proper reliquary, he could keep thoughts of her from haunting him when they were least convenient, intruding on his duties. It didn't always work, of course, but to allow himself nothing was far worse.

"There was a man brought in to the hospital today, madame," Sister Agathe said, when Lucretia saw her after the council. "A military brother of an order I've never heard of, the Poor Knights of the Cross of the Passion of Acre. He bore a broken red cross on his tunic."

"They're a new order," Lucretia recalled. "His Holiness only granted them a charter a few years ago. They escort pilgrims to the Holy Land, or so I've heard. How did he come to us?"

"He had been bitten, he said, by a very large wolf. His companions managed to drive it off in time to save his life, but the wound festered and they had to take the arm off above the elbow. His commander asked our mercy to look after his convalescence." She hesitated. "He also asked the phase of the moon, which I thought was odd, but when I told him it was waning, he seemed content."

"He's mending then, from the amputation?"

"Yes, madame. It was his sword arm. A grievous hurt for a knight in holy orders."

"Yes, it is," Lucretia said, taking the clean shift Agathe handed her. "Make sure our guest from the Poor Knights feels welcome in our house as though he were one of our own brethren. Though if he says anything more of the wolf who attacked him, I should like to hear it."

"Yes, madame."

Chapter Twenty-One

Magdeburg, Saxony
Soon after the Feast of the Holy Trinity
June, 1230

Jaufres de Courville had seen many a pretty girl in his travels these past three years. They usually came in one of two categories—those with brothers or other guardians of their virtue, and those whose virtue was easily won, either with coin or a smile and a few sweet words. The one he watched this evening on the tourney grounds of the Teutonic commandery of St. Mary's was more than simply pretty, however. She was perfect in all her attributes save one: the tall and well-armed brother who escorted her. A pity too; she was clearly an accomplished flirt, which implied she was accomplished in other skills as well, and he liked the sound of her laugh, like a cascade of silvery bells.

"Her name is Rosamund. Lovely, isn't she?"

Jaufres turned, startled. A young man—someone's squire by his youth and fine dress—stood at his elbow. Perhaps of her household, for he spoke French as well.

"I meant no insult to the lady, sir," he said. "Surely it is no offense to admire such a fair creature from afar?"

"But would you be content with admiring from afar, if perhaps the opportunity presented itself to lessen the distance? If I could... arrange... such an opportunity?"

"Ah, friend," Jaufres grinned, "what I could do with such opportunity... assuming of course, her guardian was otherwise occupied. She looks like the receptive type—"

The squire reached across, grabbed Jaufres's tunic, and pulled him bodily around and up against the wall with jarring force. Jaufres's angry protest froze in his throat when he stared into the squire's eyes, cold and dark as the inside of a tomb. *Be silent,* a voice in his head commanded, and he could not speak; *and listen,* and suddenly there was no sound in his ears but the squire's soft voice. "I see..." the squire murmured. "I could kill you for what you were thinking of her just now... but I've thought of something better. I'm going to give you what you want, Jaufres. I hope you enjoy it as much as I will...."

My dearest Rose—
By way of this missive may I introduce our young friend Jaufres, with my best wishes and most sincere affections. He tells me he is something of a poet; I trust you will find his talents to your tastes.
—A.

Rosamund folded the parchment and set it aside. It was unusual for Alexander to send her a vessel—especially a handsome young man. Still, it was never wise to spurn his gifts. "Milord tells me you are a poet, monsieur," she said, smiling.

Jaufres looked confused for a moment. "Your... lord? I—I thought he was a squire of your household. He was so young."

"He is somewhat older than he appears," she said, taking his arm. "But what sort of poetry do you favor, and in what tongue—monsieur, are you well?"

Jaufres rubbed at his eyes with one hand, wincing as if in sudden pain. He swayed on his feet for just a moment, and she held him steady; if he wondered how such a slightly built girl could do such a thing, he did not show it.

"Monsieur Jaufres? Perhaps you should sit down—"

But the spell seemed to pass; he stood straight again and smiled at her. "I—I am quite well, milady," he assured her, taking her hand and bringing it to his lips. "What kind of poetry do you most enjoy? I believe there is an entire *chanson* to be found in your eyes alone...."

So beautiful… so sweet. Alexander's body was absolutely motion-less in his chair, his eyes open and unseeing. *This* was what he had wanted for so long, to hold her, caress her without holding back—and see just how far she allowed her mortal lovers to go. Jaufres's desires were easily aroused, and felt as foreign to him as the instincts of a beast. Rosamund, however, managed his crude advances with grace, restraining his groping hands with little more than a glance and a raised eyebrow. In the end, the pleasures of Rosamund's cool touch, the sharp pain/pleasure of her fangs piercing his flesh, the ecstasy of blood and flesh that followed, was even greater than he had hoped.

But when he came back to himself, leaving Jaufres's body to find its own way back to his lodgings, it was no longer enough. He could taste blood where his fangs had pierced his lips, but it did not satisfy him. Jaufres's desires had only served to enflame his own, and his Beast was aroused, growling in frustration, having been forced to watch another Cainite satisfied while it still hungered. He rose from his chair. The weaver's daughter with dreams of the blacksmith's apprentice no longer interested him; nor did the passions of the laundress for a certain red-haired guardsman. Only one sweet throat would satisfy him now.

And this time, he would not be denied.

The company of Poor Knights of Acre who had established themselves near Magdeburg gathered around the table in the main hall, which served as both chapter-house and refectory. The estate had been left to their order in its late master's will, out of gratitude to the order's grand master and doubtless in hopes of atoning for past sins. The order prayed for the good of his soul at every morning mass.

As the only layman at the table, Otto von Murnau felt a bit like a duck in the henhouse. His fine clothes in dark blue and maroon, the decorative brass on his belt buckle and the scab-bard of his sword, even the rings on his fingers, set him apart from the brothers in their plain white wool and broken red crosses. He kept his mouth shut except to eat, and listened to the brothers discuss their plans, wondering what his own part in them might become.

"I think the Teutonic Hospital of St. Mary is the place to start." Brother Reinhardt ate awkwardly with his left hand; his right arm ended in a stump at mid-biceps. "Do you remember last year, when the cursed wolf did this—" and he half-lifted the stump, "I noted even then that the Teutonic Knights who joined our night vigils carried silver. I saw it. *They knew.*"

"Knew what?" Otto asked. "Your pardon, sir," he added, offering Herr Manfred a brief bow from the neck. "But anything out of the ordinary can be a sign of Lucifer's get—and I'm terribly curious. What vigil?"

"Brother Reinhardt was attacked by a giant wolf last winter near Brandenburg," the knights' commander explained. "The monster savaged his sword arm before his companions were able to drive it off with fire and prayer. The curse from the fangs of such a beast is such that we feared the infection had already spread, though we took the arm as soon as we could. But thanks be unto God: After three months of prayerful vigils on the night of the full moon, Brother Reinhardt showed no sign of succumbing to the curse, and was pronounced cured."

"Thanks be unto God," Otto agreed. The brothers all crossed themselves, and Otto echoed the gesture.

"How did you get dragged into the cardinal's mission, Herr Otto?" Herr Manfred asked. "You're no cleric. I know your father, in fact. Good man."

"Thank you, sir," Otto replied, as smoothly as he could. "My uncle, Brother Leopold of the Dominican Order, suggested to Grand Master Gauthier that I might be of some use to your endeavors here. I have had some experience fighting the enemies of God."

"Good, good. Experience is a good thing, harrowing as it may be. Will you be taking vows then?"

That caught Otto off guard. In fact, he wondered what exactly Gauthier had *written* in that letter. "Vows? Oh. No, sir. No, that's not why I'm here at all."

There was silence around the table. Several of the brothers gave him odd looks, as if they couldn't imagine anyone *not* wanting to jump feet first into lifelong vows of celibacy and poverty.

"Well, to be honest, lad, you've not the look of a serious fighting man about you anyway," Herr Manfred said kindly, and Otto wasn't sure whether to be relieved or insulted. "But why did Herr Gauthier send you, if not to join us in the fight?"

"I *have* fought them, sir. But that is not the reason I was sent. You've a dozen men here better with the sword than I. It's not in fighting the minions of Lucifer that I am most useful to you, though I certainly will if need arises, but in finding them in the first place."

"Finding them? Good! God's teeth, that's excellent, in fact. That's exactly what we've been needing. How do you do it?"

Otto hesitated. It was one thing to discuss the family secret with Uncle Leopold, or Cardinal Marzone's little circle of hand-picked confidants, or even Sister Teresa. It was something else to talk frankly and openly about it with a group of men he had just met, who didn't understand. But that little talent was why he was here, why the cardinal and Gauthier had been so keen on sending him north to aid the Poor Knights on their chosen mission. *Are we not all brothers in the same fight, at least in spirit?*

"It—it's awkward to explain, sir," Otto began. "It's not something I can teach. It's just something I *know*. I can identify a Cainite, a shape-changer or a witch, even if they're trying to disguise themselves, sometimes even those unfortunates who serve them. It's Our Lord's own gift, and it has never failed. You can test me if you like."

The master rubbed at his beard thoughtfully. "You can pick them out even among a crowd of good Christian folk? How?"

Otto reminded himself that Herr Gauthier himself had chosen these men, and they had to be able to trust each other if they were to accomplish God's work. He forged on ahead.

"I can smell them, sir."

Chapter Twenty-Two

Magdeburg, Saxony
The Ides of July, 1230

"The larder needs cleaning," said Fidus. "And restocking." That meant there was a body that needed to be gotten rid of. Lucien wondered sourly who'd done it this time. Usually it was Jervais, but even Fidus was careless now and then. Especially if Lucien was around to clean up the mess, and go foraging—hunting for some other unfortunate bastard no one would miss, to replace the dead one. When it came to filling their own bellies, the Tremere were the most unimaginative vampires he'd ever met. Perhaps that accounted for their dispositions. Fidus was only an apprentice, of course, but he seemed to think his Tremere blood made him inherently superior—a notion Lucien felt no obligation to reinforce. Particularly since there were some things—like foraging—that Lucien was actually far better at than the much younger Tremere.

"Lucius, are you even *listening*?" Fidus demanded. "You know what he'll say if he goes down and finds a corpse stinking the place up."

"No, Fidus," Lucien said in his sweetest voice, "what *will* he say?"

"*Lucius!*" The bellow came from the floor above. The sound of his master's voice triggered the usual rush of hope, eager anticipation and hollow dread in Lucien's unbeating heart. Not even Josselin, who had made him what he was, could engender such a mix of feelings in him anymore. But then, it wasn't Josselin's blood he'd drunk three times.

Fidus merely smiled. "Don't forget to clean the larder after he's done with you."

Lucien ignored him; his feet were already on the stairs. "Coming, Maestro!"

"Did you enjoy your visit with your sire, Lucius?" Jervais asked, when he got there. "I'm sure you've made him *very* proud, with all the things you've done."

Lucien spotted a letter lying on the table, recognized Peter's formal, angular hand, and the official rose seal. A brief letter, only a few lines—which doubtless explained his master's temper right now. *She's put him off—again.* He felt all the anticipation, the pleasure, the hope he'd first experienced at Jervais's call, turn to something cold and gelatinous and drain away into his belly, leaving only despair and a deep sense of shame.

"Of course—he doesn't *know* all the things you've done, does he?" Jervais went on, not even waiting for him to respond. "I rather suspect there's a few things you've never told him— that you would really rather he didn't learn, aren't there? Well? Aren't there?"

"Yes, Maestro," he agreed, miserably.

"But he doesn't need to know about them. It's best he thinks of you as—dare I say it—honorable as he imagines you to be, misguided, perhaps, but having the best intentions. Not the desperate little sleaze who would betray his own kin to keep them from learning what a self-centered, greedy little snot he was behind the angelic facade. And I'd like to help you with that, Lucius. I know how it is to want to prove yourself better than your sordid past would lead one to believe. But I need you to help me a little too. You can do that, can't you, my little songbird?"

It was blackmail, of course, but that wasn't what he really cared about. If he was able to help, the rest wouldn't matter any more. To help Jervais now would erase all the things in the past that haunted him; all the shame, guilt and desperate fear would melt away before his master's smile. "Yes," he cried, and he fell to his knees, grasping at the sorcerer's hand. "Yes! Oh, yes, I can help you, milord—please, tell me, I'll do it right away!"

"It's not that easy, Lucius. But let's see if you can do it. I want you to think about the Lady Rosamund. You know her far, far better than I do, of course—that's where you can help me. She must have something she hides, something she's ashamed of, a secret sin she cannot resist, some unfulfilled longing she holds deep in her heart. Tell me about that, Lucius. Tell me something about Lady Perfection that she wouldn't want me to know. You can do that for me, can't you?"

Lucien's face fell. *Rosamund.* Rosamund had been kind to him. *What can I tell him about Rosamund....*

"Well?"

"I'm *thinking*, milord, I am—she's very young, she's always been protected!" Desperately he searched his memory. Josselin loved her, of course, but Jervais could see that for himself, so that wouldn't do.

"Well, she's not so protected now, is she? Come on, Lucius. You can do better that that."

"She—she wanted Lord Jürgen to—to find her pleasing," he blurted out. "She talked of little else, even on our trip home. I got rather tired of hearing it, to be honest. I'm sure her feelings haven't changed. Even with his Highness..." His voice trailed off. Alexander frightened him. Alexander *knew*. And Rosamund hadn't said anything, but he'd known she was frightened, too. *I would be too, if I were...*

"His Highness who?" Jervais interrupted. "Lord Jürgen?"

Not so protected now. The revelation was so strong, it struck him dumb for a moment. The schemes of elders, and their fondness for re-enacting their own history. The pitch and tone of voices, even among the servants of the house—if nothing else, his musician's ear was very attuned to the quality of voices, the delicate nuances that said what words could not—

"Lucius—" Jervais started, warming up, "I *believe* I asked you a *question!*" The last word fairly shook the room, and was punctuated by a blow that split his lip and sent him sprawling, crashing into a heavy oaken table.

But for once his master's temper didn't send him cringing back on his knees; the taste of his own blood in his mouth, the twinge in his shoulder where he'd struck the worktable, were nothing compared to the incredible excitement bubbling up inside him, the sheer joy of being able to answer his master's question.

"Forgive me, milord, Maestro, but—but I only now realized it. I hadn't seen it before, but it's so obvious—well, obvious to one of us, I suppose, but you'd have to know the story. But it has to be, that's why he—"

"*Lucius!*" Jervais grabbed his tunic and hauled him up to his feet. "Talk sense! Realized *what?*"

Lucien took a deep breath. "It does make sense, Maestro. But first I have to tell you a story, so you'll see how it all fits. It's about a girl named Lorraine...."

"How many churches thus far?" Otto asked, resignedly, looking up at the shadowy hulk of the stone tower. He'd gotten used to daily mass while in Cardinal Marzone's service, but attending mass or other services seven times a day, usually at different churches as they searched for clues to their quarry, was almost more virtue than he could bear. *Forgive me, Lord, but I am not suited for such a holy life. Would it be too much to ask for some sign of our quarry this time?*

"Six," Brother Emil said cheerfully. "It's good for your soul, my friend. And if this doesn't turn up any clues, we'll put you in a novice's robe next and start attending divine office at local abbeys."

Otto managed a polite chuckle. Emil meant it as humor, but there was still the underlying message that he expected it would be only a matter of time before Otto realized where his duties really lay and took vows himself. Otto had politely declined the loan of a Poor Knight's habit and surcoat, and borrowed instead a plain cotte and mantle from his manservant Adam, so he could join the Knights at compline services at St. Sebastian's as one of their lay servants. This at least allowed him to be in their company within whispering distance—should there be anything worth whispering about—without attracting any particular notice.

They entered the church, the Poor Knights going down the right side of the church, Otto and Adam following. Uncle Leopold had been quite certain that he'd once picked up distinct devil-spoor in several Magdeburg churches, but so far Otto hadn't found a trace. Still it was the only clue they had—as far as he could tell,

Magdeburg's citizens did not habitually find mysterious bloodless or dismembered corpses, nor did children vanish off the streets at twilight. The curfew was reasonably enforced and rarely broken.

The Poor Knights weren't the only worshippers here from the military orders, however. Otto recognized the distinctive white habits and black crosses of three knights of the Teutonic Order as well, some distance back from his companions with their broken red crosses.

Otto leaned forward slightly and tapped Brother Reinhardt on the shoulder. "Brother," he whispered. "Do any of the German knights behind us look familiar to you?"

The one-armed knight glanced behind them briefly. "The younger one, perhaps. It's too dark in here to see properly."

"Maybe I should go back and check—" Otto began, but Emil shook his head.

"Not now, the service is starting. Afterwards, you scurry out as if to get our horses. We'll take a better look as they leave."

Otto scurried, as instructed, as soon as the priest finished intoning the Latin benediction. As it happened, however, the three Teutonic Knights seemed to be in no hurry to leave. As the resident canon monks filed out of the church—there being few laymen at such a late service—the German knights came forward even as Otto was moving back. He did remember at the last minute to move aside for them and humbly bow his head, as any good servant should, but he couldn't resist the temptation to inhale as they passed.

It was a mistake. The stench that wafted up from the knights' habits was foul as rotting fish; it caught in his throat and triggered a coughing fit so fierce that it brought tears to his eyes. He kept his head bowed and staggered past the knights, one of whom reached out a hand to assist him.

"Are you ill, sir?"

He shook his head and kept going, ducking around a pillar to catch his breath and wipe his eyes. *I should really be more careful what I pray for.*

Adam joined him a minute later, his expression anxious. "Milord? Are you—"

Otto waved him to silence. Brothers Emil, Mathias and

Reinhardt were close on his heels, and Otto fell in behind them as they exited the church.

"Well, *that* was quite a performance," Emil said in a low voice as soon as they stepped outside. "Does that mean we've found something at last?"

Otto took a few deep breaths, clearing his lungs, then looked around warily, even peering back into the dim church. Cainites could hear dangerously well.

"They're gone," Emil said. "The young brother asked for confession. The priest seemed quite pleased to see him, too."

"That young brother is a Cainite," Otto whispered. "I'm sure of it, as sure as I am of my own name."

"And I *do* remember him, Brothers," Reinhardt said grimly. "He's a brother-knight at the Hospital of St. Mary's. I heard the priest call him Brother Ulrich."

"Then should we assume he will likely go back there later tonight? Or should we follow him and make sure?" Mathias asked.

"It's *in there* with the *priest*," Emil growled, glaring back toward the door.

Otto laid a hand on his arm. "Brother. You said it looked as though they had met before, right? Then, as sad as it may seem, this is likely a regular meeting. The danger to the priest right now is not to his life, but his soul."

"Then what are we going to do?" Reinhardt asked, looking at Emil, who was commanding their little expedition.

Emil considered, then his eyes fell upon their horses, and the gear they'd packed in hopes of a successful hunt. "There's a blind turn in the road halfway between the west gate and St. Mary's, after you cross the bridge by the old mill," he said thoughtfully. "Let's arrange a little meeting there. Mathias, your crossbow will come in handy, I think. I want this bastard alive—he's got a lot of questions to answer."

"I feel I have been remiss in my duties as an envoy, Lady Rosamund."

The satisfaction of watching Jervais humble himself had ceased to amuse Rosamund. The man had the hateful ability to couch a threat in an apology, and she expected another to be along shortly. He rarely appeared in her embassy with anything else in mind, it seemed. "How so, Maestro?"

"Although I presented apologies for past misunderstandings, I fear that I let words alone stand where actions should have been." He dug into a pouch hanging from his belt, and pulled out a small folded square of silk, which he laid in one beefy palm and then delicately unfolded to reveal a polished silver coin the size of a penny but with unusual markings stamped in its surface. He extended his hand toward her. "Take it, milady. It's far more than it appears, of course, but I promise it can do you no harm."

Somewhat warily, she took the coin in her fingers and focused her vision on it until it was bright and clear even in the room's flickering candlelight.

"It looks like an ordinary coin," she said, looking at it closely. "Well, not entirely ordinary—not with these markings. Is this Greek?"

"Milady has a very good eye," Jervais said smoothly. "There are some Greek characters, and others of a more occult nature, given the purpose for which the coin is created."

She lifted one delicately arched eyebrow. "And what purpose is that?"

"It absorbs blood. Or, to be more precise, it absorbs the most powerful humors and energies from the blood, and so transforms it from Cainite blood with all its myriad arcane properties to something akin to merely mortal blood, having removed all those properties and drawn them into itself."

"Oh. And then what do you do with it?"

"The coin has many potential uses after that, of course, but that's not the point, milady. The *point* is that, with this coin under my tongue, I can drink the blood of any prince in all of Europe and the coin will ensure that its effect on me will be no more than if I drank from his lowliest mortal slave."

"It prevents the sealing of the blood oath, then?" She looked at the coin again, a strange hope growing within her. Could this single little coin be her salvation? Dare she even consider such a risky notion, put her faith in the same Tremere who had conspired against her and enslaved Josselin's errant childe? What price might he demand—and how had he guessed she might have need of such a thing?

"Exactly, milady. You see why it is a valuable trinket to have around. One never knows when one might find oneself in a difficult position, having no choice but to drink the blood of another of our kind. Yet, with this coin, it is possible to acquiesce gracefully, fulfill what is required, and suffer none of the anticipated ill effects."

"It is a coin of high value indeed, then, Maestro." She made as if to give it back to him, but he raised his hands, not accepting it.

"Keep it, milady," he said grandly. "A token of my sorrow for having caused you embarrassment years ago, and thanks for all your recent efforts on my behalf."

"You are most generous, Master Tremere." She studied the coin warily, as if she expected to see whatever trick was hidden within it. "But why should I trust you?"

"For the simple reason, milady, that you have no choice. Believe me, it is not at all in my interest to deceive you on so great a matter. You are, for what it's worth, my best advocate in this court—and I can indeed be generous to my friends. Keep the coin, milady. Tell me later how you value my friendship."

She could see the victory in his eyes as her fingers closed over the coin—but he was right. She had no choice. "Be sure that I will, Master Tremere," she said coolly.

Chapter Twenty-Three

Magdeburg, Saxony
Feast of St. Henry, July, 1230

*T*o *the Lady Rosamund of Islington, Ambassador of the Rose to the court of Lord Jürgen Sword-Bearer in Magdeburg:*
My dear childe,

I pray Lord Jürgen delivers this to you promptly, and that you forgive this indirect method of delivery, but from your previous letter, I feel it is most urgent that you see this letter and your guardian does not, for his suspicions are a danger to you in this matter. Therefore I have charged his lordship to put this in your own hands at some privy time, and I trust he will respect our desires, for you have said he is a Cainite of great honor.

I do not wish to alarm you unduly, but there are certain things I feel I must share with you as they may be of particular relevance to you now. You must realize, my dearest, that I was but a childe myself at the time of the Lady Lorraine's untimely death and, being so young in the blood, was not privy to the discussions of our elders. But our cousin Helene, who recalls the time more clearly than I, told me that before Lord Tristan's tragic attempt to rescue his beloved sister from Lord Alexander's hands, he had received a letter from Lorraine, which subsequently found its way into Helene's hands.

Based on what she has told me of that letter, and in light of what followed after, we are both quite certain that, by the time Tristan made his rescue attempt, Lord Alexander had already partaken of the Lady Lorraine's blood three times. However, I do not believe the reverse was true, or Tristan would never have been able to persuade her to accompany him. Unfortunately, under the circumstances, the bond of blood was no protection for her, for it only served to inflame his desire for her further, so that his anger was so much the greater as well. When first he discovered she had fled, I recall hearing that he went straight away to her rooms and tore all her gowns to tatters in his fury. It was after that he went to see the sorceress Mnemach, and the results of that you know.

You see, my darling, why this is of import. I send you this warning now, in hopes that you may receive it before it is too late. The path before you is fraught with peril, far greater than I had ever anticipated or would have desired to set before you; now you must walk it with great care, lest history repeat itself and Lorraine's fate becomes your own. Know also this: Lorraine was a fool, for she allowed herself to be ruled by her own passions rather than her wits, and she and Tristan paid the price of her folly in full measure. In that degree, at least, I believe you are better served than she, and that you will consider well the consequences of your actions even when great passion moves you. You have in all things ever been my greatest pupil, and I have every confidence you will not disappoint me even in this darkest night.

I worry now that I have sent Josselin to you, for I know there is great love between you, much as there was between Tristan and Lorraine. Yet I will not call him home, for you may yet have need of a champion beside you. As you hold his oath, I will therefore leave that decision in your hands. Remember only that the appearance of betrayal is just as dangerous to you as its actuality. Be forewarned and wise.

I remain as always, your loving sire,

—Isouda de Blaise, Queen of Love for Chartres, Blois and Anjou

"Something's wrong," Josselin said. "Do you feel it?"

Rosamund took a slow, deep breath and closed her eyes, trying to pay more attention to things she couldn't quite hear, smell or see. There it was, a slight uneasiness on the edge of her consciousness, an elusive shadow that felt distinctly wrong. Having so identified it, she could feel it even when she opened her eyes again and saw the familiar whitewashed walls of Lord Jürgen's council chamber. "Yes."

"They're singing a full mass in the church. Listen."

"For compline?" Rosamund focused her attention in the direction of the church. Yes, there it was—the full, rich sound of male voices, the rise and fall of chant. Odd, for an evening office. And then, louder, harsher on her ears, the sound of footsteps, several pairs of leather-clad feet on stone in irregular rhythm, coming closer.

She refocused hastily, snapping back to regular perceptions, rising to her feet as the doors opened and then dropping into an effortless reverence as Jürgen swept in, followed by Christof, Father Erasmus, two other brothers Rosamund did not recognize, and, much to her surprise, Brother Renaud.

"Milady Rosamund, Herr Josselin," Jürgen motioned them up. "I thank you for coming on such short notice. Please, join us."

Josselin took her hand, and led her around the far side of the long, polished table. At Jürgen's nod, he assisted Rosamund to sit at the prince's left hand, then took a seat beside her. Renaud and Father Erasmus sat down on Josselin's other side, and Christof and the two unnamed brothers sat to Lord Jürgen's right. The feeling of something wrong persisted, even in their seating arrangements; yet it took Rosamund a moment to realize who was missing.

"Brothers, I have asked Lady Rosamund and Herr Josselin to join us, for the matter before us may extend beyond our brotherhood, and I value their counsel. Milady, milord, this is Brother Hermann and Brother Rudiger, who lead other houses in our Order of the Black Cross in Saxony.

"I find myself in need of your counsel, on a matter that may present dire consequences to us all. Yet, because of the potential risk involved, I would ask that none here speak of this matter to others, either Cainite or mortal, without my leave. And Wiftet, if you will kindly just sit down—"

Rosamund didn't see exactly where the fool had come from—perhaps he had even been hiding in his lord's shadow the entire time. But now he did as he was told, and sat at the far end of the table, looking a bit abashed.

"For those of you who know our situation, I would beg your

patience as I make others here also acquainted with it. The Order of the Black Cross attends mass this night, and for many nights to come, for the souls of a number of our recently departed brethren now gathered to the bosom of Our Lord: those who fell in a grievous battle eight weeks ago in Livonia, of whom our brother Renaud has journeyed through many dangers to bring me word this evening; and for three brothers lost but two nights past here in Magdeburg, including one of my own blood."

Ulrich, destroyed? Rosamund heard the rough undertone to his voice, and felt a sudden pang of sympathy for Ulrich's sire, whose responsibilities as prince and grand master of the Order of the Black Cross did not permit him time even to attend the mass held in his childe's name. "Be assured, milord," she said, her heart leading her before her mind had even formed the words, "that I, my brother, and the Courts of Love extend our most sincere condolences to you and the order for these terrible losses, and know that their names shall be in our prayers as well."

She did not remember moving her hand—somehow as she spoke it had traveled of its own will, and now rested lightly on Jürgen's left arm where it lay on the table. It was a rather forward and personal gesture to make to a prince in front of his council, and yet to withdraw it now would be to admit the gaffe, which would be even more embarrassing.

But then Jürgen turned to her, and laid his right hand over hers. "We thank you, Lady Rosamund, for your kind words and your prayers. Both are most welcome and appreciated."

His gaze only met hers for an instant, but in that instant he had rescued her from herself, and even thanked her for it; even as he removed his hand and she reclaimed hers, something of his touch lingered in her skin, and an echo of warmth like a summer breeze touched her soul. She clasped her hands on the table in front of her to keep them from any further mischief, and forced herself to focus on Jürgen's words, not his profile.

"We will not forget what has occurred on distant battlefields," the prince continued, "but it is the latter and more recent attack that now concerns me, for this danger reaches beyond the order's own ranks to any Cainite in our realm.

"Brother Ulrich and his mortal brethren were ambushed

on the road, halfway between Magdeburg and this monastery, by a band of armed men wielding crossbows. Though they in cowardice disguised themselves, we have since identified them as members of the Order of the Poor Knights of the Cross of the Passion of Acre, an order founded and still headed by Herr Gauthier de Dampiere... whom some of us here have cause to remember with no fondness."

The name meant nothing to Rosamund, but she heard Josselin inhale softly, and saw recognition in the eyes of the other brother-commanders.

"Brother Ulrich's squire escaped the ambush, and so was able to report back to us. Having determined where his assailants took him, Brother Christof and some of the brethren, including our Brother Renaud, attempted a raid upon their house, in order to rescue our brothers."

At a nod from Jürgen, Christof picked up the story. "Our mission failed, tragically. Brother Ulrich was slain by his captors, as was another Cainite brother in our company. They were not many, but they wielded a power..." Christof paused. Rosamund could see the worry and guilt upon the knight's youthful face, and shame as well—she suspected Christof was not accustomed to failure. "A holy power similar to that wielded by Gauthier himself."

"Holy power?" Father Erasmus asked. "Just because a man does something extraordinary does not make him holy, Brother. Even if he is in the Church. Not all mortals who serve Cainites realize from what source their abilities spring."

"With all due respect, Father," Christof said, a bit tightly, "you were not there."

Jürgen raised his hand, halting further discussion on that issue. "Herr Gauthier, for those of you who have not yet had cause to learn of him, is a mortal Templar of extraordinary tenacity, who has taken upon himself a mission from God—to destroy every last one of the childer of Caine."

A French name, thought Rosamund and remembered the stories she had been told of red-robed monks hunting Cainites in Paris before her arrival. *But he's a knight, not one of the Red Brothers. Still... the Temple in Paris...*

"We first encountered him near Acre, during the last cru-sade," Christof continued. "He destroyed three of our number, including Baron Heinrich, who was our primary advocate in the Hungarian court. Since that time, Herr Gauthier has persuaded the Holy Father in Rome to bless his new order of Poor Knights, who wear a broken red cross on their tunics in honor of the frag-ment of the True Cross their Grand Master is said to have recov-ered in Acre. Officially, their mission is to protect pilgrims and holy shrines. However, it is now clear that their true purpose in fact supports their founder's vendetta against any and all Cainites whose existence he can uncover."

"And apparently he has now uncovered us," Jürgen said.

"If I may, milord," Josselin said, leaning forward.

Lord Jürgen nodded. "Speak."

"If this is the same Gauthier de Dampiere of whom I have heard tales, milord, he is not a young man. He was one of those who answered the call to crusade in the Languedoc twenty years ago, and destroyed a number of Cainites during his time there, of both high blood and low."

"Whether low blood or high," Wiftet murmured from the other end of the table, "when it spills on the ground, or runs in a dark river down the bright blade, or blows away as ash on the wind. It is all the same color, then. But the good knight gives us all the same regard in the end, and it is a most final end."

"If you will pardon the interruption, milord." The voice was feminine, low and husky, with an exotic lilt Rosamund could not identify—and to realize she was not the only woman in the room was an even greater shock. "I believe I have learned some things that you will find of interest."

A slightly built figure stood at the far end of the table, swathed and veiled from head to foot in ragged black linen. Given the man-ner in which she had simply appeared out of nowhere, and the total veiling of her face, Rosamund could guess the newcomer to be Nosferatu, in which case the veil was a mercy. Even so, Wiftet immediately got up and offered her his seat, with a gallant bow.

"Akuji, welcome." Lord Jürgen, at least, did not seem sur-prised to have a veiled stranger appearing out of nowhere at his council table.

Now she took the seat Wiftet offered and joined them at the table. "For the good news, milords, milady, Brothers, I have learned that Herr Gauthier himself is not in Magdeburg. These men are, however, here under his authority. I counted eight knightly brothers, a dozen or so squires, and thirty men-at-arms, a priest, and the expected number of other servants to maintain such a number of fighting men—a goodly number." She paused for a moment. "I fear the remainder of my news is less encouraging. Herr Gauthier has a patron high in the church—although there are but a few of them here now, the men spoke of a cardinal giving a great and holy commission to their entire order, from which they derive their determination, and their support."

"What is their commission?" Jürgen asked.

Akuji's voice took on a solemn tone, as if she was reciting the very text, save for doing it in German instead of Latin. "They are ordered to investigate, examine, and pronounce God's judgment upon those mortals who serve the cause of the Adversary by their service to such Cainites and other demons, and to seek out and destroy the damnable heresy known as Cainism. In particular, they are here to conduct an investigation—an inquisition—into the Order of the Hospital of St. Mary of the Germans in Jerusalem. They have now seen the proof of the order's contamination—bear in mind, good Father, that I use their words, not my own—with the Cainite servants of the Devil, and are even now debating whether they can deal with this infestation on their own, or must need send for the aid of their friends in Rome."

Holy Mary. Rosamund did not utter the words aloud—indeed there was not a sound at the table for the space of an *Ave* after Akuji had finished speaking.

"Brother Ulrich was not a heretic," Father Erasmus said softly. "Nor was he careless. Those he… visited… had no cause to complain of him. How then did these knights even discover him? Surely they did not lie in wait for any Teutonic knight who might be traveling back to his abbey after dark?"

"Apparently when they saw him at services that night, they recognized what he was," Akuji said. "It would not be difficult then to guess where he must be from."

"They will attempt to search the hospital here during the day if they can gain access," Jürgen said.

"They might," Christof said thoughtfully. "But not very hard. Not yet. Even during the day, they'll have no idea of how strong our defenses are. It would be foolish to charge in headlong, when they do not know our strength."

"But Herr Gauthier has never hesitated to do exactly that, as I recall," Brother Hermann put in.

"They could have learned from our captured brothers how many we are," Brother Rudiger said.

"Not from Ulrich," Christof said, firmly. "And from the squire's report, I believe Brother Benedict did not live to face their torture. For which we must thank God, for his end was therefore merciful."

Torture. Rosamund suppressed a shiver.

There was a timid rap on the door, and one of the brothers poked his head in, looking anxious. Brother Christof rose from his place and went to see what was so urgent, stepping briefly outside the room.

"Were there any of the red monks?" Josselin asked.

"Red monks?" the veiled Cainite echoed him, apparently curious.

"The Order of St. Theodosius," Josselin explained. "They wear robes of a dark red, like old blood. They have hunted our kind in France and the Languedoc for some years now—and it was rumored that they had an alliance with Herr Gauthier and his Knights of the Broken Cross. Even during the crusade in the Languedoc, he was said to be accompanied by one of that order."

"I have heard of those brothers," Rudiger said with a scowl. "They have a monastery in Bergamo. And now one near Munich, a gift of the Count von Murnau."

"There were no such monks with them," Akuji said. "For that, at least, we must thank God," Father Erasmus said.

Brother Christof returned, and the look on his young face was grave indeed. "This afternoon, the Poor Knights took the priest from St. Sebastian's church, to whom Brother Ulrich spoke his confession that evening, acting under the cardinal's authority. And—milord, I am sorry to say that Brother Richart, whom we missed at compline earlier this evening, was at St. Sebastian's at that time, and of all the canon monks in that church, they took him as well."

Several of the brother-knights crossed themselves. "We must *do* something," Hermann said. "They are not many. There must be some way of dealing with them, now, before this goes too far."

"If there were any of the damnable heretics left, we could at least point them to a more appropriate target," Christof said, taking his seat again.

"We will deal with them," Jürgen said, flatly. "I will *not* permit Gauthier and his holy rabble to destroy all we have built."

"But they cannot be dealt with—not directly," Rudiger said. "You've already lost two Cainite brothers. And if these men now have the support of Rome—"

Jürgen's fist hit the table with a heavy *thump.* "Nor will I run and hide from the very Church I serve, and in my own city!"

Rudiger glared back. "This holy rabble seeks the destruction of every last Cainite in all of Christendom! Nothing less will satisfy them! They will not stop until every last one of us is reduced to ashes!"

"And then what?" Rosamund asked. She hadn't quite meant to speak aloud, but now every other pair of eyes at the table were focused on her.

"With all due respect, milady," Rudiger snorted, "I should think that would be obvious. It won't matter if we're all ash in the sun!"

"That's a good question, though." Christof said. "They'd likely go on to other cities… other chapters of our order…."

"But they'd at least be warned, and prepared." Hermann leaned forward. "I am not afraid of a fight; I have seen what our brothers can do in battle. But we cannot fight the entire Church—not only is it tactically impossible, but we might then find ourselves opposing God!"

"This isn't the entire Church, Brother," Father Erasmus insisted. "It's one order, perhaps two if you take the Red Brothers into account, led by madmen. But cardinals, abbots, knights and monks are mortal, and we are not. We can outlast them—we always have. But I cannot believe that God Himself has ordained our destruction by their hands. We serve His purposes just as much as the living Church does."

"Well, if you *want* to be a martyr, Father—" Rudiger began.

"Enough!" Jürgen's fist hit the table again, and his glare silenced all present. "We are, I believe, agreed that to fight the Poor Knights directly is unwise, as it might well bring the power of their full order, not to mention the attention of their patron in Rome, down upon us. It goes against our very nature to hide— and since they clearly already know we are part of the Teutonic Order, hiding will only encourage them to search harder—and we have too many in our service to protect them all."

"Perhaps martyrs *are* what we need," Christof said slowly. "If, as Lady Rosamund said, they thought they *had* destroyed us all—then perhaps they would be satisfied. We could redistribute our own Order... even send a larger force to Livonia if neces- sary—and, based on what Renaud has told us, it does sound nec- essary. Now that we know their purpose, we could better hide our numbers, even those mortals in our service, if there were fewer of us in any given chapter house. The question is, how many would it take to convince them they had, in fact, succeeded in their purpose?"

"You're talking about asking your *own people* to sacrifice themselves?" Rosamund asked, horrified.

"This is *war*, milady." Rudiger said sternly. "Not a tournament."

"Nor is it chess," Jürgen returned. "While Brother Christof's suggestion is certainly one viable tactical solution, given the cir- cumstances, I am not yet ready to admit it is the only one. Still, we can take certain preparatory steps. I want the Poor Knights watched, as well—by day and by night—and those mortals in our service warned to avoid them. And if—*if*—it is possible to take one of them alive without alerting all the rest... we will do that too. Meanwhile, Brothers, all our houses should be put on alert, and told to prepare either for battle here or for crusade in Livonia."

"And if any more of our brothers fall into their hands?" Father Erasmus asked, quietly.

"I don't want there to *be* any others, until we're ready to deal with this matter once and for all." Jürgen replied. "As for Father Simon and Brother Richart... not all martyrs choose their fates. They are in God's hands now."

Josselin had been quiet as they walked back to the house. Rosamund had assumed he had been too involved watching for the possibility of an ambush by the Poor Knights to waste energy on conversation. Though their lantern was shuttered, emitting very little light, she still felt exposed, vulnerable, as if every eye could see them. She gripped Josselin's hand so tightly it must have hurt, yet he made no complaint. But when they finally reached the safety of their own haven he did not relinquish her hand, but drew her gently away from the stairs and down the hall to his own chamber, one finger on his lips for silence.

"What is it?" she whispered urgently, looking up the stairs, back down the hall as if expecting to see Poor Knights or red-robed monks bursting in on them any minute.

"What? Oh. No, no, *petite*, nothing like that—" He opened the door to his own chamber, and guided her inside, then hung the lantern from hook and opened its shutters to give them some minimal light.

"Oh, good." She almost felt silly for her fears now—or was that Josselin simply trying to soothe her? Sometimes it was hard to tell where her feelings came from when in the presence of other Cainites.

"Rosamund, we must talk." Josselin shut the door and listened for a moment to ensure no one had come downstairs to greet them.

"Talk? About what?"

He came away from the door, took her hands in his. *"Ma petite.* I don't know quite how to put this—I pray you will not think badly of me for saying it aloud, but if I do not, I don't know who else will before it's too late. You *must* be more careful. For both your sake, and his."

"What—what are you talking about, Josselin?" She broke away from him, turned away, avoiding his gaze. He followed.

"Rosamund, sweet sister. I am not blind. I can see where your heart is yearning—and it is my greatest fear that *he* will see it too."

"And what then should I do?" Rosamund demanded. "Should I then deny the feelings in my heart? Deny love? Am I nothing more than Salianna's distraction, her revenge and sacrifice for the childe she lost long ago?"

"I'm not a good one to give advice on feelings of the heart, *petite*. I wish I knew—I only know that if *he* ever sees how you look at Lord Jürgen... that worries me, Rosamund. Alexander loved Olivier, and yet, in a fit of anger, he destroyed him. He loved Lorraine, and yet, in his jealousy, he destroyed her also. And he loves you—and he will share your love with no one else."

She gave a soft, bitter laugh. "And to think it is *you* he is most jealous of—maybe he's not as good at reading hearts as you think...."

Josselin gently turned her around to face him, then lifted her chin up to meet his gaze. "Rosamund. I cannot ask you not to love—I cannot even master my own heart; how can I expect it of anyone else? Only keep it close, and secret, at least until—"

"Until Alexander makes me take the third drink, when it won't matter anymore?"

"I don't know." He sighed. "Nothing I say of late is the right thing, is it?"

"It doesn't matter, Josselin." She reached for him, slid her arms around his ribs. He enfolded her in his arms, her head against his chest, his cheek on her hair. "I am grateful for anything you say, whether I want to hear it or not."

"Then be sure, *petite*, I will always be at your side to say it, and protect you however I can."

For that moment, at least, she felt safe. And suddenly bold enough to ask him something she'd wondered about for a long time. "Who is she, Josselin?"

"—What? Who is who?"

"I do not doubt your devotion, my knight—but I also know that I am not the one who truly holds *your* heart. I never have— but someone does, am I right?"

He was silent for a few minutes, although he did not release her. "Why do you ask?" he said at last.

"Well, it *would* be nice to know I'm not alone in loving unwisely—and if the one you loved was someone you dared *admit* you loved, you would not have kept it so secret all this time. And it's been *years*, Josselin. Do you think I am blind? Do you think I didn't notice how loathe you were to leave the Languedoc, or to join the crusade against the heretics? It's someone in Esclarmonde's court, isn't it?"

"Trust me, Rosamund. You are never alone in loving unwisely—after all, if the heroines of the lays ever loved where they should, there wouldn't be much of a story, would there?"

"You're evading the question, aren't you?"

"Yes, I confess that I am." He looked down at her, his expression sober. "'When made public, love rarely endures.' You know that's true."

"Josselin, *please.*"

He hesitated, then leaned down and pressed a kiss to her forehead. "Ah, *petite.* How can I refuse you? Very well. You're right, and you're not alone; does that make you feel better?"

Then his expression grew serious again. "But at this moment it is *your* love that poses the risk, not mine. And as your kinsman, your vassal, and as one who holds you dearer than his own survival, I am asking you to *please* be very, *very* careful."

She hugged him close and promised.

Chapter Twenty-Four

Magdeburg, Saxony
Soon After the Feast of the Assumption of the
Blessed Virgin Mary, August 1230

Alexander had always been fascinated with maps. To reduce the scope of land and sea, mountains and cities to parchment, so it could be held in one's hands, reducing the journey of weeks to the width of his hand. For the past centuries, maps had been his only vision of the world outside his own domains, for traveling was not something Cainites did lightly—and a Cainite prince rarely did it at all.

But he had traveled beyond the borders of his old maps now. His newest maps showed all of the Empire, from the plain of Lombardy up to the Baltic coast, from Savoy to the west and Bohemia and Hungary in the east, even to Constantinople and Turkey. He listened to rumors and traced their sources... here was Buda-Pest, here was Prague, there was Lübeck, and there was Danzig, and Riga. He had been told that the Baltic actually froze in winter, so that the crusaders had *walked* across the sea to the island of Osel and conquered it. Now he heard—not from Jürgen directly of course, but through his own spies in the prince's much-vaunted holy order—that some barbarian savage had wiped out an entire troop of the Black Cross knights sent to destroy him. Part of him wondered how strong this Qarakh really was... and what Jürgen would do about him now.

"Your Highness?" Marques held a map in his hands. "I found this one—" He held it out so Alexander could see it. "You've not looked at it in months, milord."

"Haven't I?" Alexander took it, laid it flat on top of the others. This map showed Île de France, with Paris at the center where it should be, the towns and castles of his former vassals marked with tiny colored shields. He looked up sharply at Marques. "What are you trying to say, Marques? That you think I have forgotten Paris? *Forgotten* what he did to me, what they all did to me there?"

"No, milord," Marques said, looking down. "I know you'll never forget."

"But? I hear something unspoken, Marques. Speak."

"But how long will you wait, your Highness, before you take what is yours? How long will you let *him* put you off, ignore all you've done for him and do nothing in return?"

Alexander looked down at the map. There on the edges of his domain was the shield bearing the red and white roses of Isouda, Queen of Love for Chartres. Isouda's childe was his too, as much as Île de France and Paris… she even lay closer to hand, and yet…

—How long will you wait before you take what is yours?

"A very good question, Marques," he murmured. "A very good question indeed."

Peter was not quite asleep when he heard a familiar voice downstairs—one that was neither Josselin nor his mistress. Hastily he grabbed his shirt in the dark and pulled it on over his head, but by the time he looked up Alexander was standing at the door, a dim, shadowy figure with eyes that glittered slightly in the faint moonlight coming in the window.

"Peter. Do forgive me for interrupting your rest." Alexander entered Peter's bare little room, closed the door behind him. "It's been some time since we last talked. I hope you haven't been feeling neglected."

Peter bowed to Alexander with all the dignity he could muster, standing barefoot in only his shirt and braies. "Your Highness. We—we didn't expect you this evening—"

"No, apparently not." Alexander came closer. "Now, as I recall, it is your duty to know where your mistress *is*, at all times—just in case she should need your assistance. Therefore she is never to leave this house without you knowing about it. Am I correct thus far?"

"Yes, your Highness."

"Therefore you should be able to tell me where she is right now, since she is very clearly not *here* where she should be."

"Of course, your Highness, let me think...." In fact, he was thinking very fast indeed. "I would have written it down, of course, let me check my *vade mecum*—" His portable lap-desk sat on the floor beside the bed. He went down to one knee and opened it, fumbling after the *vade mecum* notebook he carried everywhere.

Alexander reached down, grabbed the front of Peter's shirt and lifted him up. The Cainite's eyes caught him halfway up, dark, ancient eyes in a boy's smooth face. "Now," the soft, terrible voice continued, "is the time to beg."

Peter felt a cold sweat break out over his entire body. His knees turned to water, and if Alexander hadn't been holding him up, he would have collapsed to the floor. Fear turned to shame as he felt a warm trickle running down his leg, staining his braies. Alexander's eyes bored into him. He heard a roaring in his ears, felt as though all the humors in his brain were boiling, swelling, preparing to burst out of his skull. Nothing he remembered, thought or felt could be hidden—his entire life, his memories, desires, hopes and fears were all laid bare in an instant to the ancient Cainite's demanding gaze.

He was dimly aware of voices elsewhere in the house, of Sir Thomas answering the door, admitting someone to the house: "No, milord, he's not here at the moment. No, milady isn't either—have you a message?"

When Alexander dropped Peter to the floor, he curled up into a pathetic little ball of something that had once been a man, lying in a puddle of his own piss, and begged God for forgiveness.

It was raining hard, and Lucien was soaked to the skin by the time he reached Magdeburg and the Embassy of the Rose. Jervais had been in another foul mood this evening, determined that his repeated "kindnesses" to Lady Rosamund should finally be repaid. He was only slowly learning the arts of diplomatic patience, and it seemed that Lucien always bore the brunt of the learning process. *Please, please,* Lucien pleaded with a usually less than merciful God. *Let him not be there. I can't face him again, I really can't—I can bear anything else, but not the way he looks at me....*

God, in His usual mockery of Lucien's faith, did indeed answer his prayer—when he arrived at Rosamund's embassy, Josselin was not there.

Unfortunately, someone else was.

Lucien had never met Alexander before, but he'd heard all the rumors. He was not at all happy—or surprised—to find out how many of them were true.

"So." Alexander ripped open the letter Lucien had come to deliver, ignoring the fact it was not addressed to him, and scanned the contents. "My sweet lady has not yet learned her lesson, if she is still trafficking with the Tremere. But you—" He looked up and Lucien felt a cold chill run through his blood. "You're not Tremere. Who are you?"

"No one, milord—" Lucien started to say, but his voice was no longer his own. That same voice that had once led to his first death and subsequent rebirth at Josselin's hands now betrayed him one more time, spilling the entire story of his wretched existence to the prince in whose court he had been condemned.

Alexander was still as a statue during his recitation but, when it was over, he smiled. "Ah, that explains a great deal. Now, what to do with you—"

Lucien knew it would be useless to run, but he lacked the courage to face his doom head-on. He broke for the door, but Alexander was faster yet, and thrust a dagger with a blade of polished rowan through his heart before he'd gone three steps. The only other mercy God granted him that night was that by the time his sire and Lady Rosamund returned to their haven and learned what had occurred, he and his captor were long since gone.

Jervais bani Tremere was not pleased, not at all. The good news was that he'd finally received acknowledgment of his presence, and actually been summoned to present himself formally before

Lord Jürgen's court. The bad news was that the summons had
to do with the capture of Lucien de Troyes, who had doubtless
squealed like a stuck pig about just who had been protecting
his sorry corpus for the past seventeen years. Threatening to
surrender Lucien to the Queens of Love's justice had been a useful stratagem. Actually losing him was intolerable. Although at
least this explained why he hadn't come back with an answer to
that particular message. Jervais had begun to wonder if Lucien's
sire had staked the little bastard and shoved him in a box to
save him from the big bad Tremere.

Now Lucien's sire—and indeed, what looked like all the
Cainites in Magdeburg—watched as Jervais stood before Lord
Jürgen's cold-eyed gaze and answered questions about his mis-
creant servant. There was no question of Lucien's fate, of course.
Jürgen had too many vassals watching him tonight to pay heed
to pleas for mercy, even from Rosamund's rosy lips. It was just
Lucien's poor luck to become Alexander's object lesson to his
lady on the price of dealing with the Tremere—and the sly bastard had even managed to do it in a way that Lord Jürgen would
bear the blame of the execution.

Jervais remembered what he had given Rosamund weeks
before, and hoped she would yet find it useful—as paltry an
attempt at vengeance against Alexander as it was, it was the best
he could do for the moment. He did not look at Lucien himself,
manacled hand and foot, on his knees on the wooden platform
that served as both dais and likely execution stage.

"Well, Master Tremere?" Jürgen asked.

Well, there was really nothing else he could do but put the
best face he could on it. "Your Highness," he said smoothly, "I
am shocked and grieved at the accusations against my servant
Lucien de Troyes, but I cannot in good conscience dispute or
defy the condemnation and just sentence proclaimed by the
Queen of Chartres. I therefore renounce my lordship of this
person and respectfully remand him to your justice, milord, so
that the sentence of blood may be duly carried out." He bowed.

"Very well, Maestro," Lord Jürgen said. "You may step
down." Jervais did so, and returned to his place among others
gathered there in the courtyard.

Rosamund laid her hand on Josselin's arm, hoping to soothe him. As he had in their sire's court, he had pleaded with Jürgen for Lucien to be spared, but she also knew that mercy at this point was not politically feasible—and although she would never say it to Josselin, sparing Lucien might be more cruel than kind. *Spare him for what? Eternity as a Tremere thrall? What kind of mercy is that?*

The onlookers were still, even the mortals barely breathing, as Lord Jürgen stood and surveyed the prisoner, his loyal warrior monks, and the rest of the crowd of witnesses.

"I will not dispute Queen Isouda's judgment," Jürgen said at last. "Lucien de Troyes stands under a sentence of Final Death, and that sentence must be carried out." He glanced at Rosamund. "I am sorry, milady. The sentence stands."

On the platform, Lucien was silent, his hands clenching and unclenching, his face gaunt and bloodless. The manacles on his wrists clinked softly.

"Milord." Josselin's voice rang out over the murmurings, and silenced them. "I am his sire. The right of destruction is mine."

Josselin, no, don't punish yourself—Rosamund shook her head, fighting tears.

"Do you claim that right in order to carry it out, Sir Josselin?" Jürgen asked.

"Yes, milord." Josselin said. His eyes were on Lucien, who was staring at him in turn. "I will do it, by your leave."

Jürgen studied him for a moment, and then nodded. "You have my leave. But it must be witnessed here, so that all may see the sentence was carried out."

Josselin nodded. "Thank you, milord." He mounted the platform, offered Jürgen a low, respectful bow, then glanced at Father Erasmus, standing among the Black Cross brothers. "Father. Might he have the rites?"

"Of course," the priest said, and went to kneel by Lucien's side. Rosamund could have heard what they whispered between them if she had wished, but she did not. A novice of the order brought what was needed, and Father Erasmus touched the elements of the Eucharist to Lucien's tongue—as close as any

Cainite could come to receiving the Holy Communion—and anointed his eyes, ears, nostrils, mouth, and hands with oil, then laid a hand on his head for a blessing.

The gathered witnesses were silent during the rite—likely more because of Jürgen's steady gaze over them than any respect for the prisoner's belated show of piety. When Erasmus was finished, he took Lucien's hands and raised him up to his feet. "Stand, my son," he murmured softly, "and hold fast to your faith, and may God have mercy on your soul." Then he returned to his place with the brothers, leaving Lucien to face Josselin alone.

Christof drew his sword, and offered it hilt first to Josselin, who was unarmed. Josselin accepted it, and approached Lucien, who was weeping now. Gently, he smoothed the prisoner's hair, drew him close until their foreheads touched. "Forgive me, Lucien," he whispered. "This was never what I intended for you."

"Please." Lucien's voice was barely audible even from inches away. "I'm still afraid—"

"Be at peace, my son," Josselin pressed a kiss to his childe's forehead, his fingers sliding into Lucien's hair. "It won't hurt. I promise." Then he pulled Lucien's head back and sank his fangs into the prisoner's throat.

Lucien's eyes closed with a soft sigh, and he surrendered willingly to Josselin's kiss, his knees buckling so that all that held him upright was Josselin's grip in his hair. For a long, stretched-out moment, Josselin held him there, until Rosamund wondered if he meant to drink Lucien dry, or worse....

But then Lucien's body was collapsing lifelessly to the platform, his head falling after it and rolling a short distance away. Josselin was standing over him with a bloody sword, dark tears streaming down his own cheeks; his stroke had been so fast that it was likely Lucien had never even seen it coming.

"It is done, milord," Josselin said hoarsely. Then he dropped the sword where he stood, turned and strode quickly off the platform and disappeared into the cloister beyond.

Chapter Twenty-Five

Magdeburg, Saxony
Near the Feast of St. Francis
September, 1230

Every night of the following two weeks, Rosamund rose hoping to see Peter waiting for her, his head bent over his *vade mecum*, ready to report the doings of the day. She visited him several times during the night, stroked his hair and spoke to him gently, telling him how much she missed his company. He did not, however, seem to hear. Blanche cared for him diligently, like a daughter for her father, persuading him to eat a little, helping him to the chamber pot, getting him into a clean shirt. But otherwise he would not rise from the bed.

Once Katherine had suggested, in as kindly a manner as she possessed, that perhaps Peter would not recover, that she should consider seeking another secretary. Rosamund had slapped her in sudden fury, and might have done worse had Josselin not caught her and sent the weeping servant out of the room.

That Alexander was as much to blame for Peter's deep malaise as Lucien's death, Rosamund did not doubt; not even Katherine denied that he had been here that night. Therefore when she heard horses in the yard and sensed his presence approaching, she was filled more with a sense of dread than of joy. She sent Blanche to sit with Peter and instructed her to keep the door shut, and prepared to greet her lord.

"My dearest rose," Alexander said softly. "You do not know how it grieves me to see you so sad, especially when I fear you see me as the cause, however unjustly."

"Unjustly, milord?" Rosamund failed to keep all the bitterness out of her voice. "My kinsman is executed, and my servant ill."

"It was not I who condemned him, sweet rose," Alexander murmured. "Lord Jürgen could have spared him—have you ever asked yourself why he did not? And as for your servant—no one regrets that more than I. But he failed in his duty to you, my love. He needed to be taught a lesson, which I do hope he will learn and profit from."

The tone of his voice brought Rosamund back to her senses. Peter might not be the only one Alexander thought needed lessoning. *Was Margery a lesson too?* A cold chill touched her spine. *He came looking for me, and Peter suffered for it.* "Still, milord," she managed, trying to keep her voice steady, "I wish you had left that to me, rather than depriving me of his services."

Alexander came up behind her and laid his hands on her shoulders, bending slightly to nuzzle at her neck. "Then I'll find you a new secretary, my rose. Mortals come and go in our service, Rosamund. Truly, one is very much like another, in the end." His fingers found the lacing of her cotte, and unknotted it, pulling it free.

"You're very kind, milord," Rosamund whispered, "but I am not ready to give him up just yet, when he is so… so well trained. Milord—"

He turned her around gently to face him, framed her face between his hands. "I've waited for you so long, my queen, my Venus," he whispered. "I will not wait any longer."

The hunger in his eyes sent a thrill of desire down her spine to go with the fear, and opened up a great emptiness somewhere deep in her belly. She felt her own fangs extending, aching for his flesh the way his lips and hands now ached for hers. She knew his intent then, and both feared and desired it with an intensity that frightened her. She no longer knew where her feelings were coming from, whether from her own heart or from the force of his personality overwhelming her own through his dark gaze.

It was all she could do to remember the coin Jervais had given her, to struggle to focus on finding a way to get to it before it was too late. *It's only the second... I don't absolutely need it yet... but if I don't use it now, will I have opportunity or thought for it the next time?*

Somehow she managed to settle him on the bed, while she made something of a show of disrobing herself for his pleasure—this had once held her mortal lovers spellbound, and even Alexander seemed content merely to watch her for the moment. Veiled only in her hair, she removed her rings one at a time; then, bending low over her jewelry chest, her back to him so he couldn't see, she slipped the coin under her tongue.

Then she stood upright again, slowly arranged her hair to fall over her shoulders, back and breasts in a graceful, copper-gold veil. *Venus. I must be Venus to him now....* But it was her own hunger as much as his that drew her now into his arms. His blood was as the nectar of the gods itself, sweet beyond description, flooding her veins with his power; when he took her at last, his fangs piercing her flesh, she would have given of herself until he had taken it all, such was the worship his kiss demanded of her.

Only after he had gone the following evening did she dare take the coin out from under her tongue and noticed that the coin was now strangely heavy for its size, and the once-bright silver had turned totally black.

"Rosamund—" Josselin stared at the blackened coin on its piece of silk, and shook his head incredulously. "How could you even *think* of trusting anything *he* gives you? Is that why you didn't tell me about this before—because you knew what I'd say?"

"But it worked! Look at it! It must have worked, to change color like that! I *am* sorry, Josselin. I know I should have told you. I—I didn't want to upset you, not that night. And then it... just never seemed a good time. Please forgive me?" She came up behind where he sat at the table and wrapped her arms around his neck. "Please?"

He caught her hands in his and kissed them. "Of course, *ma petite.* Our Lady knows I've done worse. And he's got a lot of damned gall thinking he can just..." His voice trailed off.

"It was only the second time," she said, sitting on the bench beside him. "So it's like I've only drunk from him once—"

"Twice, milady." The voice was hoarse, but steady. Rosamund and Josselin turned around. "Twice before last night."

"Peter!" Rosamund jumped up and ran to him, flinging her arms around him; hesitantly, the mortal enfolded her in his arms as well. "It's so good to hear your voice again—come, sit down, you're still shaking…." She guided him to the table, and Josselin pushed a bench out for Peter to sit down on.

"What do you mean, twice?" Josselin asked. "Do you know what happened here last night?"

Peter nodded. "I heard him come. Last night. And before."

"Before?" Rosamund echoed.

"Yes, milady. Last year. When he said it didn't happen. I heard him say that to you. 'It didn't happen.' And you agreed it didn't. And I wrote it down. In case he told me too, but he never did."

"It didn't happen…" Rosamund frowned and repeated it, trying to remember.

"You're sure of this, Peter?" Josselin asked.

"I wrote it down," Peter repeated. He was clutching one of his journals in one hand; he now laid it on the table and opened it to a particular page, turning it for Rosamund to read. "If—if you'll forgive me, milady. I hear everything that goes on in your chamber, if I'm awake."

Rosamund studied Peter's journal entry, then looked up at Josselin, eyes growing wider. "But if he *said* it didn't happen…."

"Then it did," Josselin repeated grimly. He looked at the blackened coin. "You were spared the effects of the oath of blood, at least this time, but Alexander—"

"—Alexander is now likely oathbound to me," Rosamund finished for him. "Holy Mary."

"It's like what Isouda said in her letter," Josselin started. "When Lorraine—"

"*I am not Lorraine!*" Rosamund shot up to her feet and slammed her hand flat on the table hard enough to make the Tremere coin jump. "I am *not* Lorraine, and you are *not* Tristan, and I will *not* hear otherwise! This is one story that will not be retold, Josselin. *It will not happen.* Don't even *think* about it! Do you understand me?"

He was silent for a long moment. "Yes, milady," he agreed at last. His retreat into formality, the sudden hurt in his eyes, was like a splash of cold water on her temper.

She sank down again on the bench and reached across to him, taking his hand. His fingers curled around hers, protectively.

"There's only one sure way to avoid the bond, Rosamund," he said at last. "At least with him. If you would accept it from m—from someone else—" He hesitated, and did not finish the thought, although Rosamund had already heard it. *From me.*

—I know there is great love between you, much as there was between Tristan and Lorraine.... As you hold his oath, I will therefore leave that decision in your hands.

"I know," Rosamund said. "But I can't. And it's not that I don't trust you, Josselin—I do, you know that. But the way our Lady's letter described it, she said Alexander had drunk from Lorraine three times, and so was bound. She *didn't* say if Lorraine had also drunk from Alexander, or if she was bound— but if she ran away with Tristan..."

Josselin finished that thought for her. "What if Tristan and Lorraine thought of that too?"

"They've made their attempts at St. Mary's twice now," Christof reported. "During the day, of course, and only two or three of them at a time. So far, they've not gotten inside. They've been watching the road, too."

"Yes, I noticed them the last time I was there." Josselin agreed. "I went around them, of course, and they never saw me."

"Josselin, you didn't say anything about that before!" Rosamund pushed down a rise of panic. *Holy Mary, Mother of God, I cannot bear to lose him too.* It had been a strain on her nerves just to walk the length of the street from their house to the priory, watching for the Poor Knights to come after them.

"Don't worry, milady," Josselin assured her. "I can see them far better than they can see me—they won't catch me by surprise."

"Still, we've had to be very careful," Christof continued.

"Our mortal agents are on alert and avoid their notice; our brothers have been given special dispensation to wear a plain black habit when they must leave the commandery. So far God has been merciful, and no more of our number have fallen into their hands. It's not quite a siege, but it's close."

"But the walls of St. Mary's are very strong," Rosamund said. "And there are only a few of them—how can they expect to lay siege?"

"Lay siege to what?" asked Wiftet. "Who?"

"The Poor Knights of Acre," Rosamund explained. "How will they lay siege to St. Mary's?"

"Like the Israelites at Jericho," Wiftet said, jumping up to his feet. He began to skip around the table where they sat. "Around and around, with horns blowing, seven times around, and then—"

"Wiftet," Father Erasmus said in a stern voice. "Stop play-acting and sit down."

"But the walls will come tumbling down!"

"That's what they said at the siege of Jerusalem, too—I wasn't there, but I did hear of it once from someone who was," Christof mused. "They fasted and prayed, and marched around the walls—and the city did fall, though the walls remained quite intact."

"But Jericho was given to the Israelites by God," Erasmus reminded them. "It was a miracle."

"Gauthier's knights would believe in miracles," Josselin pointed out. "I daresay they're even praying for one."

"So are we," Christof said wryly. "Unless it is God's will that we become ashes on the wind, and I pray that it is not."

Ashes on the wind. Olivier's hose extending out of his empty tunic, filled with ashes. Lucien's ashes mixed with bits of charred bone...

"Then perhaps they should get what they pray for," Rosamund said suddenly. "And so should we. Brother Christof, you were prepared to sacrifice your own men to give the Poor Knights the victory they need to convince them they've won—what if God gave them their victory instead, without need for your sacrifices?"

Christof gave her an odd look. "I'm not following your

thoughts, milady," he said. "Elaborate, if you will. How would God give them their victory?"

"You said it yourself, Brother," Rosamund said, trying to contain her excitement. It was a wild idea, but if the Poor Knights could be persuaded to *believe*, it might even work. "If it is *God's will* that we become ashes on the wind..."

Lord Jürgen had never been one to scoff at unorthodox tactics if they gained him what he wanted, yet Lucretia was not sure how even he would receive Rosamund's plan, which was nothing if not unorthodox. Still he listened as she explained it to him, which was to his credit.

"You're talking about abandoning St. Mary's, of course," he mused aloud when she was finished, "but that was inevitable no matter what solution we chose to pursue. They know this place now and, with the Virgin's blessing, it will be the only haven of ours they ever find, now that we know to look for them. And we are sending a greater force to Livonia next season, as you know— which will empty a good number of our houses in Saxony and send our brothers out of their reach."

"Sending them away from one danger, and into another, but at least one we can fight openly and in clear conscience," Lucretia agreed. "I confess, milord, it goes against my grain to favor deception over something more straightforward and honest, but at least her plan spares many whom we can put to better use in Livonia, or otherwise pursuing God's work."

"And have you not thought, Sister, that perhaps these Poor Knights of Gauthier's also pursue God's work?"

"I have, sir. But Father Erasmus believes them misguided. It is the Heresy they truly seek, not us. They do not understand how even Cainites play a part in the Lord's plan."

"Nor do I imagine they will listen should one of us attempt to explain it," Jürgen replied. He stroked his moustache thoughtfully. "They will not be easy to convince, these knights. They will suspect a trap; it would take a visitation from Heaven to persuade them to believe."

"With your permission, milord," Lucretia said dryly, "I believe a visitation from Heaven is exactly what she has in mind."

Chapter Twenty-Six

"Again," Father Erasmus said. "Try not to sound so French. *Nolite timere*, unless there's only one present, so that would be what?"

"*Ne timeas, quoniam exaudita est deprecatio tua*," Josselin repeated, trying to imitate the priest's pronunciation exactly. It sounded German to his ears, but he supposed the knights, being German themselves, wouldn't notice that. Rosamund's Latin was better, but Josselin had adamantly forbidden her to play this most dangerous part in their plan, and even Father Erasmus had agreed that all the angels in scripture at least *appeared* as male.

Josselin adjusted his finery, evening out the folds of the white samite hanging from his belt and smoothing the velvet mantle over his shoulders. He was unarmed, barefoot and bareheaded, his hair falling down to his shoulders, his long, flowing white raiment inspired by scriptural illuminations and Wiftet's descriptions of the costumes from Christmas plays.

Rosamund studied the effect with a careful eye. "You look like a prince of Heaven indeed—but you need a little color in your cheeks. Hold still." With a tuft of ermine fur, she brushed colored powder over his forehead, nose, cheeks, jaw line and throat, to hide the pallor of his flesh. "There. That's better."

"You'd best be going, milady," Father Erasmus told her. "Akuji will lead them here soon."

"Be careful, and God keep you safe," she wished them. But she paused for a moment to look up at the high stone walls of the unfinished Cathedral of St. Maurice and St. Catherine, soaring so high as to seem to support the very night sky, for the roof had not yet been added. *Beautiful...* It wasn't Chartres, of course, but there was still something elegant and proud in the very stone—

"*Rosamund.*" Josselin's hands rested gently on her shoulders. "I'm sorry, *petite*, but tonight is not a good night for contemplation. Go on, now."

She nodded and reluctantly allowed Peter and Thomas to lead her back to the relatively safety of the house. *Holy Mary, Mother of God, watch over him.*

"*An angel?* Which one? *Where?*"

"What did he say?"

"How did you *know*—"

"Wait, wait, Brothers!" Herr Manfred waded into the knot of Poor Knights of Acre surrounding Matthias and Reinhardt, holding his hands up for attention. "Let's have a little order here, shall we? Everyone to the chapter hall, and we'll hear it from the beginning, and then judge."

"What's happened?" Otto asked, coming in late, buckling his belt over his hastily donned tunic. Adam had awakened him at the first hint of something going on, but it was not the first time he'd nearly been left out because, as a layman, he did not share the knights' common dormitory.

"Reinhardt and Matthias saw an angel at the cathedral," Brother Gregor told him.

"The cathedral? But it's just a half-finished shell, it's not even got a roof yet, much less consecration from the bishop—" Otto followed the brothers into the chapter hall, and found himself a seat in the back.

"We were coming back from nocturns at St. Sebastian's," Brother Matthias explained, "and it was the strangest thing. Our horses stopped, just stopped, right there in the street. And then they turned and started down another street entirely! Of course, we tried to turn them, but nothing availed us—the beasts would not heed us one jot. So Brother Reinhardt suggested we see where they were leading us, because surely as God granted Balaam's ass the gift of speech, which as you know, Brother, He did, because—"

"One story at a time, Brother Matthias," Manfred interrupted. "The horses led you to the cathedral?"

"Yes, sir," Matthias continued. "Right up to the very doors—or where the doors would be if they were built, of course. And they stopped right there, where the foundations begin, and would go no farther. But Brother Reinhardt saw a light within the cathedral itself, which we thought was odd, so we went to investigate."

"And that's when you saw the angel?"

"Yes. He was standing in the choir, near where the altar will be, just beyond the crossing. There wasn't any altar, or cross, but there were candles—a whole ring of them where he stood. His raiment was white as snow, and he was beautiful, just as in the scriptures. Reinhardt and I fell to our knees right where we stood."

"Beautiful," Reinhardt murmured, softly, massaging the stump of his arm with his remaining hand. "He smiled and spoke to us."

"What did he say?" Brother Emil interrupted. He actually sounded a bit jealous, Otto thought. Why, of all the brothers in the house, did God's angel appear to these two and no other, not even Emil himself?

"Well, first he said not to be afraid, for our prayers had been heard," Matthias continued. "Then he said that God will give us the victory over the forces of the Devil, if we but followed His instructions exactly, even—even as what, Reinhardt? I fear my memory is failing, I am a poor vessel for such a holy message!"

"Even as He gave victory to the Israelites over the city of Jericho, and caused the walls to come tumbling down," Reinhardt put in, "so shall he give us victory over the minions of Hell who hide among the knights of Heaven."

That statement resulted in cheers and praises to God from the other knights, which Herr Manfred allowed for a moment before raising his hands for silence again to get the rest of the story. "What instructions, Brother Matthias?" he asked. "Whatever else your memory fails on, let it not be that."

"Oh, no, commander," Matthias assured him. "I remember that *exactly* as he told it to us."

"Milady." Jervais smiled warmly—at least as warmly as he could manage—and bowed. "What a pleasant surprise. I was expecting his Highness of course...."

Rosamund smiled apologetically. "His Highness was called away, unfortunately. He asked me to meet with you in his stead." It was even mostly true, although Lord Jürgen had sent the invitation to Jervais only at her request.

Jervais was no fool. His eyes narrowed slightly, warily. "Ah. A pity," he said smoothly. "What I had to tell him was more of a military nature, quite unsuited for such delicate ears as yours, milady. But if his Highness is occupied, perhaps I can come another time. I will bid you a good evening then, milady, and hope that his Highness will remember me again sometime in the future." He turned as if to go.

"It turned black," Rosamund said casually, and had the pleasure of seeing his departure freeze in mid-stride and his attitude shift from annoyed to amiable in the space of a single breath.

"*What* turned black, milady?" he asked, turning back again.

"I'm sure you remember." She took the little packet of silk out of a pouch at her belt and unfolded it on her hand, so that the tarnished coin was visible—she had chosen a piece of white silk to wrap it in, so the coin's change would show clearly.

"You used it," Jervais murmured, and came closer, drawn by the coin as if by a lodestone. But when he reached out one broad, fleshy hand towards it, Rosamund closed her fingers and the silk around the coin and withdrew it from his reach.

"I fear it only works one time, milady," he said softly. "I can create another, of course, but I would need that one to work from...."

That was likely a lie; he'd certainly created the first one easily enough, although how he'd known that such an amulet would be of use to her she hadn't yet determined. Still, he wanted it back, now that it had tasted Alexander's potent blood—and a good diplomat negotiated with the coin she had.

"I'm sure." Rosamund refolded the silk around the coin and kept it firmly in her hand. "What did you have to tell his Highness, Maestro? Something of a military nature, you said?"

"Yes, milady," the Tremere admitted. "I did. I understand his Highness is planning a campaign in Livonia—do not look surprised, Lady Rosamund, I'd be a poor diplomat if I didn't have a *few* other sources to bring me the news, or to know what is on his Highness's mind. His Highness is considering undertaking a crusade against the pagans on the Baltic coastlands—no surprise, as the Teutonic Order was invited there, and is already engaged. And I have heard that his Highness recently suffered a loss in that region as well. An entire troop of his much-vaunted Knights of the Black Cross, slaughtered by a barbarian warlord. Naturally, his Highness will not let such a deed go unanswered in Livonia any more than he did in Hungary—am I right thus far?"

"So far," Rosamund agreed.

"The Knights of the Black Cross are certainly brave and highly skilled," Jervais continued, "but they will find Livonia a hostile territory. The ground is treacherous, often wet and filled with bogs, dangerous for horses. In the winter, the rivers, ground and the sea itself are frozen, and the cold is bitter even for Cainite blood. The pagan tribes are treacherous as well, and cannot be trusted. This barbarian warlord, this Qarakh, now leads the Cainites in the region like a prince, and defies the crusader troops sent against him."

"Yes, I'm sure his Highness knows that much already," Rosamund said.

"And the Telyavic sorcerers that are Qarakh's allies, milady? Does his Highness know about them?"

"Sorcerers?" Rosamund raised one eyebrow. "Sorcerers of the blood?"

His eyes flicked to the silk-wrapped coin in her hand, and back again. "You do realize how important this is, Lady Rosamund," he said. "You wouldn't want Lord Jürgen to go to

Livonia unprepared for such a thing. I trust that you will convey to his Highness the willingness of House and Clan Tremere to assist him in this matter—especially when it comes to other sorcerers. Swords alone won't bring him victory—any more than they did in Hungary."

"Now, that *is* of military interest," Rosamund agreed. She seated herself on a bench, and laid the coin beside her like a promise. "Tell me more."

Chapter Twenty-Seven

Magdeburg, Saxony
Feast of St. Michael, September, 1230

Seven days. For seven days, the Poor Knights had done as their angel had bidden them: They had come in their silent procession and circled the fortified monastery that was St. Mary's, once the first day, then twice on the second, thrice on the third day, and so on for the entire week. The first day, the procession had been as the bells had rung nocturns, in the dead of the night; the second day's procession had been at lauds, in the early dawn; the third had been at prime, and so on through the monastic hours of the day. Now, the night of the eighth day had come, and the knights would be expecting the angel's promise to be fulfilled.

Brother Renaud had not been the only Black Cross novice assigned to keep watch on the Poor Knight's commandery over the past seven nights, but he had asked for tonight's vigil because of its importance, and Christof had granted it. His woodcraft was better than that of the other novices due to Sighard's training, and his night sight was keener. Several of his fellows had even said his eyes glowed red, which he remembered Sighard's doing as well.

The time given for the fulfillment of the angel's promise was nocturns as well, but apparently the Poor Knights were taking no chances—Renaud spotted two horsemen leaving the commandery's gates a full three hours before he expected the knights to assemble for their final battle. *Scouts*? They had not done this before; he wondered if perhaps the Poor Knights might deviate even further from the plan. "I'm going to follow them," he whispered to his fellow novice and watcher, Brother Tancred. "The Lord Marshal must be warned."

"We're not supposed to split up!" Tancred reminded him. "We should both go."

"And then who would be watching the gate? Rorick and Stefan are too far away to see it. You need to stay here. I'll be fine."

Tancred couldn't argue with that. "God keep you then. Be careful!"

Renaud clapped a hand on his shoulder, then slipped back through the woods to where they'd left their horses. He untied his own, then turned and realized he was no longer alone.

"Renaud," Alexander murmured. "What a fortuitous meeting this is—though not for you, perhaps.

"István, *now*."

There was the deep thrum of a bowstring. The force of the bolt drove Renaud back a step, against his horse, but it pierced lung and muscle, not his heart. Gritting his teeth against the pain, he grabbed the saddle, lifted his foot to the stirrup, and pulled himself up. A hand grabbed his belt and yanked him back down again, then threw him across the clearing and into a tree trunk with painful accuracy.

Snarling, Renaud struggled back up to his feet, drawing his sword. But Alexander was just *there*, in front of him, one fine-boned hand gripping Renaud's jaw, forcing him to meet the former prince's icy gaze. Suddenly his hand could no longer grip his sword, his legs could barely support him. Even when Alexander let go and stepped back, those cold eyes held him immobile.

The next bolt found its target; a numbing cold ran outwards from his unbeating heart to all his limbs, and he crumpled to the ground, paralyzed and helpless.

"Renaud de Joinville," Alexander said, standing over him. "Your existence was mine from the first night you tasted my childe's blood and swore your service to Olivier and to me. I may have lent you to Sighard for a time, but that did not invalidate your oath—nor allow you to dare claim this gift of immortality from another's veins. Your disloyalty and betrayal have never been forgotten, though the judgment and final penalty have been delayed until a more appropriate and auspicious time."

"Like now." Marques grabbed Renaud's tunic and dragged him to lean up against a tree, ripping the laces of Renaud's mail coif free in his haste to pull it back and bare his throat. "*Traitor.*"

On Renaud's other side, István laid aside the crossbow and drew a knife.

It was no easy task to move an army undetected, nor to abandon a long-established haven, much less leave it clearly visited by the wrath of an almighty God. Real Cainite remains being in short supply, those of mortals were disinterred and prepared for burning as well, and ashes from the kitchen hearth and black-smith's forge gathered and laid out as convincingly as possible. The mortal brothers who had volunteered to stay received special blessings and the supreme unction from Father Erasmus, and then submitted themselves to Lord Jürgen's personal direction, so that they would be able to tell their Poor Knight captors only what the *Hochmeister* wanted them to know.

Every night, a few of the rest of the Order of the Black Cross had left St. Mary's under cover of darkness, traveling in small groups with minimal baggage, and as quietly as possible. They went either to the Castle of Hundisburg, where Jürgen had established an alternate commandery, or to one of the other smaller commanderies in the north that Lord Jürgen had ordered prepared to receive them, in preparation for the upcoming and far longer journey to Livonia.

The horse was the first sign of trouble: a riderless horse trotting up the road towards St. Mary's. Its saddle and tack were of the unadorned style favored by the Black Cross, and splattered with Cainite blood. Hoping to find some sign of his rider, Christof and Josselin rode back along the road. They had barely gone a mile when Josselin pulled up, extending a hand to signal Christof as well.

"Someone's coming—" Josselin whispered and closed his eyes to listen more closely. "Two horses."

They turned their horses off into the trees, and found a

good vantage point where they could view the road ahead and remain unseen.

"There's a light," Christof said, frowning. "Damn them, I expressly ordered—"

"Those aren't our knights," Josselin interrupted. "They're mortal. Look, they're leaving the road."

"Scouts, then," Christof muttered. "I'll have to distract them, or they'll see our people."

"No, I'll do it," Josselin said. "You can get those brothers moving faster, they'll listen to you."

"Josselin—" Christof started, although he couldn't argue the logic. "Very well."

"And lend me your surcoat."

The moon was so bright, they only needed the lantern when they rode under the trees. But on such a night, they would not be the only ones abroad. And, as Otto himself had pointed out, demons knew the scriptures too, and might guess there was a reason and rhyme for the Poor Knights' activities around their walls these past seven days. Given the hour, it was foolish to assume the Cainites would wait inside their walls like captive pike in a barrel. So Brother Matthias, who knew the countryside around St. Mary's like his own name, and Otto, whose sensitive nose was becoming legendary, rode out ahead of time to ensure that events were indeed moving as the angel had foretold.

Brother Matthias pulled up his horse suddenly. "Herr Otto, look. Is it—?"

A mounted knight on a tall gray horse stood on the road ahead of them, on the other side of a narrow bridge. The knight wore full mail from head to foot and a white surcoat with the black cross of the Teutonic Order, and carried a long lance tipped with steel.

Otto looked, and sniffed the air. A sickening-sweet odor of rotting garbage reached his nostrils, and he nearly gagged. "*Yes,*" he gasped. "One of them."

"Well, then," Matthias grinned, and lifted his own lance. "God willing, I'll send the bastard right back to Hell."

On the other side of the bridge, the knight's horse stamped

and tossed its head. The knight lowered his lance. The moon-light reflected off his mail and his eyes glittered coldly in his pale face.

Otto felt a sudden sense of foreboding, as if the blood in his veins had suddenly turned to ice; he felt a sudden urge to turn his horse around and ride as fast as he could back to the safety of the commandery. "Brother, maybe we should wait for the others—"

"Have you no faith, Herr Otto?" Matthias urged his horse forward, and lowered his lance. "For Christ and the True Cross!"

Across the bridge, the gray horse held its ground, the knight unmoving as Matthias kicked his destrier into a full charge.

The Poor Knight lowered his lance and charged. "Steady, lad, steady," Josselin murmured, holding Sorel back. "Let him come to us...." In truth, he was impressed—and more than a little sur-prised. No mortal had ever withstood his gaze like this, much less mustered an attack.

The mortal knight's horse crossed the bridge, hooves pound-ing on the wooden planks.

Josselin rose up in his stirrups, his grip shifting on the lance. At just the right moment, he lifted it above his shoulder and then hurled it like a javelin with all his blood-borne strength.

The knight had no room to dodge the missile, no time to maneuver. It penetrated both his armor and his torso; he was thrown backwards out of the saddle with the force of it and landed hard on the dirt. He did not move again.

Josselin drew his sword and urged Sorel forward at the other mortal—the knight's lackey, perhaps, since he wore no habit. The blood-scent invigorated him; his fangs were already extending, the Beast whispering in his ear. *Run*, he willed the mortal as he rode towards him.

Run, or join your master.

Otto saw Matthias go flying backwards out of his saddle, and land hard on the road, the lance through his body. He crossed himself, murmured a quick prayer for the Poor Knight's soul. Then the demon knight came over the bridge, sword in hand

and teeth bared like a wolf.

Fear gripped Otto's bowels, and he had a strong urge to turn his horse and ride away as fast as he could into the night. But no Murnau had ever run from the Devil, or so his father had always said. He drew his sword. "Demon!" he cried, and kicked his horse forward.

But his horse was not trained for combat, and at the last minute it shied away from his oncoming foe, forcing him to pay as much attention to keeping his balance as defending himself from the Cainite's attack, or hitting the bastard.

The Cainite swerved towards him, and parried Otto's attempted blow with such force that he felt his hand and arm go numb. He had a closer view than he'd ever cared to of the Cainite's white fangs and cold blue eyes; the stench of the creature made his eyes run and his vision go blurry.

Then a hard, mailed fist impacted with his temple; he was aware of falling, darkness and stars as the ground rose up to meet him.

Josselin dismounted and knelt beside the fallen mortal's crumpled form; the man was stunned, blood matting his hair where Josselin had struck him. He bent closer, suddenly noticing the silk embroidery that trimmed the man's collar.

This was no servant: His clothes were too fine, the clasps and embellishments on his belt buckle and scabbard too decorative for a man connected to a monastic order. He wore mail under his tunic, too, and a ring on his finger, which bore a heraldic crest.... It was unfamiliar to Josselin, but he made a note of its design; perhaps Christof would know it.

He could see the pulse of the artery at the man's neck, steady and strong, could smell the sweet blood. A sudden hunger stabbed at him, even though he had fed earlier that same evening. This, the Beast whispered, was his rightful prey, overcome by the hunter; his prisoner, whose ransom could only be paid in blood.

Josselin bent to collect it.

Cold fingers on his cheek, touching him, examining his clothing.

Otto struggled to clear his head of fog and pain without moving or opening his eyes, tried to keep his breathing shallow as he could. *Maybe if he thinks I'm out cold he'll leave me lie…. Holy Virgin, if ever I have found favor in your sight—*

Then the Cainite half-lifted him up in his arms, letting Otto's head loll back, and he remembered too late the *real* use a Cainite might have for a helpless victim, as cold lips touched his throat.

He went stiff, fighting back too late, and the Cainite's grip tightened. There was a sharp, piercing pain as the demon's fangs stabbed into his throat, and cold terror washed over him.

And then the pleasure began. Waves of pure sensual ecstasy rippled through him from his head to his fingers and toes and back again, leaving him enthralled in a delicious languor. It was the intensity of sex, the sweetness of marzipan, the rare delight of his father's praise, and it was the seductive taste of death a little at a time as the demon suckled on his vein and drank away his life.

But it did not kill him. Instead it withdrew its sweetly paralyzing kiss and left him empty and alone, weeping on the side of the road, for the Poor Knights to find.

The sun was rising by the time the Poor Knights had finished searching St. Mary's Hospital and Commandery and cataloguing the results. The few prisoners—poor fellows—wept in their chains, and told tales of an angel stalking through the abbey with a sword of fire. The evidence they had found in the abbey bore that out, from the scorched and fallen gates and doorways to the empty, bloodstained Teutonic habits, filled with gritty ash and bits of charred bone.

"Ashes," Brother Emil was grinning in satisfaction as he held up his hand and let the ashes sift down through his fingers. "Every last one of the bastards! Not that it makes up for Matthias—not even a thousand piles of ash would do that! But this is a good start—what was the final count, Reinhardt?"

"Eighteen, Brother," Reinhardt said. "Eighteen Cainites destroyed by the power of God, just as the angel promised! Brother Matthias is smiling down on us from heaven, I'm sure. And thank God for that skittish horse of yours, Herr Otto! The creature must have thought you dead—thank the Virgin and St. Maurice you're not!"

"Yes, thank God," Otto agreed, weakly. Brother Gregor had cleaned the blood from his face, checked the dilation of his eyes, and then assured him he'd recover. His hand strayed to his throat, involuntarily; there was no mark there, no evidence of how his flesh had been violated. Nor had he mustered the courage to tell them.

Now there was a clean breeze blowing through the abbey's broken gates and, God willing, the darkness here at least had been burned out for good. But he couldn't help wondering which, if any, pile of ash was *that* demon knight, and if the Cainite's destruction had truly freed him of its spell.

No one had ever told him that the bite of a Cainite felt *good*. Now he felt soiled, unclean, and even though it had hardly been voluntary on his part, he wondered if mere confession would ever clean the stain from his soul.

Chapter Twenty-Eight

Magdeburg, Saxony
Eve of the Feast of St. Dionysius, October, 1230

The priory was quieter than she remembered it, the cloister lit only by intermittent moonlight, and the few brother-knights of the Black Cross she saw, including those two sent to escort her, wore plain black habits instead of their customary white. But they did not lead her to Jürgen's council chamber, where he usually met with her, but to a room on the floor above, which appeared to be his personal office, workroom and sleeping chamber.

"Lady Rosamund." Jürgen was wearing black also, though of a secular cut rather than a monk's habit. For some reason, that subtle difference pleased her; she did not like seeing him as a monk. "My apologies, milady, for the delay in receiving you— as you know, events of late have been somewhat harried, and have kept me from the pleasures of your company. I am aware, however, of all you and your brother have done for us of late."

"I am your Highness's loyal servant, always," she replied, curtsying. "But it was on another matter I came to speak. It seems that Master Jervais did indeed have some information regarding matters in Livonia to offer your Highness and, having now heard it myself, I think you would find it of interest. I cannot verify his report, of course, and it may be he knows even more than he told me, should your Highness ask it of him."

"That may be," Jürgen replied, thoughtfully. "My generals will be meeting after my formal court on All Souls' Night. Perhaps that might be a better time to hear your report, milady—and if we need to summon the Tremere in for more details, I am certain he will be more than willing to make himself available."

"Of course, milord," Rosamund agreed.

"I will offer more official appreciations in that court as well, but I wanted to thank you personally as well for your assistance in this difficult matter." He paused, and something in his tone, even the way his gaze flickered off to one side and back again, told her he was not yet done with all he had to say. "There was something else as well...."

Rosamund did not need to see his colors to realize this was bad news; she could hear it in his voice, and braced herself for it.

"Your report said that Brother Renaud was missing," he said somberly. "I thought you and Josselin should know—we found his remains in the woods near the Poor Knights' commandery. Brother Tancred said he had gone to follow two knights who had left ahead of the others. From what evidence remained, it appears he had been shot in the chest with a crossbow... several times. One bolt must have pierced his heart—he would not have been otherwise subdued without taking others with him."

Oh, no—poor Renaud! "I—I am sorry..." she managed. "I know Josselin will be greatly grieved to hear of it. He considered Renaud a friend. And I did as well. I never doubted him, milord—I feared it was so when Josselin told me he was missing."

"He was a friend to your seneschal also, perhaps from their time in service together."

"Yes. Renaud was close to Peter, and to Fabien also—how did you know?"

"Peter sometimes visited him at St. Mary's. I thought you knew?"

"No—but I'm not surprised. I—I'd rather he were there than—than other places he could have gone." She was having trouble speaking; her throat was tight. *Poor Peter—where else could he have gone? He dared not even weep for her.* "We have all need—needed God's comfort in these past years."

Images flickered unbidden through her mind of those whose suffering had been burned into her memory and her heart:

Renaud, weeping over poor Olivier's empty tunic; Margery coming back from Alexander's room in the early dawn, pale and wan, her eyes reddened from weeping; Peter lying curled up on the floor where Alexander had let him fall, having wet himself in his terror; and her loyal Josselin, standing over Lucien's headless corpse with a bloody blade and tears running down his cheeks, forced by duty and Alexander's malice to destroy the errant childe he had loved. And for herself, what it felt like to lie trapped by Alexander's cold arms and colder heart, to endure his caresses and fear his kiss more than the dawn....

We have all suffered, she realized, and then struggled to banish those memories before they overwhelmed her fragile self-control. *I will not cry. I must be strong.*

"Milady—is something wrong?"

I will be strong. I owe it to them to be strong, I can't fail them now, I must be—

But her tears had been dammed up far too long. One dark tear escaped, running down her cheek, and then another. Then it was as if the floodgates of her soul had opened and there was nothing she could do to stem the tide of it. Fear spiked along with grief, frustration, anguish too long bottled up inside. A sob burst free of her throat, and she turned and ran for the door.

She didn't even get halfway before she encountered an obstacle, a hard chest and strong arms that wrapped around her, then scooped her up off her feet. Jürgen carried her, still weeping, across the room and laid her gently down on the bed. "Shhh, shhh," he murmured, leaning anxiously over her. "Rosamund—no, you stay there, don't be afraid, you're safe here. Whatever it was I said—I pray you forgive me, lady, I would not hurt you for all the world, surely you know that...."

His concern bathed her with warmth, his gaze all but overpowering, so close, so focused. Her grief had to struggle to keep its grip on her, but she didn't want to let it go, not entirely, not yet. She fumbled after his hand and he let her take it, curling his fingers around hers. "Not you," she managed. "Never you—"

"Then what is it, lady? Sweet Rosamund—" His free hand stroked her hair gently, almost as if he feared to hurt her with his touch. "Let me help you."

"You can't." It was a whisper. "No one can."

He bent slightly and lifted her up in his arms, holding her against his chest. Her arms went around him almost instinctively. "Rosamund. Can't you trust me just a little?"

It felt so safe in his arms. So good to let the burdens go, let him hold her, let his soft words convince her what she so very much wanted to believe. "I do trust you, milord. It's not about trust."

"Then what is it? This—this is not like you." He touched her cheek, almost gingerly, with his fingertips, traced the line of her jaw. "Whatever troubles you, I will not allow it to continue. Did I not tell you that, should you need my protection, you had only to ask? Rosamund—"

There was something in his voice that caught at her heart—his own hurt and frustration, wanting an enemy he could fight, an obstacle he could knock down and so vanquish her grief and pain in a blow. She looked up and met his gaze, and the words that she had planned to soothe him evaporated from her tongue and vanished unsaid.

His eyes drew her in, deep and intensely blue; she had never been so close to them before. There was concern in them, and a fierce protectiveness that washed over and through her like the heat from a fire. And something else, just as dangerous as flame, and as warming: desire. She savored that for a moment, felt it touch something inside herself that she had tried so hard to keep buried and secret, coaxing it into germinating, sprouting and blossoming where he could see it too.

"Rosamund—" he murmured, and then bent his head down towards hers and kissed her.

His moustache teased her skin as his lips explored hers, upper and lower. Her hand found his chest and slid up over his shoulder and into his hair; his arms held her close, one hand sliding down the length of her back. His lips strayed, moving over her cheeks, finding the tracks of her tears and kissing them away, then returning to kiss her again. Her fangs slid free without her even willing them, lips parting for his tongue, exploring his mouth in return. There was a taste of blood....

Her hunger suddenly opened up as a bottomless void; with

a small cry she broke free and buried her face in his shoulder, trembling in her efforts to rein that hunger in, to control the blood-lust and desire that his kiss, his very presence evoked in her.

"Rosamund—?"

"You, milord, are no monk," she murmured into his tunic, and he chuckled. Somehow that evaporated the tension, and even her blood-hunger faded to something manageable, even enjoyable, hovering at a level more akin to eager anticipation than frustration.

"Would you have me be, milady?" he asked, amused. He freed one hand, reached down and began to unbuckle his belt. She laid her hand over his for a moment.

"Not for all the world," she admitted, smiling, and undid the buckle herself. His fingers proved extremely deft on the laces of her gown, and his lips as eager to explore her skin as hers were for him. This was what her soul had longed for, since the first time she had seen him standing tall and proud before his court eighteen years ago: to lie close in his arms, touch him and be touched, to feel his hand on her breast, his legs entwined with hers, his lips exploring her throat…

Yes. Oh, yes… She closed her eyes and lifted her chin, felt his lips part over the vein. Anticipation, knowing what was coming, was nearly as sweet as the kiss itself; when his fangs pierced her flesh, she gave a soft cry of ecstasy and let the rapture of it take her.

And shortly thereafter he held her close, as any true knight and lover should, and surrendered himself, body, soul and blood, to her kiss.

"You still haven't told me what was distressing you so…" he said, some time later. "But I have a feeling I know. I *will* protect you, Rosamund; you, Josselin, and your servants. There is no need for you to fear."

"And when you go to Livonia with your army," she asked, softly, "what then? Will you leave him here to watch your throne when you're gone? Or pack me in your baggage train like one of the nuns—or a camp follower?"

"Would that I had the luxury of a choice—but I cannot leave, not now. Not with him here. Once again, I must be prince rather than general, and allow Christof and Rudiger to lead my men into battle. Though I must confess—" His fingers trailed through her hair, playing with the silken length of it. "I have found another reason to hold me here as well. A different kind of ambition—and a different prize."

"Is that what you see when you look at me, Jürgen? A prize to be won, taken from Alexander?"

He propped himself up on one elbow and looked down at her, lightly caressing her cheek with the backs of his fingers. "You *are* a prize, Rosamund: a precious jewel that any king would be proud to wear in his crown, a rare and delicate flower that any gardener would cosset and protect, a beauteous lady any knight would willingly fight and die for. And you are a lady of noble blood, of such grace, beauty and wisdom as any prince would feel honored to call his queen. And I *will not* let him have you. Believe that, my sweet lady."

He meant it, Rosamund realized, and for a whole minute she let herself bask in that knowledge, the warm assurances and comfort radiating from his very presence beside her, his touch on her skin, his blood singing in her veins. "I do believe it," she whispered, and let him gather her close again. When Jürgen held her like this, it was easy to believe he could conquer the world.

"You are the Ambassador of the Rose," he murmured to her hair. "What do you think Queen Isouda would say to a proposal of alliance—an alliance of blood?"

What will Alexander say?

—He loved Lorraine, and yet, in his jealousy, he destroyed her also.... He will share your love with no one else.

"I—I am certain that my queen would favor an alliance," Rosamund murmured, because she had to say something, and she knew it was true.

"And you, Rosamund? Would that please you as well?"

His very heart was in those words, and her own heart would break if she refused him outright. "If it were possible, and my queen agreed," she said at last, "then there is nothing in all eternity that would please me more."

"Then it will please me also," he said, and bent down to kiss her again.

In the nearby church tower of St. Sebastian, the bells began ringing, calling the monks to morning prayer.

Lauds! It's nearly dawn! She started to get up, to reach for her chemise and gown. *If I hurry, I can make it, it's only a few blocks.* But Jürgen reached out and intercepted her, letting his hand slide up the length of her arm and draw her back down again beside him.

"Stay."

He was beautiful, even asleep and still as a corpse, long hair disheveled and beard untrimmed. His servants had come in and lit candles, and left a few packets of correspondence on the worktable. Rosamund wondered if they had been surprised to discover someone sharing their master's bed.

She let her fingers play across his broad chest, following the curve of muscle and bone under his pale skin, the ragged white lines of old scars. He had not been Embraced as an adolescent boy, but a man in the prime of his years, tall and strong from a mortal lifetime of wielding a sword, fighting his way through life into eternity. Even asleep he was the image of the warrior-king; when he was awake, and his eyes brilliant and alert, looking on the world as something to conquer...

His hand moved, caught hers in an instant, his grip relaxing as his eyes opened and he recognized her, his face relaxing into a smile. "Rosamund."

She felt his regard as a caress, and for a moment wanted nothing more than to fold herself back into his arms, to taste the fire of his blood on her tongue, feel his fangs in her flesh. Somehow she resisted: His blood was as sweet and potent as his smile, but neither totally overwhelmed her good sense, not yet.

"Milord. I fear I must go—I will be missed—"

He drew her hand to his lips and kissed her palm. "Alexander must learn he cannot have everything he wants," he said smoothly. "He cannot have you."

She smiled. "I meant, my servants will be concerned for me. Peter will be worried."

"We cannot let Peter worry, then."

Chapter Twenty-Nine

Magdeburg, Saxony
Feast of St. Dionysius, October, 1230

Rosamund bid her escort goodbye at the door and let herself in. Peter's office on the ground floor was empty and dark, nor was there any light showing under Josselin's door—perhaps he'd spent the day at the new commandery with the Black Cross knights. She hurried upstairs.

The solar on the floor above was dark and empty, the kitchen surprisingly deserted. She listened for a moment, but heard nothing, no murmur of conversation, no movement. Where *was* everyone? Somewhat more slowly, she went up to the third floor.

Peter's room at the top of the narrow stairs was empty as well. She went to her own, and stopped, frozen in place by what she saw within.

Her chamber looked as though it had been ransacked by the Tartar hordes. The oaken chest that had held her clothes was overturned, the lid torn off its iron hinges and smashed like so much kindling, the shutters torn away from the windows and treated the same way. The remains of the chest, the broken chairs, and the floor were draped in torn remnants of fabric and embroidered trim; even the heavy hangings around her bed had been ripped down and torn to pieces. Rosamund bent and picked up a scrap of white brocade from the floor, recognized its pattern. It had been the sleeve from her favorite cotte....

—When first he discovered she had fled, I recall hearing that he went straightaway to her rooms and tore all her gowns to tatters in his fury.

Numbly, she stepped into the room, fighting the urge to

cry, to give in to the red haze that edged her vision. Suddenly
the apparent absence of her staff, of Josselin, took on a new, far
more disturbing significance, and caused cold terror to grip her
unbeating heart. *Where are they?*

*—the appearance of betrayal is just as dangerous to you as its actu-
ality; be forewarned and wise.*

"No..." she choked, and turned to go, to search the house
for any sign—

"You weren't here," Alexander said, petulantly. "I missed
you."

She froze again, and then turned slowly back, clutching the
little scrap of brocade tightly in her fingers as if it were her only
shield. "Your Highness."

He had been sitting in a corner on the other side of her bed.
Now he rose to his feet, and came towards her. His pale cheeks
showed dark streaks and smears of bloody tears. So did the chemise he was holding in his hands. "I thought you had left me,"
he said, softly. "He wants you to leave, I know he does. And you
were both gone. I—I didn't know what to do."

His grief caused her own heart to ache. She knew what it
was like to feel abandoned by those she loved. She reached out
to him, took him into her arms, and he dropped the chemise
and held her closely. "I—I'm so sorry," she managed. "I didn't
mean to upset you, you know I wouldn't leave you!"

"I missed you so much," Alexander murmured into her ear,
and kissed her cheek before releasing her. "I will get you new
gowns, my rose, even finer ones. You didn't really like those old
ones anyway, did you?"

The green wool cotte had been a gift from Isouda, and the
white brocade had been made by her mother and sent to her in
France for her bridal chest. Josselin had brought back a piece of
blue silk velvet from Toulouse, and Margery had sewn a gown
of it for her in secret, embroidered with gold, as a surprise....

"I know you didn't like them," Alexander pressed. "And
now you can have new ones. That will be much better, don't
you think?"

*—I will give you anything you desire. What can he give you?
Nothing.*

"I do like new things, milord—"

"*You didn't like them.*" His eyes bored into hers, and suddenly the white brocade looked silly and childish, the blue velvet tawdry, and she was glad to be rid of them.

"No," she agreed. "You're right, I really didn't. I really needed some new gowns."

He smiled. "You see? I knew it—I always know what you're thinking, my love."

She suppressed a sudden sharp spike of near-panic. Fortunately, Isouda had drilled her in courtly phrases, and she did not need to think clearly in order to answer him. "Now, milord, would you take all the mystery away? What would be the challenge in that?"

"I have missed you so much, my rose," he went on. "After we parted, I couldn't stop thinking about you, not for a minute. Finsterbach is nothing but a hollow pile of stone without you to brighten its halls, and my bed is cold and lonely without you beside me. And that's when I realized how much I truly loved you. 'A true lover is constantly and without intermission possessed by the thought of his beloved.'"

It was one of the Rules of Love, although she had not realized Alexander was so conversant in them; they had seemed contrary to his nature. "There is more to love than that, milord."

"I love you," Alexander said, taking her hands. "I thought I loved you even before, but I didn't really *feel* it. But I *must* have, because I was jealous—and real jealousy always increases the feelings of love, that's what Capellanus wrote, isn't it? And it's *true*, Rosamund, because it has happened to me! Now when I look at you, even think about you—I feel such love that even the *langue d'oïl* is inadequate to express it."

The blood oath wasn't love, of course—she had heard a dozen debates in Isouda's court alone on that topic. But to Alexander, it might well *feel* like love.

"I am flattered, milord," Rosamund demurred.

"I know you'll feel it too, my love." Alexander came closer. "You will come to love me, just as I love you."

"In time, milord, of course," she demurred. "The heart cannot be hurried."

"What shall I do, my rose, to prove my love? Shall I kill those pitiful knights who have been giving Lord Jürgen such difficulties? Shall I climb a mountain of glass, or tame a dragon to be your palfrey? I would give you Paris, and Salianna's head on a pike, but—" His expression darkened, and the fury suddenly radiating out of him was enough to force her back a step in alarm. "*He* will not give me *troops* as he has promised! After all I have done for him, he *will not support me!*"

Looking for something on which to vent his fury, Alexander picked up the remains of her oaken wardrobe chest and hurled it into the wall. The heavy missile shattered and demolished the plaster between the timber beams, exposing the brick beneath and causing a shower of plaster and chunks of broken wood to fall to the floor.

Rosamund bit back a cry—better the wall than one of her people—and heard the faintest of whimpers and slight creaking from somewhere up above. *The attic. They're in the attic—I must keep him away from them. And the Poor Knights as well—I will not have him undo all we have striven for!* "Would you truly prove your love, Alexander?" she asked, thinking hard. *If she could direct him, use the bond while she could...* "You know a true lover considers nothing good except what he thinks will please his beloved. And the easy attainment of love makes it of little value. Difficulty of attainment makes it prized."

"Yes! Yes, exactly," he said, coming to her and taking her hands. "I can deny you nothing, my love. Tell me what you would have me do, and I shall do it."

This is not love, she reminded herself, as his eagerness to please warmed her heart. She had to fight down the impulse to give in to it, to treat him with the same easy affection she would offer Josselin, whose love did not come from her blood nor require anything of her in return. "I must think on it, milord," she said, and gave him her warmest smile. "You are no ordinary knight. What might prove a challenge for an ordinary man would hardly be a proper test of your love, for it would be too easy."

He gave her an almost boyish grin. "Yes. Set me a task,

milady. Then you will love me as I love you, and you will be mine forever."

"But you must let me think on it, and be patient. You can be patient, can't you?"

"Oh, yes," he assured her. "But I pray you, do not let me wait too long!" He lifted her hand to his lips, kissed her knuckles, then turned it over and kissed her palm.

So much for patience. "I must beg your leave, milord, then, to retire so I may consider—*no, milord!*"

"I have only so much patience, my love," he whispered, as he slid back her sleeve and sank his fangs into her wrist.

That which a lover takes against the will of his beloved has no relish, she told herself, but it didn't help. His desire was nearly as overwhelming as his kiss; her knees buckled, and he followed her down, suckling greedily, sending shudders of pure sensual delight shooting along her nerves and within her veins. He made little noises of satisfaction as he drank, and she could not restrain a whimper of her own, hating herself for enjoying it so, but being unable to resist it.

This is not love, this is not love, she repeated to herself over and over again, her litany of survival, of keeping her mind her own. She was still repeating it even after he ceased to drink, picked her up and laid her gently on the ruin of her bed.

"We will be so happy," he whispered to her, and kissed her forehead. Then he was gone.

She was aware of footsteps, of voices, of mortal heartbeats and the scent of blood. Familiar voices, familiar presences nearby, jarring to acute preternatural senses. Hunger stabbed at her, and the Beast growled a warning. *Go away. Leave me alone, let me die—*

"Milady—?"

"Peter, be care—*Rosamund, no!*"

Crimson flared across her vision. She snarled and leapt up, fangs bared and eyes wild with fury. But her attack was foiled. Something larger and heavier than herself slammed into her and bore her to the floor. She struggled, spitting, snarling, but her adversary was stronger than she was, and held her fast. Her fingers grabbed an arm and wrist, and she sank her fangs into unresisting flesh. Blood reached her tongue, sweet and powerful and cold, and she gulped it down, even as a trembling hand buried itself in her hair, and a hoarse voice whispered endearments in her ear.

Cainite blood. *Josselin.*

"Rosamund, listen to me, hear me. You know me, m*a petite....*"

Rosamund found herself latched on to Josselin's arm, his greater weight pinning her down, both of them sprawled on the floor in her ransacked chamber. Suddenly embarrassed, she withdrew, licked the ragged wound closed. "Please," she whispered hoarsely. "Let me up—"

"Of course." Josselin lifted himself off and glanced up at the circle of pale, frightened faces of the mortal servants. "Leave us," he said. "I promise, she'll be out to see you soon. Go."

Obediently they left, and Josselin bent over her, picking her up in his arms. She wrapped her arms around his neck and let him carry her. When he set her down again, she was a bit surprised to find herself on his bed, in his own little chamber downstairs. "Josselin—I—I'm so sorry, I didn't mean—"

"I know, *petite.* It's all right—better me than Peter, at least. I just thank God and all the saints you're—" He looked at her more closely. "What did he do?"

"Not—not that. I didn't drink, I'm still free. He—needed reassurance, I guess."

"*Bastard*—" Josselin hissed.

"Josselin, no," she said, putting her hand on his arm. "Don't even *think* it. Why don't you see it, either of you? You cannot protect me! No one can!"

"Maybe it's because we—" he stopped. "Either of *who*?"

"Jürgen," she whispered.

"Peter said you didn't come home last night."

She heard the question he did not voice, and nodded.

"You love him, don't you?"

"Yes. At least I thought I did. But—but once you taste the

blood, how do you even *know* anymore? Does it matter after that? Is it Jürgen I truly love, or Alexander, or—" She dropped her gaze, struggling with the churning of her own emotions when she looked up his face.

"Or me?" Josselin smoothed back her hair, gently. "The blood isn't love, Rosamund. You know that."

"But it feels the same," she persisted. "And if it feels like love, then what difference is there, really? If I took the third drink, it wouldn't matter anymore. I'd be happy, and never know how miserable I was—"

"No," Josselin said. "You'd know, trust me. You'd know, and yet you'd be equally convinced that the reason you were so miserable had nothing to do with *him*, because how could someone you loved so much be someone you could hate, who stole your will and your self-respect? So when you were unhappy, you'd blame yourself, and wonder what the *hell* you'd ever done wrong—"

She felt his pain at that moment as if it were her own, ached to soothe him, make it all better, do anything it took to ease the anguish that memory brought him. *His blood*, she realized, and then, *who did this to him?* And then she knew, felt it in the echoes of his blood, of the connection they shared. "Salianna."

"Yes, Salianna. A long time ago, when I still breathed. But he will be no better, Rosamund. You know he won't, you've known him long enough." He shook his head. "Love isn't just how you *feel*, Rosamund. It's what you *do*."

"Then what shall I do?"

He was silent for a long time. "I wish with all my heart I had an answer for you," he said at last. "Sleep here tonight, Rosamund, and try not to worry. I'll send Blanche and Peter down to see to you."

"What about you?"

"It won't be the first time I've slept in rougher quarters, *petite*, and the cellar is dry and secure. Rest, and think, and I'll do the same." He bent and kissed her forehead. "You are not Lorraine, and you will not let your passions run away with you."

Passions are horses. It was something Isouda had said once. Rosamund thought about it even as she was assuring Peter and Blanche—and indeed, it seemed every mortal in the household—that she was indeed unhurt and did not blame anyone for the state of her bedroom save Alexander himself. Blanche brought her a shift to sleep in, and Peter promised to see to having the room straightened up and the wall and shutters repaired as soon as possible.

Passions are horses. What was the rest of it? Josselin would know—he remembered everything—but something in her wanted to answer this one herself. Oh, yes...

—*Passions are horses, swift and strong, but you must keep them under control. They must be made to serve your needs and directed on their course, not allowed to carry you over the precipice.*

—*You have in all things ever been my greatest pupil, and I have every confidence you will not disappoint me even in this darkest night.*

"Peter," she said softly, as he was turning to go. "Leave the candle—I want to read for a while."

A familiar leather courier's pouch hung from a peg on the wall; Rosamund got it down and emptied out its contents on the table, a half-dozen thick parchment packets, each bearing a well-loved seal.

She picked one up, opened it, edged the candle closer, and began to read.

—*Lorraine was a fool... consider well the consequences of your actions even when great passion moves you.*

—*even the greatest and the least among us have their vulnerabilities as well as their strengths, and you are best served to make use of them both.*

She chewed at her lower lip and thought for a moment. Alexander's vulnerabilities... his strengths.... Pride. Courage. Tenacity. A powerful Cainite, prince and warrior doomed by his sire to be forever a boy, never a man... *Pride.* His pride had served her well before, and Jürgen's pride was no less. Would that serve her now?

—*Only be careful what mask you choose....*

She would have to be very careful indeed.

Chapter Thirty

The cotte had been Margery's, of rich blue damask, the finest thing she had owned. Blanche and Katherine resized it for her, and Peter salvaged enough of the white brocade to make a bit of trim around the collar and hem. The kirtle beneath it was the angel's white samite, and another piece of the white brocade and a scrap of the green wool were fashioned into the favor for her belt: the white rose of a Toreador ambassador. She wore her hair loose in a cascade of copper-gold waves, under the circlet Alexander had given her. And at her throat...

"Are you sure that is wise, *petite*?" Josselin asked. "I'll admit he has good taste, but still—"

She took the brooch out of its little box. It was a beautiful piece of work, a stylized gold rose on a blue enamel background. The note, with Jürgen's characteristic brevity, had simply said *For milady*, but she knew his hand. "He will expect me to wear it," she said, and pinned it on.

The great hall of Hundisburg Castle was crowded. Located seventeen miles from Magdeburg proper, Hundisburg now served as the temporary commandery of the Order of the Black Cross, and for tonight at least, Jürgen's court. Though fewer than usual of the Black Cross knights were present, there were still sufficient to make an impressive showing. Cainite lords from most of Saxony and Brandenburg were there, and the emissaries of a number of other Cainite courts, including Ignatio Lorca from Hardestadt's own household. Rosamund wondered how many of them expected Jürgen to announce his departure for the Livonian crusade. Even Jervais—who had likely not been expressly invited, but had the gall to show up anyway—lurked back near the doors.

Josselin, resplendent in his own court finery, including his blue surcoat with the three white swans, but politely unarmed, stayed close by her side as she greeted those she knew and exchanged diplomatic pleasantries. After six years in Jürgen's court, she knew almost all the regular emissaries, and even had the delight of surprising Sir Robert of Norfolk, envoy from Lord Mithras in London, with her native fluency in both English and Norman French.

"Have you thought of a quest for me, my rose?" Alexander asked her, taking her hand.

Rosamund sensed Josselin stiffening beside her, and concentrated on remaining calm, projecting reassurances. "I have, milord," she said, "but this is hardly the time—but you will know it very soon, I promise you."

"After court, then," Alexander murmured, and kissed her hand, his dark eyes remaining fixed adoringly on her face. "For I can wait no longer."

"Of course," she assured him, and then let Josselin lead her to their places, as Lord Jürgen's herald stood in front of the throne. Wiftet strutted in as well, and took his usual place on the front of the dais.

"His Highness, Jürgen von Verden the SwordBearer, Overlord of Saxony and Thuringia, Landgraf of Brandenburg and Prussia, Lord Protector of Acre, Grand Master of the Black Cross, Prince of Magdeburg!"

The Cainites and their mortal servants hardly needed prompting to bow, as Jürgen strode through the room, followed by Brother Christof, Father Erasmus and a well-armed escort of Black Cross knights. Yet, despite his monastic escort, Jürgen was once again dressed as a secular lord, much as he had been the night they had arrived six years before, his tunic emblazoned with his own red eagle, black velvet mantle trimmed with ermine and lined with scarlet silk. At his side he wore the same sword she had brought to him from France, eighteen years before.

To see him again, even though it had barely been three nights since she had lain in his arms, thrilled her to the core of her being—her warrior prince, lord and lover. She forced herself to notice Alexander as well, standing near the throne, remind herself of her purpose. *He will grant what I ask,* she reminded herself. *He must.*

"Rise," Jürgen told them, turning to face them. "We have much of importance to discuss with you this evening. The Order of the Black Cross leaves in a few weeks on crusade in Livonia, to hunt down and destroy the pagan Cainites who threaten our peace, and the peace of the German settlers and missionaries to the tribes of that land. You have doubtless heard the rumors of a barbarian warlord from the east, a wild Tartar of Gangrel blood who has claimed that land and vowed to drive all Christians out of Livonia. This insolence shall not be borne. Our holy knights have sworn to hunt down this Qarakh and destroy him, for the glory of God.

"I have every faith that they will succeed, even though I will not be leading them. My responsibility, as prince and overlord, is to remain here, and deal with the matters that cannot be handled with a troop of knights or a well-honed blade." He glanced around the room, making sure he had everyone's attention. Rosamund thought his smile started when his eyes fell upon her, but she couldn't be sure. Still he *did* smile.

"I am told that I may find myself preferring the field of battle than the deadly game of politics—but I will not shirk my duties in either arena, nor will I give ground before any foe, for that is not how God fashioned me. Yet some foes there are that require a particular kind of diligence, and I would warn you of them now."

He raised his hand, and three Black Cross brothers stepped forward. One holding up a knight's white surcoat bearing a broken red cross, the other two holding up wooden boards painted with heraldic devices. "Learn these emblems, we command you, and carry the word back to your own domains, for they represent those who would destroy us all. Avoid them, and defend yourselves with great caution—for we have learned that their patronage comes from the Curia in Rome itself. The Order of the Poor Knights of Acre is led by Gauthier de Dampiere, whose name some of you may already know. The Order of St. Theodosius, who have attacked our kind in France, Savoy and the Languedoc—know them by their robes the color of old blood. And the House von Murnau of Bavaria—patrons and supporters of the Knights of Acre and the Red Monks, at the very least, if not more. We have but recently diverted them from these my domains, and any who dare attract their notice again in my domain will reap serious consequences—so that surrendering to the torture chambers of the Poor Knights may seem the lesser hazard than facing my judgment."

A murmuring swept through the assembly. Clearly some knew one or another of the orders or the noble family that Jürgen had just named, or had heard stories of their activities. Rosamund suspected the severity of Jürgen's pronouncement was getting some commentary too. The Silence of the Blood, one of the traditional laws of their kind, already forbade Cainites from attracting undue attention from mortal authorities, but in practice, the level of its enforcement varied widely. Jürgen had just drawn a hard line, one that would be harsh indeed to enforce; yet having said it, he would now have no choice but to do so.

Jürgen let them murmur a minute or two, then signaled the knights with the emblems to remove them. "I would like to take this opportunity to publicly thank those who were instrumental in diverting the Poor Knights away from this city: Brother Christof, Father Erasmus, and the other brothers of our order, some of whom gave their very existence to defend us all; I would also like to acknowledge the valued assistance of Akuji and Wiftet—yes, that's you, Wiftet—" he added as the jester spun around on his butt and looked up at his lord with wide-eyed surprise.

"What did I do?" Wiftet cried out in dismay. "Whatever it is, milord, I'm very sorry and it will never happen again!"

There was laughter from those gathered in the hall, and Jürgen paused for a moment for it to die down before continuing. "I would also ask Herr Josselin de Poitiers and Lady Rosamund of Islington to come before me, for their particular assistance in this matter went far beyond the requirements of ambassadors to our court."

Josselin took her hand and led her up to the front. He bowed and she curtsied, trying to maintain control of her passions, lest her colors betray her to any who might be watching.

Jürgen smiled, presumably at them both, but it seemed to Rosamund that the greater warmth of it was directed to her.

"Herr Josselin," Lord Jürgen said, "you have faced many dangers on our behalf, both in Hungary and here in Magdeburg, and have done so with courage and grace, even though you had sworn no oath, nor owed us any service save that of a guest in our realm. Nor will we ask such an oath of you now. Even so, we now declare that you are a guest no longer, but a knight of our court; and as such, you are granted the right to bear arms in our presence and in our court, in our service and your queen's. Brother Christof, arm him."

Christof stepped forward, carrying Josselin's own sword belt, and buckled it around his waist. Josselin bowed. "I am honored, your Highness, by your regard and I thank you. If my oath were not already given elsewhere, please know it would be yours."

She barely listened. Her thoughts were flying too fast for the words to make sense. Perhaps there had been something in his eyes when he looked at her, or there was truth to the story that sometimes lovers who shared blood could read one another's thoughts. For whatever reason, his words of three nights before suddenly took on new meanings that somehow, in her entrancement, she had not understood before now.

—*And you, Rosamund? Would that please you as well? Then it will please me also....*

Not *would please* him, but *will*. And she realized that her sire's blessing must have already been obtained, or else he would never have asked her. She had barely been consulted. And he was about to ask her again, in front of the entire court. *In front of Alexander.*

—*Alexander must learn he cannot have everything he wants.*

Jürgen turned to her and held out his hand. "Milady Rosamund."

Josselin handed her over to him, bowed and stepped back. Jürgen smiled and kissed her hand.

—*Consider well the consequences of your actions even when great passion moves you.*

"Milady, you have graced us all with your beauty, charm and wisdom; you have done good service to me and to your queen as her ambassador to my court; and you have never failed to give me good advice, even when I was not inclined to listen."

His words were still formal in tone, but she remembered that he had himself called his proposal an alliance of state, not the joining of two lovers. *Does he really love me? Or am I a prize and nothing more?*

"Your advice and your wits have served my people and myself well in recent months during a time of great peril. Your dignity, grace and wisdom have held all this court in awe ever since your arrival. Indeed, you have long since demonstrated beyond all doubt that you are, by every measure possible, a princess already in all but name—I can think of no more pleasant or honorable duty than to rectify the last. Lady Rosamund, if you would so honor me, I would have you ever at my side, as my consort, and my queen, and let this night begin a new era of harmony and friendship between the Fiefs of the Black Cross and the Courts of Love in France."

The hall was silent as a tomb, everyone waiting for her answer. She could *feel* a icy cold radiating from her left, feel the entire room chilling as the tension among both Cainite and mortal members of the court rose to the breaking point. She could sense Josselin's sudden apprehension, his hand resting on the hilt of his sword, ready to die in her defense. And Jürgen... Jürgen waiting for the answer he expected, knowing exactly the stir he had created and relishing it, grimly proud to put Alexander in his place, not realizing he would die for it.

—*Love isn't just how you feel, Rosamund. It's what you do.*

"Your Highness, I cannot accept this honor you would do me," she said as clearly and firmly as she could, doing her best to ignore the way the sudden pained comprehension in his eyes broke her heart in two. "I am flattered that you believe me worthy of such an elevation, and I thank you for your kindness.

But I have other obligations that I must fulfill, duties to milord Alexander and his own long-delayed quest to retake his rightful throne in Paris, and those duties must take precedence over anything else."

"Of course, milady," Jürgen said, coolly. Now the source of the chill had shifted from off to her left to right in front of her, but elsewhere in the room she could all but hear the tension among the witnesses dissipating like an errant fog.

"But if I may make any claim to your Highness's favor, in light of the events of the past few months, there is a boon I would ask instead of this great honor that I cannot accept...."

It was her right, and he knew it, especially after he'd been so lavish with her praise. Jürgen nodded, though the warmth in his eyes had turned icy blue. "Ask it, milady, and we shall take it under consideration."

"Milord Alexander is an experienced general and leader of men into battle, yet here his skills are wasted, and he grows restless, waiting for the night to come when he may return to Paris in triumph. I ask, your Highness, that he be permitted to command your troops in Livonia. Let him test his strength against the barbarian warlord in your service. Let him prove himself your ally and worthy of your support."

Jürgen considered. Rosamund found herself chewing her lower lip again, a habit Isouda had never managed to break her of, and forced herself to stop. This was the quest she had hoped Alexander would accept, the boon she had planned to ask for, although Jürgen's own move in court had forced her hand in a way she had not intended.

"Milord Alexander," Jürgen said finally, acknowledging the elder's presence in his court. "Is this your wish as well, to lead troops against Qarakh and his barbarian tribes?"

It was a delicate insult, to infer she might have spoken without Alexander's express permission, but she ignored that, and turned to favor Alexander with her most charming smile.

"Yes, milord, it is." Alexander said, smiling back at her, dark eyes already alight with anticipation.

Christof leaned close to Jürgen's ear. Rosamund could just imagine what the Lord Marshal had to say about this proposal.

She did not attempt to hear what he said. Jürgen listened, and listened to the whispered opinion of Father Erasmus as well.

Finally Jürgen raised his hands for silence, and the murmur of speculation and commentary in the hall faded away. "Lord Alexander, if you will join my command staff in my private council chambers after court, we will discuss this matter further and work out the details. However, I see no reason to deny the privilege of crusade to any good Christian soul who desires to serve God by raising a sword against the infidel. Your boon is granted, milady, and I thank you."

They were dismissed. Josselin's hand under hers guided her in making her proper curtsies, and guiding her back to their places in the hall, nor did he release her hand even then, his support being all that kept her from collapsing on the spot.

—Be careful what mask you choose....

"My sweet lady, my rose," Alexander murmured, taking her hands. He had sought her out as soon as the formal court was ended, dismissing Josselin as her escort and comforting support with little more than a cool glance. "This is a worthy quest indeed you have laid before me—I swear to you, I will seek out this barbarian Qarakh and bring you back his head!"

"A worthy quest, milord," Rosamund managed, "for your success will put Lord Jürgen in your debt, and his troops will be accustomed to your command. Use this opportunity well, milord, and it may be the road back to Paris will begin with Riga." She mustered her bravest smile. "A lady needs no bloody trophies, milord. It is enough that a lover strives to please his lady's desires in all things, for then he shows his love in his submission to her will."

"You chose well this evening, and wisely." Alexander took her hands to his lips, and for a brief second she was afraid he'd take her there on the spot, there was such a hunger in his eyes. "Forgive me, my sweet rose, for ever doubting your loyalty to me. For how could such a rare jewel and beautiful lady desire to settle for a grubby provincial title, when in but a little while, she can be queen over all of France?"

With a sharp pang to her already broken heart, Rosamund realized that his words were not solely aimed at her. Lord Jürgen was standing but a short distance off, engaged in a conversation with envoys from distant fiefdoms in the west. She reminded herself that had she not spoken as she had, it was entirely possible that she, Josselin and even Jürgen himself would now be naught but ash.

"Your pardon, milord, milady." The Nosferatu monk who had first appeared at the Christmas Court before last, the one named Malachite, stood at Alexander's shoulder. He had been an infrequent visitor to Magdeburg over the intervening months, and Rosamund scolded herself for not noticing him before. He certainly did not trouble to hide his ravaged countenance, and she had to fight down an instinct to recoil. Alexander seemed unaffected by it. *No doubt he has seen worse*, Rosamund reminded herself.

Alexander's annoyance, however, faded quickly when Malachite spoke again, in a language Rosamund did not know, nor even recognize. Alexander answered him in the same tongue, and then turned to Rosamund again, and kissed her fingertips. "If you will excuse me, my love," he said, and she could hear the eagerness in his voice—whatever the Nosferatu had said, it had certainly piqued his interest. "I must begin my quest—as it seems our friend here has information of great use to me."

"Of course, milord," Rosamund agreed, hoping she didn't seem too eager herself.

Alexander turned away. The Nosferatu's eyes met hers, soft and brown, almost gentle despite the desiccated bony, sockets in which they sat. "Thank you, milady," he said in accented French. "You have done well." Rosamund got the distinct impression he meant a great deal more by those words than the courtesy of permitting his interruption of her conversation.

Malachite then walked away with Alexander, and left her to her own brooding thoughts.

Chapter Thirty-One

Alexander spread the map out on the table, and Brother Rudiger, Marques and Malachite bent closer to look at it. Christof was not present; Alexander had taken Christof's position as commander of the crusade, and Rosamund sometimes wondered if the Order's Lord Marshal would ever forgive her.

"According to the reports from the Brothers of the Sword, the pagans of Kurland have only in the past year accepted baptism in the Christian faith." Alexander traced a region on the map, around the bay and the little castle drawing that represented the city of Riga on the coast. "From those reports, it appears that the territory Qarakh's tribe now claims extends from the Kurland south and east, here, into Samogitia and Semigallia. Their tribe is nomadic, and wanders throughout this region—finding them will be our first priority."

"It's a pity we cannot know exactly where Johann was ambushed," Brother Rudiger said, looking at the little mark on the map. "Brother Renaud, God rest his soul, was certain he could find the place again. A forest near a—"

"In this vast, unmarked wilderness, Brother Rudiger, one forest likely looks like another," Alexander interrupted, coldly. "I highly doubt he stopped to take proper bearings, considering how fast he must have been running. Now, as I was saying, the tribes in the Kurland have accepted baptism, but that does not mean they can be trusted. If it is Qarakh's intent to drive

Christians out of his lands, then he must take that defeat very badly indeed."

Alexander looked up, caught Rosamund's eye for just a brief moment where she stood at the door. She smiled at him warmly. Thus encouraged, he went back to his war council with renewed enthusiasm.

Rosamund closed the door quietly and left him to his work. Then gathering her courage together as best she could, and stilling the nervous qualms in her unbeating heart, she ascended the stairs at the end of the hall. She stood outside Lord Jürgen's door for a few minutes, working up the nerve to knock.

The door opened. Jürgen looked down at her and raised one eyebrow. "Alexander is in the council chamber, milady," he said curtly. "I suggest you seek him there."

"Thank you, your Highness," she replied, keeping her voice as mild as she could, "but I was actually hoping to have a word with you—if you would indulge me, milord."

He nodded, and stepped back, holding the door open for her. "A few minutes, then," he said. "You might be missed."

"Thank you, milord," she murmured, and slipped past him into the room. He closed the door. "Milord, I—"

"There's no need to explain, milady, or apologize," he said, cutting her off simply by raising his hand. "Clearly you had to make the choice you felt was best for you. And clearly I should have known better than to make such a controversial offer publicly in court."

"Yes," she replied, dryly. "You should have."

"Your advice, milady, is ill-timed, given what we had—" He stopped, started again. "Given what you had said before. "

"And what should I have done, milord?"

"You should have *trusted* me," he insisted. "I promised I'd protect you."

"I told you, milord," she said softly. "This is not about trust." This was turning out to be every bit as bad as she thought it would be. She could feel his frustration and hurt echoing in her veins, from the blood they had shared. She could only hope that he felt something of her as well.

"I thought it was what you wanted," he said. "To be free of

Alexander, and to be with me. I knew he'd be angry, but that's why I did it in court. It's not in his interest to oppose me as long as he needs my support."

"It was not in his interest to kill his childe Olivier, who had stood loyally by him even in his exile, but he did. It was not in his interest to murder Lorraine, his consort—" She stopped herself. That story was too painful now, too personal.

"But he did," Jürgen finished for her. "I've heard the story, milady. Did she not betray him?"

"That—has been disputed, milord," she answered. "But whether she actually did or not hardly mattered, so long as he *believed* she did—by accepting the love and protection of another."

A long awkward silence fell between them, as he absorbed the obvious implications of what she had said, and she waited, anxiously, for him to speak.

"So you would rather martyr yourself than fight back, or even *try* to free yourself from him."

"What do you think I've been *doing* these past six years?" Her voice came out a good deal sharper—and louder—than she had originally intended, but his dismissal of her long struggle struck a spark against her pride. "I am not yet a martyr, milord, and I *am* still free, at least to think for myself, and love as my own heart bids me. And I will *not* give that up without a fight, neither to him nor to *you!*"

"I never *asked* you to!" Jürgen snapped back.

"Didn't you? In front of all the court?"

"No!" He looked honestly baffled. "I asked you to be my queen."

"Your prize? Taken away from Alexander like a seizing a castle after a siege? What kind of queen should I be then, who is your captive and dependent on you for her survival?"

"Never my captive, Rosamund. You *must* believe that." He sat down heavily in the chair beside his worktable. "If anything, milady, I am yours."

It was the first softening he'd shown, the first attempt at courtly language, and Rosamund had to concentrate not to give in too soon. "Indeed?" she asked, although not as coolly as she could have. "If there was one quality I was *quite* positive your Highness possessed, it was that you and you alone were always your own master."

"I suppose I have learned over the years always to convey that impression," he admitted, grudgingly, "whether it was true at the moment or not. It's a requirement of the position."

Isouda had once said something very much the same. Rosamund sat down on a bench beside the table as well. "And the truth, milord?" she asked.

"The truth? None of us is ever entirely his own master."

"I am sure that your lord sire would have been pleased to see you make an advantageous marriage," she said, not looking at him. "Or at least you seemed to believe it would have been advantageous. An alliance of state."

"I see," he said slowly. "And now you think that was my only purpose."

She didn't dare look at him now. "Was it?"

"Is that really how it seemed to you?" he asked, a bit more earnestly. "It seems I have offended you most gravely in those moments where my intention was completely the opposite! I thought you understood the—the esteem in which I have held you from the moment we met!"

"How would I have understood that, milord?" She did not need to see him to sense his distress, the emotions thrumming in her veins, although his words did not convey his feelings nearly as much as the undercurrents in his voice, and the very tension in his frame that she could see out of the corner of her eye.

The tension was too much for him to continue sitting. "How would you have me give you to understand it, milady?" he demanded, rising from the chair and striding away to the open window. "No, never mind. I've already made my missteps, I cannot take them back. I wish you had said some of these things beforehand...."

Rosamund rose and followed him, joined him at the window. "I could say much the same, milord. But I see I must have hurt you even more greatly than I feared. It is not like you to give up on any enterprise so soon. Considering you have all eternity before you, would you really abandon this one before it is hardly even begun?"

He stared out into the night, the dark shadowed streets below, the faint moonlight highlighting the distant hulk of the unfinished cathedral. "Eternity is not a very hopeful word to me at this precise moment, milady," he said. "I see only a hard road ahead in these next years. Hard and treacherous, and lonely."

"Perhaps not lonely," she murmured.

He turned toward her, studying her intently. "Perhaps? Is that the most you can give me?"

"For now, I dare not promise more, milord. I do wish it were not so—but like you, I see a hard road ahead."

"But perhaps not lonely." He smiled ruefully. "I must admire your candor once again, milady. At least you have never been one of those ladies to make promises you cannot keep. I admit a certain part of me would rather hear those promises all the same, but…I suppose only time will tell. We will have to find out the hard way, step by step."

"Indeed."

"Still, you are right… I have never turned aside from a road because it is hard, or declined a venture because its outcome is not certain. With your permission, then, I will walk this road to wherever it may lead. I will not falter again…and be assured, I will not give up."

She smiled back up at him, and was pleased to see him have to take a quick breath in reaction to her gaze. "I look forward to it, milord."

To the most noble Lady Isouda de Blaise, Queen of Love for Chartres, Blois and Anjou:

My dearest and most reverend Lady,

I hope this letter finds you well, and all in my so distant country of good heart, and blessed of God. For myself, I do not know if I am blessed or not, but must trust as ever in the grace of Our Lord and His most blessed Mother, and in my beloved Saint Margaret who has so far paid good heed to my most desperate prayers and kept me from being swallowed up. Yet God has granted me, if not deliverance, at least some reprieve, although I do not yet know to what end. Lord Alexander—for I will no longer call him by the title that is no longer his—has agreed to lead a crusade against the pagan Cainites in Livonia, at the request of Lord Jürgen. And so I am encouraged now that Alexander is gone, at least for a season. What we most feared has occurred, at least on his part, and although it frightens me, as you can well imagine, thus far I have been able to persuade him to reason. So I have perhaps only delayed the fate he intends for me, yet that delay is a season of hope, and I will cling to it with all my heart.

Rosamund set her quill aside and chewed on her lower lip. *I should tell her,* she tried to convince herself. *She would understand. She would tell me it was political necessity—not a sin. She would forgive me.*

But still, the guilt had plagued her, kept her from her daytime rest, shortened her patience and her temper. She kept imagining Alexander showing up at her doorstep, injured or suffering some terrible curse, demanding vengeance, accusing her of a worse betrayal even than infidelity. To ease her conscience, Rosamund had finally written a confession, laying out the details of her fault, her most grievous sin of omission, her silent treachery against her liege lord and would-be lover.

—And the Telyavic sorcerers that are Qarakh's allies, milady? Does his Highness know about them?

"No," she whispered fiercely, in answer to the remembered voice of the Tremere ambassador. She used a long iron poker to feed the parchment sheets of her confession to the fire on the hearth.

"No, he does not, nor does Alexander—and may God have mercy on my soul."

About the Author

Janet Trautvetter is a contributor to many supplements in the Dark Ages and Vampire: The Masquerade game lines, including Dark Ages: Inquisitor and Archons and Templars.

Curious about other Crossroad Press books?
Stop by our site:
http://www.crossroadpress.com
We offer quality writing
in digital, audio, and print formats.

www.ingramcontent.com/pod-product-compliance
Lightning Source LLC
Chambersburg PA
CBHW070858180626
46817CB00003B/819